Anne-Marie O'C
She has written play
She now live
husband and son.

[illegible] Connor was born in Bradford. [illegible] plays for theatre, radio and television. She now lives in Manchester with her [illegible] and son.

STAR STRUCK

Anne-Marie O'Connor

1 3 5 7 9 10 8 6 4 2

Published in 2009 by Ebury Press, an imprint of Ebury Publishing
A Random House Group Company

Star Struck is a work of fiction. In some cases true life figures appear but their actions and conversations are entirely fictitious. All other characters, and all names of places and descriptions of events, are the products of the author's imagination and any resemblance to actual persons or places is entirely coincidental.

The Random House Group Limited Reg. No. 954009

Addresses for companies within the Random House Group can be found at www.randomhouse.co.uk

A CIP catalogue record for this book is available from the British Library

The Random House Group Limited supports The Forest Stewardship Council (FSC), the leading international forest certification organisation. All our titles that are printed on Greenpeace approved FSC certified paper carry the FSC logo. Our paper procurement policy can be found at www.rbooks.co.uk/environment

Typeset in Adobe Caslon by Palimpsest Book Production Limited, Grangemouth, Stirlingshire

Printed in the UK by Cox & Wyman, Reading RG1 8EX

ISBN 9780091932398

Thank you to Grainne Fox for being generally all round brilliant and for working UK hours from New York – what a woman!

A big thank you to Gillian Green for her eagle editorial eye, great enthusiasm and wonderful ideas; and to everyone at Ebury who has worked on this book.

To Mum and Dad for all their invaluable help while I was writing this.

To Jack for putting up with the traffic on the M62 four times a week and being a star.

And to Steve for his love and support. Oh yes and for having a *brilliant* sense of humour. Do I get my tenner now?

To Jack

Chapter 1

Catherine Reilly was sitting in the foyer of a five-star hotel in Manchester city centre breathing rapidly with her head between her knees. Her feet, which she'd pushed into her younger sister's silver wedges that morning, looked odd from this angle. Her ankles were puffy and red and her toenails, which she had painted orange on the instruction of Lorraine Kelly, who'd informed her that silver wedges and orange nails were 'bang on trend for summer', looked like Smarties stuck on the end of cocktail sausages. She had teamed the footwear with a pink swirly-print maxi dress, which was also, on upside-down reflection, probably not a good idea.

Jo – Catherine's nineteen-year-old sister from whom she'd borrowed the outfit – was studying fashion design at college. Not just that, Jo could throw on a bin bag, wear an opened baked bean tin for a hat and still look a million dollars – she was definitely someone who could pull off a Pucci-print dress and wedges. Catherine felt that she was from a different end of the gene pool to her younger sister – not having gazelle-like legs and thick, bum-length, Angelina Jolie hair. Even if I dressed in head-to-toe couture, Catherine thought to herself, I'd still only look like change from a fiver.

As Catherine silently berated herself for not having thought about this fact sooner, she could feel someone rubbing her back. 'Thank you,' she said, weakly lifting her head.

The St John's Ambulance woman looked at her and smiled kindly. 'Thought we might need a stretcher.'

'No, I'll be fine.' Catherine felt totally disoriented. One minute she had been queuing up to receive her competition number, the next – overcome by the thought of what she was letting herself in for, auditioning for *Star Maker: Transatlantic* – she had fainted, collapsing onto a line of seats. She remembered swaying and then nothing – not until she was brought round from a tangle of chair legs. She could just imagine the crash. No gentle swooning for the likes of her, she thought. No being caught by some handsome man in naval uniform and being carried off into the distance like the final scenes of *An Officer and a Gentleman* – just a St John's Ambulance woman to bring her round. She just wasn't the sort of girl that people leapt from their seats to help – the type who always had an air of mystery about them. She smiled too much for that, even when she was trying to be mean and moody. And anyway, she looked like she could probably cope in a crisis.

Catherine was what her grandma used to refer to as a 'big girl'. She wasn't *abnormal load* big; she was just the wrong side of Top Shop. Catherine had accepted the fact that she was never going to wear skinny jeans. She was fairly sure that even her skeleton would have a hard time pulling off anything Kate Moss wore. At five foot six and a size sixteen, with shoulder-length dark brown hair and eyes that were grey or green depending on the light, Catherine thought she looked OK. Not that she spent much time dwelling on her looks; she had far more than that to worry about. That was until today, of course, when she had been queuing to get her number. She had realised that of the girls who were, like herself, in their mid-twenties there were two categories: the thin, gorgeous ones – of which there were plenty – and the deluded ones. That was when Catherine had fainted.

Star Maker was TV's most watched programme and every year it plucked one lucky person from obscurity and catapulted them to singing stardom. But this year it was set to be bigger and better than ever. It had been renamed *Star Maker: Transatlantic* and the winner was guaranteed a recording contract – not only in the UK but also the US – with all the might of Richard Forster, the impresario who created *Star Maker* behind them. Richard Forster was so scathing and reputedly so controlling that he made Simon Cowell look like Bambi. This year too they had promised to bow to the public's insatiable appetite for the audition process and were screening fourteen nights of back-to-back auditions and then going straight into the programme. *Star Maker* was taking over the autumn/winter schedule. In the past Catherine had watched the programme intrigued as to why people put themselves through the ordeal of public scrutiny. But this year she had been having a particularly bad day and, seeing the advert on the TV for this year's competition, had just applied – like someone who'd gone for a walk on Beachy Head and then, in a moment of madness, jumped over the edge.

It was a Saturday evening in the depths of winter and Catherine had been sitting in the living room watching

Ant and Dec as her father Mick loudly ate fish and chips next to her. She had felt as if she was about to crack. That morning Mick had delivered some truly awful news to Catherine and, in his time-honoured tradition of treating her as if she was able to deal with anything he threw at her, sworn her to secrecy. He had said that he didn't want the others to know – the others being her three sisters Claire, Maria and Jo. And while Catherine spent the day crying to herself after her dad's bombshell, Mick mooched around the house acting as if he had said nothing earth shattering.

'That, my friend,' Mick said, holding up a fat greasy chip, dripping in gravy so that Ant looked like he had a chip for a head, 'is a king among chips. Bloody lovely.' He dropped it into his mouth like a bird with a worm. Sometimes her father wouldn't eat for days; whenever Catherine pressed him to have some food he'd say he didn't have it in him. During these times he would usually take to his bed and only come out for the occasional toilet trip or to tell Catherine something that he had seen on *Sky News* that had filtered through his morose fug. He had been suffering from depression for years, but that day he had been in eerily high spirits. It was probably shock, Catherine thought. That was certainly what she had been suffering from.

Catherine and her father were alone in the house. Jo had been out at a friend's house, Maria was living with her fiancé Gavin, and Claire, her eldest sister, lived with her husband Paul and their two children, Rosie and Jake, near enough away to always be popping in but far enough away to not have to bother when the proverbial hit the fan.

As the adverts rolled Mick had begun to wonder out loud what he'd like for dessert – 'Angel Delight or Arctic Roll? The tyranny of choice.'

Catherine wasn't particularly interested in the finest foods Iceland had to offer, she felt as if her skull was about to shatter into a thousand pieces. As she was sitting thinking about her father an advert for this year's *Star Maker* auditions came on the TV. They were being held throughout the country but one was nearby in the centre of Manchester. An alien feeling of recklessness welled up inside Catherine. She didn't enter things like this but today she felt as if anything might happen.

While her dad chuntered on about his dessert dilemma Catherine made a mental note of the details she needed in order to enter and when Mick was tucking into his fourth slice of arctic roll, she escaped to the dining room, logged on to his computer and filled out the application form. At the bottom of the form was the question: *Why should we pick you?* She stared and stared at it. Finally she had written the only thing that she could think to write – the truth: *Because I can sing.*

Catherine could sing. The only person who had heard her voice in years was Father McGary at the local church. Catherine had been in the choir as a youngster but had left when she was sixteen, blaming her studies but privately thinking she was a bit old to be standing about wearing a ruff. When Catherine was nineteen she had bumped into Father McGary, catching him at a particularly low moment. He had just said mass for one man with a ferret tied to a bit of string and told Catherine that with congregations like that it was only a matter of time before the church closed. He said he missed hearing her sing, and she had admitted that she missed singing. And so they had agreed that she could pop along to St John's whenever she felt like it and Father McGary would open the church for her. That had been five years ago. St John's was still open and as far as she knew congregation numbers had improved, or at least ferret numbers had dwindled. She enjoyed her time at church. She wasn't religious, but having the time to herself to think and practise the songs that she wrote was the most treasured part of Catherine's week.

Catherine pressed *send*. It was so simple. Was becoming a star these days really that easy? No trawling the clubs, no building up a reputation, no getting signed to a label and then hopefully getting the public to notice you. Those days were past. Now it seemed all it took was just the click of a mouse. It made Catherine feel queasy, the idea that she had just set something in motion that might lead to untold opportunities – or abject failure.

She didn't want her dad to know what she had been up to, so – after quickly printing off the audition details – she cleared the history on the computer. It wouldn't have mattered anyway. By the time Catherine had gone back into the lounge, Mick was snoring, with arctic roll dribbling down his chin.

Catherine took a deep breath and, with the help of the St John's Ambulance lady, stood up and felt her legs go from under her again. She steadied herself on a chair. It was then that she realised she had an audience. A heavily made-up girl with ringlets and neon pink leg warmers was blowing bubblegum bubbles and swinging her left leg to the side of her head in a limbering-up motion. As her ankle made contact with her ear she held it there for a moment and said, 'You look well bad. You should go home.'

An earnest-looking young man with asymmetric hair and a muscle top looked at the girl who was still performing her stretches.

'How can you say that? She needs to be strong. Everything happens for a reason and fainting into some chairs could be a sign that she's like, totally gonna nail it today.'

Oh no, Catherine thought, I've entered a world where people say things like *'totally going to nail it'*. As the girl bent down and touched her toes and muttered 'God, whatever,' a girl, about the same age as Catherine, nudged her and smiled kindly.

'You OK?' the girl asked. She looked like a normal, everyday girl: short, brown hair, brown eyes, glasses; nothing that screamed 'Star of Tomorrow'. She was like her, Catherine thought before quickly remembering that she was dressed as a swirly pink blob.

'Just nerves I think.' Catherine smiled shyly.

'Tell me about it. I'm bricking it. Everyone here has made such an effort. I look like I've popped to the shops,' the girl said.

Catherine laughed. 'I wish I'd just worn what I usually wear.' Catherine said pulling awkwardly at the maxi dress. 'Believe me, I don't usually dress like this. I've borrowed my sister's gear and now I'm regretting it.'

'You look nice,' The girl said nodding her approval. 'I'm Kim, by the way.'

Catherine shook the girl's hand. 'I'm Catherine, pleased to meet you.'

'You too.'

Just as Catherine was about to ask Kim what she going to sing for her audition, the asymmetrical-haired youth began to sing an impromptu 'You Raise me Up' by Westlife.

Catherine looked at Kim, who was in turn staring agog, then another fancy-haired young man stepped in and began to harmonise – terribly – with fancy-haired boy number one, who looked put out that his finest moment was being interrupted. Fancy-haired boy number two had his eyes shut, oblivious, as he rattled through a dozen or so key changes until he sounded like Barry Gibb. Catherine was just about to pull Kim to one side and shuffle away from the serenade when Kim's number was called and she was pulled away by a *Star Maker* employee. Catherine was on her own. She looked desperately around for the toilet in order to make a break for it when a camera crew – on the look out for TV gold – quickly swung into action and before she knew it she was being interviewed by Jason P. Longford, TV's favourite presenter. Catherine, who was still light-headed, felt as if she was watching all of this from afar. But then a jolt of adrenalin shot through her as she realised that she was definitely being filmed.

'Well, they're certainly raising everyone up around here,' Jason P. Longford said with a fake chortle before thrusting the microphone into Catherine's face. 'You with these boys?'

'No, I just fainted and they decided to sing to me,' Catherine said truthfully.

'She doesn't look too impressed, does she, viewers?' Jason said, flashing his bright white veneers and giving a nasty glint to the camera. Catherine was stunned. It wasn't that she wasn't grateful, she just didn't think that the two guys were singing to her for any other reason than they wanted to get themselves noticed. She didn't manage to say this though; Jason wasn't letting her get a word in edgeways. 'And what are you going to sing for the judges?'

Catherine felt faint again. She shouldn't have come today. Who did she think she was? She wasn't lithe like the girl with the leggings or funky like the Westlife wannabes. The only person she'd met so far that was anything like her was Kim and she'd been whisked away from her before they'd had a chance to ponder what they were doing there. Catherine was just a girl who worked in a call centre who was so nervous she could barely stand up straight.

An old man hove into view, sidling up to Jason P. Longford, singing 'The White Cliffs of Dover' with his dentures on the end of his fingers like a ventriloquist. Catherine's mind went blank.

'Not answering questions now, have we a prima donna on our hands?' Jason asked jovially but with an undercurrent of nastiness.

Catherine's brain was just catching up with what he was saying to her, she was so mesmerised by the old man. 'Sorry, no, not at all. I'm singing "Martha's Harbour".' She said quietly.

'What's that?' Jason asked, looking at one of his researchers in such a way that Catherine feared the poor guy would be sacked if he didn't know the answer.

'It's an acoustic song by a band called All About Eve,' the researcher said, pulling his clipboard to his chest as if it would cover the obvious irritation he felt with the TV star.

Catherine caught his eye briefly – grateful that at least someone around here didn't appear certifiable. He's cute, Catherine thought, and then immediately felt bashful and looked at the floor.

For a split second Jason looked like he'd lost all interest but then he quickly rearranged his features back into his for-the-camera face. 'Fair enough, but can you do this?' he said spinning around and pointing at the octogenarian who was now tap dancing and singing 'Would You Like to Swing on a Star?' as well as playing puppets with his false teeth.

Catherine looked at him and smiled tightly. 'I wouldn't have thought so,' she said.

Jo breathed in sharply as if pulling in her stomach might save her and her family from a ten-car pile up. She'd broken one of her own sacred rules: Never Get in a Car with Claire Ever Again Ever. Not After the Last Time. The last time had been when Jo had asked for a lift to the Trafford Centre and they'd found themselves facing the wrong way on the inside lane of the M60 motorway. After that Jo decided she'd rather take the bus. Knife crime and gun crime were on the up in Manchester – if the news was to be believed – but Jo would rather take her chances with a gang of hoodies on the top-deck of the 845 than step foot into any vehicle Claire was driving. However, here she was, hurtling across Manchester at break-neck speed and it was all Catherine's doing.

'What's with the dramatics?' Claire demanded, pulling her fingers agitatedly through her honey highlighted hair.

It always amused Jo that her older sister insisted on dyeing her hair blond. The Reillys were dark haired. No point denying it. Even so, Jo did what she could to make her darkness less obvious. Jolen cream, for example. Something a really blondie – unlike Claire – wouldn't need to think about. Jolen – a hair-lightening cream – was a staple in the Reilly girls' bathroom cabinet and known simply as 'tashe cream'. On the night of her eighteenth birthday Jo had had a particularly nasty run in with a tub well past its sell-by date that her sister Maria had assured her was fine. She had applied said tashe cream as instructed but when it began to sting and then burn, Jo realised she had a problem: she'd branded a Mexican Desperado moustache shape onto her top lip. Maria had thought this hilarious. This just went to show, in Jo's opinion, what an out and out cow her sister could be. It could have been Maria with the *My Name is Earl* moustache but she didn't seem to care.

Maria claimed to know why she and her sisters were all so dark – they were Black Irish, she told Jo – she loved to think that she was something special, descended from some heady Celtic/Spanish mix. Maria liked nothing more than to talk up her own part in things. That was why, Jo thought, when Maria bragged about her job as a trolley dolly on a budget airline you'd think she was responsible for actually flying the plane.

'You've just pulled out without looking and we could have all died!' Jo shouted at Claire. Her sister's driving really did scare her witless. They were now careening across the Mancunian Way, a busy concrete flyover that straddled the city centre.

'God, you're so sensitive,' Claire said, looking straight at her as if the road and their position on it was inconsequential.

'Eyes on the road!' Jo shrieked. 'Sensitive, eh? So why's that bloke beeping his horn and giving you a wanker sign?'

'Joanna!' Mick piped up. 'I won't have any wankers on a Saturday morning.'

Jo swallowed back a giggle and tried to ignore the elbow that Maria had just jabbed into her ribs.

'Can we just get there in one piece, please? Jesus,' Maria asked loftily.

'"Jesus". "Wankers". I don't know where I got such potty-mouthed kids from,' Mick said, throwing his eyes to the heavens.

Jo was going to point out that her dad could make Gordon Ramsay blush if he put his mind to it but she decided to let it go. She had a hangover and she didn't want to enter into a pointless argument this early in the day.

The previous evening was a bit of a blur. Jo knew it involved some annoying bloke who wouldn't leave her alone while she was out trying to have a good time with her mates. He kept bothering her and trying to buy her shots of tequila. Jo hated tequila and she hated men who tried to buy her tequila. In fact she hated men who tried to buy her drinks full stop; it got on her nerves. She was only interested in men if they wanted a good laugh. She didn't need some cheesy slimeball trying to buy her Verve Cliquot and thinking he could parade her round in his sports car. Manchester seemed to be full of these sort of idiots. Jo didn't know where they got off, but she liked to tell them where she thought they should.

Her hangover meant that she hadn't been quite as on the ball as she might have been when Catherine came in, asking to ferret through her wardrobe. She should have known something was amiss when her usually dressed-down sister had asked if she could borrow her silver wedges. Where had she thought Catherine was going to wear silver wedges on a Saturday morning – Netto? Jo had pulled the quilt over her head while Catherine helped herself to some of her stuff and then managed to fall back to sleep and a nice dream about living in a bouncy castle when she had been rudely awakened by Claire.

'What the bloody hell does Maria find to do in there?' Claire said, plonking four-year-old Rosie on Jo's bed and nodding in the direction of the bathroom.

'Pluck her monobrow?' Jo offered sitting up in bed and looking at her alarm clock. 'What the hell are you doing in my bedroom, getting on my nerves at eleven o'clock in the morning?'

'You're a cheeky sod, do you know that?' Claire asked, eyeballing Jo. 'We're hiding.'

'From who?'

Rosie jumped down off the bed and began playing with Jo's jewellery on her dressing table. 'Go into Aunty Catherine's room, Rosie, she's got well better stuff than me.' Claire threw Jo a look. 'What?' Jo asked with mock innocence. Rosie ran into her aunt Catherine's room.

Even though Claire had left home years ago, as soon as she was back in the house she resumed big sister duties and thought that she could take over the place and order Jo around. Jo didn't hold it against Claire, she had her own life when their mother had left and she'd always made sure that Jo was looked after, taking her out for the day when she was younger and letting her stop over at her house whenever she wanted. She was married to Paul who wasn't the brightest tool in the box but he was nice enough if a little dull – his only topics of conversation seemed to be about Manchester United or the traffic on the M60.

Actually, Jo quite liked Claire – it was Maria who got on her nerves – but it made her laugh that her eldest sister thought that as soon as she turned up order was restored. It was obvious to anyone who stepped foot into the Reilly household that the person who had held the family together since their mum had left eight years ago was Catherine.

'Anyway,' Claire sighed. 'It's Dad. That's who we're hiding from.'

'Why?'

'Rosie just said, "Eurgh, Grandad – poo!" and then I had to pretend to him that she wanted one, rather than she was indicating that he smelt of it.'

'Dad? Does he?'

'Well, he stinks of something. Who's looking after him?'

'What do you mean, "Who's looking after him?" He's a grown man. I'm fed up with all this pussy-footing-round-poor-Dad routine. He needs to get his bloody act together. I'm telling you, he gets right on my wick.'

'Catherine's meant to sort him out, where is she?' Claire

asked, as if she hadn't listened to a word her sister had just said.

'If she's got any sense, she's gone out. Anyway, why's she meant to look after him? I know she does, but that's just because she's a massive mug.'

Jo had run out of patience with her dad's demands years ago and wished that her older sister would do the same. But for some reason, one that Jo couldn't fathom, Catherine seemed beholden to her father, especially lately. Only last week Mick had decided on a whim that he wanted to go kite flying on Saddleworth Moor and Catherine had willingly obliged. Jo couldn't think of anything worse than getting tangled up in the strings of a box kite, with her hair whipped by the wind and sticking to her lipgloss, just because her dad had decided he needed a new hobby.

A sound like someone bouncing on a trampoline was coming from Catherine's room. Claire jumped up to investigate, throwing Jo a look of annoyance as she went. Jo threw the quilt covers back and slowly followed her sister. She arrived at Catherine's bedroom door to find Rosie jumping up and down on the bed.

'This is Aunty Catherine's room, darling, you wouldn't like it if she came round and bounced on your bed,' Claire was saying.

'Would,' Rosie said.

Fair enough, thought Jo. She was four, she probably would.

Rosie jumped backwards and landed on the bed with a thump. Jo held her breath, it was hard to tell sometimes if her niece was going to laugh or cry. Whatever she did, Claire would no doubt give her a round of applause and a medal. Rosie was spoilt in Jo's opinion, Claire was way too soft with her. They were in luck this time – Rosie burst into a fit of giggles and Claire clapped approvingly.

'Come on, petal, let's have you.' Claire said, trying to coax Rosie off the bed.

'Just pick her up.' Jo said.

'All right, Super Nanny.'

'What?' Jo asked innocently.

'When I need childcare tips, I won't be coming to a hungover nineteen-year-old for them.'

'Oooh!' Jo said camply. 'Anyway, I was watching a programme on Sky the other day about kids; this nanny was saying that you've got to be cruel to be kind.'

'Well, when you've got your own, Mary sodding Poppins, feel free to be as cruel-to-be-kind as you want.'

'Are you allowed to say "sodding" in front of Rosie, or will she have to go and see a child psychologist by the end of the week?' Jo asked, smiling with mock-sweetness.

Claire pulled a face at her younger sister. As they bickered, Rosie picked a piece of paper out from under Catherine's pillow and began playing with it, scrunching it into a ball.

'Can Mummy have that?' Claire asked.

Rosie giggled and screwed it up even more.

Jo shook her head at her sister and said to her niece, 'That's mine, thank you,' and whipped the paper from her hands. Rosie looked crestfallen. 'It could be important,' Jo said, sitting on the edge of the bed reading whatever was written on the paper as Rosie jumped down next to her. 'Oh. My. God.'

'What?' Claire asked, intrigued before evidently her

conscience got the better of her and she pretended that she had been beginning a sentence. 'What . . . ever that is put it back now. This is Catherine's room.'

'She's at the *Star Maker* auditions,' Jo said. She couldn't quite believe it. Her sister, the quiet one, the reliable one, the not-exactly-Leona-Lewis one was at the *Star Maker* auditions?

'Catherine? What for?' Claire asked, seemingly as amazed as Jo by this revelation.

'Well . . . she does have a good voice,' Jo said tentatively.

'When was the last time you heard her sing?' Claire asked. 'Ten years ago in choir. She could sound like a strangled cat now for all we know.' Claire paused for a moment and looked seriously at Jo, 'They'll annihilate her,' she said gravely.

'Come on now, that's a bit harsh.' Jo replied.

'She's hardly Kylie, is she?'

'You are so tight!' Jo said, shaking her head.

'I'm not tight, I'm right.'

'Nice saying.' Jo said, impressed. She turned her attention back to the piece of paper. 'She still writes songs,' Jo said, staring at the audition acceptance form. 'Dad told me.'

'Really?' Claire looked shocked. 'I'm surprised he even noticed.'

Jo knew what she meant. Since his wife left him, their dad had become more and more insular, moping around for years until he was finally diagnosed with clinical depression. Their mother, Karen, when told of Mick's illness had said, 'Depression? He's depressed himself with the sound of his own voice.' The milk of human kindness didn't exactly run over where their mother was concerned. Jo didn't care what her mother thought, or at least she didn't want to care what her mother thought.

'We've got to stop her,' Claire said, jumping up.

'Why?'

'Because the last thing Catherine needs is Richard Forster telling her she's useless,' Claire said.

Richard Forster was the Svengali judge who had created *Star Maker*. He had achieved fame and fortune on both sides of the Atlantic creating pop stars and dashing the dreams of hopefuls during televised auditions. He was nearing retirement age but due to a team of cosmetic surgeons and great make-up artists he looked somewhere in his late forties or early fifties.

'We could just go and cheer her on,' Jo said, looking at Claire hopefully. Anything for a day out, she thought.

'Get dressed,' Claire said. 'We'll figure it out when we get there.'

And this was how Jo had come to break one of her most important rules. No one else had a car. Maria's ex-fiancé Gavin had taken theirs as part of their break-up settlement. He got the car, she got the ten-foot-high, Posh and Becks-style professional picture of the two of them entwined and kissing. Jo couldn't help thinking that Gavin had come out of the deal far better off than Maria, especially as they all had to look at it every day sitting at the top of the stairs. Maria was very sensitive about the picture and when Jo teased her about it she bit her head off and told her that someone had bought it from eBay and she was waiting for them to pick it up. Jo couldn't wait to clap eyes on the nutter that would part with their hard-earned cash for that pictorial monstrosity. So Jo couldn't drive, Maria had no car and Mick was everything-phobic, including driving. That left Claire to chauffeur them all unsafely to the venue of the *Star Maker* auditions.

Mick looked out of the window at the Manchester skyline and sighed, 'I can't believe she didn't tell us.'

Her dad loved sighing, Jo thought. He would often string a load of sighs together so they sounded like one big ongoing outtake of breath. Jo once told an ex-boyfriend that there was no point in coming round to her house to meet anyone because her dad just sat in the corner sounding like a pressure cooker and they wouldn't be able to hear themselves think.

'I wonder what she's going to sing?' Jo pondered.

'They'll crucify her,' Maria said matter-of-factly.

'No they won't,' Jo snapped. Jo didn't want to enter into one of Maria's bitch-fests. Maria got off on other people's misery – or so it seemed to Jo. What Jo couldn't work out about Maria was how so many other people actually seemed to like her. People from work were always ringing up, she had at least one billion friends on Facebook and when it was her birthday she didn't just go out for a drink or a bite to eat – no; it was a five-day, Liz Hurley's wedding-esque affair, with different themes and venues. Last year she'd had a night out in Manchester, a night out in Blackpool and a weekend in Magaluf. Jo thought that she'd rather stab herself in the eye than spend a weekend in Shag a Muff with her sister and her so-called mates but she'd kept quiet and bought her an iTunes voucher.

Jo often wondered why Maria was so popular without

coming up with much of an answer. As far as Jo could see it was as if the nastier and more cutting Maria was with people, the more they wanted to be her friend. It was classic school-bully behaviour and Jo saw it as her civic duty to pull her sister up at any given opportunity, seeing as no one else had the bottle to. 'I wonder what she's going to sing?' Jo asked again.

'R. Kelly, "Flying without Wings",' Maria said.

Jo burst out laughing. 'More like that's what you'd sing, you wrong 'un. I can just see you up there, all moony-eyed at the judges, thinking you were the dog's bollocks.' Jo shut her eyes and began crooning in a high-pitched voice.

Maria punched her in the arm. 'Piss-taker.'

Mick tutted his disapproval at the language.

Jo shoved her back. 'Deluded R. Kelly lover!'

'Will you two give up!' Claire shouted from the driver's seat. Jo and Maria piped down as Claire began slapping the satnav angrily. 'No, I do not want Peter Street in Abergavenny; I want Peter Street in bloody Manchester.'

Jo bit her lip. She wanted to laugh but knew that she would be shouted at and in making Claire shout would distract her even further and they'd no doubt end up under the wheels of a tram. They all sat in barely held silence as Claire pulled up to a red light by Piccadilly train station and waited impatiently as if the whole traffic system was designed to be against her.

Jo's thoughts turned to how this was all going to play out when they got where they were going. What exactly did they think they were doing? What were they going to do when they got there – run in and put a hood over

Catherine's head and kidnap her, IRA-style? Catherine wasn't answering her phone and Jo wasn't sure she would take too kindly to her family turning up and demanding that she not put herself through a public audition. Maybe they should just support her, Jo thought. But then Jo didn't really get a vote where family decisions were concerned – as the youngest she was always treated as the baby without any of the usual perks. She wasn't even allowed the odd teenage strop without someone pulling her up and telling her how hard it had been for them when they were younger – like her three sisters had grown up in a Dickens' novel or something. They're not that much older than me, for God's sake! she thought. Catherine was twenty-four, Maria was twenty-eight and Claire – first in line to the Reilly throne – was thirty-three. As much as Jo tried to put her point across and make the others see that she did sometimes know what she was talking about, she felt that her opinion was never really taken on board by her older sisters. Today would be no exception. She knew what would happen as soon as they arrived at the auditions: Claire would take charge and everyone else would fall into line. It was just the way things were.

Claire rounded a corner in fifth gear and Jo lurched to the side, squashing poor Rosie who had been sitting quietly minding her own business all the way into town. 'Sorry, Rosie,' Jo said, putting a protective arm around her niece.

'That's it! There!' Claire said, screeching to a halt outside a five-star hotel.

'You can't just drop us off here,' Maria said. They had stopped on double yellow lines and were being waved at by an angry-looking man in a high-visibility jacket.

'Right, you lot go in and I'll park up. I'll be one minute.'

Jo jumped out and helped Rosie out of the car. She looked across at the sea of people who were packed inside the building. 'We'll never find her in there,' she said to Maria.

'We bloody well will,' Mick countered defiantly.

Jo looked at her father's disgruntled expression. She had a feeling that daddy dearest didn't want Catherine – his carer – going anywhere anytime soon.

Andy Short wasn't short. He was six foot two and his skinny frame and shock of black hair made him look even taller. He heard the line 'You're not very short are you?' nearly every time he was introduced to someone. He had grown to think this odd; like saying 'You're not very black are you?' to Jack Black.

Andy worked in TV. 'Our Andy works in telly,' he would often hear his mum say proudly. Then she would pause for effect and add the killer punch, the one that got even the most hardened and snobby of her I-don't-care-that-your-son-works-in-TV friends staring at him with admiration. 'He's working on *Star Maker*.'

Once this bit of juicy information was out of the bag everyone always asked the same question, 'What's Richard Forster like?' The real answer to that was that he had a penchant for young girls and many of the hopefuls who came through the doors found themselves being promised the earth and invited back to his palatial hotel suite in whichever city they were auditioning that week. But Andy never told anyone this. Neither did any other crew member, not just because it was unprofessional and sounded like sour grapes, but more importantly because Cherie Forster – Richard's wife and one of the other judges – was such a formidable character that everyone assumed she'd find out who'd snitched on her husband and they'd never work anywhere in the world again, ever.

Andy lived in south Manchester in the suburb of Withington with his parents, something he had vowed to change this year. He was definitely going to get his own place. He loved his mum and dad dearly but his mum had a habit of vacuuming at least three times a day and other people's legs had less rights than the vacuum in her domain. As a result Andy always had bruises on his ankles where his mother had feverishly gone at them with the Dyson. He wanted his own flat and the right to never vacuum again if he so wished. Withington was populated with students and young professionals and, although Andy had left school at seventeen, coming from an area like this made him feel that he had to do something exciting with his life. He couldn't spend the rest of his life pulling pints in the bar where he had worked for the past four years, listening to students rattling on about how drunk they had got the previous evening and pretending they didn't revise.

Andy had always wanted to be a cameraman. And when his uncle Norman had said that he knew someone who knew someone who knew someone who'd once worked on *Coronation Street*, Andy had taken his number and made enough enquiries – and sat through enough interviews that led to nothing – to get himself a job as a runner on the new series of *Star Maker*. A runner was – as the title suggested – someone who did most of the running around that was required behind the scenes on a TV show. The job of a runner wasn't suited to anyone with prima donna tendencies. You had to be prepared to do anything, Andy had quickly learnt. He had heard some horror stories from other runners – one girl had told him that she had to organise a different prostitute every night for a 'happily married' star she had worked with. But until this week Andy hadn't really had to deal with any egos. He had just got on with his job and had been responsible for shepherding the weird and the wonderful as they came in their droves to audition for *Star Maker*. He loved the opportunity he was being given and couldn't believe that he was paid – albeit a pittance – to go to work every day and do something he enjoyed. But in the past few days that feeling had changed, ever since he had been given the role of general dogsbody to Jason P. Longford.

Jason P. Longford was thirty-six, good-looking – if a little David Dickinson on the colour chart, gay but pretending to be straight for his housewife audience, and ruthlessly clawing his way to the top of the TV tree. He had landed the roll of *Star Maker* presenter, ousting Bramble Bergdorf, the pretty but ineffectual daughter of a rock star, who had hosted the show the previous year. This was Jason's ticket into the big time and he was constantly looking for his next opportunity to upstage all around him but for some reason, one which was lost on Andy, he was a huge hit with the public. Yesterday and today Andy had found himself obeying an exhausting list of demands from Jason. He rattled off conflicting orders like machine-gun fire: 'Get me a latte.' 'I didn't order a latte, I ordered a cappuccino.' 'Where is the running list for today?' 'I didn't ask for a running list, I know exactly what we're meant to be doing.' 'Wear green tomorrow, it's my lucky colour.' 'Why are you wearing green? You look like an elf.'

Today, as the audition room had filled with people, Jason had scoured it from behind a screen so that no one could see they were being observed, like a velociraptor hunting its prey. He had already pounced on a few people who in his opinion would make good TV: a man who had an industrial weed spray pack on his back and had been singing the theme from *Ghostbusters* and a girl who had brought her own dry ice machine. Now he was grabbing Andy by the elbow and dragging him towards a poor girl who had just fainted.

'Plain Jane alert!' Jason said, beckoning his crew to follow him.

Jason had a theory that normal-looking people tried harder for the cameras, if they were pug ugly then even better. The girl who had fainted was now being harmonised to death by some Justin Timberlake wannabes. Andy thought momentarily that she wasn't anything like a plain Jane, she was quite pretty, even if she did look like a little washed out.

Then Jason snapped, 'Camera on me.' And they were off: Jason turned on the charm and was performing for his public. He actually said 'my public' without a trace of irony. Andy was sure that even Maria Carey would be less of a diva than Jason. When Jason asked the girl what song she was going to sing, Andy was surprised to hear her say 'Martha's Harbour', a song that his mum used to listen to when he was younger. Jason obviously hadn't a clue what she was talking about – if it wasn't a Barbara Streisand number he always looked a bit lost – but Andy was excited. It made a change from 'Unchained Melody' and 'Wind Beneath My Wings'. When Jason turned round and hissed at him, demanding to know who had sung this song, Andy told him – All About Eve. And as Jason looked at Andy as if he was as much of a freak for knowing the song as the fainting girl for wanting to sing it, Andy caught her eye momentarily. It was the first time in the short while he'd worked on *Star Maker* that he'd seen someone who didn't have a hunger for fame in their eyes. She just looked terrified.

Jason clicked his fingers across his throat to indicate to the camera crew to stop filming. He glared at Catherine. 'God, love, I'm not being funny but you're going to have to pull your finger out of your dull arse if you want to get anywhere in this competition. You're up against the likes of her, for Christ's sake.' He pointed to a doll-like starlet standing nearby. 'And the prize is a recording contract in the US, not two weeks' cabaret in Skeggy.'

Andy was mortified. He stared wide-eyed at the girl and wanted to announce to the room that the views of Jason P. Longford did not necessarily reflect those unfortunate enough to have to work with him.

'Oh,' she said quietly and looked at her hands.

'Just saying, darling. You've got thirty seconds to impress in there and when you meet me, you should be switching on the charm.'

Andy could tell that Jason was losing interest in her and that the old man next to him who was GF (in production speak this meant Great For, as in *great for* TV) was taking centre stage with his false-teeth puppetry. Jason was asking him about his life, trying to extract a story. The TV presenter's tack with old people was to always go for the sob story, no matter how eccentric, they were bound to have a recently dead dog or a recently dead wife or have been dropped out of an aeroplane over Dunkirk in the war and had a peg leg ever since. It always went down well with the producers, so when he was outrageously nasty to nervous young women it was brushed over because he was, on the whole, great at his job.

The poor girl looked crushed. Andy wanted to tell her to ignore Jason, he was a nasty piece of work, and to just go into the audition and give it her all. But he was being beckoned by Jason. Andy grabbed her wrist before he was dragged away and whispered, 'Sorry about that.' He really was; he felt terrible. He didn't understand what this Jason guy got out of his personal swipes at people. The girl looked up and a fat tear rolled down her cheek. She wiped it away.

'It's OK.' She said and smiled sadly. But Andy knew it wasn't OK, it was just the way things were.

Over an hour had passed since Jason P. Longford had told Catherine exactly what he thought and his comments still stung. She had had her preliminary audition. Contrary to popular belief only about twenty per cent of people who attended the auditions ever got to face Richard Forster and the other judges. The rest were auditioned and sent away by TV producers who were clearly looking for more than talent; they were looking for people who would be good to watch. Catherine didn't think that there was anything particularly earth shatteringly special about her that would make them put her through; all she really had was her voice. Catherine had tried to get a smile from the three prelim judges but they had simply raised their heads from their notes when she started to sing, then told her she was through. She thought she had done quite well and the cute clipboard guy had stopped her on the way out and said, 'That was amazing', but he might have just been trying to be nice, embarrassed that he hadn't stepped in when his boss was being so rude. A lot of other hopefuls were exiting the first audition crying, having been told *Thanks, but no thanks*, but the lucky ones like Catherine had been given a golden ticket which meant that they were through to see the judges. She looked around hoping that she might spot Kim who she'd briefly met earlier, but there was no sign of her. Catherine assumed that she must have received a 'no' and gone home disappointed.

Now Catherine was sitting on her own and dwelling on what Jason P. Longford had said to her. Why would someone say something so rude? Catherine felt foolish. He always seemed so nice on TV. Jason presented his own mid-morning show and was always incredibly generous to his guests. Maybe it's me, Catherine thought. She knew she needed to stop dwelling on this, there were bigger things to worry about – the fact that she was going to sing in front of the *Star Maker* judges any moment now being one of them.

The judging panel comprised of Richard Forster, his wife Cherie, Lionel Peters, the famous Broadway producer and Carrie Ward, an American recording star who was married to a famous American footballer who couldn't seem to keep himself out of the tabloids – and they were formidable. She hoped that she wasn't going to faint again.

An old lady wearing a baby-pink gown and a little diamante bow in her hair sat beside Catherine. 'Would you like a boiled sweetie, love?'

Catherine smiled gratefully and took one. 'Thank you,' she said, putting the sweet in her mouth and savouring the liquorice flavour. 'You look lovely, by the way,' Catherine added.

The old lady had obviously made a real effort. Her make-up was flawless and her nails beautifully manicured. She carefully placed her boiled sweets back in her handbag, looked up as Jason P. Longford re-entered the room and watched him as he played to the audience. 'Not everyone thinks so,' she said, looking straight at Jason. 'I always thought he was a nice man on the telly until today.'

'Why, did he say something?' Catherine asked, hoping he hadn't but knowing he probably had.

'He said, "So what brings you here then, love?" And I says, "Well, I like the show and I like to sing so I applied." And he says, "Right . . . you a widow?" I says, that no, my husband dropped me off and he's gone round B&Q for the afternoon – well, I knew my Harold wouldn't be doing with all this – and he says, "No one died recently?" So I looked at him and said, "Not that I know of." And he looks at me like I've just crawled out from under a stone and says, "Bloody hell, love, you could've made something up." Then he turns to one of those fellows that's with him and says, "Who wants to see an old bag with no sob story?" And just while I'm standing there thinking what a rude man he was he said, "And what's with the dress, she looks like she's been dug up." Dug up! I was ever so upset.'

Catherine was sitting open-mouthed. Who did this man think he was? Even Richard Forster wasn't this nasty to people, even though that was what he was famous for – he was just at the blunt end of honest. Catherine looked at the old lady sitting sadly next to her and suddenly she was on her feet and heading in the direction of Jason P. Longford. He was in the middle of having his picture taken with some of the other entrants but Catherine knew that if she stopped she'd lose her momentum and wouldn't say anything.

'Why were you so rude to that lady over there?' she asked loudly.

Jason looked around as if checking to see who she was speaking to. When he realised it was him, he looked at the guy with the clipboard and said, 'Nutter alert. Get security.' But the clipboard guy didn't move.

'You are rude. You were rude to me and you were very rude to that lady,' Catherine continued.

'I said, get security.'

The clipboard guy walked forward and took Catherine by the arm and pulled her away. 'Listen,' he whispered, 'you've got through to see the judges, don't blow it, he's not worth it.'

'He's horrible,' she shouted over her shoulder. She would never have been this brave on her own behalf but she couldn't believe that this so called 'personality' had been so nasty to an old lady.

'Yes, he is,' the clipboard guy agreed.

'And you work for him.'

'Yes, unfortunately I do.'

'Jason P. Longford is an exceptionally rude man!' Catherine shouted to the room full of hopefuls.

Jason looked around and shook his head as if to indicate that Catherine was just another person in a long line of unhinged people he had to deal with.

'Number 4695, Catherine Reilly!' the woman ushering people into the audition room shouted. Catherine heard her name and looked down at her number.

'That's you, go,' the clipboard guy said with a gentle shove.

Catherine noticed that he looked worriedly over to Jason. Jason saw that she was heading for the audition room and sped off in the direction of the door, beating her to it, barring her way in.

'Wait there,' he said menacingly, slamming the door behind him. Catherine's heart sank, he was bound to sabotage it for her, but she wasn't just going to leave now. As she jigged nervously from one foot to the other, the large automatic doors to the hotel opened and a row of familiar faces emerged: Maria, Jo, and her father. Her niece Rosie was there too – which meant that Claire couldn't be far behind. Catherine stared in horror. Her family didn't see her as they scoured the room.

Before she had time to think, Jason P. Longford came out of the audition room. She was sure he was about to say that the judges didn't want to see her but instead he whispered in her ear, 'I've put in a good word, psycho. Don't fuck it up.'

Catherine was frozen to the spot. Why had she made an enemy out of this nasty piece of work? She wanted to say something back but her mind was blank. The door opened and one of the producers ushered her into the room. Cameras were pointing at her as she walked in shakily and stood the centre of the room. There, staring back at her, were four of the most famous faces in TV. Catherine's legs turned to jelly.

'So . . . Catherine.' Richard Forster said looking down at his crib sheet. 'Why do you think you're a star?'

'Er . . .' She was lost for words. 'I don't.'

The judges threw looks to one another. Cherie Forster stepped in. 'This is *Star Maker*,' she said sarcastically.

'Sorry.' Catherine gathered herself. 'I just want to sing.' She was trying to sound honest; she didn't think she was a star. People like her stayed at home and read *Heat* magazine; they didn't appear in it.

'And what are you going to sing for us today?' Carrie Ward asked.

Catherine looked at her. The woman was impossibly beautiful. She had silky blond hair and dewy honey coloured skin with pinched pink cheeks. *She* looked like a true star. Catherine shuffled nervously. She felt like a frump.

'"Martha's Harbour".'

'I love that song,' Richard said. The others nodded approvingly. That was good enough for Catherine. 'When you're ready, Catherine . . .'

She was just about to begin when the door flew open and her family ran in.

'What's that about? She just looked straight at us and did one!' Maria said, indignantly pushing through the crowds of people waiting to audition.

Jo grabbed her arm. 'You don't think she might be totally mortified that we've all just rocked up, by any chance?' she said, trying to present her sister with a bit of sense.

'Her? Embarrassed of us? Why?'

'Let me think,' Jo said, looking at her dad as he picked a remnant of his breakfast out of his beard, inspected it and then popped it in his mouth.

'So what are we doing here if we're not going to stick up for her?' Claire asked.

Jo looked at Claire, who looked different somehow. She had only just joined them after parking the car but she was wild-eyed with excitement. Jo could tell that her sister was getting caught up in the atmosphere. If she wasn't careful, she'd be the one bursting through the audition doors and singing 'Somewhere Over the Rainbow'. 'What's up with you? You look half-demented.'

'Nothing's wrong with me, I'm just taking things in. Look!' Claire shrieked, star struck. 'There's Jason P. Longford.' Claire set off in the direction of the TV presenter. The rest of the family followed. Jo thought for a moment about what to do and then, deciding that she really couldn't do anything other than wait for Catherine to come back out, followed them.

When she arrived at the doors to the audition room Claire had already struck up conversation with Jason P. Longford. 'We just love your show.'

'Vomit, Claire. Stop bum kissing.' Jo said, sweeping past the TV presenter and sticking her ear against the audition room doors.

'Can you hear her?' Maria asked.

Jo shook her head. She could hear voices but no singing.

'And who is this beautiful lady?' Jason P. Longford said, sidling up to Jo. Jo's eyebrow shot to the top of her forehead.

'Bleurgh,' she said, folding her arms across her chest.

Maria stepped in, speaking quickly over Jo, who knew Maria would be like this as soon as she clapped eyes on someone she'd seen on the telly. If there was a casting couch there Jo was sure that Maria would lie on it, legs akimbo, shouting 'Take me Jason you big hunk of famous love!'

'She's our sister. The youngest. Everyone says she looks like Angelina Jolie,' Maria gushed.

'Maria, for the love of God!' Jo seethed. She didn't look anything like Angelina Jolie in her opinion. She had the same sort of hair and big lips – which Jo thought made her look more like a sucker-fish than a film star – and bright blue eyes, but all of her sisters had bright blue eyes. She didn't get what the deal was. Jo wasn't stupid; she knew that something had happened when she was sixteen. Until then she had always been too tall and too skinny for any of the boys at school to look at her twice. But on returning to school after the six weeks' holidays that year, all of the boys in her year suddenly seemed to notice her. It was as if she had somehow grown into her features. Well, they could get stuffed, Jo had thought. And that had pretty much been her attitude to men ever since. If they were only interested in how she looked then she wasn't interested in them. It didn't seem to put them off though, annoyingly. Even clearly gay ones like this Jason guy.

'And you're here for the girl in there?' Jason asked, as if there must be some mistake.

'Yeah,' Jo said. 'She's our sister.'

'She's your sister?' Jason asked, shocked.

'Yes.' Jo was losing patience.

'Really?' he said, raising his eyebrows to the researcher guy next to him.

'What?' Jo asked, her eyes narrowing.

'Well, you don't look like her,' Jason snapped. They glared at one another for a moment until Claire cut in.

'I'm Claire, this is Maria, Jo, my daughter Rosie and our dad Mick and we're all here to support Catherine.' Maria chirped, as if she was introducing the Reillys on *Family Fortunes.*

'And where's Mum?'

'She buggered off when I was twelve,' Jo began.

'Joanna,' Mick hissed. Her father often complained about Karen and blamed her for his lot in life, but the fact of the matter was he was still in love with her and he didn't take kindly to anyone slagging her off. Anyone other than him, that was.

'She's in Chorlton!' Claire shouted loudly over Jo, kicking her to shut her up.

Jason P. Longford looked at them for a moment weighing them up. 'Please do not swear,' he said witheringly.

Jo began to sense her dad's agitation. He didn't like crowds and he didn't like his routine being upset and yet here he was being thrown into a room with hundreds of people. She could feel that he was about to say something.

'We don't think she's doing the right thing,' Mick piped up.

'Dad!' Jo said through gritted teeth.

'Do you want to go in?' Jason asked, pointing at the audition room.

Jo looked at the presenter. Why would he let them in there?

'Yes, I think that's a good idea,' Claire said, speaking for the family. Jo couldn't believe it. Jason opened the door and nodded them in. It all happened so quickly. The others fell into the room and Jo felt she had no option but to follow. And there they were, the famous judges all staring at them. Jo had a sudden flash of clarity and realised what they must look like: the Manchester Hillbillies. She'd seen it time and again on this show – the half-wit contestant who couldn't sing for toffee being defended by their quarter-wit family members. Not that she thought Catherine was a halfwit but still . . . Catherine was also staring at them. Jo could tell from her sister's face that she wasn't appreciating the family's show of unity.

Sorry! Jo mouthed.

'Who have we here?' Richard Forster asked.

Jo was about to speak for her family, afraid that Claire would have such a gush fest she'd collapse in a heap on the floor, but her dad beat her to it.

'We know your game,' Mick said, waggling his finger at the music mogul.

'Dad!' Catherine hissed.

'This is your dad?' Richard asked neutrally. He didn't have to say anything else, Mick was digging his own grave unaided.

'Hey you, mouth.' Mick said, as if he was taking on a hoody at the corner shop. 'I don't want you pulling her to pieces because she doesn't look the part and hasn't got a note in her head.' Mick jutted his bristled chin out defiantly; something that he did when he was trying to look important. Jo thought it made him look like Uncle Albert from *Only Fools and Horses.*

'Did you really just say that?' Catherine asked, utterly exasperated.

'Hi, Richard.' Maria said, with a small girly wave, as if there was only her and Richard Forster in the room. Jo cracked out laughing.

'"Hi, Richard",' Jo said, mimicking her sister. 'What are you doing, you div? D'you think he's going to ask you out because . . . well, I don't know what . . . because you're here?'

'I'm just saying hello,' Maria snapped.

'Embarrassment,' Jo said, shaking her head.

'Has she sung yet?' Claire asked someone wearing a head-microphone and holding a clipboard. Jo couldn't believe that Claire was talking about Catherine as if she wasn't there.

'No, she hasn't.' Richard Forster said tersely. 'And with you lot bleating on I'm quite sure she's not going to want to. Could you all leave, please?'

Jo and her sisters stared at the judge. He was serious. Jo glanced at Catherine, who was standing with eyes to the floor, her cheeks burning crimson. Oh God, Jo thought, we are officially the family from hell.

'Fine, we know when we're not wanted. Come on, Catherine,' Mick said.

'Not her. You lot,' Richard Forster said with a dismissive flick of his hand.

Jo grabbed her father by the shoulders and pushed him

bodily out of the room. Claire and Maria looked dumbfounded, as if they thought that while they were there they might have been asked to do a turn. Jo thought that she had her father under control, but he wasn't going quietly.

'I knew Colonel Tom Parker,' Mick barked over his shoulder. 'Gentleman, he was. Not like you, you robber baron.'

What the bloody hell is a robber baron? Jo thought, her heart racing as she tried her best to limit the damage her father was causing.

'He'd have had you out of the music business quicker than you could say Chico Time,' Mick continued.

Jo shoved her dad out of the audition room and, ensuring that Rosie was still with them, turned and grabbed her two sisters by their arms and pulled them unwillingly away from their fifteen minutes of fame.

'Bloody hell, you've got your work cut out,' Richard Forster said. 'Right, where were we? When you're ready, Catherine.'

Catherine was mortified. She wanted to bolt for the door but she was here now. Her throat had dried up, thanks to her family descending en masse, and she was shaking like a leaf. Cherie Forster tapped her pen on the desk impatiently; Lionel Peters – who looked like a wise old wizard with his pointy beard and long greying mane – had put his hands behind his head and leaned back in his chair, his face neutral, but Carrie Ward smiled warmly and said, 'Take your time Catherine.'

Catherine swallowed hard and began to sing. Her voice

was sweet and strong but she knew that nerves were getting the better of her. She put her hand to her throat as if this would stop the reverberation that she was sure they could all hear. As she reached the end of the verse she looked at Carrie Ward and there was something in her eyes – a willing for her to succeed – that made Catherine think that maybe she was doing well. This gave her the confidence she needed and she pushed on; giving her all to the chorus. She could hear her voice now resonating around the room. She was finally beginning to enjoy herself when Richard Forster waved his hand in the air and said, 'Thank you, thank you.'

Catherine stopped dead and blood rushed again to her cheeks. She touched her face and in that moment had a strange recollection of trying to fry an egg on the pavement as a child because she'd seen it done on *Record Breakers* – it hadn't worked but she was sure if she cracked one on her face now it would fry in seconds.

'Lionel?' Richard said, looking for the impresario's opinion on Catherine.

'To be honest, I could take it or leave it,' he said with a shrug. Catherine stared at him numbly.

Carrie Ward hit her hand on the table and looked at him open mouthed. 'Are you kidding? That was beautiful!' she said.

'Cherie?' Richard turned to his wife.

Cherie paused and looked at Catherine. Catherine could hear the blood rushing in her ears, like listening to the sea in a seashell. 'You were very nervous.' She paused. Catherine nodded. 'I'm not sure you're ready for this competition.'

Catherine hung her head. She was probably right. When she looked up the judges were staring back at her. She couldn't work out why for a moment and then realised that they expected her to list all of the reasons why she was right for this competition. But she couldn't and she wasn't about to beg. She could sing OK but she wasn't sure that this public grilling was something she could face every week. She opened her mouth to speak but Richard Forster had had enough.

'Look, I'm in agreement with Cherie. I think if we put you through, you'd crack.'

'I wouldn't, I promise.' Catherine said, tears welling in her eyes and her voice shaking as if to cruelly prove the judges' point that she wasn't in control of her emotions.

'Lionel?'

'It's a no from me.'

'Cherie?'

'You're a sweet girl with a big smile,' She paused and the look on her face suggested she was torn as to whether to put Catherine through or not. 'But I'm afraid it's a no from me.'

Right, thank you, if you could just arrange for the floor to open up and swallow me that would be great, Catherine thought.

'Carrie?'

'Absolutely one hundred per cent yes! We've just put some one through who was dressed as a giraffe and you're turning her down?'

Good point, Catherine thought.

'Thank you,' Richard said. He definitely wore the trousers around here.

Carrie had one last go at defending Catherine. 'She's twenty-four. If we send her away she'll be too old for the category next year.' Catherine knew that it was the unspoken rule that the only successful *Star Maker* winners were the ones who came from the under-twenty-five category. The public wants its stars to be youthful.

Richard Forster looked at her, thought for a moment and then proceeded to sum things up for Catherine. 'Here's the thing,' he said – Catherine wasn't sure she wanted to hear the thing – 'you can sing. And there's definitely something about you, but – as Cherie said – I'm not sure you're ready for this competition. America will be extremely tough.'

Catherine hung her head waiting for the inevitable.

'It's a no, Catherine.'

Catherine was gutted, in the most extreme sense of the word. It was exactly like all her guts had been ripped out of her and dumped on the floor. Her family would *definitely* be on the TV with their performance and she would become a laughing stock. A rejected laughing stock. She nodded meekly and headed for the door. The short walk felt like a day-long trek.

Jason P. Longford pounced on her as soon as she came out of the audition room. The camera was rolling and he was charm personified. 'Catherine, how did it go?'

She shook her head, unable to reply.

'Was it a no?' He asked, oozing fake compassion.

Catherine nodded and walked off. Jason followed her with his crew. 'What did Richard say?'

'He said no.'

Catherine discerned a look of glee from Jason. She

turned away from him – catching the eye of the clipboard guy from earlier. He gave her what she thought to be a look of sympathy. She'd had enough of people's sympathy for one day. It was her family feeling sorry for her that had made her so nervous in the first place. She walked away from Jason and could hear him saying, 'What's her problem, miserable cow?' He was obviously off-air again. Catherine sloped towards the door thinking that this was all her own stupid fault. Who did she think she was? Someone good enough to do well on a show like this? She swallowed back tears and wished that she'd never got out of bed that morning.

'Dum. Dum. Dum. Another one bites the dust . . .' Andy was watching Jason P. Longford move his body with a distinct lack of rhythm, as he sang in celebration at having orchestrated another person's exit from the competition. It was like watching an embarrassing uncle trying to body pop.

'What you looking at?' he snapped at Andy.

'Nothing,' Andy said, averting his gaze.

The door to the audition room opened and Richard Forster stuck his head out. The crowds of people waiting to audition became visibly excited at his presence. 'Can I have a word?' he said. Andy and the rest of the crew went to follow him but Richard said, 'On your own.'

Jason gulped and followed the man who, for the moment, was responsible for his career. Andy stood outside the audition room and could hear muffled, raised voices and snatches of conversation. He didn't want to appear as if he was listening in, but that was absolutely what he was doing. Richard Forster's voice dominated the proceedings.

'When they're obviously good, don't let their idiot family lose it for them just for TV ratings . . . I know what I said, but there's enough lunatics out there without breaking good people who've come to audition . . . unless they're totally OTT, I don't know . . . like they're toothless and playing a banjo, then no more families in the audition room! We're turning into a freak show and this is going out in America, not just here. It needs to be about talent.'

Richard calmed down and then began saying something else to Jason, which Andy could barely hear. Then Jason's voice: 'It won't happen again . . . absolutely, absolutely . . . yes, straight away.' Andy stifled a laugh at the sound of Jason's grovelling.

A few moments later, Jason came out of the audition room, smoothed his shirt down and stretched his neck from side to side as if limbering up. He looked at Andy. 'They want to see that bloody girl again.'

'Really?' Andy asked, surprised.

'Am I standing here telling lies for the sake of it? Of course, really. Go find her. And don't come back without her.'

Catherine, still stunned by her family's performance, was standing in the taxi bay of the hotel, shivering in the cold drizzly Manchester weather and wishing that Claire would hurry up. She had just called her sister and pleaded with her to turn around and pick her up. It didn't take much pleading. Claire was rightly contrite. Thankfully, they hadn't got far and Claire soon screeched to a halt outside the hotel – the scene of Catherine's shame.

Catherine was soaked. She hadn't thought to dress for the rain. *God knows why*, she thought. Twenty-four years in Manchester should have taught her that the chances of rain were high even if a drought of Biblical proportions was predicted.

'What happened?' Jo asked, excited.

'Don't ask.'

'Oh my God, were you booted off? The shame,' Maria said.

'Thanks for the understanding.'

'But we'll be on telly looking like wrong 'uns now,' Maria complained.

'And that's Catherine's fault, how?' Jo asked. Then something seemed to occur to her. 'Eh, maybe they'll get us back to be on the final show, you know like they do with all the divs who can't sing. How top would that be?'

'Not very top at all,' Catherine said quietly.

No one seemed to notice she was angry. Her family were so thick-skinned that Catherine would probably have to murder one of them for the others to notice she was annoyed.

'Sorry, Catherine,' Jo said, nudging her sister affectionately. 'You're right. Not top at all.'

Catherine looked at Jo. It was OK for her, a knock like this was nothing to Jo. She breezed through life. Catherine only wished that she were one of life's breezers.

Catherine couldn't catch her father's eye. She knew he was annoyed that she hadn't told him of her plans to audition. 'Well, I'm glad that's done and dusted is all I can say,' Mick muttered.

'And all I can say, Dad . . .' Catherine said bravely, 'is who the hell is Colonel Tom Parker?'

'Who . . . what . . . who the . . .' Mick stammered as if he was utterly agog at his daughter's lack of knowledge. 'Only Elvis's bloody manager, that's who!'

'Elvis Presley?'

'What other Elvis is there?' Mick asked, outraged.

'Costello?' Claire said.

'Who's bothered about Elvis Costello? Jesus H. Corbett,' Mick said, shaking his head in disgust.

'So, you knew him well then, did you, Dad? Elvis's manager?' Jo asked.

'Like that,' Mick said, prodding his entwined fingers in Jo's direction.

'Where did you meet him?'

'Brighouse.'

Catherine closed her eyes and took a deep breath. The fact that she had just had possibly the worst morning of her life seemed lost on her family. 'Can we go please?' she asked.

'I need the lav,' Mick said, clambering out of the car.

'No, Dad. Not in there.' Catherine didn't want her dad trying to get back into the hotel.

'I've got my disability badge with me, what are they going to do, chuck me out? I'll go to the *Manchester Evening News* with it if I have to.' Mick was always threatening to go to the *Manchester Evening News*. It didn't matter how unreasonable he was being about something, he naturally assumed that he was somehow fighting the corner of the little man. He'd once been arrested and cautioned for staging a sit-in and singing 'We Shall Overcome' at Central Library because they'd tried to charge him twenty-six pence for returning a Jamie Oliver cookbook two weeks late. Catherine thought this was an odd choice of book for her father to borrow seeing as he didn't seem to know how to turn the cooker on. When the police were pulling him through the doors of the library for causing a scene, he had shouted to anyone who'd listen, 'Get me the *Manchester Evening News* on the phone!'

Just as Mick was getting out of the passenger door, someone ran up to the side of the car. Catherine stretched to see who it was. It was the cute clipboard guy who worked with Jason P. Longford.

'Thank God I caught you.'

'Me?' said Mick.

'Yeah, Dad, the world revolves round you,' Jo quipped.

'No, Catherine.' The clipboard guy looked at her. Catherine put her hand to her chest; she was shocked. 'Richard Forster wants you to come back in, have some time to calm down and forget what happened earlier and do the audition again.'

Catherine was speechless. Maria wasn't. 'Oh my God! That is so brilliant, come on, let's go!'

'I'm under strict instructions – it's just Catherine, I'm afraid.'

Catherine looked at Claire, Maria, Jo, Rosie and then at her dad standing forlornly on the pavement. 'Go on, Catherine. Go for it,' Claire urged.

Jo nodded in agreement. 'Seriously, sis. Off you go. Break a leg. You'll make a dead good fake celebrity. I'll come to Nobu with you and hang out with Chantelle if you want.'

Catherine smiled. 'Thanks Jo, you're a trooper.'

'Any time.'

'We'll come and get you when you're ready.' Claire said. Catherine looked at her sisters. Could this be support from her family?

'Good luck, Aunty Catherine,' Rosie said sweetly.

Even Maria managed a half-generous smile and said, 'They must have thought you were good for something if they're asking you back.'

Catherine got out of the car and looked at her dad, hoping for an iota of encouragement, but he didn't look at her. Instead he turned his attention to the guy with the clipboard and said, 'Any chance of using the bog?'

'I'm Andy, by the way,' the clipboard guy said to Catherine, putting his hand out for her to shake. 'I'm really sorry about what happened with Jason earlier.'

Catherine shook his hand. It was one of those moments where she wished he hadn't put his hand out and she could tell he was thinking the same. They shook hands limply and then both laughed, embarrassed. 'He's horrible,' Catherine said about Jason. She wasn't going to dwell on the embarrassing handshake.

'Yes, he is.'

'But you still work for him.'

'I haven't got any choice. Believe me, if I did I'd swap in a heartbeat,' Andy said.

'Jason P. Longford.' Catherine mused over the name. 'What's the P for?'

'Penis, I think.' Andy deadpanned. Catherine cracked out laughing.

'It suits him.'

'He's awful, but I can deal with awful if it means I get to do something good with my life. *Star Maker* only runs until Christmas, then after that I can hopefully work on another show.' Andy went on to explain to Catherine a bit about his frantic job. Catherine found herself laughing at his anecdotes.

They reached the entrance to the hotel again and Andy opened the door. Catherine stepped through, thanking him. She couldn't remember the last time someone had opened a door for her; mostly people hadn't realised she was there. Just being back in the waiting room made Catherine nervous again. 'I'll have to wait hours, won't I?' she said to Andy.

'I don't think so. I only said the thing about you having a few hours before you went in again for your family's benefit. I hope you don't mind. They seem pretty persistent and if they'd have come back in with you I think I might have been sacked.'

Catherine laughed, mortified by her family. Then, the fact that she had been asked to come back in hit her and she was suddenly overwhelmed. She gripped Andy's arm.

'Are you OK?' he asked.

She took a deep breath. 'Yes. Sorry.'

'You nearly cut off my blood supply.'

Catherine shut her eyes and told herself to get her act together. This was a huge opportunity and she wasn't going to blow it a second time. She could feel that other people in the audition room were looking at her, wondering why she was getting special treatment. She tried to block them out.

'Oh God,' Andy whispered. Catherine looked up to see Jason P. Longford heading over to them at speed.

'Here she is! Here she is!' he announced at the top of his lungs as if he and Catherine were long-lost best friends. He put his arm around her, something which made Catherine's shoulders shoot up to her ears. He squeezed so hard that it made Catherine yelp involuntarily. 'Coming through. Coming through,' Jason said clearing a way through the crowds. 'Lady with a second chance.' The camera crew followed her, and Catherine looked round for Andy and caught his eye. 'Good luck,' he mouthed. Jason forced her through the audition room doors.

'Back again. *Déjà vu!*' he said to the judges with such fake cheer that Catherine was sure he was going to snap and kill someone any moment. '*Voila!*' he said, posturing like a magician's assistant.

'Thank you, Jason. That'll be all,' Richard said. Then he turned and said off-microphone to one of the producers, 'Can we cut him out of this section if we use this?' The producer nodded. 'Good,' Richard said.

It seemed that Catherine and Andy weren't the only ones not to be enamoured by Jason Penis Longford.

'Right,' Richard said, looking up at Catherine. 'We've had a change of heart. I like you. I think you've got something, but I think that you were far too nervous because of your family. Do you think giving you a second chance is the right thing to do?'

'Absolutely,' Catherine said. As she was standing there,

having been given that second chance, she suddenly knew that she could do this.

'Off you go then,' Richard Forster said, giving her the nod to start.

Catherine began to sing. She could feel the pitch of her voice, low and strong to begin with, dipping breathily in the verse and soaring sweetly in the chorus. She knew every word and note inside out, she had sung this song a thousand times, and in her imagination had performed it on countless occasions. It felt like her own song; her own words. This time around, singing this song as it should be sung was as natural to Catherine as breathing. She finished the last chorus and realised she had been allowed to sing the song all the way through. She looked at the judges, feeling as if she had just emerged from a trance. Her heart thumped heavily in her chest. Now was the moment of truth.

Carrie Ward spoke first. 'That was just beautiful.' Catherine could see that she had tears in her eyes. She hoped that was a good thing.

Next up was Cherie Forster. 'Well, all I can say is I'm glad we brought you back and I disagree wholeheartedly with what Richard said earlier. A voice like yours would be a breath of fresh air in America.' She threw her husband a look. He didn't respond.

Lionel was nodding next to her. 'I have to agree. I'll eat my previous words; that was a brilliant performance.'

Catherine eyes were darting between the judges, she was trying to take in what they were saying but it just didn't seem to compute. Her gaze landed on Richard Forster.

'So, Catherine . . .' he paused for what seemed like an

eternity. 'Your first audition was a little shaky but we decided to bring you back because we thought that you might have something.' He paused again. Catherine's legs were shaking, barely holding her up. 'And I have to say that I think you have, I can't put my finger on it, but there's something about you.' He paused again, the suspense was killing Catherine. 'And that performance was one of the best auditions I've ever seen. You were sensational.' Catherine clapped her hands to her mouth. 'So here's the moment of truth . . . Carrie?'

'Again. One hundred per cent, yes.'

'Lionel?'

'It's a yes from me.'

'Cherie?'

'If I get you in my category, we've won. Yes! Yes! Yes!'

'Catherine?' Richard paused again. Catherine thought she was going to collapse with anticipation. 'You're through to Boot Camp.'

Catherine jumped in the air, 'Thank you so much!' she said. She was about to run over to the judges but then collected herself and ran out of the audition room. Jason tried to get hold of her for an interview but she ran straight towards the first friendly face she saw: Andy. 'I'm through!' she squealed and threw her arms around him, squeezing him tightly. He hugged her back. Then suddenly the moment had gone and as excited as she was, Catherine realised she was hugging a virtual stranger. 'Sorry,' she said, embarrassed, pulling away. But Andy didn't seem to mind. In fact he was beaming and it seemed that he was just about to say something when Jason got his Vulcan-like grip on Catherine's arm and pulled her into camera shot.

'Get over here, you'd better get used to this if you're going to be famous,' he hissed.

She wasn't going to be famous, she thought. Not her – was she? But even as she tried to make her way through the other hopefuls who were now surrounding her, waiting to hear her good luck story, Catherine had the disconcerting feeling that things might never be the same again.

Chapter 2

'Well, well. Saturday evening mass; we'll make a good Catholic of you yet.' Father McGary smiled at Catherine.

She had been sitting at the back of church throughout the service having left the house for some fresh air and headed to the only place where – up until today – she had felt welcome to sing. Father McGary was a portly man with a big shock of greying ginger hair and thick Deidre Barlow glasses. Catherine often wondered how he'd ended up with a pair of glasses that were so obviously meant for a female face but she'd never asked him. Anyway, they kind of suited him.

'I just needed a bit of time out of the house,' Catherine explained. 'I've had a bit of a mad day.'

'You and me both. The church roof has pigeons lofting in it and I've been up a ladder with a sweeping brush trying to get at them for the best part of the afternoon,' Father McGary said. 'What have you been up to? Is your father demanding to be pushed in his bed from Land's End to John O'Groats?'

Catherine laughed. Over the past few years, as Catherine had come to the church to practise her singing, she and the priest had built up a good rapport and she had slowly begun to confide in him about her role within her family. She knew that Father McGary felt that she took too much on with her father but he never pushed the issue, he just made the odd wry comment that made her think.

'No, I went to the *Star Maker* auditions,' Catherine said, wincing slightly as she delivered the news. She was half expecting Father McGary to either not know what she was talking about or to be disgusted with her. Would he think that it was shows like that that were adding to the moral bankruptcy of the nation and that she'd need to go to confession and repent immediately?

'I nearly went myself!' Father McGary exclaimed excitedly, smacking Catherine on the arm. 'I had the form filled out and everything. I thought, they've never had a priest on before. I'll be the first one.'

Catherine laughed. 'What were you going to sing?'

'"When Doves Cry" by Prince.'

Catherine almost laughed again but when she realised that Father McGary was serious she swallowed it.

'I didn't know you could sing, Father.'

'I can't, I haven't a note in my head, but it looks like a nice day out, and like I said, I'd have been the first priest. I'd have got myself and the parish noticed and that way more people might come to mass. More people might put money in the collection and I might get the roof fixed and not find myself up to my elbows in pigeon poo on a regular basis.' Father McGary's warped logic somehow made perfect sense to Catherine. 'So, tell me, how did you get on? Did you get to meet that Forster fella?'

Catherine told Father McGary all about her day and the fact that she was now through to the Boot Camp stage of the competition. He sat listening to the story, taking it all in with glee. 'I'm delighted for you!' he said, ruffling Catherine's hair as if she were a toddler. Something about the priest's unconditional support touched Catherine and tears sprang to her eyes.

'Eh, no crying now. What are the tears for?'

Catherine shrugged, she wasn't entirely sure. She thought a moment. 'I'm just worried I suppose . . .'

'Worried about what?'

'My dad. How he'll cope while I'm away.'

'Your father will be fine. Always has been, always will be.'

'But he's poorly,' Catherine said and then immediately felt guilty. Should she even be saying this? After all, her father had sworn her to secrecy. But she had kept the secret for long enough and it was beginning to feel like carrying a ton weight around.

'He's always poorly, isn't he? He's had everything under the sun for as long as I've known him.' Mick had lived in Father McGary's parish since he was a boy and he was something of a notorious character around the area. Her father only attended church for 'hatches, matches and dispatches' as he liked to call christenings, weddings and funerals, but Father McGary knew all about Mick; everyone, it seemed, knew all about Mick.

'He's got cancer,' Catherine said, her voice barely audible.

Father McGary blessed himself. 'Oh Catherine, I'm so sorry. When did you find this out?'

'He told me months ago.'

'Well, I see lots of people who have cancer and pull through.'

Catherine leant forward and began to cry. She didn't

want the priest to see her like this; she didn't want anyone to see her like this.

'What type of cancer is it?' Father McGary asked gently.

Catherine lifted her head up and looked at him. She knew that this was going to sound like a ridiculous answer but it was the truth. 'I really don't know.'

'He never said when he came home from the hospital?'

'No, he just told me that he has cancer and that he can feel it inside of him all of the time and whenever he goes to the hospital he comes home and it's bad news. They don't seem to be able to treat it, whatever it is.'

'And has there been any word from your mother about this?' the priest probed gently.

'No. I doubt Dad would want her to know.'

Father McGary looked as if he was about to say something but then thought better of it. 'What have your sisters said?' he asked instead.

Catherine knew again that this was going to sound ridiculous once she said it out loud. 'Dad's asked me not to tell them.'

Father McGary took this in and nodded his head even though his body language made him look as if he should be shaking it in disgust. 'And has he given any reason for this?'

'Not really. We don't really talk about stuff. He just trusts me . . .' Catherine trailed off, thinking that she was sounding a lot like a wet lettuce.

'That may be the case, but he can't burden you with something like this. What has he said about your success today? I'm assuming you'll have to leave him to go off to the competition, what has he said about that?'

'Oh, he's been fine really. He's quite encouraging actually,' Catherine said, without being able to meet Father McGary's gaze. She was like some poor battered wife who when confronted about her latest black eye, claimed to have walked into a door.

'That's good to hear.'

Catherine nodded and stood up. She was sure that Father McGary didn't believe her, but she didn't want to tell him how her father had really reacted to the news that she was through to the next stage of the nation's most watched competition – like a five-year-old in a sulk. 'Thanks, Father, I just wanted to tell you how I'd got on, you know, with you letting me sing here and everything.'

'Don't be daft. You'd better come back and sing here when you're rich and famous.'

'I will,' she nodded.

Catherine left the church and walked along the road in the direction of her house. She felt a warm glow from the priest's reaction. It had been nice to tell someone who knew how much this meant to her. Catherine loved music and singing and Father McGary seemed to understand this. Over the time that she had been using the church to practise she had discussed her musical tastes with the priest on numerous occasions. Telling him how she had first become interested in pop music when she was five or six when Claire used to listen to Madonna and New Kids on the Block. As she got older Claire graduated onto bands like REM and Nirvana and Catherine used to listen to her CDs when her sister was out working at her Saturday job at Tesco. As Catherine grew up and her musical taste developed she found herself becoming fascinated by the lyrics as much as by the music. Bands like Radiohead, Doves and Elbow sat alongside singers like Beth Orton, PJ Harvey and Tori Amos in her CD collection. While everyone else at school was listening to the Spice Girls and Take That, Catherine was listening to songs of heartbreak, loss and longing. These songs spoke to her even though she hadn't experienced anything like this at the time, but somehow she knew how it felt.

When her mother left home these songs meant more to her than ever. She didn't need a boyfriend to break her heart, she had a mother who'd done that for her. Not that Catherine ever said anything to anyone, she was too much of a peacemaker for that; add to this the fact that she felt she had to keep things on an even keel at home for poor Jo who had only been twelve at the time of their mother's departure. So her own feelings towards her mum were channelled into the songs she wrote herself, she was just too lacking in confidence to ever sing them to anyone. Catherine hoped that this competition might give her the confidence she needed to push herself forward.

As Catherine neared the end of the street she turned around. She was a couple of hundred yards away from the church now but she could still see the silhouette of Father McGary standing waiting; checking to see that she was OK.

'Here she is, Mariah Carey,' Mick said, as Catherine came through the door. 'I got me own tea, thanks.' Mick was sitting in front of the TV with a plate of beans on toast on his lap.

'How's me putting the toast in the toaster, popping it,

spreading butter on it, warming the beans, putting them on the toast and then putting the plate on your knee, you getting your own tea?' Jo asked, pulling her hair into a ponytail and smearing lip balm on her lips. 'I don't know how you put up with him, it's like living with Dot Cotton.'

'You have to listen to him too,' Catherine reminded her.

'Not really. I'm usually out, which is where I'm going now.'

'Out where?' Mick asked.

'Out out.'

'You're not going anywhere until I know where you're going.'

'OK.' Jo grabbed a pen. She scribbled something on a piece of paper and handed it to her father. 'Here's the address.'

Mick looked at it satisfied for a moment until he realised it was a joke address. '999 Letsbe Avenue. Very funny, Joanna. Very smart.'

Jo smiled sweetly. 'I'm off to tell everyone my sister's going to be famous. Bye!'

'Where are you going?' Mick asked, and then demanded, exasperatedly, from Catherine, 'Where's she going?'

'Jo, we're not meant to say anything in case it gets in the papers . . .' Catherine said weakly, before letting her sister go. She knew no one would be interested in her – what sort of story did she have that the *News of the World* would want to splash across the front page: BOOT CAMP GIRL LETS DAD SORT HIS OWN TEA OUT SHOCKER? She didn't think so.

Catherine sat down in the chair opposite her dad. After her conversation with Father McGary she wanted to ask Mick what cancer he had and why he didn't want her to mention it to anyone. But sitting here now, actually face to face with him, she knew she couldn't. They didn't have huge heartfelt conversations like some family from *Home and Away*. She just needed to make sure that he understood that she was going to be away for a few days at Boot Camp and in that time she wouldn't be able to help him.

'Dad, you know I'm going away.'

'Don't worry about me . . .'

'Well I do, so I'm just saying.'

'Pass me my pills, will you?'

Catherine went to the drawer where her dad secreted his stash of pills. He took five pills three times a day, each one looked big enough to tranquilise a horse. Catherine sat and watched as Mick tipped each one dramatically back into his mouth.

'So, I'm just wondering . . . who's going to look after you?' Catherine asked.

The question hung in the air as Mick motored his way through his tablets. When he had finished throwing down the last one he began to cough – a daily pill-taking routine – like a cat with fur balls. Catherine waited for him to finish. He looked at her.

'What?'

'I was saying, who is going to look after you?'

'I can look after myself,' Mick said, turning his attention back to the TV.

Catherine took a deep breath. 'But you ring me at least fifteen times a day. How will you be able to look after yourself?'

'Who rings you fifteen times a day?'

'You do, Dad!' Catherine said, frustrated. It was true. As soon as she left the house Mick would make his first call of the day to ask her where something was or to tell her something he'd discovered.

Maria came into the living room in a cloud of perfume, wearing a silver backless dress and six-inch high heels. Her chestnut hair was scraped back and her make-up was perfectly in place, if a little bit caked on. She was pretty but she just couldn't leave the house without a face full of MAC. Maria would look much better, Catherine often thought, if she just applied less slap.

'Maria, when I'm at Boot Camp, will you be able to take care of Dad?'

'He's big enough and daft enough to take care of himself, aren't you?' Maria said, hunting through the ornamental jars on top of the fireplace. 'Have you seen my cash card?'

'No. Listen, he needs help . . .'

'I am here, you know,' Mick pointed out.

'And I won't be able to speak to him whenever he wants to call me.'

'Then he'll have to talk to one of us, won't he?' Maria said, pulling out drawing pins, reels of cotton and a piece of chalk. 'Why have we got chalk? Who uses chalk? This house is like a jumble sale.' Maria spied something on the floor near to where Mick was sitting. 'There it is,' she said, picking up her cash card. 'Right, I'm off out. Don't wait up.' She ran out, slamming the door hard behind her.

'See, like she's bothered if I'm OK or not,' Mick grumbled.

'Well, it might help if she knew about . . . your illness.'

Catherine couldn't bring herself to say 'cancer'. Just the word made it feel more scary and real than it already was.

'I don't want them knowing,' Mick said.

'But why, Dad? Why only tell me?'

Mick turned and looked at his daughter. 'Because I suppose I think it's you and me against the world, Cath.'

Catherine hung her head, she didn't want her dad to see that she was on the verge of tears. The only person who had ever called her Cath was her mum. But it had been a long time since she'd left and a long time since anyone had referred to her as Cath. 'It's not, Dad. The others want to help too.' Or at least they would if they knew, she thought.

'I don't really think so,' Mick shook his head.

Catherine felt deflated and back to square one. As other candidates were excitedly preparing for the experience of their lives, Catherine was trying to sort out childcare for her own father. There was nothing for it, she was going to have to grab the bull by the horns and make her sisters listen – it was only a few days and she'd be back, it wasn't as if she stood a chance of making it to the finals. She called Claire. She was sensible; she'd know what to do.

'Yep,' Claire said breathlessly when she picked up the phone.

'It's about Dad, Claire. I'm going to need some help while I'm away.'

There was an impatient pause. Then Claire said, 'And?'

'And I was hoping, you know, because you're the eldest and everything—'

'And I'm the one with two kids and a husband . . .'

'I know that, Claire, but I just thought that you might be able to sort Dad out.'

'Well, as Dad would say, you know what thought did.' Claire snapped.

Catherine could never remember what it was exactly that thought did do. Something to do with muck carts and weddings, but she never really knew what that was meant to mean.

'All right, don't snap. Have I caught you at a bad time?'

'You could say that. Jake's got nits and they're hopping off his head and Rosie's freaking out, so I'm sorry but looking after Dad is not top of my list of priorities.'

'OK,' Catherine said quietly. 'Sorry.'

'Listen,' Claire said, her voice softening. 'I think you need to give yourself a break. Dad runs rings around you because you let him. If you leave him to his own devices then he'll have no alternative but to sort himself out, will he?'

'No, you're right.' Catherine said, wishing that she could tell her sister the truth about their dad, then maybe she'd understand her concern. 'Thanks, Claire. And good luck with the nits,' she added.

Jo was sitting in a dingy pub near Manchester University. She and her friends always came to this area of town – the drinks were cheaper than in the city centre and the men more scared of talking to women, which meant that she and her friends were generally left alone to get on with the important business of having a good time. She was sitting with her best friends Cara and Rachel and she was making them wait for her news.

'Come on then . . .' Cara said.

'I don't know if you're ready for gossip this good,' Jo said, taking a sip of her pint and shaking her head as if by withholding the information she had she was actually doing her friends a favour.

'You've bigged it up so much that unless you're going out with Orlando Bloom it's going to look like poor news,' Rachel said, but Jo could tell she was dying to know what she had to say.

'My friends, faith in me you have lost.'

'Listen Yoda, spill it, or move on.'

A smile played on Jo's lips. 'You know our Catherine . . .'

'Yes,' Rachel and Cara said in unison. She knew what they were thinking, *yes, your sister, the boring one . . .*

'Well, she went for an audition today.'

'An audition for what?' Rachel asked.

Jo knew this was going to be good. They would never think in a million years that Catherine would have a talent for singing.

'Oh, a little singing competition . . .' Jo said, watching Rachel and Cara roll their eyes at one another, '. . . called *Star Maker*.'

'No!' Rachel gasped.

'Way!' Cara finished for her.

'Yes. Way.' Jo nodded.

'Did she get to meet the judges?'

'She didn't just get to meet them . . . she got through.'

'What?' Cara and Rachel screeched.

'Boot Camp. My sister is going to be famous. Well, maybe not famous, maybe seen once and then booted off but you get the drift . . . But you're not allowed to say anything or I'm dead meat. The show controls all the press stuff. We've all got to sign confidentiality agreements which means that Richard Forster can eat our spleens if we blab anything to the press if she gets down to the finals.'

Cara and Rachel looked at each other and burst out laughing. 'Whoa! Back up. How has that happened?' Cara asked.

'She can sing,' Jo said. And then she remembered the really good bit of the story. 'And I'm probably going to be on telly.'

'Why? Because you're just so goddamn photogenic?' Cara asked.

Jo shoved her. Her friends always teased her about her looks.

'Don't be a div. No because we went in there – the whole family!' As Jo told the story Cara and Rachel roared with laughter. Jo loved telling her friends stories, they always appreciated them and always egged her on to elaborate. She had been looking forward to imparting this priceless anecdote all day.

'All of you?' Cara asked.

'The entire Reilly clan?' Rachel added.

'The lot of us. Dad included.'

Cara and Rachel let this piece of information settle and then burst out laughing again.

'Yes, Mick Reilly got out of his pit long enough to get himself on national TV,' Jo said, finishing her drink with a flourish. Jo went on to tell the girls about the total show they'd made of themselves and how her father had shouted at Richard Forster.

'What's a robber baron?' Cara asked, wiping tears from her eyes.

'That's what we said,' Jo replied. 'So our Catherine is off to Boot Camp . . .'

'What's going to happen with your dad? She does everything for him, doesn't she?'

'I'm going to show him a picture of his arse and his elbow and once he's worked out which is which, he's on his own,' Jo said, rising from her seat. 'Another drink? All this business of having a famous sister is making me thirsty,' she said, smiling before heading for the bar.

Chapter 3

The day of Boot Camp finally arrived. The last few weeks had seemed like months; in which time Catherine had become something of a local celebrity. The *Star Maker* people had made her sign all sorts of legal documents, stating who she could and couldn't talk to, stressing how important it was that people didn't know what was going on behind the scenes. But they had informed her that it was fine to tell people that she was going to Boot Camp. Until then she hadn't even thought about the repercussions of telling people her good news. People weren't just interested in it, it seemed, they somehow felt that they had a vested interest in Catherine's future. Because *Star Maker* was such a national institution, Catherine quickly realised, people saw her success in getting through to the next stage as somehow their own success. They knew her, they were pleased for her and therefore they were now involved in the whole process. She didn't begrudge anyone feeling this way; on the contrary she was delighted to have people support her. It was just odd to be the centre of attention for once. She wasn't quite sure how she felt about it yet.

It had started when she had to ask at work for time off. Catherine worked in a call centre in Trafford Park, an industrial area that stretched from the M60 ring road to Old Trafford. The most exciting thing that had happened to anyone on her team in the last five years was when her colleague Ray had appeared on *Eggheads*. He had come a cropper against Judith Keppel and still hadn't got over it. He would wander around work, muttering 'The Hoover Dam'. Catherine didn't know what that meant but it obviously upset Ray.

When Catherine asked her boss Gloria for time off and told her the reason, Gloria had been so excited that she had screamed and spilled Slim Fast all over her keyboard. 'Take all the time you need,' Gloria said. 'As long as we get tickets to the live finals.'

Catherine didn't think she'd get that far but she promised Gloria that she'd do her best and asked Gloria if, in return, she'd keep quiet about her impending time off.

'Of course! You know me, take everything to the grave,' Gloria had said conspiratorially, crossing her heart and winking. However, Gloria didn't get as far as the grave with this particular secret; the next day Catherine had arrived at work to be greeted by a huge make-shift banner draped on the outside of her office building with 'Catherine Reilly – our *Star Maker* Winner!' written in ten-foot-high letters. When Catherine arrived at her desk Gloria shouted 'Now!' and everyone tried to let off party poppers, with mixed results; some refused to pop, some popped loudly with streamers landing on the banks of PCs and Ray's went off in his eye, meaning he had to fill out an occupational health form and spend the morning in the sick bay.

'I couldn't help it, Catherine, I'm just so pleased for you!' Gloria said.

Catherine couldn't be angry with her. Gloria was lovely;

Catherine couldn't ask for a nicer boss. But it did mean that Catherine's little secret was soon the talk of Manchester.

The *Manchester Evening News* had called, asking if they could write an article about Catherine. Mick had naturally thought that the phone call was for him – the *Manchester Evening News* was finally on the phone – and had been hugely disappointed to discover that it was his daughter they were interested in and not the latest letter of complaint he had submitted to them about footballers parking on double yellow lines. Catherine had been given a number by the *Star Maker* producers to call if she had any questions before Boot Camp, so she had rung and asked them if it was OK to speak to the paper. They agreed and Catherine found herself on the front cover. MANCHESTER GIRL HAS STAR QUALITY the headline read, with a picture of her at the side. Jo had run home with the paper waving it for everyone to see. In the past few weeks Jo had been almost more excited about Catherine's impending trip to Boot Camp than she was herself. Jo had laid the paper out on the table and she, Maria and Catherine had gathered around. Mick had been feeding his goldfish. When Jo began to read the article she realised that Mick wasn't paying attention. 'Eh, Dad. You coming to look at this, or what?' Jo had asked.

'I'll read it after,' Mick had sniffed, dropping a pinch of fish flakes into the goldfish bowl.

'Suit yourself,' Jo replied, turning back to the article. Catherine hadn't been able to concentrate on the words. She just wished that her dad could be happy for her, or at least feel that he could tell one of the others what he was going through so that they could help.

Now the day had arrived for Catherine to leave for Boot Camp and Mick was still in truculent form.

'If he says, "Don't mind me," one more time I'm going to boot him,' Jo said.

Jo had taken the day off college to drive down with Claire and Catherine to the manor house in the wilds of the Cotswolds where Boot Camp was held. She was glad of the day off, her tutor was getting on her nerves at the moment. Jo was in the middle of a project that her tutor said should draw inspiration from the early post-war couture of Christian Dior and team it with fabrics used in space flight to give it a futuristic twist. Jo had decided that this sounded like a load of bollocks and that she was going to design a collection inspired by Alexis Carrington Colby Dexter – Joan Collin's character in Dynasty, one of Jo's re-run TV heroes, and one of the people Jo would like to be for a day – and there wasn't going to be a square inch of Teflon near it.

Maria had been unable to change her shift and was absolutely gutted. She had headed off to the airport with a face like thunder that morning after telling Catherine that she had to call them if anything, and she meant *anything*, happened. Catherine knew that the fact that she was involved in *Star Maker* and Maria wasn't was killing her sister. Not that Maria could sing, or would ever have entered the competition – she just thought that she deserved better than the hand she'd been dealt in life; that she shouldn't be serving people teas, coffees and Beyoncé Knowles' latest perfume on a plane but that she should be sitting in first class being served herself. Claire called it 'a misplaced sense of entitlement'. Jo called it 'delusional nob-head behaviour'. Catherine thought that the truth lay somewhere in between.

Claire had deposited Jake and Rosie with her mother-in-law and was busy packing the boot with Catherine's belongings. Catherine had been informed by one of the *Star Maker* producers that she needed to bring at least four changes of clothes as they didn't want them wearing the same thing every day. Jo had taken Catherine to Primark and – as she had put it – 'done a number on her'. Catherine was now kitted out in the latest fashions and all for less than fifty pounds. If she'd known that her sister had been so good at choosing clothes that flattered her, she'd have dragged her into town years ago.

Catherine decided, as her father was obviously avoiding being alone with her, it was time for her to take him to one side and talk to him before he left. She waited until he needed to use the toilet and then followed him upstairs, sitting on the landing until he had finished.

'You scared the bloody life out of me!' Mick exclaimed, clutching his heart.

'Can I have a word?'

'Antidisestablishmentarianism.'

Catherine sighed. 'Very good, Dad. Not that sort of word. I need to talk to you about the . . .' she found it hard to say, '. . . cancer.'

Mick's eyes darted around, checking to see if anyone was within earshot. 'Not here.' He grabbed Catherine by the arm and pulled her into her bedroom. He shut the door, flopped on the bed and put his head in his hands. 'What do you want to know?'

'Anything. You won't let me come to the doctors

with you, you won't tell me what's going on. You keep saying you're going to be fine, but I don't even know if you mean it.'

'You're going anyway, doesn't matter what's up with me.'

'Dad, don't be like that . . .'

'Don't be like what?'

'That. Making me feel guilty.'

'I'm not making you feel anything. I'm just saying . . .'

'What sort of cancer is it?' Catherine asked gently.

Mick tapped his stomach.

'Stomach cancer?'

'I don't want to talk about it, and neither should you. You're going off on a big adventure, don't worry about me.'

'Let me tell Claire. I want her to keep an eye on you.'

'I don't want Claire knowing. You can call me from this place, can't you? It's not a prison camp.'

'We're not allowed our mobile phones in case anyone takes pictures and sells them to the papers. They don't have a problem with people knowing who's gone into Boot Camp, it's who's coming out the other side they're worried about. So it's all secretive. Bonkers, I know, but that's the way it is.'

Every time Catherine told anyone anything about Boot Camp it made her, for a moment, step out of herself and think *Did I just say that?* It all seemed so surreal. She still couldn't believe that any of this was happening to her.

'So how am I expected to contact you if there's an emergency?'

'What sort of emergency? Do you need me to stay here, Dad?' Catherine grabbed her dad's hand. If things really were as serious as he seemed to be suggesting, and

Catherine was the only person that Mick felt that he could trust, then she couldn't go away and leave him.

The door burst open. It was Jo.

'Why are you asking if he needs you to stay here?' she demanded.

Catherine shot her dad a look. Was that all Jo had heard him say?

'Because she's being daft,' Mick said. ''Course I don't. I'm all for her going, aren't I, Catherine? Off you go and don't worry about me.'

'Christ, that record's well stuck,' Jo said, grabbing Catherine's arm. 'Come on, we have to set off now or you're going to be late.'

'I'll call when I get there,' Catherine promised. Mick hung his head. She wanted her dad to look at her to wish her well, but he just stared at the floor.

'Bloody hell, Catherine, you're only going for a week!' Jo said and then seemed to remember that she should have more faith in her sister. 'Well, initially.' She looked at her father. 'So are you going to say good luck to Catherine then?'

'Who's going to be here with me today?' Mick asked.

Catherine's heart sank. She really would have liked him to wish her luck, but he couldn't. He was just worried about himself. As always, everything in Mick's life revolved around Mick.

'No one, but the *Corrie* omnibus is on; get stuck into that,' Jo said flippantly.

'All heart, you, Joanna.'

'Why, thank you.'

'That was sarcasm. You're not all heart. You're the

opposite. Heart*less*. I'm all right, Jack, sod the rest of you. That's you.'

'Did you hear that Catherine? I'm all right, Jack? That's me all over isn't it? Doesn't sound like anyone else who happens to be in this room . . .' Jo said, glaring back at her father.

'Yes, her an' all.' Mick jabbed a finger in Catherine's direction. 'The pair of you. No heart. Just thinking of yourselves. No wonder your mother left,' Mick said.

Catherine's mouth dropped open. How dare he? She did everything he asked of her and just because she was doing something for herself for once he threw this accusation at her. Catherine couldn't believe it, it was one thing for her father to be deluded, but she didn't expect him to be this cruel just because he felt abandoned. Jo stared, wide-eyed, at her father. She was obviously in shock at his accusation, too.

Something clicked inside of Catherine. The guilt at having to leave her father to look after himself had been weighing heavy since she had been successful at the auditions and Mick had been pulling out every stop to maintain her guilt. But this, calling her heartless and blaming them for their mother's departure, was low. She couldn't believe he could say something like this. If anyone drove Karen away it was him, because he was even more self-centred than Karen. All Mick ever thought about was himself. Never Claire and his grandchildren, or Jo and her college work, or Maria and her – Catherine stalled thinking about what was important to Maria – Maria and her make-up. Why was everything always about him? Why couldn't he be happy for her to go away for a few days? It wasn't like she was going to Pontin's, she had the opportunity of a lifetime here and what did her dad want her to do? She thought she'd ask him. 'Do you want me to stay, Dad?'

'You are not doing anything of the—' Catherine dug her fingers into Jo's arm, stopping her mid-sentence.

'That would be very nice, Catherine,' Mick said.

Catherine stood staring at her dad. He was serious.

'You mean it, don't you?' Catherine asked. 'You would seriously let me squander this one opportunity to do something amazing to sit here with you . . .'

'Watching the *Corrie* omnibus,' Jo added helpfully.

'. . . when the others will be back this evening and I'll be back in a few days' time.'

Mick changed tack. 'It's just a lot of commercial rubbish this *Star Maker* thing, Catherine, and I don't want you being used up and spat out by these TV companies.'

'What are you on about?' Catherine asked angrily. Jo's eyes widened, she wasn't used to Catherine raising her voice. 'You don't know the first thing about TV companies, you don't know the first thing about anything. You just sit here, spouting off from your chair and I'm supposed to listen to you. You haven't once said you're pleased for me getting through the auditions, you haven't once asked me about singing. I'm not expecting a big hug and you to say you're proud of me . . .'

'Yeah, steady on, Catherine, we're not American,' Jo said.

'. . . but you've actively discouraged me. What sort of dad does that? I know you're not well.'

'What's up with you?' Jo asked peering at her father.

Catherine opened her mouth to say, to get it out in the open that their father had cancer but stopped short – it wasn't her place to tell the others. She looked at her dad, hoping that he would take this opportunity to be honest.

'Depression,' Mick said quickly.

'Bloody hell, we all know that,' Jo said, rolling her eyes. 'You've had that for years. I don't think Catherine staying here for the next few days is going to cheer you up.'

'I'm going, Dad,' Catherine said resolutely. 'I'll not be far away.'

'A four-hour car journey,' Mick said morosely.

'Two hours,' Jo corrected.

Catherine didn't want to leave her dad but perhaps it would do him good. It was what Jo had been saying for ages. Her dad, she said, was too dependent on Catherine and, she said, Claire and Maria quite liked it that way. Catherine had always rubbished the idea but recently it had become increasingly obvious that maybe her sister was right. Catherine had always thought that looking after her father had naturally fallen to her and that if she ever, for some reason, needed to go away then Claire and Maria would step up to the mark and help out. But since she had been given the place at Boot Camp this hadn't seemed to be the case. Both sisters wanted her to go on *Star Maker* because they wanted to know all of the backstage gossip, but neither of them seemed particularly interested in looking after Mick in her absence. Jo had also told Catherine that no one should have to sort Mick out. He was wallowing in self-pity and the longer he was molly-coddled, the longer he would remain that way. Catherine realised now that this was absolutely true with regards to his depression. Cancer, on the other hand, was a different thing altogether. But she didn't think that a week would make any different. He wasn't in hospital and he certainly didn't seem to be at death's door. Catherine hated having to think like this but with her dad refusing to wish her well Catherine had to think about this as rationally as she could.

'Say good luck to Catherine,' Jo insisted.

'Break a leg,' Mick shrugged.

Catherine breathed a sigh of relief. This was the first time that he had said anything remotely encouraging to her about going to *Star Maker* Boot Camp.

'What's that about? Break a leg?' Jo asked angrily.

'It's a saying Jo, he's not being literal,' Catherine said.

'Oh.' It wasn't often there was a gap in Jo's cultural references and she clearly didn't like it when there was.

'Theatre saying,' Mick said knowledgeably. 'Never wish anyone luck and never mention the Scottish play.'

'Ah, *Macbeth*.' Jo said, happy that she was back on track with her father's references.

'Don't mention the Scottish play!' Mick shouted.

'Jesus, mind my eardrums.' Jo rubbed the side of her head. 'Who d'you think you are? Ian McKellen?'

'It's OK, Dad. I don't believe all that superstition stuff,' Catherine reassured him.

'Well, you should,' Mick snapped, walking past her, back into the bathroom.

Catherine watched him shut the door and looked at Jo. When he had said 'Break a leg' there had been the tiniest glimmer of hope for Catherine. That he really did wish her well. But now he was sulking in the bathroom, and she knew that he really didn't want her to do well at all, he just wanted her here with him.

'That's it, Dad, give it out with one hand, take it away with the other,' Jo shouted. She turned to Catherine. 'Selfish old sod. Ignore him. He'll just stew in his own juices until we get back.' Jo headed down the stairs.

Catherine looked at the closed bathroom door. She was about to say something to her dad but couldn't think of anything more to say. She turned around and walked down the stairs with a heavy heart. She just wanted her dad to be proud of her, but maybe Jo was right, he wasn't capable of ever thinking about anyone but himself.

Chapter 4

'Catherine, wake up. We're here.' Jo said, shaking her sister. No way were they letting their sister stay in a place like this for a week, it was amazing; a huge turreted castle at the end of a tree-lined drive.

Catherine opened her eyes. 'Oh my God.'

'Oh my God is right. Look at this place! It's like the Playboy Mansion.'

'How do you know what the Playboy Mansion looks like?' Claire asked.

'Because I watch *Girls of the Playboy Mansion*, duh!' Jo said.

Jo loved the show. The idea that a load of girls a few years older than her would hang around with manky octogenarian Heff and his smoking jacket made her laugh out loud. She found it fascinating. It was like Bruce Forsyth trying to set up home with Girls Aloud and then expecting them to get their bits out and 'entertain' whoever came to the door.

Girls of the Playboy Mansion was one of Jo's favourite TV shows along with *America's Next Top Model*, where a group of would-be American models all lived in a house together. From what Jo could gather they didn't do much modelling. But they did do a lot of crying and back biting which made excellent TV; Jo Sky-plussed every episode. But her absolute favourite was *Dog the Bounty Hunter*. This was where a be-mulleted American went out and caught 'felons' (they weren't proper felons, just smack heads who'd gone looking for a fix instead of attending their parole hearing) who had 'jumped bail'. Jo knew all the lingo. Dog thanked God a lot and told said felons (smack heads) that they should be thankful to their 'momma' because their 'momma loved them, no madder what'. It was the same thing every week and was, in Jo's opinion, TV gold. She had often thought that if she didn't turn out to be a world-famous fashion designer she might set up her own bounty hunting service. Although she didn't think that quite so many Mancunian mothers would pay for the safe return of their smack head sons as LA mothers. That was why American was the land of opportunity, Jo thought wistfully.

'You watch such a load of rubbish on the telly,' Claire sniffed.

'And you watch *Heartbeat* – what's that about?'

'It's about a little Yorkshire village in the 1950s,' Claire said matter-of-factly.

'Not what's the show about, I mean, what's you watching it about? I know what it's about, it's about Green Grass getting his car stuck in some cow muck to hilarious consequences while Cliff Richard and the Shadows sing and we all sit around thinking what a lovely time we had in the fifties, forgetting how shit-boring it actually was then, and how women were second-class citizens and everyone just ate luncheon meat and no one even knew what a panini was . . . Anyway ITV have canned it. Thank God.'

'I can't believe we're here,' Catherine said in awe, snapping Jo out of her *Heartbeat* diatribe.

Jo looked at the huge manor house in front of her. 'I can't believe we're here, either. And you're going to be staying here!' Jo squealed and punched Catherine on the leg and then had to apologise because she'd made a red mark.

Claire looked around for somewhere to park the car when a man came towards them dressed in a black suit and speaking into a walkie-talkie.

Claire wound down the window. 'The man at the lodge told us to park up here,' Claire said.

About five miles back, at the beginning of the drive, a man stationed in what could be termed a booth, but was in fact bigger than the Reilly's house, told them to drive to the front of the manor house, park the car and ask for someone called Will.

'I'm Will. And you're Catherine Reilly and you're in the . . .' Will looked down at the clipboard he was carrying, 'under twenty-fives, girls category. Great. Follow me.'

'Ace,' Jo said bounding out of the car.

'Hi, Catherine, very pleased to meet you,' Will said, putting his hand out for Jo to shake.

'Oh, I'm not Catherine. That's her.' Jo pointed at her sister.

'Hi,' Catherine said, dragging her bag out of the boot and putting her hand out for Will to shake.

'Oh, hi.' Will said and then looked at Jo and Claire as if he was wondering where they thought they were going.

'Can't wait to see your room.' Jo said setting off in the direction of the imposing entrance.

'Er, excuse me, only the people signed up for Boot Camp are allowed on the premises. Security and all that.'

'Come on,' Jo said, pointing to her face. 'Does this face look like that of a security risk?' Will didn't answer. 'All right then, what about that face?' Jo said, pointing at Claire.

'I'm sorry, ladies, but only Catherine is allowed in.'

'Bloody hell! I just want to ask Richard Forster how he gets his hair so black and his chest so shiny,' Jo said.

'Right you, come on, back in the car.' Claire instructed her youngest sister.

'Are you sure they can't come in?' Catherine asked.

Jo felt sorry for her sister. She needed something to feel guilty about, if it wasn't her dad it was her and Claire not being let in to have a nosy at the *Star Maker* judges.

'Don't worry about it, Catherine. We won't let Will into our mansion when you're rich and famous. Sorry, Will.'

'That's a shame,' Will said sarcastically.

Jo quite liked a man with a bit of sarcasm about him. 'For you it is. It'll be ace. Right, come on then Claire, back to Manchester.'

Jo linked her sister's arm and guided her back to the car. Catherine was standing with her suitcase at her side. Jo looked at her sister. She looked like someone who was staring at their big chance – her eyes almost danced. Jo walked over to her and gave her a quick hug. They weren't a touchy-feely family but this definitely warranted a hug.

'Even though *Will* won't let us in,' Jo said, looking over her shoulder at Will who was standing with his eyebrow arched at Jo, 'we don't mind. Good luck, Catherine. Knock their socks off in there.'

'Thanks, Jo.'

Jo and Claire stood by the car and watched Catherine walk towards her new home for the coming days.

Claire turned to Jo. 'How do you think she'll do?'

'Dunno. She's as good a chance as anyone I suppose.'

Jo really hoped she had. Catherine deserved a break, and not necessarily an all-singing-all-dancing break with a guaranteed route to overnight success. Just a break from their dad would be a start.

Catherine turned around and waved. Claire and Jo waved back. Will waved too, in a sarcastic bye-now-off-you-two-go way. Jo kept waving to Catherine with her left hand and with her right hand merrily flicked two fingers at Will. He reciprocated. Jo was quite pleased, she would have expected men who worked in TV to be total saps but he seemed all right, Catherine could have a laugh with him at least, Jo thought. Better than all the *High School Musical* wannabes who got through on things like this. Catherine turned around and waved one last time before she went through the door.

'It's like *Stars in Their Eyes*,' Claire observed.

'It's not though, Claire, is it? It's a bit more impressive than that.'

Jo climbed into the passenger seat and wondered what news Catherine would have for them next time they saw her.

Andy was sharing a poky room with a guy called Jesse. Their room wasn't just something you could describe as a broom cupboard – it was a broom cupboard; the brooms had been removed and replaced by beds. Andy had envisaged a palatial velvet-pelmeted room when he had been told that he would be staying at the Boot Camp mansion. Maybe even a four-poster bed. As it was he was sandwiched into a single bed so close to Jesse's that if he turned over in the night he ended up spooning him. All of the decent rooms were occupied by the *Star Maker* hopefuls. And even they were three and four to a room. They were all currently in the process of arriving, expecting glamour but finding that the reality wasn't exactly how things were portrayed on TV.

The past four weeks had flown by for Andy. In preparation for the upcoming Boot Camp, Andy and the other runners had been drafted to the house and were briefed on all aspects of the show. The most important rule that was stressed to everyone working on *Star Maker* was that whatever happened in the house stayed in the house. Will, the head of production, told them that in the past there had been threesomes, drug taking and a near fatal incident in the pool, which had since been drained. He said that when you put a lot of young, more-often-than-not egotistical people in a confined space, sparks naturally fly. These things were never leaked to the papers and anything that was, the odd affair, the odd hissy fit, was carefully crafted by the *Star Maker* PR team.

Each person picked to come to Boot Camp was made to sign a number of legal documents and anyone trying to step outside the boundaries of these agreements would find themselves in serious trouble. They were also made to sign away any rights to their music; and this wasn't just in the eventuality of them being a success on the programme and securing a recording deal. Anyone given exposure by *Star Maker* was deemed *Star Maker* property.

So even if they were sent home at Boot Camp stage they were bound to *Star Maker* Inc. for two years from the release of their first single, meaning that they wouldn't earn anything until their third year of success. It was a Faustian pact – most singers don't have a shelf life of more than two years – but one that few turned down; the opportunity to hit the big time was too big a draw.

Andy felt like he was learning so much about the music and entertainment business, and not all of it he liked. But he couldn't help thinking that as much as this sort of show chewed up and spat out people with dreams and ambitions, it did sort the wheat from the chaff. The really talented people always seemed to survive. He wondered if that really was the case behind the scenes or if it was just how things were presented on TV and he would see a different side over the coming weeks.

One thing Andy had been grateful for over the past month was the absence of Jason P. Longford. As there was no presenting to be done, Jason was sunning himself in Barbados as the personal guest of Michael Winner. That was a dinner party Andy wouldn't want to be invited to. He could just imagine the pair of them, barking orders at the staff until everyone in a service role was a quivering wreck.

'We're late,' Jesse said, sticking his head into the broom cupboard. 'The under-twenty-five girls are arriving and there's some fit ones.' Andy rolled off his bed and then rolled off Jesse's bed and fell out of the door. They had been briefed on what was happening today. The under-twenty-five boys had arrived this morning, the under-twenty-five girls were to arrive before three and the over-twenty-fives, both male and female, were due to arrive after five. They would all have dinner together this evening and then the judges would arrive by helicopter tomorrow and they would start. The judges didn't stay in the manor house, they were tucked away in a bolt hole about ten miles away. They were flown in for the day and then flown out again. The show liked to portray the judges as being very hands on but Andy had been told this really did differ from judge to judge. Carrie Ward was an unknown quantity being the new kid on the block. Cherie Forster wasn't quite so hands on, but was extremely professional and made sure that she knew everything there was to know about the people narrowed down to be in the category she represented. Lionel was also in his first year. Last year Richard Forster had staged a coup and kicked off Cassandra Barker, the ex-rock star and outspoken lynch-pin of the show and Perry White, an Australian music producer who seemed to get on everyone's nerves but was great at spotting raw talent. No one ever thought that Richard would have the balls to get rid of Cassandra – rumours had been rife about an affair between the two and that Cherie wanted her out – but he did. And despite her many attempts to defame him since, Richard had come out of it looking poised and businesslike and she had come out of it looking like a shrieking banshee. Perry, on the other hand, whenever asked about Richard Forster was nothing but gracious. And as he was bobbing around on a yacht in Monte Carlo for the summer this year, courtesy of the *Star Maker* creator, what else would he be other than gracious? Forster drafted Lionel and Carrie in because of their experience and because he had a sixth sense for whom the public would enjoy as a judge.

The one recurring criticism levelled at Richard Forster was that he didn't spend much time at all with the people in his category. He had so many other commitments that *Star Maker* was just another project in his schedule. He had made quite a few gaffs in last year's show and had made a promise to himself and the crew to be more attentive. He kept forgetting his singers' names to the point where he looked like he was losing interest in his own production. This year, Andy had been told, Richard's PA was to spend half an hour before each live show, running through the names of each singer, their background, and strengths and weaknesses so that he seemed on camera to be as sharp as he was famed to be.

Andy followed Jesse along the dark, imposing, wood-lined corridors. Jesse and Andy were getting on well. Jesse was twenty-three, short but good-looking and totally at ease with his height and his name. Andy had asked him if he was named after Jesse James. 'Everyone asks me that. My mum just liked the name,' he said with a shrug. They had quickly grown to like one another and it didn't take long before they were both sharing jokes about the mad world that they had stumbled into. Jesse was from a similar working-class background to Andy, albeit in East London, and he had come through a Lottery-funded TV mentoring scheme to get his job as a runner. Jesse hadn't had the pleasure of meeting Jason P. Longford but Andy had told him all about him. Andy was hoping that he wouldn't be assigned to work with Jason on his return. He was sure that there was something he could make himself seem indispensable at before Jason's return, which was rumoured to be tomorrow.

Jesse and Andy walked down the sweeping staircase that led to the main entrance of the manor house. It was like a cross between Hogwarts and Brideshead. There were moose heads on the walls and various coats of arms. There were pictures of landed gentry from bygone eras and what could only be described as road-kill sitting stuffed on the large oak dresser by the door leading to the main dining area. 'That thing gives me the evils,' Jesse said.

Andy shuddered, it did seem to be staring at them. 'What is it?'

'A ferret?'

Andy laughed. 'A ferret? Where do you live where you think that's a ferret?'

'Dunno, mate. Somewhere where we don't have 'em for pets.'

'We don't have a ferret for a pet. Or a whippet for that matter.'

'Never been down t'pit?' Jesse asked in a purposefully bad northern accent.

'Never. But I know that that thing there is not a ferret. It's a fox, isn't it?'

Jesse studied it for a moment, 'Nah, that's no fox.'

He looked at Andy and they both cracked up laughing. 'We should have our own nature programme.'

'David Attenborough, me,' Jesse agreed.

The large wooden entrance door swung open and Will walked in. 'Got another Boot Camper,' he said to Andy. 'Can you take her to room ten, please.'

'Yep. Follow me,' Andy said and then realised that the girl standing behind him was Catherine.

'Hi!' Andy said, happy to see a familiar face.

'Oh, hi. How are you?' Catherine asked.

'Good. Great. Yeah. Oh sorry, this is Jesse.'

Jesse stuck out his hand. 'Pleased to meet you.'

'You too.' Catherine took his hand.

'Let me get your bags,' Jesse offered.

'Oh yeah, your bags,' Andy said, but Jesse had already made a grab for them.

Andy felt awkward. It had been a month since he had seen Catherine and he didn't really know what to say. 'So, how've you been?'

'Good, yeah. You?'

'Yeah, good. Just living here in a broom cupboard with Jesse.'

'Oh, is your room small?'

'No. Not small,' Jesse stopped and put Catherine's bags down to give his hand gestures maximum effect. 'It is tiny. Like this,' he said, making the shape of a small box. 'And me and Andy like each other but we didn't expect to end up having a little cuddle every night, did we, And?'

Andy laughed. 'No.'

'So, Catherine, what are you going to sing for us?'

'Sorry?'

'Don't look so surprised. You've got to sing for us when you get to your room, it's a *Star Maker* initiation. Everyone does it.'

Catherine looked wide-eyed at Andy. 'Is he serious?'

Jesse nodded behind her back.

'Er, yes.'

'He's not. I can tell by your face,' Catherine said smiling.

'OK, he's winding you up,' Andy admitted.

'You are rubbish, mate!' Jesse said.

Yes, Andy thought, I am. This happened every time they showed anyone female to their room – even old ladies who had got through on the strength of a bad Gracie Fields impression – Jesse went into full flirt mode and Andy ended up standing there like his lanky, less impressive sidekick.

Jesse bantered his way up to the room and Catherine seemed to relax into her surroundings.

'How's the family?' Andy asked.

'What, you know each other from home?' Jesse said, confused.

'No.'

'No.' Catherine and Andy spoke at the same time and then both laughed, embarrassed.

'My family came into my audition and made a show of themselves.'

Andy was about to put her mind at ease and say that it happens all the time when Jesse piped up, 'Are you the one with the mad dad?'

Catherine seemed to think about it for a moment. 'Erm, yes. That would be me.'

'Good effort,' Jesse said, impressed.

They arrived outside the room that Catherine would be staying in for the week. There was a huge bed in the middle of the room, that had obviously been there for years and then there were five other temporary beds dotted around.

'Sorry, everyone has to share.'

'No problem. I totally expected that to be the case,' Catherine said, throwing her bag down on one of the makeshift beds. The toilet flushed in the en-suite bathroom, the door swung open and a statuesque, finely featured redhead stormed into the room.

'You were expecting to share? I wasn't.' She clicked her fingers at Catherine. 'And don't even think about the big bed, it's taken.'

Catherine spun round and pulled a *What the hell?* face at Andy and Jesse.

'This is Star,' Andy said, with a knowing nod to Catherine.

'Star?'

'Changed her name by deed poll,' Jesse whispered in Catherine's ear.

Star clearly overheard. 'Yes, I did change my name, so what?'

Jesse shrugged, 'Yeah, so what, who cares? Right?'

'Right.'

Jesse winked at Andy and then asked, 'What was your name before it was Star?'

'It's a secret.'

'Was it Beryl?'

'Shut up.'

'You look like a Beryl.'

'And you look like a twat.'

Jesse creased over laughing and then put his hand out for Andy to high-five. Andy did, but he always felt a bit limp when he high-fived anyone. It wasn't really in his nature; he much preferred a good old-fashioned British handshake. You know where you are with a handshake, he thought. 'You're going to have a great time in here with Beryl. Enjoy.'

'Thanks,' Catherine said, looking as if she really didn't want to be left alone with Star.

'Dinner's at six this evening in the main room. You can meet everyone else in your category. Is there anything else you need while we're here?' He could tell what she was thinking – *Don't leave me here* – but they had to go. They were charged with ferrying all newcomers to their rooms throughout the day.

'No, I'll be fine.'

'See you later,' Andy said, smiling at Catherine.

'See you, thanks.'

'No problem,' Jesse said. Catherine smiled shyly. Why the bloody hell did every female seem to immediately fancy Jesse? Andy thought but then remembered it was because he was funny, smart, good-looking and knew how to talk to the opposite sex. Andy didn't think he could lay claim to any of these qualities; he had to face up to the fact that he was one of life's wing-men.

Catherine had envisaged getting to her room, having a bath and relaxing on her bed until it was time to meet the other contestants. She hadn't bargained on having to spend the afternoon with Star, who had all the charm of Rudolph Hess. Star was now stretched out on the one and only double bed, wearing a silk nightgown with her hair in a knotted towel and slices of cucumbers placed on her eyelids. Where had the cucumber come from? Catherine wondered. She must have brought it from home. That was dedication to the beauty cause, Catherine thought. She opened the door to the en-suite. She wasn't getting much conversation out of Star so she though she might have a soak in the bath anyway and then get ready for the evening ahead.

'Is my bath ready?' Star enquired as if Catherine was one of her members of staff.

'Er, oh yes. It's overflowing.'

'Can you turn it off for me?'

Catherine did. She couldn't believe she did, but she did. There was something about Star's tone that made Catherine immediately obedient. She wondered how Jo would fare in this situation; she'd probably be pulling Star around the room in a headlock by now.

'Where are you from?' Catherine asked, trying to see if being amiable might have an effect on Star's frosty demeanour.

'New York, London, Paris, Beijing, Bangkok, Ljubljana. I've lived everywhere. I'm a citizen of the world.'

'Oh right.' Catherine said. She didn't really know what else to say. It would be interesting to talk about these different places with somebody normal but Star, it was becoming quickly clear, took every conversation as an opportunity to be objectionable.

'And you?'

'Flixton in Manchester.'

'Oh God, don't you find that everyone nowadays is from Manchester,' Star sighed heavily. 'I blame Oasis. Even people from bloody Newcastle claim to be from Manchester, it's like "Get over it, that is *so* nineties".' Star threw her legs off the bed as if she was descending from a horse side saddle and peeled the cucumbers from her eyes. 'So are you any good at singing?'

'Er, I'm OK, I think.'

'They haven't put you through on the sympathy vote then? I mean it happens . . .'

Catherine looked at Star. Who did this girl think she was? They were both there on the strength of their auditions, but Star's assuredness of her own superiority over Catherine was breathtaking. 'Yes it does. And what about you, can you sing?'

Star looked at Catherine as if she were simple. 'Yes, of course I can. I went to Sylvia Young.'

'What's that?' Catherine asked.

'What's that? What's that?' Star spluttered as if she'd just choked on one of her pieces of cucumber. 'It's only London's premier stage school, that's bloody all. We're talking Billy Piper and Emma Bunton here.'

'Right. And was it good?'

'Of course it was good, it cost ten grand a year to go there, that's how good it was.'

'But what I mean is was it good for you, did you enjoy it?'

Star glared at Catherine as if she thought this girl really needed a few lessons in life. 'You don't get anywhere in this business by just enjoying yourself.'

Catherine paused for a moment and then said exactly what popped into her head, it seemed to be good enough for Star so she thought she'd try it. 'Are you having a bad day?' It wasn't often that Catherine came across people like Star and she was really hoping that the rest of the people in this competition weren't like this or she might have to go home.

'Am I what?'

'You're being really rude. So I'm just wondering if you're having a bad day?'

Jo always said that Catherine could get the truth out of anyone; that she was like a CIA interrogator. Jo seemed to think that when Catherine was riled she didn't lose her temper she just tried to find out what was wrong with the other person and did so in such a calm and systematic fashion that people just rolled over and told her everything.

'This isn't rude,' Star said pointing at herself as if she could increase her rudeness levels at a finger click.

'It is from where I'm standing.'

'Listen, if I were being rude, you'd know about it. Anyway, I haven't come here to find a new best friend. I've come here to win.'

'Well, good for you.' Catherine shot Star a look as she made her way over to the bathroom door, 'I'm Catherine by the way,' she said as Star grabbed the door handle.

'What?' she asked, stopping in her tracks.

'My name's Catherine. I know you don't care but I'm just saying.'

'Oh. Right. Hi.'

'Enjoy your bath.'

'I will.'

What a witch, Catherine thought, throwing her suitcase on her bed and unzipping it. She hoped that the other girls in the room had a bit more charm about them than that stage-school brat.

'Here you go . . .'

Catherine turned around. Jesse and Andy were standing in the corridor again.

'Found another one for your room looking a bit lost . . .' Jesse said.

Catherine peered over his shoulder hoping the new girl would be better company that Star was shaping up to be.

'Oh my God!' Catherine exclaimed, 'Kim!'

'Catherine!' Kim ran towards her and gave a genuine hug. They then pulled apart and, slightly embarrassed by their own enthusiasm for seeing one another, tried to explain themselves to Jesse and Andy.

'We met at the auditions in Manchester,' Kim said.

'I didn't think I'd see you again.' As soon as she'd said it, Catherine put her hand to her mouth. 'I didn't mean it like that, I didn't think I'd get through is what I meant to say, and I didn't know if you had . . .'

'Don't worry, I know what you meant,' Kim said kindly. 'Thanks lads for the tour. Oh and Jesse, you've got to stop with the full-on flirt! It's exhausting!' Kim said, winking.

'Me, flirting?' Jesse turned to Andy as if he was genuinely shocked.

'Bye!' Kim said, waving them away.

Once Andy and Jesse had departed, Andy smiling and Jesse with his tail between his legs, Kim turned her attention to Catherine. 'He's something else, isn't he?'

'He's friendly enough, just a bit. . . .'

'Much?' Kim asked.

'Yes, I suppose.' Catherine admitted. When she had walked to the room with Jesse and Andy she had wanted Jesse to pipe down a bit so that Andy could get a word in edgeways.

'His mate's quite cute in that Oh-my-God-girls-scare-the-living-daylights-out-of-me way.'

'Is he?' Catherine said pretending she hadn't noticed.

'So, tell me, has it been mad at home? My mum and dad are all over the shop because I've got through to Boot Camp. My mum's had posters made up and forced everyone to put them in their windows saying Vote Kim! The shame, I'll get kicked out tomorrow and have to go home and say, "Er, hello everyone, can you take your posters down please, I'm off back to work in the pub. But if you need a pint I can sort that out for you."'

Catherine laughed. 'So you work in a pub?'

'Yep,' Kim said, throwing her bag on the double bed, 'The Dog and Gun. The landlord reckons it's called that because it's full of dogs and working there makes you want to shoot yourself. He needs to pack up and move to Spain and stop just talking about it, the miserable sod.' Kim jumped up onto Star's bed. 'This is comfy. Are you in this one?'

Catherine shook her head and pointed in the direction of the bathroom. Kim quickly realised that Catherine was indicating that whoever was in the bathroom was a bit of a nightmare. She jumped down from the bed and went and stood next to Catherine so that she could whisper the details to her.

'Oh!' Kim said, once she had been filled in on Star's personality and self-promoted credentials. 'She sounds lovely, can't wait to meet her.'

Catherine and Kim chatted amiably as the room began to fill up. Kim was from Bradford and she and Catherine compared notes about appearing in the local newspaper. Kim said that she had been put in a star costume and positioned outside the town hall and told to give them a big thumbs up for the camera. On the day the piece appeared on the front page of the *Bradford Telegraph and Argus* she had received over five hundred text messages. 'People from school who wouldn't have said hello in the street had got my number and were now my new best friend.'

This chimed with Catherine. She had received a call from a girl called Veronica Kenny. The last time she'd spoken to Veronica was when they were fifteen and she had asked Catherine what she was looking at and if she wanted her face smashing in. Veronica only ever seemed to do two things: threaten to smash people's faces in, and *actually* smash people's faces in. The fact that Catherine had older sisters and could run faster than Veronica was the only thing that saved her. But now Veronica wanted to go for a drink with Catherine and catch up on old times. Catherine had made her excuses, sure that even if Veronica did just want some free *Star Maker* tickets if Catherine made it to the finals, then she would still find some reason to smash Catherine's face in.

The new girls who were arriving all grabbed a bed, unpacked their stuff and then joined Kim and Catherine for a chat. There was Marissa, a chatty young mum from London, Heidi, a shy, wide-eyed nineteen-year-old from the north-east and Jill, a student from Sheffield.

It had been almost an hour since Star had taken herself off to bathe and there was still no sign of her appearing. 'I really need the loo,' Jill said.

Marissa got to her feet and hammered on the door. 'You all right in there, doll? You've not drowned have you?'

Kim and Catherine looked at one another and burst

out laughing. There was no response from the bathroom; Marissa turned to the other girls and shrugged. She was halfway through asking, 'What d'you think we should . . .' when the door burst open and Star glared at them all.

'It's not a bloody dorm, yeah? I was just after a bit of peace and quiet.'

'Pleased to meet you too, love.' Marissa said sarcastically.

'No you're not. And don't pretend you are.' Star said folding her willowy arms across her chest. 'We're all here for the same reason: to win.'

'I'm not. I'm here because I got a few days off work.' Kim said, raising a laugh from the other girls.

'You say that now, but if you get down to the finals – and with that attitude I doubt you could win a bet never mind an international singing competition – then you'll change your tune. It's dog-eat-dog and don't let anyone tell you any different.'

The other five girls looked at one another in horrified-but-about-to-laugh silence. Then Kim said, 'Well you're a little ray of sunshine aren't you?' Catherine burst out laughing and the others joined in.

Star glared at them with pure venom. 'And you don't want to cross me,' Star said viciously, but only Catherine seemed to hear her, the others were too busy laughing.

It was five to six and Catherine was ready to go down to the meet-and-greet dinner. She was so nervous that her stomach was performing flip-flops. She envisaged a great banqueting hall where they would feast on a ten-course dinner while each in turn getting to sit next to Richard

Forster and tell him everything about themselves. He would naturally be interested in each and every story and by the end of the night everyone would have bonded and no one would want to leave. The others were equally nervous, all except Star, who was refusing to join them. 'I'll be down when I'm ready,' she said, with a dismissive wave of her hand.

The five girls walked excitedly through the many corridors leading to the main hall but when they arrived, Catherine's heart sank. Unlike the cornucopia of food and fine wine that Catherine had been expecting, there was a running buffet of badly presented finger-food. 'Looks like mum's been to Iceland,' Kim whispered to Catherine. The room was filling up with the other *Star Maker* hopefuls, all dressed to the nines, all looking as disappointed as Catherine felt.

'Can I have everyone's attention?' A pretty young blonde with trendy hair and – Catherine had to look closely but yes, she wasn't seeing things – legwarmers with penguins skating on them, was shouting to everyone from the raised platform at one end of the hall. 'Right guys, welcome to *Star Maker*. Help yourselves to food and bubbly, well, it's cava, but we all love a bit of cava, don't we?'

There were some excited whoops from some of the other girls in the audience. 'Unfortunately Richard and Cherie Forster won't be here tonight but Carrie and Lionel will be coming down to wish you all well.' There was an audible sigh from the crowd. Everyone wanted to meet Richard Forster, that was what they were here for.

'Oh well, let's get stuck into the cava.' Kim said raising a plastic cup to the others.

Catherine picked up something that looked suspiciously like a turkey twizzler and bit into it. She chewed for a moment and then wondered if it would be really rude if she spat it out. She quickly decided that necessity overruled politeness and put a napkin over her mouth and removed the offending turkey matter. Turkey twizzlers reminded Catherine of her dad. For a moment Catherine thought that most girls would have nice things that reminded them of their fathers: a favourite story they were read as a child, walks in the countryside, a certain aftershave. Turkey twizzlers were probably not topping the list for most girls and their connection to their dad. But Mick loved them. On their own, in a sandwich, in a salad. He even had them as a starter when he was feeling posh. Catherine liked it when he was in a turkey twizzler phase. It meant that he was eating, and when he was eating it meant he wasn't depressed. Or at least wasn't as depressed as he could be.

As the others began to tuck into the food and drink Catherine thought that she should ring home and check that her dad was OK. Mobile phones were banned, but she knew that there was a pay phone somewhere they were allowed to use. Jesse walked past as she was wondering where it could be.

'Jesse?'

He turned and smiled. 'Hi, Catherine, isn't it?'

'Yes, just wondering. Is there a payphone I could use? My dad's not been well and I just need to call home and check that he's OK.'

''Course, follow me,' he said, nodding towards the end of the hall.

Catherine and Jesse fought their way through the packed room. Jesse turned around and put his hand on Catherine's back so that she could get through the crowd more easily. She felt slightly uncomfortable; she never really knew what to do with men who were super confident. She never really had much cause to concern herself with them, they didn't usually talk to her.

Jesse led Catherine down a dark corridor and rounded a corner. 'No one really knows about this one. There's a queue a mile long at the official telephones, everyone ringing Mummy and Daddy to tell them how fantastic it is here.'

'Thanks.' Catherine fumbled in her pocket for some change but Jesse swiped a card along the phone's card reader. 'There you go, free call.'

'Thank you.'

'In fact keep it. I've got two for some reason. Just don't tell anyone,' Jesse smiled.

'That's really kind of you.'

'Hope your dad's OK,' Jesse said sincerely.

Catherine watched him walk away before punching in her home number. What a nice guy, she thought. Catherine waited for someone to pick up the phone. Surely Jo would be home by now? It had been over five hours since she had said goodbye to her sisters.

'Hello,' Jo said, sounding out of breath.

'It's me.'

'Hi, how's it going? How's Richard Forster? Loving himself?'

'We haven't met them, he's not here tonight.'

'How shit is that?'

'I know. How's Dad?'

'He's fine.'

'No, I'm bloody well not!' Mick shouted in the background.

'Yes, he is,' Jo said, sounding as if she was physically restraining her father.

'Jo, what are you doing?'

'Pushing Dad away by the head.' Her voice sounded strained.

'What's wrong with him?'

'Nothing's wrong with him. Nothing a good kick wouldn't sort out.'

'Did you just kick him?'

'No.'

'She just kicked me!' Mick wailed.

'He's fine. Claire's coming round in a minute. If you call again, I'm not answering. He's fine.'

'Can I speak to him?'

'Bloody hell, Dad!' Jo shouted as the phone was wrenched from her hand.

'Catherine,' Mick said breathlessly. 'This one doesn't know where anything is. She's bossy and she doesn't listen to me.'

'Where's your violin?' Jo asked sarcastically.

'Dad, you need to tell Jo what's going on,' Catherine said as quietly as she possibly could, 'She just thinks you're being a mard arse.'

'No.'

'Tell her.'

'No.'

'Dad, this is really hard for me.'

'You'll be back soon.'

'God, Dad, you're so encouraging,' Catherine could hear Jo say. 'She might not be, so you'd better start behaving because I for one am not listening to your shit from now till Catherine gets the Christmas number one.'

'Ow!' Mick complained, then Jo came to the phone.

'He's fine. Get off my leg, Dad! Seriously, Catherine, go and don't be ringing here every two seconds.'

Jo put the phone down. Catherine stood for a moment listening to the dial tone. She redialled but the phone was off the hook. She took out a piece of paper with Jo's mobile number on it, there was no point ringing her dad's, he never answered it; she stared at it for a moment and then re-pocketed it. Jo wouldn't answer even if she did call. Catherine turned around and headed back to the hall, she was going to throw herself into the turkey twizzlers and sparkling wine and try to enjoy herself.

Chapter 5

Andy had been ushered into a room by Will, his supervisor, and asked to take a seat. Will had said that he'd be back in a moment but that had been over half an hour ago. Andy stood up and walked to the other side of the solid oak desk that took up one half of the wood-panelled room. On the wall was the mounted head of a deer. Andy peered up the deer's nostrils and noticed there was something lodged inside. He looked closer, it couldn't be what he thought it was . . . could it? He slowly moved his index finger towards the deer's nose, like ET phoning home, and touched the hard, bristly stuffed skin. Suddenly the door flew open and Andy nearly shot through the roof with shock.

'Yes, it is a camera,' Richard Forster said.

'I'm really sorry, I was just having a look around and then I thought I saw something shoved up there but I—sorry.' Andy trailed off. His mind was racing; there was a camera in the room. That had probably been filming him for the past half hour. Was that legal? Why was it there? Had they been hoping to catch him weeing in the desk drawer like on *Builders from Hell*?

'They're all over the place, ' Richard admitted as though this was perfectly normal practice. 'We need to make sure that we know who we're working with and that whoever we put through in the competition is totally on board with the ethos of *Star Maker*.'

'Right.' Andy nodded, feeling like a minion being shown around Dr Evil's lair.

'Look, I know it's not great having secret cameras around but we've had so many tabloid journos try and get in here that we've had to make the place as watertight as possible.'

'Is it legal?'

'It's all in your contract,' Richard Forster locked his dark brown eyes on Andy. 'You did read your contract?'

'Yeah, of course . . .' Andy said with a shrug. *Did anyone ever read a contract?* What was it going to say, you're hired, and if you're no good, you're fired? He certainly didn't expect the small print to explain that at any time he could be under video surveillance.

'Of course . . . you didn't,' Richard said, with a knowing smile.

Bloody hell, Andy thought, that voice, that look; Andy felt the room crackle with this man's personality. Andy wouldn't have been able to explain it to anyone – least of all to any of his mates – but he felt it. It was the pull of the super powerful. Richard Forster had a reputation as a hard-nosed businessman, a ruthless entrepreneur and an arrogant opinionated individual. Until now Andy had never understood how this combination had women falling at his feet. Richard was always being voted among the sexiest men of the year in whatever hormone-driven poll was out that particular week. But sitting here in the full glare of Richard's charm and arrogance – and his total disregard for ethics, evidenced by having a CCTV camera stuffed in a deer's snout – Andy suddenly got what all the fuss was about. If Richard told him that he was now his slave for life Andy would have probably agreed to it without much fuss. In fact he probably had already unwittingly signed up to it in his contract.

'Work contracts, I know how it is; you look at your hours, what you're being paid and then you sign. Am I right?'

'Yeah, you are,' Andy said blushing, feeling like a teenage girl on a first date, wishing he could say something funnier or smarter. He was going to need a fan like a Geisha if he didn't get his act together soon.

'So, you're probably wondering why you're here.'

'Yes, I am,' Andy said in a high-pitched squeak. He wanted to cough and repeat the sentence in a deep James Earl Jones voice. He gathered himself. 'You're not meant to be here tonight, are you?'

'No, but Cherie and I have decided that this is the best way to conduct the first night. Let all the rabble get together, get pissed on cheap plonk . . .'

'And see who makes a fool of themselves?' Andy finished. That was more like it, he thought, one step ahead of this game.

'No,' Richard shook his head emphatically. 'The cameras are there to see who complains. See who the divas are. See who we don't need in this competition and who we do. As you know from the auditions, we don't just put people through with good voices.'

No shit, Andy thought, remembering the woman who had turned up on a pogo stick singing 'O Fortuna' from *Carmina Burana* and had been ushered through to Boot Camp despite the fact she couldn't sing for toffee.

'They need a story,' Richard continued. 'The audience at home needs to connect with them. But at this stage *we* need to get a feel for who is going to be hard to manage and when no one's watching people show their true colours. We can afford one or two Mariahs every year, they make good TV, but we can't have an entire line up of them. They become hard to manage and when they're booted off they go straight to the papers and that makes the live shows that they all have to perform at in the new year pretty unbearable for the other contestants.'

'Right,' Andy said nodding, wondering where he was going to fit into all of this.

'And you're going to come with me, Will, Cherie and JP and have a look behind the scenes at the antics of our wannabes. Is that OK with you? Will said you were good to work with and could be trusted.'

Andy nodded. It all sounded a bit like playing God, but he was all for a bit of people watching. 'Yes, great. Who's JP by the way?'

'Jason P. Longford,' Richard said, looking quizzically at Andy as if he had just forgotten the name of a life-long friend. 'There's not much on camera stuff for him to do but he wouldn't miss all the backtabbing that happens at Boot Camp for the world.'

I bet he wouldn't, Andy thought, rising from his chair and following TV's most powerful man into the adjoining room.

Waiting for them were Cherie, Jason and Will, sitting in front of a bank of monitors, watching the party that seemed to be now in full swing downstairs.

'Well, well, nice to see you again, erm . . .' Jason said.

He took a deep breath and clicked his fingers and scrunched his eyes shut, 'Sorry, it'll come to me . . .'

The great trick of the friendless, Andy thought, pretend you're so popular that you have a million different names in your head and you couldn't possibly fit another one in.

'Andy.'

'That's right,' Jason said smiling, pleased with himself.

Andy realised that this was the shape of things to come for the duration of the competition.

'Look at those girls . . .' Cherie said.

Two young women who Andy vaguely recognised because he had escorted them to their rooms were now French kissing on the table where the buffet food had been laid out.

'Been done before,' Richard said wearily.

'Not like you to complain.' Cherie threw a withering look at her husband. Richard matched her look. Andy couldn't believe he was standing between the two most talked about people in TV and seemed to be witnessing first-hand what everyone assumed – that they didn't like one another very much.

'Anything interesting popped up?'

'Not really,' Cherie said, pushing her chair away from the monitors. 'Just the usual. A thirty-five-year-old guy from Kent has been sent home for stealing.'

'What did he steal?'

'A paperweight.'

'No!' Andy exclaimed. Everyone turned around and stared at him. 'Sorry, it just seems like madness that anyone would get through to Boot Camp and then jeopardise their chances by stealing something.'

'Especially a bloody paperweight,' Richard said with a wry laugh.

'It's the same every year. Some one caught stealing, someone with drugs, someone caught shagging in the toilets . . .' Cherie's withering gaze settled on Richard; he pretended not to notice.

'There's that bloody girl!' Jason said, then clapped his hands to his mouth.

Andy looked at the screen. Catherine was standing with her roommate Kim, both looking awkward, both holding their glasses of lukewarm wine to their chests.

Richard turned to him. 'I thought we'd cleared things up on the day. She can sing. You can get off her case until we see how she fares over the next couple of days.'

'Sorry,' Jason said quietly.

Andy watched Catherine; suddenly Jesse hove into view. He whispered something to Catherine, then she nodded and laughed and he kissed her on the cheek before walking off again. Kim shoved an elbow in Catherine's ribs and Catherine shook her head. Brill, Andy thought, Mr Smooth performing his smooth operations and he couldn't even tell him that he'd seen him because Richard Forster had sworn him to secrecy about the hidden cameras.

'So, Andy, you're probably wondering what you're doing here?' Richard looked at him.

'Erm, kind of.' He had to admit it had crossed his mind.

'We just want to know who you think is going to cause problems and who the public will like. We're here year in year out and we get inured to the whole process. We need someone with fresh eyes.'

Andy nodded, while secretly not quite believing he was somehow being invited into the inner sanctum of the country's favourite TV show. Suddenly Star came into view. She was wearing next to nothing. The best way to describe the outfit Andy thought, was a bikini with a piece of fishing net stuck to the knickers. She walked across the room as if she was the main event that everyone had been waiting for. She helped herself to a glass of free plonk and looked around with withering disdain. Everyone else in the room had come to a standstill and were now staring at this bikini-clad creature – she simply stared back. No mean feat staring down a crowd of hundreds. Then she did something that Andy wasn't expecting and neither was Cherie, Will, Jason or Richard. She turned to where the hidden camera watching the room was secreted, blew them a kiss and winked.

'How does she know it's there?' 'Who the bloody hell is she?' 'Quick, get Lionel and Carrie on, get them to distract everyone's attention.' Richard, Will and Cherie spoke over one another.

'That's Star,' Andy said. 'I was going to point out that she was probably going to be a nightmare but you can see that for yourselves, I suppose.'

'She's got bottle, I'll give her that,' Richard said.

'Make sure that's all you give her,' Cherie hissed, before turning to Will and saying, 'Carrie and Lionel are ready, go with them now!'

Catherine awoke with a start and checked the room. Everyone else was asleep. As she lay in bed, easing herself into wakefulness, she tried to work out what had woken her so suddenly. Maybe it was the quiet. The manor house was miles from anywhere and was surrounded by acres of manicured grounds. More likely, though, it was the enormity of the day ahead that had woken Catherine; today was their big day. Each bedroom had been assigned a mentor for the day and Catherine's bedroom had been given Carrie Ward. They would all have to sing two different numbers, one of their choice and one that was pre-selected for them, before lunch. At 1 p.m. they were to be taken into a room and half of the hopefuls would be sent home. The same thing would take place again in the afternoon so that by the end of day one ninety-six contestants would go through to day two. Day two took the same format until, at the end of the day, there would be twenty-four hopefuls in the four different categories. Catherine was in the under-twenty-five category but only by the skin of her teeth; there were some boys and girls there who didn't look old enough to have a Saturday job. Catherine lay awake, thinking about the intensity of the process.

On the TV it always seemed as if the contestants were at Boot Camp for weeks, being painstakingly whittled down. The truth was it was far quicker and harsher than that. It really was the embodiment of Andy Warhol's idea that everyone had fifteen minutes of fame. Catherine really hoped she could earn her place in the competition and hang around and at least make it to half an hour.

Someone stirred behind Catherine, she looked around to see who was up; it was Star. Catherine shut her eyes and pretended to be asleep. She didn't want to have to suffer the full blast of a one-to-one with Star this early in the morning. The night before Star had made an absolute show of herself – as far as Catherine was concerned – but Star didn't care, it seemed that all she was interested in was being noticed. She had entered the room dressed like a stripper and then had proceeded to writhe around in the middle of the floor, pointing at a potted plant and saying to the others, 'I know they're watching, they're always watching,' like some paranoid maniac.

'You still don't believe me about the cameras, do you?' Star asked. Catherine kept her eyes jammed shut, hoping she was talking to someone else. 'They were watching us last night. That's how it works, they want people who are going to make great TV and I'm going to make great TV. I know because a friend of my old voice coach told me.' Star said assuredly.

Catherine quickly opened one eye to see if she was talking to someone else. 'See, I knew you were awake.'

'Oh, hi!' Catherine said, embarking on a particularly bad fake yawn.

'You don't have to pretend to have just woken up.'

Bloody hell, Catherine thought, what was wrong with this girl? Didn't she understand social constructs? I pretend to have woken up, you pretend to not have noticed that I was awake and ignoring you – everyone's happy. Star evidently hadn't grown up in a house like Catherine's where everything was swept under the carpet and nobody talked about anything, ever. Other than Jo, of course. 'I haven't,' Catherine lied, 'I always yawn for ages in the morning.'

'Right,' Star said, clearly not believing a word. She jumped out of bed and quickly threw on a silver spandex all in one that was a cross between a futuristic leotard and

Kylie's hot pants. Catherine looked at her. 'What?' Star asked.

'Are you wearing that to breakfast?'

Star looked at Catherine as if she had just found her on the sole of her shoe. 'Don't be ridiculous,' she paused, 'I'm going for a run.'

Of course, thought Catherine. Silly me.

Andy was standing with Will, waiting for the three hundred and eighty-four hopefuls to flood into the main hall and be divided up into their prospective groups. The previous day's events were still very much fresh in his mind. He had a list of people that he now knew would be going home even if they came into the room and sang like Whitney Houston. Last night Richard Forster told Andy that he was taking no chances this year, because this would be the biggest show ever. Whoever made it down to the final twelve had to cope with live finals in New York up against the best twelve singers that the US had to offer and he wasn't going to leave it to chance and a good rendition of 'Rehab'.

Jesse came sprinting over. Andy hadn't seen him that morning; Jesse had been up with the lark, going for a long run in the grounds. Andy hadn't bothered to join him. He didn't want to look like Crazy Legs Crane going for a run with Usain Bolt. 'Wait while I tell you, she was only out running this morning in the skimpiest outfit ever. You could hang coats on her . . .'

'Who?' Andy interjected. One thing he was learning quickly about his new friend was that he was a fan of imparting far too much information.

'Star. She is well fit.'

Andy looked at him. Life wasn't fair. People like Jesse thought every woman in the world was 'well fit' and it seemed that every woman in the world thought that he was 'well fit' in return.

'She's also well mad,' Andy commented.

'Yeah, but them well mad girls are always good in the sack,' Jesse said with a knowing wink. 'Anyway, she'll be out of here tonight, she's too harsh with the others for them to keep her in. You know what they like – loads of people hugging and kissing each other and being best mates.'

No, she won't, Andy thought. She's on the list. In fact Star was top of the list to stay. Richard had put a few other names on as they had sat secretly observing the contestants the previous night. But this morning he would decide who was going through.

'Here come the girls . . .' Jesse began to sing.

Andy looked up to see Kim, Catherine, Marissa, Heidi and Jill heading towards them. They were all dressed in similar outfits of jeans, flat pumps, long T-shirts and scarves. Andy didn't really understand the new trend for girls wearing scarves in the middle of summer. But then again, Andy didn't understand much about girls full stop. The girls filed past them and smiled in turn at Jesse. Catherine bowed her head, gave Jesse an awkward smile and then looked up at Andy and said, 'Hi.'

'Hi.'

'How's it going?' she asked.

'Yeah, good. You?'

'Fine. Nervous about this though.'

''Course. I bet you are.' Andy stood frozen, wanting to

say something funny or cool, but coming up with nothing witty he said, 'Best of British.'

'Thanks.' Catherine half smiled and walked off. Was that a half smile of friendship or a half smile of sympathy? Andy wondered.

Jesse helped him quickly arrive at a conclusion. 'Best of British? What are you? A spitfire pilot?' He laughed, putting his arm around Andy as if he really needed some guidance.

'Did that sound bad?'

'You like her, don't you?' Jesse said, peering at Andy, an impish smile flickering on his lips.

'No,' Andy said, feeling his face burn. Andy hated the fact that he blushed. He had always blushed, it had been an affliction from childhood that he had never quite grown out of. Never mind the eyes being the window to the soul, in his case it was his cheeks. If you wanted to know if he liked someone or was embarrassed or if he was uncomfortable in a situation, all you had to do was look at his face and then you had your answer.

'Yeah, you do,' Jesse said, nodding his head like a wise old sage.

'No, I don't!' Andy shouted.

'Easy. Bloody hell You'll burst a vessel, mate. So what if you do?' Jesse said with a shrug. 'She's nice.'

Great, Andy thought. Jesse likes Catherine, too.

Evidently, Jesse sensed Andy's obvious unease. 'Go for it, if you like her, say something to her. She might be out of here by tonight.'

'But . . . I thought you liked her.' As soon as he said it Andy knew that he sounded like a child in a playground.

Jesse squeezed Andy's shoulder. 'Sort it out, Andy. I like everyone. Doesn't mean I'm going to piss on another man's rhubarb.'

Andy smiled gratefully.

'Anyway,' Jesse gestured in the direction of Star, who had just rounded the corner wearing a pink leather catsuit, 'I've got madder fish to fry.'

Catherine nervously went over both songs she would sing that day in her head all morning, unlike Star who, once she had returned from her early morning run had proceeded to curl in a ball inside of a sleeping bag and then frantically wriggle her way out. When Kim asked what the hell she thought she was doing, Star snottily explained that every morning she 're-birthed' herself. Catherine had hidden in the toilets until her fit of giggles subsided.

As they gathered in the hall and Star joined them, tugging at her ill-advised leather catsuit, Kim dug an elbow in Catherine's ribs. 'What the bloody hell is she wearing?'

'It's interesting,' Catherine admitted.

'Interesting is right. It's riding up at the back *and* the front.'

Kim was right. Star's catsuit was cutting into her in the most unflattering way.

'Camel hoof alert,' Marissa leaned forward and whispered to Kim and Catherine. Kim sniggered. Catherine shifted uncomfortably. Star was a div, there was no doubt about it, but she didn't want to start ganging up on the girl.

'I should tell her,' Catherine said, making a move towards Star.

Kim caught her shoulder. 'She'll bite your head off, you know what she's like.'

Catherine shrugged, 'Yeah but . . .' She relented, Kim was probably right.

'She's probably done it on purpose, I mean Britney Spears is always being photographed with her bits out, a tight catsuit's probably really conservative nowadays and we just haven't been reading enough *Heat* magazine.'

Catherine laughed. Kim was right, she was judging Star by her own standards.

The room had filled up with all of the contestants from the previous evening. There were a few sore heads and a number of shifty looks being exchanged between different boys and girls. The two girls who had put on the lesbian floor show the previous evening were standing as far apart as it was possible to stand with their eyes cast to the floor.

Will the producer took to the stage. 'Right, everyone. This is where things get serious. Firstly, can I just point out that this isn't a youth club and that the requests for the morning after pill that we've had from a few of you isn't something we can sort out. That's something you'll have to arrange yourselves when you leave. The latest you'll be here is tomorrow night so it's up to you to make that decision yourselves.'

Catherine took a deep breath. There was something so flippant and harsh about what Will had just said that it jolted her. She suddenly realised that they weren't there for a cosy few days; this was business and anyone who thought otherwise was kidding themselves.

'Right. Let me introduce you to your judges.'

Carrie Ward came out from behind the screen. Everyone cheered. 'Oh I love her,' Kim said. Catherine agreed. Everyone loved Carrie Ward. This was her first year in the UK working on *Star Maker: Transatlantic.* She had previously been one of the judges on the US *Star Maker* show but now the two were being brought together she had been brought over to work with the British contestants. She was always kind to her contestants in the US show, but always seemed to know what she was doing, gave them good song choices and stood by them.

'I hope we get her.' Catherine smiled at Kim's assumption; Kim blushed and corrected herself. 'You know, if we get through. What am I on about? I'll probably be packing my bag in two hours.'

'Hi, everyone,' Carrie said in her lilting Deep South accent. 'I'm really pleased to be here with you guys and it was so nice to meet so many of you last night. Good luck with the auditions and my advice is just to go for it.'

Lionel Peters stepped out onto the stage. Everyone cheered again but not quite as enthusiastically as they had done for Carrie. 'So, I'm not as popular then, I see?' Lionel said with a smile. 'Fine, I don't mind. Right, I want to hear good, tight auditions from everyone. No one is born entitled to success and fame, you have to work for it.'

There was more applause, then Cherie Forster stepped out onto the stage. Suddenly the crowd erupted, this was beginning to feel real now: the Forsters were here.

'Hello, everyone,' Cherie said in her sweet girly voice that could turn in an instant into a bitchy growl. 'I just want you all to do you best, I can't ask for any more. And relax and enjoy your performances.'

Cherie stood alongside Carrie and Lionel. The atmosphere in the room had reached fever pitch as everyone excitedly waited for Richard Forster to make an appearance. He stepped onto the stage and there was cheering, screaming and floor stomping. A couple of guys at the side of Catherine began whooping and shouting, 'Whoops, there he is, Whoops, there he is.' Catherine cringed slightly. She didn't like huge public displays of emotion, which was why she could never bring herself to enjoy going to a football match when her dad tried to drag her to see Manchester United whenever he was well enough and had managed to get tickets. Grown men shouting put Catherine on edge for some reason. She realised she should get used to all this, and fast, if she was going to stick around in this competition; there would be far more whooping and hollering to come.

'Right, guys!' Richard shouted over the crowd. 'You've made it this far, just give it your best shot. First up are the under-twenty-five girls. Could you all come forward, please?'

Catherine felt suddenly sick. This was it. The people from the other categories filed into the chairs that had been arranged facing the stage and one by one each girl was called to the stage. Catherine could feel sweat pricking her brow. She needed to get her nerves under control; she had quite a wait as they were going up alphabetically. The first few girls shook with performance anxiety and crashed out of their songs as a result. They were given a second chance but Catherine felt that they had blown it. As each girl was called they seemed to grow in confidence, if not in talent. Catherine began to think that being near the end of the alphabet wasn't such a bad thing.

'Kim Nevin,' Will shouted.

Catherine looked over at Kim and winked. She felt nervous for her new friend as she walked up onto the stage. And then she realised that she didn't have a clue whether Kim could sing or not. What if she opened her mouth and was tone deaf? Catherine sat for a moment clutching her stomach, hoping that Kim was good. She didn't have to wait or worry for too long – as soon as Kim began to sing 'Somebody Else's Guy' by Jocelyn Brown, it became clear that she wasn't just good, she was great. Her voice sounded like it should belong to a soul diva, not someone who was five foot nothing from Bradford. Richard Forster, who had been sitting slumped in his chair, suddenly sat up and looked around at the seated hopefuls to gather their reaction. Everyone was fixated on the tiny northerner with the huge voice. Kim finished the last bar and everyone cheered. Catherine got to her feet clapping, she was so proud of her new friend. She looked around to see the only person not clapping was Star, sitting with a scowl on her face. Catherine shook her head, the girl was proving impossible to like.

'If you keep that up, you'll be heading for the final,' Carrie said.

'Brilliant. Thank you . . .' Lionel looked at his notes. 'Kim. I must remember that name.'

'You've just blown the cobwebs off this competition,' Cherie said with a smile.

'Well done, Kim, can't wait to see what more you've got,' Richard said looking genuinely pleased.

Kim clutched her hands to her chest and ran excitedly from the stage. 'Oh my God!' she whispered as she sat down next to Catherine, 'I can't believe their comments.'

'I can't believe your voice!' Catherine said honestly, 'you were amazing.'

'Thanks,' Kim said shyly. Everyone was looking at her. She sunk down in her chair. Catherine thought that she was really going to have to pull something out of the bag with her performance now. Her friend was great, she didn't want to look like the loser sidekick.

The next few girls called to the stage were all good, but no one impressed the judges like Kim had.

'Star Prichard,' Will shouted.

'It's just Star, I don't use my surname.' Star said, flouncing up to the stage, as much as a person could flounce wearing a squeaky leather catsuit.

'I think you need oiling,' Cherie said cuttingly in her baby-sweet voice.

'You don't use your surname?' Carrie asked.

'No. Do any of the great singers? Madonna, Prince . . .' Star scrunched her face up, evidently trying to think of another superstar known by just one name. 'Kylie.'

'Minogue,' Cherie offered helpfully.

'Yes, but she's just Kylie, really.'

'What are you going to sing for us today, darling?' Richard asked, obviously trying to hurry things along.

'"Nessun Dorma",' Star said matter-of-factly.

'Bloody hell,' Kim said, sinking down in her chair.

'Right . . .' Richard said. 'It's an interesting choice for a pop competition, but off you go.'

Catherine held her breath. Star was such an exhibitionist that she was sure that this would be an over-the-top, disastrous performance. But what Star did next surprised everyone in the room. She might have been dressed like Britney on acid but she sang like Catherine Jenkins; her voice was beautiful and pure. It was sweet and gentle through the verses, rising to an almighty emotional crescendo. Everyone in the room jumped to their feet and applauded as Star took a bow. Catherine was standing with her mouth open. Star was unpredictable, that much she had to give her. The judges' comments reflected the audience's exuberant reaction.

Richard Forster rounded up the comments. 'I'd like to see more versatility from you, I need to hear that operatic voice lend itself to other genres of music. But I have to say, that was an outstanding performance.'

Star beamed, delighted with herself. She then looked at the crowd and arched an eyebrow.

'Did she just give an entire room a dirty look?' Kim whispered.

'Catherine Reilly,' Will shouted.

Crap, Catherine thought, how am I going to follow that?

'Good luck,' Kim nudged her.

Catherine stood up, feeling sick and dizzy. She hoped that her nerves didn't get the better of her. She couldn't afford to let that happen. Her roommates had all given great performances on the first go. Catherine walked towards the stage. I'm going to do this for Dad, she thought. He's ill and he could do with some good news. She so desperately wanted him to be proud of her and to know that she was good and was doing this for a reason. She stood on the stage and looked out at the four-hundred-strong audience.

'The family didn't follow you this time?' Richard asked.

Catherine shook her head. He was smiling, right, that was a joke, Catherine thought, not knowing whether to laugh or start singing. She was sure she was doing a very good impression of a startled bunny.

'When you're ready, Catherine,' Richard said.

Catherine closed her eyes and pretended that she was the only person in the room. That she was back at church practising alone with only the pigeons nesting in the roof for company. She had decided to sing the Sinead O'Connor hit 'Nothing Compares 2 U'. She knew when to sing gently at the beginning, when to punch through the lyrics in the chorus, when to let rip with emotion and when to hold back. She opened her eyes as she finished the verse and chorus that was required of her. Everyone in the room was applauding and cheering, which was a good sign, but Catherine didn't know if it was good enough for the judges.

'That, Catherine . . .' Richard Forster paused for effect, 'was really, really good.'

'Thank you,' Catherine said.

'Totally,' Carrie agreed.

'Really beautiful.' Cherie nodded.

'You're one to watch for me,' Lionel said, nodding his head in agreement.

Catherine hurried from the stage and sat down beside Kim. Catherine felt a tap on her shoulder and turned round to see Star looking at her. Catherine – thinking that Star was about to congratulate her on her performance – said, 'Well done, Star. You were great.'

'Thanks. I know.' Star didn't reciprocate the compliment. 'Looks like the competition's on with us three, doesn't it?'

Kim's eyes narrowed. 'If that's the way you want to play it, then yes, it is.' She turned around and folded her arms.

Catherine joined her, feeling terrible. She didn't like making enemies but it seemed Star wasn't giving her much choice.

'Right!' Will shouted to the 384 hopefuls. 'We're going to call your name out, you'll come to the front in groups of twelve and we'll tell you whether you have made it through to the next round. Those who have, please take a seat again, those who haven't, go back to your rooms, collect your stuff and we'll arrange for you to get home.'

Catherine looked at Kim, alarmed; that was quick. In ten minutes she might be calling Claire and asking her to make the long trip from Manchester. But then again, what did she expect? It was a competition.

The first twelve people in the firing line went up. Among them was a woman in her sixties who had put in a sterling performance of 'Penny Arcade' – a Roy Orbison classic, so she had informed the judges – replete with barmy dancing and arm waving, a teenage girl who had sung 'Thank You' by Dido and a young guy who had really impressed the judges with his rendition of 'Stand By Me', but Catherine wasn't sure looked that he looked like a pop star. Catherine really couldn't tell if they were going through or not. She looked at Kim, who shrugged. She didn't know either. The line up themselves didn't have a clue, they were all staring at one another to see if they could spot an obvious failure or stand-out performer in the group.

'Guys, thank you for your time and efforts but unfortunately on this occasion it's a no.'

Catherine's stomach sank for them. The young Dido girl started to cry, a few of the others hung their heads and shuffled off the stage, only the woman in her sixties seemed unperturbed. 'I had a lovely time, Richard love, thank you.'

'No problem, sweetheart.' Richard nodded his special nod that Catherine had noticed he reserved for ladies past the menopause.

The next group went up. This time Catherine was sure they were all going through, they had been great. 'We'll see you all again this afternoon!' Carrie informed them. They all jumped around, screaming with excitement.

'Guys, there's three more stages before we get to our final twenty-four, don't get too excited,' Richard said. They all piped down and shuffled off the stage.

Next up was a group that had a really strong line up; each one had performed well. Catherine looked at Kim and said wisely, 'They're through.' Kim nodded her agreement.

'Sorry guys, it's a no,' Richard said.

Catherine shot up in her chair. 'Bloody hell, I wasn't expecting that.'

'Bye bye,' Star said nastily. Kim shot her a look. 'What? They could all sing but none of them had star quality, did they?'

'I think I might be going home,' Catherine said, looking at the sorry group as they trundled off the stage. The next group were an odd bunch; some had been fantastic, some had been mediocre. Catherine decided to give up trying to work out which way it would go. Will called the final names for the group. 'Star Prichard.' Star stood up and walked towards the stage as if she owned the manor and everyone else there was her servant.

'Guys . . .' Richard paused for the camera, 'we'll see you this afternoon.' Everyone except Star jumped for joy. She just walked offstage, totally assured of her right to be in this competition.

'She's unbelievable,' Kim said, shaking her head.

'Catherine Reilly,' Will announced. Catherine stood shakily and walked to the front of the hall. She watched the others in her group and seeing other people who had impressed the judges head up to the front didn't make her feel any better. Good singers were already packing their bags to go home. 'And Kim Nevin,' Will said finally. Kim had been great so maybe they'd done enough to get through. If not, they'd be going home together.

Richard looked at them all with the poker face that Catherine had seen him use so many times on TV. 'I'm sorry, guys . . .' Catherine's stomach hit her feet, '. . . you're going to have to do it all again this afternoon.'

It took Catherine a moment to realise this meant they were through. Kim ran over and hugged her. 'One hundred and ninety-two down, one hundred and ninety-one to go.' Catherine did a quick calculation in her head; she was about to correct Kim and say 'One hundred and ninety to go.' Leaving – in her wildest dreams – her and Kim in the final. But she stopped herself short. Maybe Kim did mean one hundred and ninety-one to go and Catherine – although they were getting along really well – was still just another competitor?

'What am I on about?' Kim said suddenly. 'One hundred and ninety to go. Me and you get to the final and you win, that'd do me just fine.'

Catherine beamed at her new friend. 'Don't be daft; I'd like you to win.'

She genuinely meant it. Wherever she went out of the competition didn't really matter to her as she never thought she'd even get this far. Catherine was relieved to have met someone like Kim, someone who knew what friendship was and wasn't going to let the silly business of competition get in the way of what was really important in life.

Chapter 6

'I can get it for you if you want,' Jo volunteered kindly as her dad sat watching the telly in a sulk. He hadn't spoken for over an hour, other than to tell her how ill he was.

'Get what?' Mick asked, evidently pleased that his moaning seemed to be working and Jo was about to do something for him.

'Your violin.'

Mick narrowed his eyes at his daughter. 'You're a piece of work you, Joanna.'

'Takes one to know one . . .'

'I don't know where we got you from sometimes, I really don't.' Jo knew what was coming next. 'And then I remember where I got you from . . .'

Your mother, Jo mouthed as her father said simultaneously, 'Your mother.'

'That's right, Dad, that where I came from: Mum,' Jo said wearily.

She bent down and inspected her toes. She was using the few spare hours before she went to bed to paint her nails and give herself a mini-facial. She had carefully checked the instructions on the packet of the face pack, unlike last time. A few months ago she had stolen one of Maria's free passes to the gym and decided that she was going to make like a lady-who-lunches and wear a face pack in the sauna. Unfortunately, the face pack she had purchased was a self-heating one; which coupled with the heat from the sauna was a lethal combination. Jo had fled the sauna clutching her face and screaming – like the melting witch in *The Wizard of Oz* – and had dived into the pool, scattering a group of pensioners who had been minding their own business, enjoying an aqua-aerobics class.

'Speaking of Mum . . .' Jo said, she knew it was like picking a scab but she couldn't help herself, 'have you heard anything from her?'

'Me? Why would I hear from her?' Mick asked, shifting uncomfortably in his chair.

'I'm just asking.'

'Well, don't be daft.' Mick tutted and stared at the TV.

'I'm not being daft. I've not heard from her either.'

Mick looked out of the corner of his eye at his daughter and then resumed watching the TV. Jo couldn't work out what that look was about. Was he trying to work out if she was secretly seeing Karen and wasn't telling him? That certainly wasn't the case. The last time Jo had seen her mum was a year ago, in a dodgy coffee shop in Urmston called the Acropolis. The name always amused Jo; there wasn't anything remotely Greek about either the Acropolis coffee shop or Urmston. She thought they could at least try to spice things up once in a while by serving Ouzo or smashing a few plates, but they just served bad cheese butties and weak tea. Jo had insisted on the venue, she knew it would annoy her mum – who thought she was way above Urmston these days – and that was the way Jo liked it, because Karen liked to call the shots, not the other way round.

Mick might call Jo a piece of work, but Karen was the original article. She had left when Jo was twelve to set up home in Chorlton with Jay, whom she'd been having an affair with for less than two months. Jay always corrected anyone who called him just a plain old artist. 'Conceptual artist,' he would say. 'Piss artist,' Jo had countered last time she had seen him, eighteen months ago. Her abiding memory of Jay was that he smelt of old booze and cigarettes and was always waiting for a grant from the Arts Council. His last 'exhibition' had taken place in his and her mum's house. It had been entitled *Loss* and consisted of a turquoise ten-foot synthetic moulding of Jay's penis. Jo had asked why it was turquoise. Jay had said that it represented the Id. After that Jo didn't think that there was any point ever speaking to him again.

Karen had agreed to meet her youngest daughter in the Acropolis in Urmston after Jo had refused to get the bus to Chorlton. Chorlton was full of people like her mum and Jay and Jo hated the place. It was all artists and bohemians and bongo-playing hippies with more money than sense who'd bought their houses for ten pence in 1990 and were now sitting on a small fortune. Jay hadn't even bothered to buy his house for ten pence; he'd inherited it from his dad. This meant that he and Karen could sit around doing whatever they pleased and not have to worry about working a nine-to-five job, as everything was paid for. This didn't stop Karen always claiming to have no money or to be always on the lookout for something free, but it did mean that no one really listened anymore when she went into 'poor me' mode.

The meeting had been fraught. Karen told Jo that she

wanted to apologise for leaving her when she was young but that Jo needed to understand that Mick had been impossible to live with and that she and Jay had a sexual connection. (Puke, Jo had thought at the time. Who needs to hear that from their mum?) She then said that Jo couldn't blame her for wanting her own life; that she had given up years of her life for her kids. Jo had pointed out that that was surely the point of parenthood and you couldn't just up-sticks because you felt there was more life in Chorlton with a halfwit artist. Karen had called Jo selfish, Jo had called her mother a sad old cow and the owner of the Acropolis had asked them to keep their voices down.

Jo had run from the coffee shop all the way home and when she had burst through the door in floods of tears Catherine hugged her and stroked her hair and let her shout about how shit their mum was. Catherine had always been there for Jo to let off steam about their mother. She had stepped in to pick up the pieces when Karen left and had become more of a mother to Jo than Karen would ever be. Claire had already moved in with Paul and they were in the process of planning their wedding when Karen announced her departure, which led to Claire cancelling the church and the meringue dress and booking a flight to the Dominican Republic with Paul, where they were married with only a cocktail waiter as a witness. Maria was living with her first boyfriend Kyle and although she couldn't believe her mum had left home, didn't want to get to involved, so it was left to Catherine to look after Jo and their dad.

Mick hadn't always been a disaster zone. He used to

be fun, or at least that was how Jo remembered it. Mick had worked as a fork-lift truck driver at the Kellogg's factory in Trafford Park. He liked his job and his workmates and used to come home with lots of free cereal and stories about sending new workers to ask for a 'long stand'. But when Karen left, Mick began to decline. He went on the sick immediately and then never really went back. His sense of humour somehow turned in on himself and where before he would find the fun in things and enjoy taking the piss out of himself and others, he became bitter and sarcastic before – for a while – he stopped communicating altogether. Jo knew that Catherine tried to shelter her from her father's unsettling depression, but she guessed what was going on.

Karen would come home from time to time and have Jo over to stay but as the years went by it became strained and Jo didn't want to share her mum's new life because she didn't really try to include her daughters in it. Karen wasn't like her friends' mums, Jo came to realise, her natural instinct was to look after herself rather than her kids. It wasn't that she was Cruella De Vil, it was just that she felt that she had done her bit and thought that they should all be thankful to her for sticking around as long as she had. Jo had once flipped and demanded to know if she had been an accident, it would stand to reason as there was a five-year age gap between her and Catherine. Mick had told Jo sourly that she had been a miracle as far as he was concerned, which led Jo to have doubts as to whether Mick was even her real father. Once Catherine had calmed her down and pointed out that she looked even more like a Reilly than Mick did, Jo had decided that she needed to overcome this Jeremy Kyle moment in her life and put some distance between herself and her mum. She didn't want to be hurt by Karen anymore. So she had decided that every time she saw her mum she would act indifferent. It made Jo really sad, but she decided it was the only way to deal with someone who could leave a twelve-year-old child in the care of her not much older sister.

Jo had always tried not to take Catherine for granted. It had been hard sometimes, when she wanted to shout at her mum or dad but Catherine had been the only person there to listen. She knew that Catherine needed her own life; that she shouldn't be bound to the family home for ever just because their dad needed something to fill the wife-shaped hole in his life. This was why she wasn't about to let her father's incessant sulking derail Catherine's chances on *Star Maker*.

'D'you think Mum'll pop back up when Catherine gets on the telly?' Jo wondered. 'She'd love that wouldn't she? A half-famous daughter.'

'Yes, she would,' Mick agreed, almost cheerfully.

What was that about she wondered? God, he was deluded. Did he think that Karen would now pop along to see Catherine on *Star Maker* and then somehow decide that she'd made a terrible mistake and that she really should be with her smelly, depressed ex-husband? Jo needed to burst her father's bubble before he wandered any further into Cloud Cuckoo Land.

'Yes and that Jay'd love nothing better than a bit of free national publicity for one of his "Exhibitions".' Jo stressed the word sarcastically and sketched quotes in the air with her middle and index fingers.

Mick sunk back in his chair with a face like a smacked backside. 'Wouldn't he just? Probably paint his John Thomas and run around onstage, the big show off.'

Jo laughed. 'Yeah, he'd probably make a public appeal to the British Museum, see if they wanted to mount it after he's gone.'

Mick laughed too. 'I'll mount it for him, the bloody berk.'

Jo looked at her dad for a moment. It wasn't often they laughed together; it was a shame the only thing they ever seemed to bond over was slagging off Jay the Nob.

'You think she's going to do all right in this competition don't you, our Catherine?' Mick said, turning to face Jo.

'I don't know. But I hope so. Be ace, Catherine all famous and us getting into swish parties. She might even let you come if you put a smile on your face.'

Mick soured again. 'Unlike you, I'm not all starry-eyed about these things. I know they're a racket. They use the likes of our Catherine.'

Jo couldn't listen to him anymore. He had to bring everything down to his miserable level. 'And what's the alternative, Dad?' Jo asked, standing over her father, her hands on her hips.

'She was happy enough here,' Mick said, refusing to catch Jo's eye.

Jo shook her head in disbelief. 'What? So she stays here and sorts you out? That's the alternative? I'd take my chances with the evil pop machine if I were her.'

'We all know what you'd do: look after number one.'

'God! That is rich coming from you. I'm not looking

after number one; I'm just being a teenager. I go to college, I come home, I eat cereal for my tea because I can't be arsed cooking and I think about getting my tongue pierced every now and again and then decide it's a bad idea. I'm not the devil incarnate – I'm normal. You, on the other hand, you're different to most dads I know. *They* work, *they* look after their kids, not the other way round.'

'I'm ill!' Mick shouted.

'So you keep saying. You take pills every day but you never say what for. You stay in bed, you moan and shriek and carry on but you never actually say what's wrong with you, do you?'

'You don't care what's wrong with me; I could be lying in a ditch . . .'

'What does that mean? Lying in a ditch? What ditch, where?'

'It's a figure of speech,' Mick huffed.

'Well, talk sense, Dad, you're doing my head in!' In the corner of the room the land line began to ring. Mick looked at Jo. 'I'll get it, might be Catherine. Don't want you putting a downer on everything.'

'Hello.'

'Hi, Jo.'

'Catherine, how've you got on?' Jo's stomach knotted, she was so nervous for her sister.

'I'm through to the last forty-eight!' Catherine squealed.

'Oh my God!' Jo jumped up and down. Mick folded his arms across his chest knowing that whatever Catherine was telling Jo, it wasn't good news for him. Jo took a deep breath. 'Dad, Catherine's down to the last forty-eight. From four hundred!'

'Well done, love,' Mick said flatly.

'How is he?' Catherine asked.

'Miserable.' Jo said shooting a look at her father.

Jo heard Catherine take a deep breath. 'Jo, can you go to your room with your mobile and I'll call you from there?'

'Yes. Why?'

'Don't ask. I don't want Dad getting suspicious, I'll call back in half an hour.'

'Good luck for tomorrow!' Jo said brightly. She hung up the phone.

'Was she asking how I was then?' Mick asked as Jo gathered her beauty treatments and mobile phone and headed for the door.

'Yes, course she was. She's having the time of her life, doing really well in *Star Maker* and she just wants to know about you because you are obviously all she thinks about,' Jo said, slamming the living-room door behind her and heading to her bedroom to wait for Catherine's call.

Catherine had sung her heart out at the afternoon auditions but the competition was becoming tougher and she wasn't sure she had made the cut. So when she was told by Richard Forster that her and the others in her group – which included Star and Kim this time – had sailed through to the next round, Catherine had been ecstatic. Marissa, Heidi and Jill hadn't been so lucky. Jill had gone out that morning while the other two made it through to the afternoon auditions only to be told it was time to go. But Star and Kim were still in the running.

'I can't wait to get to America, they're going to love

me.' Star had said modestly. 'I think that I might ask Barack Obama to appear in one of my videos . . .' She added, as an afterthought, as if the president had nothing better to do.

Kim had tapped the side of her head and rolled her eyes to Catherine. Star really was deluded; her only saving grace was that she was in the right place and doing all the right things to ensure that her delusions might not be so far-fetched after all.

As Catherine sang through the songs for the following day in her head, Catherine began to think about things at home. Only twenty-four hours ago the idea of her getting through to the final twelve had seemed like a pipe dream by now she was down to the last forty-eight it was a possibility, albeit slim. Her dad was sick with cancer and she needed to support him and if she couldn't be there to do it, then someone else would have to step in. What if his condition worsened though? Then what would she do? Catherine didn't know who to turn to and so she decided, with a heavy heart, that she should tell Jo. She'd toyed with the idea of telling Claire but Claire had enough on her plate with her own family. She knew Maria wouldn't know what to do with a conversation that didn't revolve around herself, but Jo – although still a teenager and completely barking in some respects – really had her head screwed on.

Catherine allowed Jo enough time to get to her bedroom and then dialled her mobile number. If Mick found out what she was doing he would freak and Catherine would feel terrible, so she needed to make sure that Jo was on her own.

'Yo!' Jo said breathlessly into the phone.

'Yo.' Catherine always felt like someone's sad uncle trying to be cool when she said things like 'Yo!' She wasn't a 'Yo' person. She was more of a 'How do you do?' person. She would probably have been better suited to post-war Britain, with its politeness and its rations and its make-do-and-mend mentality than the early twenty-first century with its 'Yo's and its text speak.

'Ha! Catherine, you sound like a nob when you say "Yo".'

Catherine sighed. 'I know. Thanks.'

'No prob. So, what's up?'

'Jo, how's dad been?' Catherine asked cautiously.

'I told you, *Les Miserables*.'

'Right . . .'

'Although he did manage to laugh when we talked about the Nob.'

Catherine half-smiled, if there was one thing that could unite the Reillys it was a general dislike of Jay.

'Why, what did you expect?' Jo asked.

'Has he been taking his tablets?'

'Yeah, he loves them doesn't he? "Oh pass me my one o'clocks, Jo, if I don't take these my spleen'll fall out." "Oh Jo, quick, I've stopped rattling, pass me my three o'clocks, my bowel's packed in again." What they all for anyway?'

Catherine cleared her throat, could she really say it? She must. 'Cancer,' she whispered.

Jo fell silent and then said, 'What?' as if she hadn't heard Catherine correctly.

Catherine took a breath; she felt a rush of relief followed by guilt, but there was no going back now. 'Dad's got cancer. He didn't want to worry anyone so he only told me,' Catherine explained, 'but I think it's serious.'

'Of course it's bloody serious, it's bloody cancer!' Jo spat into the phone.

'All right, Jo. Keep your voice down.'

'My voice is down!'

'Jo, it isn't.' Catherine winced, hoping that her dad was in his usual place – in front of the TV with the volume turned up.

'Sorry,' Jo said finally. 'I'm just totally shocked, that's all.'

'You can't say anything to him. He'll kill me if he finds out I've told you, I just don't know what to do. He won't give me any details at all. He sort of hinted it was stomach cancer but all he's really said is that it wasn't good and he didn't want to trouble anyone.'

'I'll find out what sort it is, don't you worry,' Jo said, sounding like she was already making plans to pin her father against the wall and take him to task about keeping this quiet.

'Please, Jo, you know what he's like. He stresses, he can't take things like this. I've been really thinking about it and I just know that it'll make him worse. If he thinks I've told you, he'll assume I've told the others. And then it'll suddenly feel really real and make his condition worse.'

'God, I hate him sometimes!' Jo shouted.

'Jo, please!' Catherine pleaded. She waited for Jo to say something but there was silence from the other end of the phone.

'Jo? You OK?' Jo was rarely stuck for something to say. 'Are you crying?'

'What did we do to deserve this, Catherine?' Jo asked, her voice cracking. Catherine wasn't used to hearing her sister so serious, but then again she wasn't used to telling her that their dad had cancer. 'We've got the shittest mum in Manchester and a dad that could be dying for all we know but is so fucked in the head that we can't even talk to him about it because we'll make it worse.'

'Sorry . . . I shouldn't have said anything.' Catherine wound the telephone cord round her hand and peered down the corridor checking she was alone. Thank God she had been shown this pay phone, she wouldn't want everyone hearing this news at the other public phones.

'Of course you should, don't be silly,' Jo said gently. 'I'm just mad that's all. Mad and sad. Shit combination.'

'I know,' Catherine agreed. She felt terrible too. Suddenly she knew that she needed to do something about it, not pass the buck to Jo, but do something herself. 'Listen, I shouldn't even be having this conversation, what am I thinking?' Catherine's mind was whirring. 'I'm coming home. I need to be there. I need to help Dad. Who do I think I am, swanning round this mansion singing Mariah Carey songs?'

'You're going nowhere,' Jo said firmly. 'You're staying there and you're getting as far as you can. Then, and only then, are you coming home. Don't worry about Dad, I'll sort him.'

'No, I can't, Jo, I should be there.'

'Catherine, if you come home I'll tell everyone that Dad has cancer.'

'You wouldn't . . .'

'I won't have to because you're staying there and you're

going to just see how you get on, OK? If you get through to the finals then we'll talk about what to do, but only then. Yes? Look, I know you think I'm still twelve and you need to mother me but you don't. I'm perfectly capable of looking after myself and misery-arse Dad too.'

Catherine wound the telephone cord around her fingers, fighting back the hot tears that had sprung to her eyes.

'I know what you gave up for us when Mum left . . .'

'I didn't give up anything really . . .' Catherine cut in.

'Yes you did. You could have had a life and then you didn't.'

'Thanks.'

'Sorry,' Jo backtracked. 'You know what I mean.'

Catherine was trying to hold back her emotions but found herself sobbing. She didn't want her younger sister to think that she'd ever given anything up to look after the family but it must be obvious to everyone that she had. That was why she had never pursued any of her own interests. Why she had hidden her love of music and just settled into a job that was easy and meant that she was near home. That way she could be home each evening to make tea and help Jo with her homework or their dad with whatever harebrained project he had taken up to prevent him from pining over their mum.

'Yes?' Jo asked again. Catherine wasn't used to people doing things for her, especially her little sister.

'Yes,' she said quietly.

'Right, go and put Flixton on the map. Preferably somewhere good, like next to Monaco.'

Catherine laughed despite her tears, 'Thanks Jo.'

'And I won't say anything until you come back, OK?'

'OK, bye.' Catherine hung the phone on the hook and wiped her eyes. What she really wanted to do was crawl into bed and sob her eyes out but she couldn't do that. Star would probably be hovering over her giving her advice on how best to cry.

'Are you OK?' a voice behind Catherine asked. For a split second she thought it was Jesse; he was the only person that knew she used this phone. When she turned around she saw that it was Andy.

'Yes, fine,' Catherine said, surreptitiously wiping her eyes.

Andy looked at her curiously and then looked at his feet; they both knew she wasn't all right.

'Just stuff at home, you know.'

'How's everything going with your group?' Andy changed the subject.

'Good, they all seem . . . nice.'

'Star still being charming?' Andy asked as he smiled. His eyes twinkled and little dimples appeared at the corner of his mouth. Cute, Catherine thought.

'She should contact the UN, they could do with someone like her as an ambassador,' Catherine said.

'They should send her in with the troops,' Andy warmed to the theme. 'She'd be brilliant on peace-keeping missions.'

'I can just see her in Sierra Leone,' Catherine agreed with a smile, 'telling everyone that if they just stopped squabbling and just talked about *her* then things would naturally sort themselves out.'

Andy laughed out loud. Catherine shyly looked at her hands, not sure what to say next.

'So, you're down to the last forty-eight? Good going.'

'Thank you.'

'You've got a great voice. And a really great chance of doing well.'

'Do you think?' Catherine looked at him. She wondered if he knew something she didn't, but the earnest look on his face suggested that he was just being kind. 'We'll see.'

Catherine decided that she needed to stop talking about herself and turn the conversation to Andy. He was probably sick to death of listening to people talking about themselves, about their ambition, their talent, their 'journey'. Everyone seemed extremely keen to be on a 'journey'. Even the woman with the Roy Orbison song had said that she felt that learning the dance to 'Penny Arcade' had been part of her 'journey'. Catherine thought that it was a bit grand to be calling it a journey after being booted out at the first hurdle. It was more of a trip, surely, or a little outing maybe.

'So how are you finding working on *Star Maker*?' she asked. She really didn't know how other people managed to flirt. She was utterly hopeless at it. In all other aspects of her life – home, work, dealing with door-to-door salesmen – she knew where she was. But when it came to members of the opposite sex she had chosen to bow out early, aged seventeen, when she had been first let down by her one and only boyfriend, Darren Gleeson. Darren had made a big play for Catherine; asking her out after they had been partnered together on the lighting rig at the annual school play. Darren had taken her to the cinema and to Frankie and Benny's (the height of sophistication at the time). He also informed Catherine that he was an expert at removing a girl's bra with one hand because he'd practised on his sister – which was so wrong that warning bells should have rung, she realised with hindsight.

Darren had been intensely interested in Catherine for the four weeks they were together; writing her poems, buying her fluffy toys and then as quickly as he had become interested, he became wholly uninterested and moved on to a girl called Jenny Addison, leaving Catherine feeling silly and rejected. She hadn't bothered since then. She knew this probably seemed harsh to other people, that she would cloister herself in this way, but she didn't want to be hurt and so didn't put herself in situations where the chance might arise. She always marvelled at girls who could just get off with someone and then get up next morning and think nothing of it. She wasn't wired that way. Anyway she knew that boys fancied girls like Jo and Maria who had confidence in spades, not girls like her and besides she had too much on her plate with her dad and now with singing to be thinking about romance. She had decided to leave the relationship stuff to the big girls and getting on with what she was good at, namely staying in the background and looking out for other people.

'It's good, yeah. Bit weird, doesn't feel quite the same as pulling pints . . .' Andy saw the look of confusion on Catherine's face. 'Crap job I had a while ago,' he said by way of explanation. 'But it's good.'

Catherine and Andy began to walk along the corridor. Andy took a sideways glance at Catherine. She paused, sensing that he was going to say something, but he didn't. Then he did it again, Catherine looked at him. He took a deep breath. 'Listen, tell me to sod off if you want but you looked really upset when you were on the phone and I know what it's like here: you don't know anyone, there's no one you feel like you can speak to, it's a bit of a weird environment . . .' Andy stopped, he looked like he was regretting ever opening his mouth. 'I suppose what I'm saying is that if you need to talk about anything then I'm good at listening,' he said with a small shrug.

Normally Catherine would have clammed up and nodded her appreciation but she was so stressed about her father and her role at home that she did need to speak to someone and Andy seemed so kind and willing to listen that it seemed like the most natural thing in the world to open up to him. 'My dad's got cancer.'

Andy's hands fell to his side helplessly. 'Oh God, Catherine . . . I'm really sorry.'

'So not only is he mad and inappropriate,' she said referring to the one and only time Andy had met her father, 'he's really poorly,' she said, her voice cracking.

Andy put his hand on her arm. Catherine began to cry in earnest now. She didn't want to dissolve into floods of tears but it seemed she had no choice. She needed to get this out and poor Andy, who she barely knew, was getting the brunt of it. He stepped closer to her, she hung her head; she didn't want this poor guy to have to see her like this. He put his free hand on her other arm. 'I'm so sorry, that must be awful.'

'It is because I look after him and I've come here . . . but I don't look after him because of the cancer, that's a newish thing, I just look after him because he's got depression and I'm sort of the only one at home, except Jo, she's good, she tries but she's only young and she's got her own life.' Catherine sniffed back her snotty tears and wiped her nose with the back of her hand. She looked up at Andy. 'Why am I telling you all this? I'm sorry. I just . . . I just needed to say something I suppose,' Catherine said. She didn't really know what else to say.

'Right,' Andy said awkwardly, 'I'm rubbish at this sort of thing, so I'm just going to come straight out with it. Would you like a hug?'

'Would I what?' Catherine asked, making sure he hadn't just asked her if she'd like a mug or a jug before she threw her arms around him.

'Oh God, sorry, I just thought you looked like you could do with a hug.'

'That would be really lovely,' Catherine said sheepishly.

Andy moved closer and wrapped his arms around her. They stood there, motionless for a few moments as she felt his warmth and basked in the comfort of this small intimacy. Then Andy pulled away. 'You OK?'

Catherine nodded, 'Yes, thank you.'

'Do you need another one?'

Right now Catherine wanted to curl up in Andy's arms for the rest of her life, he was so kind and lovely and seemed to know what to say and when to say it. She was just about to say 'yes please' when Jesse rounded the corner.

'What are you two up to round here? Sneaking around?'

'No, we're not doing anything.' Andy protested a little too much.

Catherine stood, her arms by her side, staring at her feet as if she'd just been caught behind the bike sheds by a teacher.

'I was just using the phone and then Andy came round

and I—' Catherine broke off, as Jesse stood there, his eyebrow arched.

'Anyways, I'm just looking for you to tell you that you're needed in your room. Richard Forster's planning a visit and he wants you, Kim and Star to see him.'

'God, really?' Catherine asked. She was going to have to pull herself together.

'Yep. Come on,' Jesse said, spinning on his heel and marching ahead.

'Go on, good luck,' Andy said, winking at Catherine. Catherine smiled gratefully and headed off to her room.

Since when do I wink? Andy felt a stab of mortification as he walked back to his and Jesse's cupboard. Since when do I volunteer to hug people? There it was, that stab again. It was all right for people like Jesse, he could get away with stuff like that. He was smooth, women liked him; he looked like a hunk of manhood. Andy looked more like a clothes prop with a wig on and he knew that that look didn't lend itself to great sweeping Lemar-type love gestures. He couldn't tell if Catherine thought he was an idiot. She seemed quite pleased that he had intervened. But then again maybe he'd just caught her at a very low moment and she was back in her room wondering why she'd just let that beanpole of a runner touch her.

Will approached Andy. 'Just the guy. How's it going?'

'Erm, OK. You?'

'Great.'

'Can I catch you for a few minutes about . . .' Will threw his wrist out and looked at his white Chanel J12 watch, '. . . nine? Richard should have finished with the girls by then.'

'Oh yeah, Jesse said he was going in to speak to them.'

'Yeah, he likes all of them, but he just needs to have a word, you know, see what else they have to offer, other than their voices.'

Andy nodded. 'OK, where are we meeting?'

'Production room. Don't let any of the contestants see you. We're deciding the final twenty-four.'

'Cool, I'll be there.' Andy said, still marvelling at the fact that he was being allowed into the inner sanctum.

Andy let himself into his box room. If only the Great British Public knew that this was how their favourite show was decided. All of the heart-wrenching knife-edge auditions were just a con – from what Andy could gather, who was worthy of a place in the show was decided on sob story, controversy, personality and voice, in that order. And he was going to help.

'So Star, tell me your story,' Richard Forster said, shooting his cuffs and holding his head to one side. A very tanned head at that, Catherine observed. It had been bugging Catherine for a bit. In real life Richard didn't really look like *himself,* or at least how he appeared on TV. He looked like someone else, and then it occurred to her, he didn't look like someone else, he looked like some*thing* else: a magician. If he ever fell on hard times – not likely with the universal success of *Star Maker* – he could always ply his trade sawing someone in two or producing a dove from behind their ear.

'I went to the Sylvia Young School,' Star said with such gravitas that it seemed she thought that this information should see Richard roll over and start salivating.

He obviously sensed this. 'Who hasn't?' he retorted.

'OK . . .' Star said, gathering herself. 'Well, I told one of your researchers this but I haven't heard it mentioned since and I think it is key to who I am,' Star said, clutching her hand to her chest dramatically.

Kim sighed and lay down on her bed. She had stopped even pretending to humour Star. Richard looked over at Kim. His eye flickered, he spotted something. Catherine couldn't work out what, but she could tell that the cogs were whirring.

'Well, I was put though Silvia Young by my uncle . . .'

So far, so ordinary, Catherine thought. A family benefactor, this must happen a lot to people like Star; it was no biggy. But Catherine could tell from the look on Star's face that she was holding something back, something she evidently thought was solid TV gold.

Star took a deep breath and bit her bottom lip, looking out of the window as if trying to compose herself. '. . . because I went to live with him when my mum and dad died in a car crash when I was nine.' She delivered this news like someone who knew the answer to the million-pound question on *Who Wants to be a Millionaire*, not like someone who had suffered a terrible family tragedy at an early age.

Richard Forster nodded. 'Well, that is sad. I'm truly sorry to hear that, Star.'

He was being genuine, Catherine realised. Of course, he would have to have a heart of stone not to think that Star's background was sad. It didn't mean he wouldn't capitalise on it for the purpose of the show and Star knew it. Catherine suddenly felt sick. Is this what it took? Taking your family's personal tragedies and laying them bare for all to see. Well, she certainly wasn't about to do that. She didn't care if it meant she was going home tomorrow.

'I'm sorry about that, Star. That's awful,' Catherine said. She hadn't taken the greatest liking to the girl but she couldn't let this pass without saying something.

'It's OK,' Star said with a shrug. Catherine didn't know if she was trying to put on a brave face or if it really was OK. She didn't seem too perturbed by her situation.

'And you Kim, tell me about you.'

'Well, there's not a lot to tell. I work in a bar, I used to sing at the karaoke every week and people kept telling me to enter and then, when my brother went to Iraq . . .'

'Your brother is in the army?'

'Was.'

Richard looked at her like a lion who had just sensed something juicy to eat in the undergrowth.

'Yes, he's left now. Works at Tesco,' Kim said. Catherine watched her study the great Richard Forster for a moment. 'Did you want me to say he's had his leg blown off and that's why I'm here?' Kim asked. 'That hearing me sing is the only thing that gets him out of bed in the morning and stops the Basra flashbacks?'

Catherine cringed, she didn't think that taking Richard to task in this way would do Kim any favours.

'All I want to hear about is you, thank you,' he said, his glacial composure remaining intact.

Kim weighed him up for a moment. 'Well, he works at Tesco and I work in a pub. No sob story. Sorry,' Kim said with a sweet smile.

'Thank you, Kim.' Richard gave her a bemused look.

Star was sitting on her bed, rubbing hand cream into her cuticles and giving Kim a look that suggested she thought she was an idiot.

'And Catherine. We met your family . . .' Catherine winced at the thought of her dad and his performance in front of the judges. She hoped to God when the programme was aired in three weeks time that they didn't make it onto the screen, though she had a feeling that it was just too good a *Star Maker* moment to end up on the cutting-room floor. 'So we know a little bit about you,' Richard continued. 'But is there anything else you think we should know, anything that gives a bit more colour to who you are?'

Catherine thought for a moment. There was nothing she would hate more than people finding out that her father suffered from depression and cancer and that she helped look after him.

'I work in a call centre and live at home and I like singing.' This was all true, Catherine thought, no lies here, just not the whole truth.

'One of our crew said something about your mother . . .' Richard looked at Catherine for a reaction.

Oh God, she thought, what about my mother, what? Keep a straight face, don't give anything away.

'My mother?' Catherine asked neutrally. 'She's just a normal mum.'

OK, that was definitely a lie.

'Right.' Richard nodded his head. 'That's fine. Just wondering.' He got to his feet. 'Well girls, we'll see you tomorrow.'

Catherine was about to show Richard to the door but Star jumped in front of her. 'If you need to know anything else about me, just ask,' Star said to Richard.

He looked her straight in the eye and said, 'Thank you Star, I will.'

She shut the door behind him and waited for a few moments until he was well away from the room. Then she looked at Kim and Catherine and said disparagingly, 'Well, you two have totally fucked your chances.'

Catherine was taken aback. She had just been about to ask Star what it had been like for her when her mum had died. 'How have we?'

'You bored him to tears,' she informed Catherine, before turning to Kim. 'And you made him look like an idiot. Nice going.'

'What's the alternative?' Kim asked. 'He uses the shit things that have happened in our lives to cobble together a reason why we're on the show.'

Star's eyes bore into Kim. Catherine held her breath; Star was well within her rights to be offended by Kim's insensitive words. 'That's not the alternative, it's the only way to get on in this competition,' Star said, walking towards the bathroom.

'So you don't mind using your mum's memory in this way?'

Catherine nearly crawled under the bed. She fully expected Star to explode. 'My mum's memory?' Star sneered, 'Don't be a complete dupe, Kim. She's not dead, she lives in Fulham. But she's totally not bothered about pretending she's not my mum. I mean this competition is too important to fuck up and Mum thought that saying they were dead was the best way to go.' Star flicked her hair over her shoulder and stared pointedly at Kim.

Catherine and Kim were sitting open mouthed. Star opened the door to the bathroom and looked at them both. 'What?' she said finally, as if she couldn't believe they were taking exception to what she had done. But both Catherine and Kim were speechless. They really couldn't believe that Star would stoop so low.

Andy was sitting in his chair trying to disguise the fact he was ill at ease in the presence of Cherie Forster and his boss, Will. He had decided to mirror Will's posture and was sitting with his leg lolled casually over the arm of his chair. Will looked cool sitting like this, Andy quickly admitted to himself as his long leg hung limply over the chair-arm, because Will *was* cool. He was six foot, totally in proportion, had a five o'clock shadow that George Michael would have fought him for and a manner about him that suggested everyone should either fancy him or like him for being a great bloke. Andy just looked like a stick man who'd been drawn badly into a chair. He swung his leg back round and planted his feet firmly on the floor.

'You all right?' Will asked.

'Yeah, fine.' Andy said, stretching his arms above his head and yawning. He had no idea why, but whenever he was nervous and trying to appear nonchalant, he yawned. He really needed to stop being such a bag of nerves, but this was a rather special fair-enough-to-be-a-bag-of-nerves situation he now found himself in. Cherie looked at Andy as if he was irritating her. He stopped yawning. The door opened.

'Well, I know the under-twenty-fives,' Richard announced, sitting on the edge of the desk.

Please say Catherine, Andy thought. She really deserves a break and she's nice.

'Star has to go through.'

'Oh God,' Cherie groaned.

'Come on, she's very attractive . . .'

Cherie threw her husband a look that could have cut him in two, but he chose to ignore it.

'She's got a great voice . . .'

'And it's operatic, there's no other girl singing like her.' Will said, getting behind Richard.

'And . . .' Richard paused and then a cunning smile spread across his face, '. . . her parents died in a car crash and she's been brought up by her uncle.'

'Bingo,' Cherie said, nodding resignedly.

'Bingo indeed, my love,' Richard said, winking at his wife. She didn't seem to appreciate the wink.

'Great,' Will said excitedly. Great? Andy thought. The girl's parents are dead and this is great somehow? 'So who else?'

'Well, Therese has to go through.' Andy thought for a moment, he didn't remember any Therese.

'Who?' Neither did Cherie, it seemed.

'Pre-Raphaelite hair, sang like Alanis Morrisette.'

'Oh, I liked her, yes, very good.' Andy hadn't met Therese and didn't remember her audition; he must have been elsewhere at the time. Richard named three more girls, Carly, Sierra and Julie, all of whom had really impressed the judges. Andy had to admit that they had all been excellent but this meant that there was only room for one other person. Who would they choose between Kim and Catherine? It had to be one or the other, they had both performed brilliantly.

'And lastly it has to be Kim,' Richard said, his flat pronouncement shattering the hopes of countless girls. Andy's heart sank.

'Kim? What's her story?'

'She hasn't got one, she's just got attitude and that's what we need. She made me laugh actually, her brother had been in Iraq and the way she said it I assumed he was dead and actually he's working in Tesco's . . .'

'What about Catherine?' Andy heard himself say.

'Pardon?'

'Catherine.' Andy tried to swallow his nerves. Think, what did she do that sets her apart? 'She was really good but you sent her away and then gave her a second chance,' he said, warming to his convictions. 'The public will love that. And then she had the whole family come in and argue with you.'

'But there's nothing else there,' Richard said, his mind evidently made up. 'She's a bit of a damp squib.'

'But she isn't, she has a great voice and really deserves a chance.'

'Andy, we've got ballsy girls with attitude, we've got one with the voice of an angel and a dead mother, we've got one who was brought up in care, one who's mum's in prison and you want me to put Catherine through who works in a call centre and cites reading as one of her interests.'

Catherine was going out, Andy knew. She would go into the next day her spirits high and she would be sent home crushed, to deal with her sick father and to watch the others on the TV living the life that she had a chance at if she'd only pushed herself forward a bit more.

'She *has* got a story,' Andy blurted. He knew he shouldn't be saying this, it wasn't information about his own home life that he was divulging, it was a girl he barely knew who had entrusted him with a secret, but if he didn't say something now she was going home.

'She hasn't, Andy, I asked her,' Richard said, as if Andy was becoming tiresome.

'Her dad's got cancer,' he blurted out.

Richard thought about it for a moment then said, 'Well, it's obviously not something she wants anyone to know about, otherwise she would have told me, wouldn't she?'

'And depression. And she's been his carer for years. And she practically raised her younger sister.'

Richard looked at his wife with a glint in his eye that suggested that they may have struck gold. 'What do you think?'

'I think that if we run the VT of her dad bursting into the room and then we find out later that he has cancer then we have a genuine human interest story. People will watch Catherine because they'll really care about her. Beats whatshername with the mother in the clink.'

Richard thought about it. 'I'm not sure. She needs to be more honest with us.'

'That's true,' Cherie said, 'But I don't think that you confronting her now is a good idea, Richard. You forget that you put the fear of God in people,' Cherie said. 'Give her a little bit more time to think about it.'

'The fear of God?' Richard asked, looking to Andy for confirmation.

Andy gulped. 'Er, you are a bit scary sometimes.' Andy silently berated himself for sounding like a minion. He coughed, 'But with regards to Catherine,' he said trying to regain his composure, 'put her through and I'm sure she'll tell you. She just needs to trust people. It's not something you want to admit straight away to the entire nation.'

Richard looked at him as if he didn't quite understand what he had said. Of course, Andy thought; people throw themselves at Richard every week, opening up about the most painful episodes in their life, just to get a taste of fame. He didn't think Catherine was like this somehow. Andy was worried. Catherine could never know that this meeting had taken place, but if she didn't admit what was going on at home, she might find herself back there far sooner than Andy hoped. He had to get her to say something or he had to get Richard to give her a chance. He wasn't sure which was the easier option; he didn't fancy either.

'I'm sorry,' Richard said, shaking his head, 'We can't put her through on the strength that she *might*, one day, want to tell us her story. It just won't work.'

Cherie sighed. 'I disagree,' she said.

'Well, that might be the case, my sweet,' Richard said, demonstrating with dripping sarcasm that he definitely wore the trousers in their working relationship. 'But it's not going to happen.'

Andy's heart sank but he shrugged and said, 'OK that's fine.' What else could he say?

'What's up with you?' Mick asked.

Why the bloody hell have I agreed not to say anything

to Dad? Not even agreed, actually come up with the idea?

'Nothing.' Jo said trying to act casual when what she really wanted to do was take her dad by the hand and ask him what was going on.

'You're perched on the chair peering at me. It's unnerving.' Mick huffed, not taking his eyes off the Saturday TV offering.

Jo stood up quickly as if that somehow negated her perching and peering. 'Can I get you a cup of tea?' she asked.

'Why?' Mick shot her a look.

'Why? Because I'd like to.'

'Why would you like to?'

'Bloody hell, Dad, I'd just like to, OK?'

'Two sugars.'

'I know you take two sugars.' Even with the knowledge that her dad had cancer, Jo couldn't help being short with him. He was unbelievable.

'Well, it's that sodding long since you've made me one that I thought you might have forgotten.'

Jo bit her tongue. 'OK. Two sugars,' she said, marching into the kitchen.

Jo put the kettle on and stood looking out of the kitchen window into the back garden. It had been a warm summer's day and the sun was just setting behind the trees. The back garden hadn't changed since Jo was a little girl. It was only a small patch of grass but as kids it had been big enough to play a game of two-a-side and to put their blow up paddling pool in on days like today. The garden was overlooked to one side by the next-door neighbour in the adjoining semi, an old lady called Ann

(Spitting Annie, Mick called her, on account of her bad dentures and his claims that she left him drenched every time he spoke to her). To the other side there was a tall fence and the old garage which Mick used to house all sorts of rubbish that was one day – if he was to be believed – going to make him a small fortune at a car boot sale. The garden of 16 Verdun Road, Flixton was further enclosed by a tall wrought-iron gate and was a safe secluded oasis from the hustle and bustle of the rest of the world, which, to a child living on a main road, seemed to begin at their front door.

Jo looked down at the mug that she had pulled from the cupboard and the teabag that she had thrown into it. There were large splodges of water surrounding the cup and in the teabags. Jo realised that she was crying. She grabbed some kitchen roll and dabbed her face. Suddenly the back door flew open, making her jump.

'If I get another pissed bloke asking me if I want to join the mile-high club, I'll fucking scream,' Maria said, throwing her overnight bag into the kitchen and slamming the door behind her.

'You're not on the flight long enough to get as high as a mile are you? I'd have thought it was more like the forty-foot club.' Jo had to be quick-witted. She couldn't let Maria see that she was upset and if she hadn't immediately slagged her off as she walked through the door, Maria would have known that something was wrong and Jo really couldn't face a conversation with Maria about her dad. She needed to keep this to herself until Catherine got back. It was Catherine's call as to when and how they confronted Mick about his illness. Anyway, Maria would only make a huge drama out of it and make matters worse.

'I've been working in Premium Economy I'll have you know,' Maria said witheringly.

'What d'you get in Premium Economy? Packet of peanuts and a life vest?'

'Shut your face . . .' Maria began, but then noticed something. 'What are you doing?'

'Making a cup of tea.' Jo said, without catching her sister's eye.

'You don't drink tea.' Maria's eyes narrowed.

'It's for Dad.'

Maria was on Jo like a velociraptor spying its prey. 'What's wrong with you?'

Nothing.' Jo snapped, mashing the teabag at the side of the cup and pushing past her sister to get to the pedal bin.

'What's up with *him*?' Maria said, closing in.

'Nothing's wrong with him. He's watching *Martin Clunes Sings Abba* in there. I was going round the twist so I decided I'd be nice to him and make him a cup of tea.'

'You're never nice to him.'

'I am today.'

'Something's going on.'

'Nothing's going on. Not with us. You on the other hand . . .' Jo said, trying to divert attention away from her and her dad.

'What?' Maria asked puzzled.

'Have you got jaundice?' Jo asked innocently.

'No, you cheeky cow, I've had a spray tan.'

'You look like an Oompa Loompa.'

'I do not!' Maria shouted in horror. She ran from the kitchen and thundered up the stairs to check the damage.

Lucky escape, Jo thought. Maria would spend so long inspecting herself in the mirror that hopefully, by the time she came back down, she would have forgotten about the cup of tea and Jo could lie low. Then all she had to do was try not to say anything to her dad until Catherine returned. Unless he seemed to be suffering in any way and then she was stepping in, promise or no promise. She didn't know what she would do or say but after a moment's thought she knew that she'd do what she always did – cross that bridge when she came to it.

Catherine's nerves were in shreds. Forty-eight hopefuls had walked into the audition room this morning and twenty-four would be going home. Catherine had been given 'The Power of Love' by Jennifer Rush to sing at this morning's auditions. She wasn't a massive fan of the song but she had practised it in the small practice rooms at the far end of the manor. This afternoon, though, they had to pick two of their favourite songs to sing and Catherine had been toying with a number of songs in her head, but she kept coming back to material that she had written herself. She didn't know what the *Star Maker* policy was on singing their own songs. Catherine was sure there was some complicated reason why it might be frowned upon but she thought that she'd just go ahead, sing the song and worry about it later. It was her voice that they were interested in surely, not the song that she chose. Catherine loved writing songs and she felt that the songs that she wrote suited her voice well, whereas with other people's songs she often felt as though she was pretending to be someone she wasn't. Not that she minded singing some of the greatest songs ever written, it was just that her voice was so specific in timbre that she couldn't belt out huge bursting show stoppers like Kim could. She preferred sweet, heartbreaking songs.

The judges filed into the room and the air around her suddenly tightened. This was serious now and everyone felt the change in atmosphere. When there were four hundred people in the room it was still exciting, but the prospect of getting through felt vague and distant. Now it was a distinct possibility for the people in this room that they would be one of the twelve through to the New York finals of *Star Maker*. Catherine looked around and wondered who in the room would win and would no doubt go on to be a huge recording artist. Her gaze fell on Star. It would probably be her, Catherine thought wearily. As irritating and utterly charmless as she was, she was the sort of person that people talked about. Catherine wasn't. She didn't stick in people's heads. She was one of those people that old acquaintances said, 'How are *you*?' to while they racked their brains for a name.

Catherine sat down next to Kim and listened as Richard Forster gave them all a pep talk. She was getting used to the pattern of his inspirational speeches. The poor man, he probably didn't know what day of the week it was. He had arrived in from LA two days ago and was due in Chicago in two days' time. He was responsible for not only fronting *Star Maker* in the US and the UK but executive producing the show in twenty different countries. He probably gave these 'Give it your best' speeches in his sleep. As Richard Forster received rapturous applause and whoops from the remaining forty-eight – something else he was probably so used to that if he wasn't whooped and hollered at least twice a day he probably wondered what was wrong – Catherine felt a tap on her shoulder. She turned around to see Andy smiling at her.

'Hi!' she said enthusiastically.

'Everything OK?' Andy asked. He seemed to be matching her enthusiasm.

'Yes, fine. Just nervous. You know.'

'Course.' Andy said sitting down. 'You OK about last night though? Your dad, I mean.'

'Yes. I'm sorry about that,' Catherine said, looking down at her hands. 'You caught me at a bad moment.'

'It's OK. You shouldn't keep it bottled up you know.'

Catherine laughed drily, Andy didn't know Mick Reilly. 'If I told anyone my dad would go spare. He's going to hit the roof when he finds out Jo knows, never mind anyone else.'

'But you could tell people here . . . if you needed to.'

Catherine looked up, confused. 'Why would I need to?'

'Well, you wouldn't, but I'm just saying they're all really supportive and kind here and everything and if you needed to tell people, well you could . . .' Andy trailed off as if he didn't really believe what he was saying.

Catherine looked at the ruthless Richard and his waspish wife Cherie and the *Star Maker* crew who were sitting around all enjoying their jobs but very much there for themselves and thought that this was definitely an odd thing for Andy to say.

'Right OK, I'll bear it in mind.'

'Good, yes, do,' Andy nodded emphatically. 'Anyway . . .' He paused as if he was plucking up the courage to say something.

'Yes?' Catherine looked at him half smiling, half wondering what he was going to come out with next.

'I was just wondering and I'm rubbish at this,' Andy's cheeks flushed red. 'There we go, right on cue, red cheeks . . .'

'I get that too. It's awful, isn't it?'

'It certainly is. It makes you feel like everyone can read your mind,' Andy said touching his face.

'That's what I think!' Catherine said, agreeing excitedly.

'Everything all right at the back?' A voice bellowed from the front of the room. It was Richard Forster.

'Sorry, yes, everything's fine,' Catherine said, her face burning brightly. She looked at Andy and the redness of his face and they both tried in vain to bury their laughter.

'What a pair,' Andy whispered.

They quickly composed themselves and everyone went back to listening to the person auditioning. When Catherine felt that the attention was definitely off them again she looked at Andy. 'What were you going to say?' she whispered.

'I was going to ask if you'd like to meet up with me for a drink sometime?'

'Really?' Catherine felt herself redden again. 'A drink?'

'A drink, a date, whatever.' Andy felt flustered. 'No pressure.'

Catherine smiled at him and did something that her

usual self would never do. She grabbed Andy's hand and squeezed it. 'I'd love to,' she grinned.

'Catherine Reilly!' A runner that Catherine didn't recognise shouted. It was the third time that day that she had been called to perform in front of the judges but she still reacted like she'd been shot when her name was called. Catherine's heart thumped heavily as she got to her feet. 'Good luck.' Kim whispered. Catherine's bum was numb from all of the sitting around and waiting. She had got off to what she considered to be a shaky start that morning with her rendition of 'The Power of Love'. It was a big song that required a big voice. Catherine had tried to give it her own interpretation but the judges didn't seem too impressed. Richard had said that it was a 'little reedy' for him. Catherine wasn't altogether sure what that meant, but she knew it wasn't good. Her second performance, an hour ago, had been 'The Wichita Lineman' by Glen Campbell. Richard Forster had sat up in his chair after the performance and said, 'Well, Catherine, I can see a lot of blank faces here, whose music knowledge starts and stops at "Angels" by Robbie Williams, but that is one of my favourite songs and that performance was great. You're back in the race.' Catherine had breathed an enormous sigh of relief and returned to her seat.

There were other girls in her category that Catherine thought had performed better than her over both songs. One girl called Julie had given a particularly brilliant performance of 'Gimme Shelter' by the Rolling Stones and then had received a standing ovation for her interpretation of 'Daniel' by Elton John; she was bound to get through, Catherine thought.

Catherine stood up and walked towards the stage. She didn't think she'd ever get used to the utter dread that she felt as she went up to perform in front of the judges. She and Kim had discussed it, they both felt the same. Star didn't seem to suffer from nerves, she just glided up, performed, thought she was brilliant and then sat back down again.

'And what are you going to sing for us, Catherine?' Lionel asked. The judges took it in turns to speak to the hopefuls at they came up to sing. Andy had explained that they strictly rotate who does the talking and that each judge was contractually obliged to speak for a certain amount of time. This was so that no one judge received more airtime than another. This, of course, didn't include Richard. He was above joint and equal contracts. He ran the show.

'I'm going to sing a song called "The Sleeping Man".'

'And who's that by?'

Catherine was about to admit the truth, that she'd written the song, but she bottled it at the last minute, knowing that Richard would probably have something to say about her singing her own work at this crucial stage in the competition.

'Mary Devoy,' Catherine said confidently, giving her grandmother's maiden name.

'Who?' Richard asked.

'She's an Irish singer,' Catherine said matter-of-factly.

Lionel nodded confidently as if he'd been listening to this Mary Devoy character all of his life.

'Off you go,' Richard said.

Catherine began to sing. She couldn't believe she was singing one of her own songs. She had sung this a thousand times in the church and in her head at work as she had sat at her desk waiting for the next call to drop through into her headset. When she finished the ballad she looked out at the judges.

'Thank you, Catherine, that was truly great,' Lionel said.

'Beautiful,' Carrie agreed.

'You had a shaky start this morning, Catherine, but that was sensational,' Cherie said nodding her head emphatically.

Catherine looked at Richard, looking for his definitive seal of approval. He was scribbling something on a piece of paper. 'Well, I don't know who this Mary woman is, but she should get out of Ireland more often. That song was great.'

'Thank you,' Catherine said, quietly buoyed by the praise but hoping that she hadn't just jeopardised her chances in the competition.

She walked back to her seat, taking her place next to Kim. This was something you didn't see on the TV – the waiting. They sang for maybe ten minutes each a day but they spent at least ten hours waiting around. Not that Catherine minded but if she had known she would have brought a book. On TV it always looked so fast and frenetic. Even the off-the-cuff quips that Richard Forster dished out were repeated so that the producers made sure they had the best shot of him delivering his cutting comments. One comment that morning – when Richard has said that a girl sang like Johnny Vegas in a frock – had been picked up by the producers and had to be repeated twenty times, with the camera circling Richard until they had it from all angles. The whole thing had taken an hour and the poor girl had had to stand on the stage and react every time the remark was repeated. At the beginning she had been crying; by the end she was simply rolling her eyes and willing them to just get on with things.

The last few remaining candidates got up to sing. Some lost their nerve when they had been consistently good for the past few days, other pulled out the performance of their lives when they had been patchy in their previous attempts. Catherine really didn't know who the judges were going to put through. She just didn't think that she would be one of the ones picked. She was sure she didn't have the star quality that some of the others had.

'Jo, for God's sake, get in!' Claire shouted from the car. Paul was standing by the side of the car with Rosie and Jake. He was wearing a Manchester United away top, stonewashed jeans and lace-up shoes. His hair was slicked down to one side. Jo made a mental note to offer Claire a makeover for her husband's birthday.

'I'm coming. Bloody hell,' she shouted back to her sister before turning her attention back to her dad over whom she'd been fussing since he'd got up this morning. 'So I've made you a jacket potato.'

'You've pricked a spud with a fork and put it near the microwave, that's hardly making me a jacket potato, is it?' Mick grumped.

Jo breathed in and closed her eyes, mustering patience. 'I've opened the bloody beans and put them in a pan for you, all you have to do is turn the hob on and microwave the spud. Do you want me to eat it for you as well?'

'Just go. All this fussing doesn't suit you, Joanna.'

'Have you had your tablets today?' she asked, thinking that when she and Catherine got back they needed to sit their father down and have a good talk about his illness and what they were going to do.

'Why are you bothered?' Mick asked, his eyes narrowing.

'Why am I bothered? Good question,' Jo snapped. She was trying to be nice to her dad but he didn't help matters, being such a miserable old sod. 'Go inside and eat your spud and we'll be back in about six hours. Hopefully with a smiling Catherine.'

'She won't want to know us when she's famous,' Mick said morosely.

'It's a wonder she wants anything to do with you now.' Jo muttered walking towards Claire's car.

'What?' Mick shouted after her.

'Nothing.'

Claire stuck her head out of the window again but before she had chance to say anything Jo shouted, 'OK, I'm coming.'

'All right, Jo?' Paul said as Jo walked over to the car.

'How's tricks, Paul?'

'Not bad. Off to the park with the terrorists,' Paul said, nodding at the kids. Rosie and Jake jumped around, holding their dad's hands.

'You walking back home?'

'The other car's in the garage. Anyway I'm not risking the M60. It's murder at the minute, lanes blocked, road works, you name it. You know, there was even a cow on it the other day.'

'They've probably moved it now though, eh?' Jo said.

The joke was lost on Paul. 'I can't take that risk,' he answered.

Jo smiled tightly, 'All right then, have a nice day.'

She kissed her niece and nephew and as she was about to jump in the front seat Maria ran towards her – as much as Maria ran anywhere, it was more of a fast totter – and jumped in the front seat. 'What d'you think you're doing?' Jo shrieked.

'Coming with you. Changed my flight. I'm not missing this again, am I?'

'Get in the back. I was here first,' Jo said.

'I think you'll find *I* was. By about eight years.'

'Jesus. The age card. You play it when it suits you but when you're out in town it's "Tell everyone I'm twenty-two."' Maria refused to budge from the front seat. 'Nob-head!' Jo shouted, hammering on the window.

Claire jumped out and leaned across the roof. 'Get in the bloody car or I'm leaving you here,' she said, pulling rank.

'Brilliant. Just bloody brilliant,' Jo muttered, climbing into the back seat and taking her place, as always, at the bottom of the pecking order.

Chapter 7

Andy knew the final twenty-four, which was why – since asking Catherine out for a drink – he had avoided talking to her. He knew that she was going home. She wasn't going to tell the likes of Richard Forster about her father's illness to have him splash it all over his TV show for the nation to see. He had also made a valiant attempt to get Richard to put her through and just hope that she would tell them her story when she got to the house of the judge who would be mentoring her group. But he knew that Richard wasn't having any of it. He needed people who wanted to tell their story. Catherine wasn't one of them. He had hoped that today might see a few change of hearts, as some of the people they hadn't added to the list had put in spectacular performances. None more so than Catherine. But her first performance hadn't been brilliant and as a result she had given the judges all the reason they needed to send her packing.

Andy was standing in the room where the hopefuls were seated waiting to be called through to see the judges. He felt his knees go from under him; someone had pushed their own knees into the back of his legs. Catherine giggled. 'Hi. Avoiding me?' she asked.

'God, no! Hi. Avoiding you . . . what? No. Don't be daft,' Andy said with a big smile. He wasn't avoiding her;

he really liked her. He just didn't like knowing that he knew her fate and she didn't.

'You'll still come out for a drink even if I don't get through, won't you?' Catherine asked shyly.

'Of course I will,' Andy said and was about to say, 'Don't be silly, of course you'll get through.' But he couldn't bring himself to lie. It wouldn't do either of them any good.

'Good, because I'm sure I'm going home. I've had a right laugh, though,' Catherine said genuinely.

Andy wanted to run in to Richard and strike out one of the names on his list and replace it with Catherine's. 'Listen, I'd better go in the other room, they're calling people in.'

Andy went through and watched Star, Kim and Sierra walk in front of the judges. Andy felt desperately sorry for Catherine. She should be up there with Star and Kim.

'Girls?' Richard Forster said with his trademark minute-long pause. 'You're coming to London.' They all jumped around, squealing. Richard Forster was to mentor the under-twenty-five girls and they were to stay at his Mayfair mansion. Richard looked down at his list.

'Carly Leadbetter, Therese Hornby and Catherine Reilly, please.' Andy looked up in shock. Julie was meant to be in this group, not Catherine. He waited, his heart thumping as Jesse brought the girls through from the other room.

'I'm really sorry, but only six girls can come to London with me,' Richard said. 'And I'm afraid you're going to have to go home.' Catherine's shoulders sank. Carly put her hands to her face in despair; Therese looked at Richard waiting to see if that was it, her chance at the big time scuppered. Andy couldn't believe it. Maybe he had changed his mind and not put any of them through. But a sly smile broke across Richard Forster's face. 'Because you're going to have to pack your cases to come to London!' he said.

'Yes!' Andy said and punched the air. He quickly realised he was drawing stares, he was meant to be neutral, after all.

'Oh my God!' Carly shouted and hugged Therese.

Catherine stood looking confused, she didn't seem to know whether that meant that she was through or not.

'We're through, we're through!' Therese grabbed Catherine's hand in a bid to make her understand.

'We're through?' Catherine said, shaking her head in disbelief. She looked out at the audience and caught Andy's eye. *I'm through!* she mouthed excitedly.

I know, Andy mouthed back. Thank God, he thought. But there was still a feeling of dread that he would have to deal with sooner or later. He knew that his enthusiasm to get Catherine through to the next round would come back to haunt him.

'What is it with you and services, Claire?' Jo asked, as they stood in line at the Marks and Spencer food outlet. It was the third service station they had stopped at on the way to collect Catherine. Having bought a coffee in the first and a sandwich in the second, Claire was now buying a bucket of mini flapjacks.

'They used to be really bad when I was a kid – like a Russian work camp canteen – but now they've got M&S food in them, I just can't resist.'

'Right. You big weirdo.'

'Check your phone.'

'I keep checking it. Jesus. She'd ring if she knew anything, wouldn't she?'

Claire had been badgering Jo all the way down to see if Catherine had called. She had forgotten her phone. Jo didn't know how this was possible. Her own phone went everywhere with her. She'd never forget it, or forget to charge it. Claire, on the other hand, was always leaving it behind or letting the batteries run down. But then Jo had to let her off. She was in her thirties after all; she was getting on a bit.

Jo was convinced that Catherine hadn't got through to the final twenty-four. She would surely know by now. They were meant to be told by three o'clock and their family members had been told to pick them up at five.

Maria joined them. She had been standing in front of the crisp display for the past five minutes and was clutching a packet of prawn cocktail crisps. 'Can you get me these?' she whispered, passing the crisps to Claire as if she was handling hardcore porn.

'I didn't think you ate "carbs".' Jo hated people who said 'carbs'. They were always the sort of people who went to the gym at six in the morning and had Hollywood bikini waxes. Maria said 'carbs'.

'I don't.'

'So how do you manage a packet of crisps then?'

'I lick them,' Maria said, as if this was perfectly normal.

'You just said that out loud, you do know that, don't you?' Jo couldn't believe Maria.

'Duh! Yeah!'

'Just checking, because you said it as if I was the stupid one.'

'You are.'

'You lick crisps! Are you related to me? Is she, Claire? Was she adopted?'

'No, she's all ours,' Claire said, moving up in the queue.

'You're weird too,' Maria countered.

'How am I weird?' Jo demanded to know.

'How are you weird? You hate Dad but all of a sudden you're being nice to him. What's that about, if you're not a complete odd ball?'

'I can be nice to Dad if I want.'

'Course you can,' Maria agreed. 'You just never are.'

Jo didn't care if Maria thought she was weird, that would be like being called a racist by a member of the BNP, but something shifted with Jo as they moved up to the front of the queue. This conversation was annoying her. There were far more important things to think about than how Maria chose to conduct her weird eating habits. Jo knew she was looking for a reason to tell her sisters about her dad. She knew that she had promised Catherine but the secret was weighing heavy on her and anyway, she needed her sisters to know what she and Catherine knew, that way they could all confront their father together when they got back and make him tell them how serious his cancer was. She knew that Catherine would be annoyed at first but she would realise that it was something they all needed to know about, not deal with in isolation.

'Dad's got cancer,' Jo blurted out.

The woman behind the counter scanning the flapjacks and prawn cocktail crisps flinched for a moment before asking, 'Would you like a carrier bag? They're five pence.'

'No!' Claire snapped, before remembering her manners. 'Thank you.' She turned her attention back to Jo. 'What?'

'Catherine told me. Last night. It's true. She's known for months but he's sworn her to secrecy.'

'Oh my God.' Maria said, clutching at her stomach. 'I think I'm going to be sick.' She ran off in the direction of the toilet. Jo and Claire watched her go. Jo was about to say something about her making room for her crisp flavouring but now was not the time for sarcastic comments, even if it did concern Maria.

Claire pulled the car up in front of the manor house. They still hadn't heard from Catherine and assumed that this was because she hadn't got through to the next round. The mood was already sombre in the car. It wasn't often that the Reilly sisters had a serious conversation, but that was what they had had for the last half hour of the journey. Maria and Claire had been angry at first that Catherine had kept this from them, but Jo had convinced them to see reason and think about how their father would have put pressure on her. Eventually they had agreed that Jo was right. Mick would have put his daughter in such a position that she would have felt she couldn't tell a soul. Catherine must have felt terrible keeping this to herself.

A few rejected-looking auditionees wandered out of the front door of the manor house. One girl burst into floods of tears as her father hugged and consoled her. Jo looked at Claire; they didn't need to say anything, they were both thinking the same thing: Poor Catherine.

'Come on then, let's get it over with,' Maria said, getting out of the car.

'Are we allowed in? We weren't last time.'

'We are now there's nothing to see, they're all on their way home,' Maria said confidently. 'Anyway, if they're going to chuck us out they'll chuck us out, won't they?' she added.

Good point, Jo thought. She liked getting into places where she had no right being.

'We don't know that she's not through yet, Maria.'

'Come on . . . She'd have called if she'd got through. Anyway, she might be relieved. She'll want to look after Dad at a time like this.'

'Why does Catherine have to do it? Why can't you do it? Why can't I do it? Why does it have to be her?' Jo asked angrily.

'I'm just saying, Jo. Get off your teenage high horse.'

'I'm not on a high horse. You just hope that she's coming home because you can't be arsed with all the hassle.'

'That is so out of order.' Maria shoved Jo, Jo shoved her back. 'If Dad's seriously ill I will be there, who are you to say I won't?' Maria said, with another push.

'Don't push me,' Jo seethed.

'Well, don't push me either,' Maria squared up to Jo.

Claire pulled them apart. 'Will you two knock it on the head?'

Jo could have happily thumped Maria, but realising they were drawing stares from disappointed *Star Maker* contestants suddenly made her stop her bickering.

They walked towards the entrance. 'We might as well go in, there's no sign of her,' Jo said, wanting to have a good nosey around the premises.

'I don't think we're allowed are we? Won't security tell us off?' Claire said.

'We were checked in at the gate, they know we're family anyway . . .' Jo said, marching up to the door. She pushed it open and walked in. There was no one to tell them they couldn't enter so she turned and beckoned to her sisters to join her. They trotted behind her along the vast wood-panelled corridors. Jo had no idea where she was going, but she was enjoying getting lost in such a palace.

Jo turned a corner into a huge formal dining room and sitting, perched on the edge of a priceless dining table, so massive it looked as if it could seat about a thousand people, was Richard Forster talking to none other than her sister Catherine. Jo coughed. She didn't really know what else to do. Maria and Claire stood behind her as if they were doing the conga.

Catherine looked up, blushing when she saw her sisters. 'Hi!'

'How did you do?' Jo asked, crossing every digit she had.

'I got through to the next round. I'm going to London. I'm in Richard's group.'

Jo heard Claire and Maria gasp and then all three sisters ran forward and hugged Catherine tightly, jumping around squealing.

Claire was so excited that she did something so out of character it made Jo burst out laughing. She grabbed Richard Forster by the head, kissed him on the forehead and said, 'You beauty.'

Richard was clearly taken aback but laughed and struck up a conversation with Claire and a very star-struck Maria.

'I know, I can't believe it,' Catherine said excitedly to Jo. And then quietly added, 'But what about Dad?'

Jo looked around. She knew she was probably going to

dampen the mood slightly, but she wanted to reassure her sister. 'It's OK, Catherine, you're fine to go. We'll sort Dad out. I've told them.'

'You've told them?' Catherine asked, shocked.

'I had to, Catherine, what were we going to do?' Jo asked, as Catherine marched past her and out of the room.

'You promised,' she shouted at Jo.

'Catherine, come back!' Jo followed her sister, kicking herself for telling Catherine now that her sisters knew about Dad. She could at least have waited until they were in the car. Given Catherine a few minutes to savour her success. Jo couldn't believe that she had managed to spoil the one time in Catherine's life when she had achieved something special by bringing her down to earth with a big fat bang.

camped out and caught a bus toward [illegible] her next. It's OK, Catherine, you're fine [illegible]. We'll [illegible] Dad [illegible] told them.

"You're not alone," Catherine [illegible] smiled.

That [illegible] Catherine [illegible] were going to [illegible], a Catherine [illegible] had [illegible] of the [illegible].

The [illegible] and [illegible] started [illegible].

Catherine [illegible] for [illegible] felt [illegible], [illegible] now that [illegible] about Dad. She [illegible] until they were [illegible] Catherine a few minutes [illegible] her [illegible] to [illegible] believe that she had [illegible] to [illegible] life which she had [illegible] something [illegible] by [illegible] down to earth, with [illegible].

Chapter 8

The four-bedroom semi where Catherine had grown up seemed smaller somehow on her return. The through lounge and dining room seemed even more cluttered with Mick's knick-knacks than usual. Catherine usually kept a daily vigil over what her father acquired and what he kept. Jo said that Mick would end up on *A Life of Grime* – a documentary about environmental health inspectors – if he wasn't careful. He seemed to think he was going to become an eBay millionaire, but was hampered by the fact that he couldn't bear to let anything go. There were old football programmes that had been brought up from the cellar, a motorbike engine that was half polished, half dripping in grease next to the TV and a taxidermy squirrel that looked rather startled by the whole experience. The home felt small, especially now that Maria was back. Catherine often wondered how they'd all managed to fit in the house, growing up. The one good thing about the Reilly residence was that Mick had bought it for less than a thousand pounds years ago and the mortgage had been paid off well before Karen left. Mick had given his wife some form of severance money when she left and she wasn't entitled to anything else. So at least they had a secure home throughout Mick's years of unemployment.

Catherine was lying in bed, looking at her ceiling. The excitement of the afternoon had all but faded. She couldn't believe that Jo had told Maria and Claire about dad. She had been so angry with Jo on the way home, but it was hard to keep up that level of anger when everyone around her was a) concerned for their father and b) about to burst with excitement because their sister was going to spend the weekend with Richard Forster.

When she had arrived home Mick had come to the door. Catherine didn't know if she could tell him. Being excited about being through to the next stage of the competition felt totally inappropriate.

'She's through!' Claire had said excitedly, doing her best impression of someone who didn't know her dad had cancer.

'Good lass,' Mick said and nodded sadly as if he'd already lost Catherine.

Later, when she managed to get him on his own, she said, 'I don't have to go, Dad.'

'I can't hold you back,' Mick had said ambiguously. She didn't know if he meant he didn't want to hold her back or he had no choice, she would go anyway.

Claire and Maria had behaved so oddly – Claire made her dad some toast and Maria changed the channel for him – that Catherine had to ask Claire to go home and Maria to go out before Mick cottoned on to the fact that they all knew.

Catherine looked up at the ceiling and at the comforting little cobweb that had hung in the corner since she was a little girl, since before their mum had left home. Catherine never removed it because she liked it being there. It made her feel safe – stupid really – that her one constant in life was a cobweb in the corner of her room.

She had stared at that cobweb on Christmas eves as a child, waiting excitedly for the hours to tick by and to be allowed downstairs to see if Santa had been. She had stared at it the night before her GCSE exams, going over everything she could remember about *Twelfth Night* and Boyle's Law and The Potsdam Conference. She had stared at it the night that she had been unceremoniously chucked by Darren Gleeson. And she had stared at it the night that her mum left home to live with Jay in Chorlton, listening to her dad crying downstairs as he sank a bottle of whisky and listened to 'You Picked a Fine Time to Leave Me, Lucille' over and over. Now she was lying staring at the cobweb and thinking that if she went ahead with taking her place in the *Star Maker* competition and her father became seriously ill, she would never forgive herself. It was her that he depended on, not the others. He trusted her. She knew where everything was that he needed. Jo would forget to give him his tablets and Maria would lose her patience with him and Claire would go home when he got too cantankerous for her, which was a given as he couldn't go ten minutes without a bout of cantankerousness. She really didn't know what to do.

'Hello.' Jo pushed the door open.

'Hi.'

'Would you like me to feed you some grapes? Or get you a big feather fan?'

'No thanks.'

'Come on . . . you're nearly famous. You need to start with some diva demands or you'll never get into Boujis.'

'What's Boujis?'

'A nightclub that Prince Harry's always falling out of

in London – you probably get dragged there with Richard. Note I'm calling him "Richard" now, because he's my mate.' Jo looked around the room as if she was searching for something to comment on. 'Right,' she said finally, 'I'm a nob, I know that, but I think that this isn't something that can be kept secret.'

Catherine wanted to be angry with Jo, to tell her that she had no right telling their sisters without consulting her first, but Jo was right. It wasn't something that should be kept secret. At least not between them. Whether they told their dad today that they all knew was an entirely different matter. Catherine didn't think it would do him any good to know that everyone knew. But she had a feeling that things were now out of her hands.

'I know.' Catherine nodded.

'You can't wrap him in cotton wool. You know what he's like, he'd be making you feel bad about something anyway. At least he's got something proper.'

'Jo!' Catherine said, sitting up angrily, 'What a thing to say.'

'Look, I'm not being tight, I'm just saying that sometimes people come through in the face of absurdity.'

'Adversity.'

'What did I say?'

'Absur— it doesn't matter, go on.'

'You know, you hear these stories of people who are just normal and then all of a sudden they find this hidden strength, you know, picking cars off kids that have been crushed, that sort of thing.'

'Yeah, but Dad's not normal. He's not been well for years.'

'No, he's not been well according to him. It's all in his head. Now with the . . .' Jo swallowed hard, '. . . cancer, he has something real to fight.'

'I don't know, Jo. I just think he's going to pieces.'

'Well, all the more reason to confront him about it. Tell him we'll help him.'

'He wants me, though.'

'What for? Balloon rides over the Serengeti?'

'He said something about going on the big wheel in town.'

'That's what I like about Dad, sets his sights high.'

'If something happens to him I'll never forgive myself.'

Jo stood up and took Catherine's Calvin Klein perfume and sprayed it up her jumper. 'What does that mean? You are going to London next week if I have to take you myself.'

'I don't know.'

'I do. This bullshit stops now.'

'Why? What are you doing?'

Jo walked towards the door. 'Never mind what I'm doing. Get your beauty sleep. You're going to be on the telly.'

'Jo?' Jo turned around and looked at Catherine. 'Put the perfume back, it cost me twenty quid.'

Jo was always rooting around, seeing if there was anything worth pinching.

She laughed, knowing she'd been caught red-handed. 'Damn. So near, yet so far.'

Catherine smiled at her sister. You had to love her for trying. Her phone began to ring. Catherine looked at the number, didn't recognise it and didn't know who would want to call her at eleven in the evening anyway. She looked at it for a moment, thinking that she should let it go through to voicemail, but curiosity got the better of her. 'Hello?'

'Catherine Reilly?' a woman asked. Catherine didn't recognise the voice.

'Yes.'

'How does it feel to be going to London?'

'Who is this?'

'It must be a thrill to be in Richard Forster's group.'

Catherine had been warned by the producers that they would start to receive calls from the press. That they would call anyone who had got through to Boot Camp and pretend that they knew that they were through whether they were or weren't. They would then cobble together a story based on the disparate facts they were given.

'Who is this?'

'The other girls in your group are really excited about going.'

Catherine wanted to put the phone down, but she was too polite. She was like this at work in the call centre, someone could be screaming blue murder at her and she'd still be nice to them. If Jo had taken this call she would pretend to be a phone sex line until the person on the other end got bored or offended or enjoyed it so much they had to go anyway.

'I'm very sorry, but I'm going to put the phone down now. Thank you for calling.'

Catherine pressed the cancel button on her phone tentatively, as if a bomb would be detonated as soon as she touched it. Once the call was cancelled she put the phone under her pillow. It rang again immediately.

Catherine tried to ignore it. It rang again. When the phone rang for the tenth time she switched it off and threw it across the room. She put her head on her pillow, but it would be another three hours before she finally fell asleep.

Jo was sitting at the breakfast bar in the kitchen flanked by Maria and Claire when Catherine appeared at the door.

'What are you lot doing?' Catherine asked, rubbing her eyes.

Jo took a deep breath and scrunched her eyes shut and gabbled an explanation. She didn't want Catherine to be angry with her, but after last night, when her sister seemed to be wavering about whether to go to London, Jo thought that she needed to take drastic action. 'We need to tell Dad. We're all agreed. We're going to confront him.'

'Tell him that we know and that we need a plan of action to help him. There's no point in us all sneaking around pretending that nothing's going on and we're all hunky dory,' Claire said.

'What do you mean, tell him?' Catherine looked at her three sisters, sitting in a row as if they were there to interview her.

'Tell him. Just tell him,' Maria said, as if Catherine was stupid and she was the brains behind all of this.

'Like on *Dog the Bounty Hunter*,' Jo said, thinking that this was the most helpful way of explaining things to Catherine. 'We're going to do an "intervention",' she said, in her best American accent.

'He's going to flip his lid,' Catherine said, sitting down with a thump.

'He's not going to flip anything,' Claire replied, getting up and pouring water into the teapot. 'Tea?'

'Please.'

'What's he going to do? Run away and stay somewhere else? He'll moan at you for telling us, but he'll moan anyway, won't he?'

'Telling you what?' Mick suddenly appeared at the door.

Jo stared at her dad. This had been her idea, she couldn't let her bottle desert her now. 'Dad, can you take a seat?' she asked politely.

Too politely, she was never this nice to him. He looked at her and then at his other three daughters. 'Come on then, Witches of Eastwick, spit it out.'

'You know we worry about you . . .' Maria said.

Mick's face suggested he didn't think anything of the sort.

'And we just want to do what's best for you . . .' Claire added.

Catherine let out a sigh. 'They know you've got cancer. I told Jo because I was worried and I was going away and then she told the others because she didn't want to be the only one that knew and now they've—' Catherine corrected herself, '*we've* decided that we need to speak to you about it.'

'Who the bloody hell do you lot think you are?' Mick asked, simultaneously scratching his beard and rearranging himself.

Claire pulled herself up to her full five foot eight. 'Your daughters!' she shouted.

Mick stared at her, taken aback. 'Now you might not

like the fact that we are bothered about what happens to you, but we are. And we are not going to let you do this on your own . . .'

'I wasn't doing it on my own. You were helping me.'

'And that's why we all know now,' Jo joined in. 'So that Catherine doesn't have to deal with it on her own.'

'It's me with the cancer, not her,' Mick said, walking over to the cupboard and pulling down a packet of Rice Krispies and thumping them on the work surface.

'Yeah?' Jo asked angrily. She really couldn't believe her dad's attitude sometimes, he loved wallowing in self-pity. Maybe her theory that this might give him an extra boost in life was totally wrong. Maybe all it would do was make him feel even sorrier for himself. 'Well, it's her with the once-in-a-lifetime opportunity and she's not cocking it up just because you want her here at your beck and call.'

'Her?' he said, throwing his hand in Catherine's direction as if swatting flies. 'What does she do anyway? Bugger all, from what I can see, except for swanning off to some talent competition and not giving a stuff about me.'

Jo looked over at Catherine, who was standing open-mouthed, her eyes watery.

'She looks after you, you selfish sod. She's your carer,' Claire said.

'I haven't got a bloody carer.'

'What is she then, Dad?' Jo demanded. 'She does everything for you. What's that if it's not a carer?'

'A mug?' Catherine said quietly.

Jo, Claire and Maria turned and stared at their sister.

'What?' Mick asked. Jo couldn't believe that Catherine

had said it; good for her. Though, she thought, her dad really did treat her like one sometimes.

'How can you say that?' Mick asked, turning around and slamming the cereal packet on the counter.

'How can I not after what you've just said?'

'I'll tell you who's a mug, shall I? Me, for trusting you,' Mick spat at Catherine.

Jo thought that her dad's anger was far more acute than the situation warranted. 'All right, you,' Jo shouted, 'chill your beans. We all know now so that's it. You can cry all you want, Dad, but we know. So what now?'

'Nothing now.'

'Wrong answer,' Claire said, walking over to her father. 'What sort of cancer is it, Dad? Where is it being treated, what have the doctors told you? And is there anything else we should know?'

Jo could tell that Claire was trying to be calm and caring with Mick, but he really would try the patience of a saint.

Mick put his hand to his stomach. 'It's stomach cancer.'

'And where are you being treated?' Claire's voice softened.

Mick thought for a moment. 'Withington.'

'Withington Hospital?'

'No,' he corrected. 'Christie's. Christie's Cancer Hospital in Withington.'

'And what have the doctors said?' Maria asked quietly.

Jo couldn't remember a time when she had seen her sister look so concerned.

'They talk in riddles that lot. I don't know if I'm coming or going with them.'

'When's your next appointment?'

Mick turned his back on his daughters and buried his head in his hands. 'Next week. A week on Monday,' he said.

Catherine looked at Jo. 'That's when I'm away.'

'We know,' Jo replied, 'we'll go with him.'

'You'll do nothing of the sort,' Mick said defiantly.

Maria walked over to her dad and, taking his hand guided him to a seat, placed a cup of tea in front of him and poured milk on his Rice Krispies. 'Yes, we will, Dad. We'll all be there for you.'

Mick gazed around at his daughters, a look of genuine wonderment on his face. 'But you've got work and stuff. You don't want to be bothering with me.'

'Yes, we do,' Claire said defiantly.

'Course we do,' Maria said.

'Despite what you might think, you daft old goat, we do love you,' Catherine said.

'Yeah, Dad, we'll come with you,' Jo offered. 'I'll even be nice to you.'

'Good girl,' Mick said with a wink, suddenly perking up. 'Pop us some toast in then, will you love and stick the radio on. United have got an early kick off.'

Jo looked at Catherine and raised an eyebrow. *Was he serious?* She walked over and grabbed some Milk Roll and shoved it in the toaster, wondering if it was her that was mean-spirited or whether her dad was just a born piss-taker, whatever life threw at him.

Catherine returned to her room and flopped on her bed. She was so mad with her dad, but so guilty at the same time at having to leave him, that her head felt as if it was filled with static and she couldn't think straight. Jo was right; he was selfish. He didn't care about her, all he really cared about was himself, which had been perfectly demonstrated by the way he had reacted when he had been confronted by his daughters – indignation followed by what Catherine could only describe as delight at the fact that his other daughters now seemed willing to pander to his needs. What an awful thing to think about her own father, Catherine thought, as she pulled out her suitcase again and began to pack for London. But it was true. He was sitting downstairs now being treated like the Maharajah because he had cancer and he actually seemed to be revelling in it.

Catherine tried to put herself in his place. He was probably frightened and felt all alone and thought no one else would want to know, she reasoned. Now that her sisters knew, he was just glad that it was out in the open. But the way he was behaving downstairs seemed more self-centred than that. He was just pleased to be the centre of attention for a change. Something that he had been striving towards for years, but had never actually achieved.

Catherine gathered up all of the clothes that Jo had helped her choose, which she had washed and ironed as soon as she returned from Boot Camp, and folded them neatly in her case. She looked at her reflection in the mirror. She had lost weight over the past few weeks, the excitement and the stress of the auditions, then the run up to Boot Camp, had made Catherine lose her appetite, something she never thought could happen to her. She'd always marvelled at those girls who said things like, 'I forgot to eat lunch.' How did someone forget to eat lunch? But now she kind of understood. Her stomach didn't seem to want to ask her brain for food. It seemed to have disconnected itself from its hunger sensors and hooked itself up with the panic and adrenalin sensors. Instead of being hungry it just churned with worry about her dad, about the next stage in the competition, about how she would come across on TV.

Catherine's phone began to ring. It was Andy. She had been wondering if he was going to call and had been coming up with excuses over the past twenty-four hours as to why he might not. He was busy, he had other things to do, he'd probably decided against it as soon as he'd left Boot Camp.

'Hello?' she said in a voice that suggested she didn't know who was calling. Why do that, she wondered? She'd taken his number, she knew it was him, but here she was acting all casual as if there were so many Andys in her phone book she didn't know which one was ringing at any given time.

'Catherine? It's Andy.'

'Oh, hi Andy.' You know it's him!

'I didn't know if my number came up, it sometimes comes up as private number . . .'

Now poor Andy was having to enter into her pretence with her. Catherine wanted to kick herself. She really needed Jo to script her when it came to talking to men; she seemed incapable of doing it properly on her own.

'No, er, yes it didn't . . . I mean, no. Er . . .' Catherine laughed nervously, what was she on about?

Thankfully, Andy laughed too. 'Shall we start again?' he asked kindly.

'Go on then,' Catherine said gratefully.

'Hi, Catherine, it's Andy.'

'Hi, Andy.'

'How are you?'

'Good. And you?'

'Great. I'm just ringing about that drink.' Andy sounded as nervous as Catherine felt.

'Oh right, yes the drink. Well, it'll have to be after I get back from London now,' she said and then corrected herself. 'Sorry, what I meant is, I'd love to, but obviously I've got to go to London.'

'It might not have to wait until you get back from there . . . because I'm coming too!'

'No way!' Catherine shrieked and then realised that her enthusiasm might scare Andy off. 'I mean,' she coughed, mocking herself, speaking again but this time in a low calm voice, 'No way.'

'Yep. They've drafted me in. Jason P. Longford likes me, apparently. Is that a good thing or a bad thing?'

Catherine laughed. 'A bit of both, I think.'

'So, I get to see you go through to the finals and then obviously win the whole show.'

Catherine smiled. 'Thanks for the vote of confidence, but I think Star is the natural-born winner of *Star Maker* this year, unless there's some American talent that's better at singing and even more assured of their own greatness.'

'Whatever. But we can go along for the ride though, can't we?'

Catherine felt giddy, as if he was inviting her to be part of his exclusive gang, her and him against the world. 'Yes,' she laughed, 'we can.'

Chapter 9

Catherine had never been to London. She knew that that probably made her sound like a hick, but she hadn't. There hadn't ever really been a time when the opportunity had arisen. Once her dad had decided that he had to go to see an exhibition by the artist Velázquez, but a week before they were due to go Mick had read an article about the artist in the *Mail on Sunday* and told Catherine that they weren't 'going all the way to London to see some doodles by a piss-taking Spaniard.' And that had been the end of that.

Catherine hadn't known what to expect on her first visit to the capital, but she knew that this trip, courtesy of *Star Maker*, would be far more exciting than it would have been had she accompanied her father. She and Kim, who had travelled on the train together, were met at the station by a chauffeur-driven car and were whisked through the streets of London. Catherine and Kim excitedly chattered as they looked out of the window at Green Park. 'Look, the Ritz!' Kim shouted as the car slowed. 'Are we staying here?' she asked.

'No, where you're staying is far better that that,' the chauffeur said with a smile. A few minutes later he pulled the car around the corner and came to a stop at some electronic gates.

'Oh my God, you can not be serious!' Kim squealed. Ahead of them was a huge white Edwardian villa.

'It's like a palace,' Catherine whispered, totally overawed. 'Is this where we're staying?' She really couldn't believe it. The Cotswolds place had been nice but in London, for some reason, she thought they might get put up in a Travel Lodge somewhere on the outskirts and be shipped in to the centre for filming.

'Here you are, girls,' the chauffeur turned round and announced with a smile, 'Chez Forster.'

'This is amazing!' Catherine looked out at the manicured front lawn and the ivy that was creeping around the huge front door.

'Fifteen bedrooms in there. Looks smaller from here, doesn't it?' the chauffeur commented.

'No, it looks massive!' Kim squealed.

'You're a bit more impressed than the last girl I dropped off. She just stuck her nose in the air and said it was like her mum's gaff.'

Catherine and Kim looked at one another. 'Star,' they said simultaneously.

They were taken through into the first reception room of the house and were allocated their room on the third floor. It was all very glamorous to begin with, as they inspected the huge bathroom and jumped around on their beds with their Egyptian cotton sheets. But as they were taken through into their audition groups and put through their paces it became apparent that they weren't going to have any time to enjoy their luxury surroundings.

Catherine, Kim and Star were kept in one room all day. They were informed that the six girls from America that they would be competing against were here, but that they wouldn't meet them until the following day because it was felt that they might be a distraction. They were then each given a song to sing, with no opportunity to change if they didn't think it suited their voice. Catherine had been allocated 'Sitting on the Dock of the Bay' by Otis Redding. At first she had panicked, but as she practised it over and over she realised that it really suited her voice. She wanted to sing her own songs but knew that for the moment she should just sing what she was asked to sing.

Star had complained about her song choice, only to be told by the vocal coach that she had better get used to being allocated songs if she was to get through to the finals, as all of the songs had already been chosen. During Boot Camp they had been allowed to choose their own songs, but now – as the competition hotted up – the contestants' performances were dictated by the judges. Catherine had thought this was odd – how could they know what would suit different singers' voices? But she was so busy that the thought soon left her head and she resumed singing.

As they fell into bed at the end of a long day, Kim looked over at Catherine and said, 'Looks a lot more glamorous on the telly, doesn't it?'

Catherine didn't want to badmouth the show. She'd had a great day and it was glamorous to her, but she hated to disagree with people. 'I suppose it can't be glamour twenty-four seven, can it? Anyway, we're not here to have a glamorous time, we're here so that they can make the show and make it look like we're having a glamorous time.'

'True,' Kim lapsed into thought.

'And we get to climb into the best bed ever at night and open the curtains and look out at a Mayfair garden in the morning.'

'I suppose,' Kim said. 'But *Star Maker* is just a machine at the end of the day.'

'Oh God, you sound like my dad.'

'Is that a bad thing, then?'

'He's just partial to a conspiracy theory or two, likes to think that this is a machine that's sole purpose is to chew up people with a dream to sing and spit them out the other end.'

'Cheery then, your dad?'

Catherine caught the lump in her throat. 'He's just a bit gloomy. The glass isn't even half empty. It's just empty.'

There was silence in the room as Catherine tried not to get upset about her dad, but soon tears began to roll down her cheeks.

'Are you OK? You sound like you're crying,' Kim said gently.

Catherine propped herself up in the bed and wondered momentarily if she should keep what was happening at home to herself. Then she saw Kim looking kindly at her and knew that she could trust her new friend with anything. The two girls sat talking until the early hours of the morning and Catherine told her everything about her dad, about her family, about her concerns about being in this competition. Kim listened and reassured Catherine that what she was doing was absolutely the right thing. And as Catherine drifted off to sleep she was struck by the thought that being behind the scenes of *Star Maker* might not being as glitzy as she may have imagined, but she was sure that she'd made a great friend in Kim.

Andy had been at the London studios of *Star Maker* for two days, working alongside Jason P. Longford as he went through his scripts and barked orders. Jesse had been flown to the US to work alongside Carrie Ward and had been frantically texting Andy to try to make him jealous. Andy didn't give two hoots, he loved London and he loved his job. He was finding the texts amusing though, as Jesse was adamant that Carrie Ward was falling for his charms and was bound to leave her rich, handsome husband for him.

Jason had taken a back seat at Boot Camp but he was now in full, egomaniacal flow. He didn't want to spend too much time hanging around London with the under-twenty-fives he said, he wanted to get to St. Tropez where Lionel was entertaining the over-twenty-five women, or Long Island where Carrie Ward was mentoring the under-twenty-five boys, or better still The Beverley Hills Hotel, where Cherie Forster was looking after the over-twenty-five men. Andy hadn't had the heart to point out that he was fairly sure that Jason had to stay in Europe for the time being, recording in the UK and France until the live finals.

'Who wants to be in scabby London?' Jason had asked disparagingly.

Me for one, Andy thought. He had only been to London a handful of times and was in awe of the place. He loved wandering along the small streets near the City with names like Pudding Lane and Bowler Street. Just walking along the banks of the Thames made him feel that – despite tabloid claims that it was going to the dogs – this was a great country. He wasn't totally daft, he knew that London had a seedy underbelly like every other major city in the world. But it also had Tower Bridge, Beefeaters and the Houses of Parliament.

'I like London. And the house where the contestants are staying is meant to be really amazing,' Andy said, thinking that he should at least offer some defence.

'Yeah, if you're some gauche Russian billionaire, maybe,' Jason said queenily.

Andy hadn't spent a huge amount of time in Jason's company but he thought that the taste of a gauche Russian billionaire would have been right up his street. Jason struck Andy as the sort of man who'd have his teeth replaced with gold dentures if he had the money.

Andy wanted to get over to Forsters' house so that he could say hello to Catherine. Acting all casual of course, as if he was just popping in to say hi because he was that at-ease kind of guy. Then he would suggest a drink in London before they both headed back. He had already asked Will if he would sign him into Soho House and he'd agreed. He wasn't sure if Soho House was any good. It sounded like a block of council flats, but Will seemed to think it was the place to take someone to impress them and he was happy to take his advice.

'Let's get over there now and then I can get on my way to somewhere half decent. What's my schedule?' Jason asked, clicking his fingers. Andy raised an eyebrow but Jason didn't notice.

'You're here until one, then you fly to St Tropez this

afternoon and then . . .' Andy flicked through the schedule. That was it, it was blank. 'I think that's it.'

'What about America?' Jason threw his arms in the air. Richard Forster had walked into the room; Jason was too busy having a hissy fit to notice him.

'Tom Sorenson is doing the US end of things, of course,' Richard informed Jason.

Andy took a deep breath. If there was one thing worse, he was learning, than being in the presence of Richard Forster as he bollocked Jason, it was watching Jason squirm from the bollocking he was receiving.

'Oh, of course, yes,' Jason said. 'Tom. He really is a brilliant presenter. The camera goes on and he lights up the room. Really. You should see him in action.' Jason said over-enthusiastically to Andy. Andy could tell Jason hated his American counterpart.

'Time's tight, Jason. I thought your agent would have been through all this with you. You stay here and Tom stays in the US.'

'But what about the live finals?' Jason asked with ill-disguised career panic.

'You'll be there,' Richard said reassuringly. 'Bloody hell, doesn't he listen to anything?' Richard asked Andy.

Andy felt like a gooseberry in between the two. He wished that Jason would pay some attention to his schedule and that Richard wouldn't be so searingly frank. Although he had to concur with Richard's frustration: how Jason had a successful career he didn't know; he wouldn't have been able to find his way out of a paper bag without the help of an assistant.

'Anyway, it's Andy I was looking for.' Richard said,

thrusting his hands into his trouser pockets and rocking on his heels, something that anyone wishing to imitate Richard always did. Andy couldn't quite believe how much he did this in real life.

'Er, yes,' Andy said, putting the schedule down nervously and following Richard out of the room, leaving Jason standing alone.

'Right,' Richard said, in his brusque time-is-money way. 'Catherine. There's been no mention of the dad's cancer, so I'm going to say something to her today.'

Andy turned pale. 'I don't think she'd appreciate it.'

'Look, I'm not some Machiavellian arsehole, but I've got a show to run and I think that she would benefit from having this out in the open. These things get out, it's better if we help her manage it. Anyway, it makes her far more appealing,' Richard said with a shrug. 'A sad but true fact.' He reacted to the drawn look on Andy's face. 'Don't blame me, blame the British public.'

'I don't think it's a great idea,' Andy pushed.

'We'll just have to ask her, won't we?' Richard locked eyes with Andy.

Andy knew that if he wanted to keep his job he had better stop talking right now.

When she'd seen *Star Maker* in the past Catherine had always thought that when the competition got to this stage wherever they were filming was self-contained. Last year, the contestants had been whisked off to Richard's place in the Caribbean and had been shown singing around the piano inside and then performing on his sea-front terrace outside. Well, there was certainly no Caribbean for the under-twenty-five girls this year, but the filming was to be split between two places. They were filmed inside the house practising and then they were whisked off to the TV studios in West London where a mock up of a huge ballroom had been constructed for the auditions. Catherine couldn't understand at first why they didn't just use of one the many huge rooms in the house, but apparently the acoustics were wrong and it didn't look right on the TV.

This was the reason that Catherine and the other contestants found themselves rattling around the back of a minibus on their way to film the 'rehearsals'. Sierra, Therese and Carly were sitting on the front row of seats and Catherine, Star and Kim were sitting together on the back. As much as Star irritated the hell out of both Catherine and Kim, it seemed they were lumped with her. Having shared a room with her at Boot Camp it seemed to be a case of 'she's an idiot but she's our idiot'. The girls had all been rehearsing for hours but were now going to run through a scripted rehearsal. Everyone agreed it seemed like a total waste of time, but recognised that they didn't know much about how TV shows worked, so they just had to accept that there was a sensible reason for doing things this way.

'I'm nervous about meeting the Americans,' Kim admitted.

'What's to be nervous about? They're just human like us,' Star stated.

Catherine and Kim shared a look. Catherine had to stare out of the window and concentrate on the passing scenery so as not to laugh at Star's assertion that she was human.

'They'll be good though, won't they? American singers are always better than British singers,' Kim said.

'No, actually, not true,' Star said, as if this was her chosen specialist subject. 'America is far bigger than the UK, so they have a far bigger pool of talent to pull from, but you only have to look at people like Adele, Amy Winehouse and Duffy to see that we are more than capable of producing world-class home-grown talent.'

Kim looked at Catherine with a smirk. 'Here endeth the lesson.'

For once Catherine agreed with Star. 'Actually, I think she's right. I think that we do have great singers and I don't necessarily think that American singers are better.'

'Oooh, best mates,' Kim said mockingly.

Catherine felt awkward. She wasn't being anyone's best mate; she just thought that Star had a point.

'I didn't mean anything, I just think that she has a point . . .' Catherine said quietly.

'And I do have a point,' Star said firmly.

Kim slapped Catherine on the leg. 'Bloody hell. Only joking,' she said, but Catherine wasn't so sure. Kim was great, but she could be matter-of-fact to the point of cutting sometimes.

A few moments later the awkward silence was interrupted by the driver. 'Here we are, girls.'

The barrier lifted at the gateway to the studios and the driver parked the minibus outside the back entrance. A moment later Will was at the side of the bus, ushering the girls into the building. 'This is glamorous,' Sierra complained.

'We've got other girls going in the front as decoys. Now stop moaning and go through, you'll be singing in a minute,' Will said, shaking his head.

'Decoys?' Catherine asked.

'We have to use decoys so that the press don't find out who's down to the last six, or last twelve if you include the Americans. We hire twenty-four girls from a model agency, twelve for here, twelve for the US, and everywhere you go, they go. It's a pain in the arse but it throws the papers off the scent.'

Catherine and the others followed Will, trying to keep up as he powered into the building and along a corridor. 'You have to do that for each category?' Kim asked, trying to take in her surroundings as well as concentrate on Will's reply. On the walls were pictures of famous people who had appeared at the studio over the years.

'Yep. Total ball-ache.'

The girls were lead through a number of doors that could only be accessed by a security card until it felt as if they were being brought into the bowels of the building.

'Where are we going?' Star moaned. 'My Choos are killing me,' she said.

'Don't you pronounce shoe in a funny way,' Will said, oblivious.

'My Choos! My bloody Jimmy Choos!'

'All right. Keep your knickers on,' Will said. 'Right, here we are, girls.' He showed them into a room that at eye level looked like a ballroom, but with the slightest of neck tilts looked exactly like what it was, a TV set. There were boom mikes and glaring lights dangling from the ceiling and the room was surrounded by cameras. Catherine gulped; this was the first time she'd been on a real TV set. In her previous auditions, although they had been constantly filmed, it hadn't been this obvious. 'And here are the American girls,' Will said, gesturing to the six young ladies sitting on chairs, nervously waiting. 'Shoneeka, Lindsay, Freya, Jenny, Petra and Meagan, meet Kim, Catherine, Star, Sierra, Therese and Carly.' The girls all nodded, weighing one another up. Catherine had expected the Americans to be super-confident and scary, but on very first impressions they seemed as nervous as she felt.

'OK, girls. There's no real time to get to know each other at the moment. We need to get on,' Will told them. 'What we will be doing after this is having you learn a few lines and pretend that you've been together for a few days and that you're all getting on famously. Get you to hug one another, that sort of thing.'

Gasps and laughs went around the room, 'You're not serious?' one of the American girls asked incredulously.

'I certainly am. The public wants to see bonding and camaraderie. Unfortunately we haven't got the time or the budget for that to develop naturally.'

'But that's dishonest!' Kim said righteously.

'Come on, you don't honestly think that people on reality TV have the time or the inclination to become best friends, do you?' Will asked. Catherine couldn't believe that he didn't seem the slightest bit phased by his own cynicism. 'It is a competition, you know. Not a love-in. Right, where's my right-hand man with the run-through sheets?' Will said, looking around.

Andy stepped forward into the light. Catherine, for some reason that she couldn't quite explain herself, felt like clapping. That would have looked really cool, wouldn't it? she chastised herself, clapping like a seal just because someone you quite like has entered the room. But she knew it was more than that. She *really* liked Andy, and he seemed to like her. And she felt that they were somehow in this together. They seemed to share the same sensibility about things. She hadn't known him long, but she just sensed she could trust him.

Andy saw her and smiled shyly. He looked great, Catherine thought. She could tell that he wasn't aware of how attractive he was. Andy was very tall, but obviously thought himself too tall, which he wasn't. He had broad shoulders and slender hips and a shock of hair that made him look dishevelled in a sexy way. She knew that if anyone pointed this out to him that he would probably blush, a thought which made Catherine smile involuntarily.

Catherine waved a small wave and looked over at Andy as Will went through what they were all expected to do this afternoon. Once Will announced that they were all to sit down and wait for their name to be called, Andy walked towards Catherine. She felt giddy but tried to pretend that she was a composed Ice Queen.

'Hi,' Andy said.

'Hello,' Catherine replied. Ice Queen, Ice Queen! she told herself.

'You look nice . . .' Andy blushed. 'Have they done something with your hair and make-up?'

'No, I did it myself, they want us to look natural until

we get to the live finals, *if* we get to the live finals should I say, I've never had my make-up done . . . well, I have, when my sister Jo wants to practise on someone . . . and then we got to choose something to wear . . . well sort of, they kind of told us what we were wearing and then we could say if we really didn't like it, but I quite like this.' Catherine pulled the green skirt that she was wearing out to one side, like a little girl about to curtsey in front of royalty. She was out of breath and flushed red; so much for the Ice Queen act.

'You look very nice.' Andy smiled appreciatively.

'Thanks.' Catherine paused for a moment and then had to fill the air. 'Sorry for gabbling. I think I'm nervous. And I sometimes get a bit gabbly when I'm nervous. Is that a word? Gabbly?'

The first time that Catherine realised that Star was standing behind her listening to all of this was when she felt a hand on her arm and then the sensation of being yanked away from Andy. Star pulled her to the side of the studio and looked at Catherine seriously. 'I had to save you from yourself there. You were making *me* blush,' Star said. Catherine wanted to tell her she had a cheek, thinking that she could intervene in this way, but actually she was glad. Someone needed to, before she talked herself into such a frenzy that she just exploded, right there in front of Andy's eyes.

'Calm down, walk back over to him and ask him how he's been. And then . . .' Star lowered her voice. Catherine thought she was going to impart some amazing worldly knowledge and leant in to hear it, '. . . let him get a word in edgeways.'

Catherine nodded. Star might be the stroppiest, most self-absorbed person she'd ever met, but she seemed to know what she was talking about when it came to conversing with the opposite sex. 'Thanks,' Catherine said appreciatively. It was obvious advice, but advice that she needed all the same.

She walked back over to Andy and said, 'Sorry, where was I? That's right, I was going to ask you how you've been.'

Andy began to tell Catherine what he had been doing since he'd arrived and she bit hard on her tongue so that she didn't begin to bore the poor guy to tears again.

Andy was midway through telling Catherine that he had had to stand outside in his underpants the previous evening when the fire alarm had gone off in the hotel where he was staying, when his voice suddenly dropped and, after checking that no one else was listening, he said, 'Can I have a word with you?'

'We are having a word,' Catherine said earnestly, before quickly realising that he meant about something more serious than standing in the street in his undies.

'Yes, what is it?'

'I did something the other day and now I feel terrible about it . . .'

'What?' Catherine said, she really couldn't think what it could be that he felt he had to explain himself to her. Before he had a chance to say, Will came over and guided Catherine away from Andy.

'Richard needs a quick word before we shoot,' Will said.

Catherine turned around to see that Andy was standing looking after her, ashen-faced.

* * *

Catherine was guided into a room where Richard Forster was talking to one of the production staff who Catherine didn't recognise and where Shoneeka and Star were seated, going over their scripts with the resident media coach, a lady called Serena Crabtree. Catherine hadn't known what a media coach was until she had entered this competition. When the contestants had been introduced to Serena for the first time, she had explained exactly what her role entailed. 'I take someone who might otherwise go on national TV and put their foot firmly in their mouth and I ensure that they keep their foot as far away from their mouth as possible. That's the top and bottom of it.' Catherine had since learned that there was far more to the role than that and that Serena was on hand to advise on posture, body language and voice projection, among many other things.

'This is some bullshit,' Shoneeka said, hitting the script she had been given.

Catherine flinched. She didn't think shouting at the media coach was a good idea, no matter how strongly you felt about something. Shoneeka was a petite black girl with a rich soulful voice and she was insisting to Serena that she didn't want to follow the script as she had been pitch perfect all morning in rehearsals. From what Catherine could gather, her script was instructing that halfway through her rendition of 'Respect' by Aretha Franklin, she was going to have to fluff her words and hit the white grand piano that was being played to accompany her in frustration.

'Well, at least you don't have to cry and say that this song reminds you of your mother,' Star said, rolling her eyes at Serena. 'I wouldn't mind, but it's about a bloody rat!' Star had been asked to sing 'Ben' by Michael Jackson.

Catherine felt odd. She hadn't been given any instructions yet. In her script she had to sing her allocated song, whereas everyone else was with a vocal coach or a media coach and now Richard Forster wanted a word. This didn't add up. Will, who had been briefly distracted by one of the runners asking him a list of questions, before dashing off to action them, now turned his attention back to Catherine.

'Why does Richard want a word with me, Will?' she asked.

'Dunno. Think it's something he wants for your script.'

Richard was sitting inside a dressing room looking through some papers while a make-up artist put the finishing touches to his cheeks. He looked strangely like a ventriloquist's dummy with his full make-up on, his eyebrows seemed too heavy for his face. A cigarette was burning in an ashtray next to him, despite the fact that smoking was banned indoors. Catherine thought that it must be weird to exist in a bubble like Richard, where he could pretty much do what he wanted anywhere in the world.

'Fancy a coffee, Catherine?' he asked, beckoning her inside and indicating for her to close the door.

'Please,' she said nervously.

'Take a seat.' He sensed her unease. 'There's no need to be nervous. I just need to speak to you about something.'

Catherine sank into the swivel chair opposite Richard. He poured coffee from the jug behind him and, placing the cup down, stared at Catherine intently.

'I'm not going to beat about the bush, Catherine. I know about your home situation.'

'What home situat—?'

'I know that you look after your dad. And I know that he has cancer.'

Catherine felt as if someone had just punched her off the chair. 'How . . . what . . . I never told anyone . . .' she stammered.

Richard let her sit for a moment with what he had just said. *Kim,* Catherine thought. She could feel the anger boiling up inside her. She couldn't believe it. Why would she do that? She might have thought she was helping Catherine, but surely she realised that she'd rather get by on her own merits than because of a sob story.

'Kim told you . . .'

'Catherine, if you look after your dad and he is ill – and I'm only saying this for your own good – you need to say so on the show.'

'I am not using my dad's illness to further my time in this competition.'

'It will come out, Catherine, these things always do. I just think that as a human interest story it really is lovely and I don't know why you're so ashamed of it.'

'I'm not, he is,' Catherine snapped.

'Your father's ashamed?'

'Yes. He doesn't want anyone to know. And that means anyone. He didn't even want my sisters knowing. He's not going to want it announcing on prime-time telly, is he?'

Catherine's stomach tensed, her legs weakened; she felt pressurised to do something that she really wasn't comfortable doing.

'No. Maybe not, but I just thought that it might be something you'd consider.'

'I won't.' Catherine was not going to back down on this.

'That's fine, then. These things do have a way of coming out, though.'

'Well, no one knows except my family and you and Kim . . .' Catherine said and then added bravely, '. . . so if it does come out then I know where from, don't I?'

'Good. We've cleared that up.' Richard said, nodding at Catherine.

'So nothing will be said.'

'Not from me. That will be all, Catherine. Have a good audition.'

'Thank you.'

'Oh, Catherine . . .' Richard stopped her, '. . . I wouldn't want you accusing the wrong person over this. It wasn't Kim who told me; it was Andy.'

'Right,' Catherine said, leaving the room, hoping that Richard Forster hadn't seen her hand shaking as she grasped the door handle. Catherine was horrified – why would Andy tell them? She thought she could trust him. She didn't like the way that Richard Forster had just volunteered this information either – the way that everything just seemed to be business to him – but that was the least of her worries for the time being. Catherine gathered herself for a moment outside of the office and then, seeing Andy standing with Will and Jason P. Longford, stormed over to him.

'Oh Christ, did they really put her through?' Jason asked, as Catherine stormed towards them.

Andy had just seen her walk out of the meeting room and now he felt sick. She knew.

'I really thought they might have seen sense but no, every years it's the same "stick her through . . . everyone loves a girl next door" crap. Well I, for one, bloody don't. Let's have some decent glamour, for cock's sake!'

'Can I have a word?' Catherine asked, without even looking at Jason or Will.

Andy nodded.

'You, lady, have got a nerve. There's a pecking order on shows like this and you are down here . . .' Jason pointed at the floor. 'So when you come up to the presenter and the production team, a bit of courtesy might be nice.'

Catherine looked at Jason. She was evidently fuming. 'Oh, why don't you just shut up?' she asked angrily.

That was a very good question, one that Andy wished he'd had the courage to ask himself. But he knew he couldn't be too impressed with the question because the angry manner in which it was asked was, he knew, all down to him.

'Why don't I what?' Jason reeled around, his hand to his chest; well and truly flabbergasted.

'You heard,' Catherine said, marching past them and looking at Andy.

He quickly followed her. He could feel Jason hot on his heels. 'What are you doing?' he asked the TV host.

'This will make great telly.' Behind him a camera was getting his kit together – Jason had obviously beckoned him across.

'This will not make great telly, Jason. This is private. End of.'

Jason sneered at Andy. 'You are proving a little more difficult to work with than I thought you'd be.'

'Well, the same goes, Jason.' Andy walked away, throwing a look at Jason that suggested he didn't follow him. Andy finally caught up with Catherine in the corridor.

'Catherine, I'm so sorry.'

'So you admit it then? You told them about my dad?'

'I know it was the wrong thing to do and that it was none of my business but I thought they were going to throw you out of Boot Camp because they didn't think you had enough to sell you to the public.'

'Sell me to the public? Do they teach you rubbish like that at TV school?'

'I didn't go to TV school. I'm not sure it exists even.' Andy realised his attempt at light humour was completely misplaced as soon as the words were out of his mouth.

'Really. If this is such a joke to you then I'm sorry, but it isn't to me. This is my family and my life and I'd thank you not to go using it like some bloody currency to get me a bit further in this bloody competition.'

Andy felt terrible and he knew that what Catherine was saying was right, but he wasn't going to stand here and let her shout at him and not at least tell her to stop. 'There's no need to be so angry, if you don't want it to go any further then it won't. They just won't use it. But you might not get through, that's all. And I was only trying to help.'

'Thanks for nothing, Andy. I really don't need help like that.' Catherine turned on her heel and stormed off.

Andy was left feeling terrible. 'I'm sorry,' he said quietly, but he knew that she was so mad with him that no amount of apologies was going to get her to see why he did what he did.

When Andy got back to the main studio, Jason was waiting for him. 'What's up with fat arse?'

Andy glared at him. 'What?'

'Your mate, fat arse . . .'

'She has not got a fat arse. Why say something like that?'

'Whatever . . . anyway, what's her problem? She came storming through here like a woman possessed.'

'Nothing's wrong,' Andy lied.

'Lover's tiff?' Jason asked meanly.

'No.'

'Well, whatever's wrong with her, she'd better straighten her face out or she won't be going anywhere.'

'Look, I've just put my foot in it massively with her, OK? Can we just leave it at that?'

'And she hates you?'

'I'd say that, wouldn't you?'

'I wouldn't waste my time on someone like her; go for one of the American girls. That way you can have a bit of a fling and dump her after the live finals.'

Andy looked at Jason and tried to work out how to reply to this. He had to tread carefully, after all he was, technically, his boss. Then again, he was also a nob. 'Right, thanks. That's really good advice,' Andy lied.

'I'm great when it comes to relationships. I just have this sixth sense about what to do. Friends always come and ask my advice,' Jason said.

And so humble, Andy thought. 'Have you got a boyfriend at the moment?' Andy asked conversationally.

Jason's face clouded over and suddenly it seemed as if all the air was being sucked from the room. Jason turned puce. Andy stood stock-still, waiting for the fallout to his question.

'Boyfriend? Boyfriend? Don't you read the papers?' he hissed. 'Number thirteen most fanciable male in *Cosmo*, number eight in *Heat's* Hot One Hundred and number one Housewife Hotty in *Take a Break*.'

Andy would have pointed out that all this made no difference to anything, but Jason wasn't having any of it. He was livid.

'Sorry, I just thought . . .'

'Well, get your facts straight before you open your trap next time.'

'Sorry.' Andy could feel himself blushing profusely.

'So you should be,' Jason said, storming off. Andy thought that he was probably in for a rough ride over the next few weeks, working with this TV prima donna.

Catherine was preparing to stand in front of Richard Forster. She had already performed in front of him three times today and now she was back to hear her fate. She wasn't nervous because she knew she was going home. While Kim was busy tying herself in knots, wondering what he had made of her performance and even Star had shown some uncharacteristic self-doubt and had pulled her own final performance apart, wondering if she could do better, Catherine knew that she didn't have to worry because her fate was sealed. She hadn't even cared when she'd been asked to sing three songs which didn't suit her voice at all because she knew it was all part of the show – engineered because they had to send her home and she couldn't be seen to be singing well. If it hadn't been for the fact that she knew that the contract she had signed stated that she had to be there, then Catherine would have quietly left the studio and made her way to the bus station.

Catherine had thought that Andy might make an attempt to talk to her again, but he hadn't. He had stayed as far away from her as possible. Probably for the best, she thought morosely. At least she wouldn't have to speak to him again after today. Catherine thought about what had happened today and how sad she felt at the discovery that this really was how these competitions operated. Oh well, at least she'd got to stay in the Cotswolds and in a Mayfair mansion for a few nanoseconds.

Catherine could hear Star's squeals of jubilation. 'She's through,' Kim whispered.

The other girls all looked at one another. If Star was through, that was one less place for everyone else.

'Therese, please,' Will shouted and Therese followed him.

The others all wished her luck as she walked off petrified, to hear her fate.

A few minutes later Therese was back, crying, shaking her head, indicating that she didn't want to talk about it. Catherine felt terrible for her, poor girl. That would be her in a minute, she just knew. Although she wouldn't be crying like that because already knew what was in store for her.

'Kim, please!' Catherine gave her friend a huge hug and waved her off. She felt far more nervous for Kim than she did for herself. As she stood waiting, Andy rounded the corner. He looked as if he was about to say something to her, but Catherine shut her eyes tight and when she opened them again, he had gone. Kim was with Richard Forster while he deliberated her fate for far longer than both Star and Therese. Just as Catherine was wondering if they hadn't witnessed her reaction and she had been whisked away, she heard a piercing shriek and Kim shouting, 'Oh my God, thank you so much, I won't let you down.'

So Star and Kim, her original roommates, were through, Catherine thought sadly, knowing that she wouldn't be joining them. As much of a total pain as Star was, it would be fun to see her in full flight in New York.

Carly was called next and Sierra stood looking terrified at Catherine. They didn't speak; there wasn't much to say. If Carly got through then they were both going home; if she didn't, then it was between the two of them. Carly's sobs could be heard and then a runner went past them in a hurry asking where the trained first aider was.

'I'm a trained first aider,' Catherine said and quickly followed the runner. But once she was standing in the mock ballroom, Carly was sitting up and catching her breath.

'She's fine, she's fine,' Will was saying as a gaggle of production staff stood around her. Catherine slunk back to the corridor where she had been waiting. She was relieved she hadn't had to perform CPR. It might have looked like a terribly cheesy attempt to gain favour with the judges: look at me I might not want to exploit my dad's illness, but I windsurf, abseil and perform mouth-to-mouth in my spare time.

When the commotion had died down and poor rejected Carly was carted off, Will popped his head around the door. 'Catherine, please.'

Sierra gave her a kiss on the cheek and wished her luck, which of course she didn't mean, but she had to say. Catherine walked back into the mock ballroom and took her place on the seat next to Richard Forster. She smiled tightly at Richard.

'Well, Catherine . . .' he said, looking at her intently. Catherine could feel the eyes of twenty different lights, sound and camera operators watching her. Please put me out of my misery, she thought, '. . . you've surprised me. I have to say that you are made of strong stuff.'

Catherine looked at him, her eyes were drawn to his Thunderbirds brow and the more she told herself not to stare at it, the more she couldn't help it. 'I don't really think I am . . .'

'You have an amazing voice, there is no doubt about it. And, as you know, I wasn't sure if the public would connect with you. But you know what?' he asked, employing his trademark agonising pause, 'I do. I think that you have a steely determination that might not have been seen by the public yet, but I've seen it, so I'm taking a punt. Catherine . . .'

Catherine could feel her chest tightening. Was he really going to say what she thought he was going to say?

'You're coming to New York.'

'Oh my God!' Catherine said feeling the blood rush to her head. She jumped to her feet and kissed Richard Forster. She could hear a squealing that seemed to come from far away and then realised it was her. 'I can't believe it!'

And then she had to sit down because her legs had turned to jelly.

There was screaming and crying coming from the corridor – it was Sierra who had obviously just realised she wasn't going through. Catherine put her hands to her mouth feeling terrible for her fellow competitor.

'Can we cut that out – whatshername crying?' Richard asked the director. 'Or better still, get it on camera and then bring her through. Won't do any harm to have a twist on how someone finds out, will it?'

Catherine knew that she should be horrified by this cut-throat attitude, but she wasn't. Richard couldn't be all that bad if he had decided to take on board what he knew about her family life and not air it. And anyway, Catherine was too delighted and too shocked to discover that she was in the finals to worry too much about the way in which Richard Forster handled people who had just been rejected.

Kim, Star and Catherine all stood staring at one another. Kim and Catherine had spent the last five minutes jumping around the room squealing. Even Star had dropped the frosty knickers routine for a moment to give the other two a hug.

'What happens now?' Kim asked excitedly.

'They just said wait here, didn't they?' Star said. 'No doubt so that they can ship out the other poor sods and get them to go cry somewhere that's not on *Star Maker* property.'

The door opened and Richard Forster and Will walked in. 'Well, girls, excited?' Richard asked.

'Yeah!' the girls replied in unison.

'So you should be, it is exciting. Right, I'm going to hand over to Will now and I'll see you girls in New York in three days' time.'

Catherine's heart sank. While Kim was gleefully jabbering about New York and Star was acting as if she was so over it because she used to live there, Catherine was thinking about how her dad was going to react to the news. She was barely going to have time to say goodbye at this rate. Maybe he could come to New York with her; maybe she could fly back during the week. She was going to ask Will what her options were, if indeed she had any. She couldn't quit now, she knew that Jo wouldn't let her. It was too good an opportunity to squander.

'Right, girls,' Will looked at his watch. 'At 5 p.m. you're booked in with Nicky Clarke for a hair cut and our make-up team here will give you a makeover. We've got Leighton doing your nails. Then you'll be filming your body shots this evening. After which we'll be doing our own interviews with you to give as press releases.'

Catherine tried to keep up with the information she was being fed.

'What do you mean, "body shots"?' Kim asked, beating Catherine to it.

'You know on the finals where you see the contestants and they've got a new hair do and look a million dollars compared to how they looked in the auditions and there's a wind machine blowing their hair? Well, that's your body shots. Then we get a few words from you now because it's good to capture the excitement of being told you're in the finals. Right, I'll go get the girls you're up against.' Will walked out to collect the American girls.

'Oh God, I'd almost forgotten about them,' Star said. 'I hope that Shoneeka doesn't get through. She thinks she's bloody amazing.' Catherine and Kim looked at one another. 'And before you start,' Star said, seeing the look, 'I don't think I'm bloody amazing.'

'No,' Kim said, 'you *know* you're bloody amazing.'

Star pulled a face at Kim, pretending to be annoyed and then gave them both an uncharacteristic smile. 'Congratulations on getting to the final.'

Catherine was taken aback. 'Wow, thanks Star.'

'No problem,' she said, pulling out a compact from her bag and beginning to powder her forehead. Catherine waited for Star to say something else, something that took away the kind sentiment of her last comment, but she didn't.

A moment later, Will was back with the Americans. Freya and Meagan walked into the room, quickly followed by Shoneeka. Catherine shot a glance towards Star who rolled her eyes. As the others hugged and made polite, delighted conversation, Shoneeka squared up to Star and said, 'I'd keep them eyeballs of yours from rolling around if I was you.'

'What?' Star asked, as if she didn't know what she was talking about.

'You heard me. I don't want any attitude.'

'That's interesting, because you're giving plenty out.'

Shoneeka stepped further towards Star. Star stood her ground. Will got between them, 'Ladies, ladies. You're through to the finals. Let's just enjoy it, yes?'

'OK,' Star and Shoneeka agreed without cutting their look away from one another.

'Star just can't help making friends everywhere she goes,' Kim whispered to Catherine.

Catherine and the girls had been chauffeur-driven through the rush-hour traffic to Harrods and had been ushered through the store by security guards to the lifts and up to the Beauty Spa. Catherine was getting a taste for being chauffeur-driven everywhere – it was nice having someone drive you around, she thought. In fact, having someone else do anything for her was a novelty. She kept having momentary panics where she would think that she should be doing something for her dad and then relaxing when she remembered he was being taken care of and so was she.

She hadn't had time to speak to her family but had sent Jo, Maria and Claire a text saying that she would be back tomorrow morning with a camera crew and had been bombarded with texts ever since to find out if she was through or not. She desperately wanted to tell them, but it was in the contract that at this stage each contestant went back and told their family on camera. Catherine wasn't so sure her father would take too kindly to this intrusion. She had tried to talk to him about it before she left but he just said, 'I'll cross that media intrusion bridge when I come to it.' Jo had pointed out that he'd spent his life trying to get the media to intrude on him, but he had just pretended to not hear.

Will had told the girls that while they were having their beauty treatments they should not under any circumstances tell anyone about why they were there. After an hour and a half of being massaged and buffed and painted, Catherine and the others emerged with perfectly manicured hands and feet. Catherine had never had her nails painted before and felt like fanning her hands in front of her face like a coquettish Edwardian lady. They were then whisked through town to the hair salon, which had been opened after hours especially for the girls. Catherine's black hair, which she usually dyed herself with Nice 'n' Easy, was expertly put into foils and low-lighted with Ebony Night and Cherry Oak. When the stylist spun her around in her chair to see the finished look, Catherine barely recognised herself. She had hair like Demi Moore. She was sure that the moment she tried to style it herself she would end up with hair more like Russell Brand, but for now Catherine thought it looked great.

The past couple of hours had been fun and had also allowed the three English girls to get to know a bit about the Americans. Star had been wise enough to give Shoneeka a wide berth and Catherine had spoken to Freya and Meagan. Meagan was from the Mid-West and was gently spoken and enjoying every minute of being in London under such glamorous circumstances. Freya was from Vermont and reminded Catherine of Gwyneth Paltrow. She was a university graduate and had been to London a number of times, which, considering she was American, Catherine thought to be terribly exotic. And then there was Shoneeka. She was from Baltimore and thought that London was cold and that Harrods was overpriced. She had cheered up though when they drove through the streets of London, pointing out sights that she'd seen on the TV and telling Catherine that she had once thought that Buckingham Palace wasn't actually a real place.

Back at the studios Catherine was put into make-up and after half an hour of having more make-up applied that even Maria would dare to wear, she was ready to be dressed and film her body shots. The stylist poured her into a black Roberto Cavalli body con dress. Catherine felt that if she breathed out people would start asking her when she was due. But once she saw her reflection in the mirror, she saw that all the styling had worked; she barely recognised herself. She looked sophisticated and sexy.

'I'd vote for you,' Kim said, walking over. Kim was dressed in a slashed shoulder All Saints dress with patent peep-toe pixie boots. Her hair had been cut into a spiky crop and her eye make-up was dark and sultry.

'Look at you!' Catherine exclaimed. She felt a sudden pang of guilt about thinking that it was Kim who had told Richard about her father, but forced it from her mind.

'Look at you, more like!' Kim said, hugging her friend.

'Look at me, more like!' Star said, stepping out of the shadows looking like Lily Col, in a black sequinned flapper dress.

'Modest as ever,' Catherine said.

'Come on now, girlies, lighten up,' Star said, as if all of the back-biting and sniping had been part of an act. 'We're all through.'

'You're a weirdo,' Kim said.

'Takes one to know one,' Star smiled.

Catherine was taken through for her body shots and as she awkwardly moved and smiled lots of pictures were taken. After five minutes of watching her mug to camera the director had obviously had enough and decided to help her out. He walked over and started pulling her around. He placed one leg in front of the other, her left hand on her hip and instructed her to close her mouth and push her bottom lip out with her tongue. 'It'll give you a great pout,' he told her. When she saw the finished shots she realised that it had. She looked like a model. Wait until I tell Jo, she thought. She'd laugh. Jo said that whenever Catherine was photographed, she always looked like someone who'd just escaped from their carer.

After the photo and film shoot, the girls were taken to a restaurant that overlooked the Mayor of London's office and Tower Bridge. They were shown to a private room and treated, along with their decoy models, to a lavish dinner with cocktails and champagne.

Before they were seated Richard Forster approached Catherine with a woman who had arms like Madonna and one of those shiny faces that lots of celebrities had, which meant it was impossible to tell their age other than she was somewhere between thirty-five and sixty.

'Hi, Catherine,' Richard said, turning to the lady at his side. 'This is Antonia. She's a personal trainer and nutritionist and will be putting you through your paces over the next couple of weeks.'

Catherine felt embarrassed. Did she need putting through her paces? She tugged self-consciously on her hair. She could feel Antonia looking her over critically, no doubt wondering how she was going to make Catherine's size fourteen pear shape into a hipless size eight.

'I'll leave you to it,' Richard said and turned and began speaking to someone behind him. Catherine smiled uneasily.

'What training regime do you have at the moment?' Antonia asked earnestly.

Pick Kit Kat up, put to mouth, bite, chew, swallow, repeat until finished, Catherine thought, but decided it was best not to say. 'I don't really have one as such.'

'Don't worry.' Antonia spoke with a nasal New York accent. 'We can fix that. OK, tonight, steak and salad, no dressing. Then from here on in, one thousand calories a day, eighty/twenty protein to carb.'

Catherine didn't know what this meant so just nodded.

'Don't worry, I'll email you a spread sheet with all the details. Then, when we get to New York, an hour each morning in the gym. Mostly core strength and fat burning. Not too many weights, don't want you bulking up.'

God forbid, Catherine thought, glancing at Antonia's arms again. Will walked past; Antonia grabbed him. 'Will, have you got the times for the veneers when the guys arrive in New York?'

Veneers? Catherine thought. Is this something to do with antique sideboards?

Will thought for a moment. 'These guys get in at ten and the dentist is due at midday.'

'Oh, OK. Won't have time for a run that day, those things kill.' She looked at Catherine. 'On the upside though, you won't be able to eat for two days.'

Catherine was alarmed. 'What are veneers?' she asked when Will had walked away.

'Da Vinci veneers?' Antonia looked at Catherine, waiting for her to register. Catherine shook her head. 'New teeth basically.'

'New teeth!' Catherine exclaimed.

'Yes, of course. You Brits all look like snaggle-toothed freaks when you get to the States; we have to have you looking your best for the small screen.'

'Do we have to have anything else . . .' Catherine flapped her hand up and down her body '. . . done?'

Antonia had become distracted by someone behind Catherine that she evidently needed to speak to. 'What? No honey, just the exercise, the food and the teeth. The Botox and the facelifts are for the over-twenty-fives.' Catherine's mouth fell open. 'Listen, great to meet you, see you in New York.' Antonia marched off but then, remembering something, spun around and said to Catherine so that anyone within earshot could hear, 'If all else fails we'll get you some lipo on your hips and stomach.'

'OK!' Catherine said shrilly.

She looked around. Everyone else was engrossed in conversation so she decided to take her seat at the table. She wasn't very good when it came to mingling. She would ask someone something and become acutely aware of the social situation she found herself in and then not be able to concentrate on what the person was saying, because she was too busy thinking of the next question to ask so that they didn't fall into a dreaded silence. She saw Andy walk in and immediately cast her eyes to the floor, she couldn't speak to him, not now. Maybe later, she thought as she headed for her seat. Unfortunately for Catherine, Jason P. Longford had been seated next to her.

As the champagne flowed, Catherine began to think that maybe Andy deserved a second chance. He was a nice guy – he had probably said what he had about her father for the right reasons and anyway, it hadn't done her any harm in the end. She was building up the courage to go and speak to him when Jason, who had been engrossed in conversation with Star, turned to her. 'So Andy, you like him?'

Catherine was taken aback by the question, 'Well, I might but . . .'

Jason looked around and then lowered his head towards Catherine's. 'Look, I don't want this going any further, but he flirts with everyone. And I mean *everyone*. He was knocking off one of the other runners until you lot turned up and then I think he just thought that he'd better align himself with someone who was going to do well. I know he comes across as a nice guy but that's part of the act, I'm just saying because I've seen things like this happen too many times. Civilians come into the world of TV and get their fingers burned . . .'

Catherine stared at Jason. He had to be lying. Andy wasn't some cad about town.

'He's a great guy,' Jason continued, 'just playing the field. Lots of guys in TV are like that, they get to box above their weight, if you get my drift. I just wouldn't want you getting involved and it affecting your performance.'

'No. Well, thanks for the heads up,' Catherine said, stunned. She didn't know what to think. She didn't particularly like Jason and she didn't particularly trust him but why would he lie about something like this? On the other hand, she already *knew* that she couldn't trust Andy after he had gone behind her back to tell Richard Forster something she had told him in confidence. Catherine looked along the table to where Andy was sitting. He was chatting to two of the decoy girls. When he saw her looking over he smiled and waved. Catherine looked away, embarrassed and annoyed. He had some nerve, she thought.

There was a bank of photographers waiting outside for the full two hours that the *Star Maker* entourage were in the restaurant. Will stood looking out of the window. 'This is the start of things to come, girls,' he said, mock-ominously. 'Best get you out of the back.'

But as they filed out of the restaurant and out through the tradesman's entrance, the paparazzi rounded the corner, cameras flashing. Clearly they must have been tipped off. Catherine felt a hand on her back and she was bundled into a car. She looked up to see Andy.

'I'm sorry,' he said, as the driver put his foot down and drove through the crowd of photographers.

'Don't be.'

'But I didn't mean to upset you.'

'It's fine,' Catherine said. 'Just leave me alone.'

'Is that what you really want?'

'Yes please,' Catherine stared out of the window.

'OK.'

Catherine wanted to be excited with Andy, to tell him that it was so mad to have photographers trying to get a picture of her, to have him bundle her in a car and take off through the streets of London. But he had betrayed her trust and if what Jason said was true, this was just what he was like anyway. Why wouldn't he be? He worked in television, he was used to this shiny way of life. He probably had a different girl every week. Catherine decided to remain silent until they arrived back in Mayfair where she politely, but with a distinct distance, told Andy that she would see him in New York.

Jo was sitting on the chair-arm wearing one of her own creations; a pink jumpsuit with shoulder pads and sky-high heels. She had decided that if anyone asked she would say she was channelling Lady Ga Ga meets Grace Jones. Her hair was scraped back from her face and she was wearing her favourite chandelier earrings. She jumped onto the settee, then back again to the armchair, crossing her legs.

'Will you sit still?' Maria hissed and then smiled politely at the cameraman in the corner of the room. She was wearing a tight pair of black satin trousers and a revealing white blouse.

'I don't know where to sit, I'm so excited. Where's Dad?'

'I've shouted for him, he'd better hurry up, she'll be here any minute,' Claire said, licking her hand and pawing Rosie's chocolate-smeared face with it. 'Who's given you chocolate?'

'I know, Claire, she's only allowed liquidised kumquats,' Jo said, pulling out a bag of Maltesers. 'But these taste so good it was cruel not to, wasn't it Rosie?'

'I like Maltesers, Mummy,' Rosie said, with a sweet smile.

Claire looked as if she wanted to kill Jo, which made Jo smile. Paul was trying to get Jake to sit still but he was charging around the room pretending to be an aeroplane.

'God, I'll get him,' Maria said impatiently, getting up from her seat.

Catherine was due through the door any minute to

announce whether she was through to the finals of *Star Maker* or not and Mick was making sure that he was still the star turn.

'Dad, hurr—' Maria shouted, opening the door.

'I'm here, no need to shout in my face.' Mick bustled into the room. He was wearing some fisherman pants that Maria had brought him back from a trip to Thailand and a T-shirt that looked older than he was, which had *Jaw Jaw is Better than War War* written on it.

'Get changed,' Claire demanded, without any pleasantries.

'Good day to you, too,' Mick nodded at his eldest daughter.

'This isn't about you, so go get changed!'

'That's what I said,' Jo agreed. She had been arguing with her dad all morning. In fact she'd been arguing with her dad since Catherine had left for London. It had only been two days but it felt like a lifetime. He wouldn't talk to her about his medication or his hospital treatment, he expected his dinner on the table when he wanted it and cups of tea to be made at a moment's notice. Jo's patience was worn thin.

'What's wrong with these?' he asked, looking down at his trousers.

'You look like MC Hammer,' Jo informed him.

'No time, they're here,' the cameraman said.

'Stand behind the settee,' Claire said.

'He needs to bob down behind the settee, then we'll just see him from the neck up,' Jo advised.

'I'm staying put. This is my sofa and I'm parking my arse on it.' Mick flopped into the chair like a truculent teen.

The door flew open and Catherine bounded in, there was a moment as she paused and they all stared at her and then she said, 'I'm through!'

Everyone jumped to their feet and cheered. Jo ran over and hugged her sister, Rosie and Jake carried on cheering, giddy with excitement. Claire and Maria came over and hugged Catherine. Only Mick hung back. Jo looked at him, willing him not to embarrass them all on TV again. Willing him to say something nice to Catherine.

Finally he walked forward and hugged his daughter. 'I'm proud of you, lass,' he said.

Catherine burst into tears, quickly followed by Claire. Even Jo, who prided herself on rarely crying, felt a lump rise in her throat. She knew that what her dad had just said to Catherine would mean the world to her.

Chapter 10

'If another twat asks me for my autograph I am going to scream.' Jason P. Longford threw himself into the seat next to Andy and pushed his Ray Bans back onto his head. Andy could see the tan lines from his sun-bed goggles. Two whole people had asked Jason for his autograph. It hardly made him David Beckham. Andy fastened his seat belt and scanned the safety leaflet.

'No point reading that. If this baby goes down, put your head between your knees and kiss your arse goodbye.' Jason laughed at his own brilliant joke.

Andy slapped a smile on his face and wanted to ask one of the cabin crew if there was any room on the wing. He was dreading the trip to New York. Yes, it would be exciting and yes, lots of people would kill to work on *Star Maker*, but Andy hated letting people down and he knew that was exactly what he had done to Catherine. He had decided that he was going to be pleasant to her when he saw her, but that it was best if he just avoided her. He didn't want to jeopardise her chances in the competition by cornering her and trying to get her to like him again, anyway that just seemed desperate. Andy was going to go to New York, do his job and try to enjoy it.

Will boarded the plane and looked around to see who else from production was on board. Thank God, thought

Andy, Will could talk to Jason and maybe Andy would get a bit of peace.

'Will!' Jason shouted.

Three girls were next to board the aircraft. One of them did a double take when she saw Jason. She whispered something to her friends. Andy couldn't make out what was being said but Jason arched his eyebrow at Andy as if to say, do you see what I have to put up with? Andy slid down in his seat and could hear the girls whispering, 'You ask him.' 'No you ask him.' This was just going to make Jason's head swell to the size of a giant watermelon.

One of the girls approached. She was pretty and young, something that would please Jason as he was so vain that he liked it when good-looking people paid him attention. 'Excuse me?' the girl said nervously.

'Yes,' Jason said, without removing his glasses.

'My friends and I were just wondering if we could have your autograph?'

Jason sighed and then looked at the girl. 'Have you got a pen?' he asked, as if the attention bored him. Will looked at Andy through the gap in the seats and shook his head.

'I'll just get one.' The girl scurried off.

'I thought you didn't want to sign anymore autographs,' Andy commented.

'No, I said that if I was asked for another autograph I'd scream. But look, I just need to remember that something as small as an autograph from Jason P. Longford can make a person's day, week, or maybe even month.'

'It could make their year,' Will said from the seat in

front, turning and catching Andy's eye. Andy forced himself not to laugh.

'It could . . .' Jason agreed seriously. 'It really could.'

The girl came back holding a pen and a piece of scrap paper. 'I'm sorry, it's the only paper we had.'

'Right,' Jason said, regarding it with disdain.

'Could you put something like, "To Jane and Lucy, *Supermarket Sweep's* biggest fans, love Dale."'

Andy thought he was going to swallow his own tongue, he was trying so hard not to laugh. He could see the seat in front shaking where Will was laughing.

'Dale?' Jason screeched, '*Supermarket Sweep*?' His voice went higher still. 'Do you think I'm Dale Bloody Winton?' His voice was by now so shrill that Andy was sure that if there were any dogs in the hold they would be covering their ears with their paws.

'Well, yes. Aren't you?' the girl asked, bewildered.

'Am I friggery. I'm twenty years younger than him for a start!'

'All right, keep your wig on.' The girl snatched the pen from Jason and walked back down the aisle. 'It's not him; he's just some nobody with an attitude problem,' the girl said loudly to her mates.

Andy couldn't believe what happened next, it was so embarrassing that it made him wish that Boeing 767s were fitted with ejector seats. Jason got to his feet and took his glasses off and shouted down the plane to the girls, 'I'm Jason P. Longford you . . .' he was so angry he struggled to find the words '. . . set of tits!'

A mocking cheer went up from the other passengers

on the plane as Jason thumped down into his seat in an absolute strop.

'Who, mate?' the autograph hunter shouted back. 'Never heard of you!'

'Get me to New York now!' Jason shouted at Andy, as if he was flying the plane.

'All right, Jason, we'll be setting off in a minute,' he replied, trying to be reassuring as a chant of 'Who are you? Who are you?' began to grow until it sounded like everyone on the plane was chanting at Jason. Andy buried his head in his hands. This was going to be the longest seven hours of his life.

Catherine was sitting in the passenger seat of Claire's car, driving towards Manchester airport. She was meeting Kim at departures and they were flying together to join the other contestants at Heathrow, where they would all depart for New York.

Jo was singing 'New York, New York', for what must have been the twentieth time that day. She accompanied it by kicking her legs through the space between the front seats in the car.

'Stop it! I can't see when you kick your foot up,' Claire grumbled, as she pulled the car into the airport.

'I can't believe you're going to New York! And not just going to New York, you're like going to New York!'

'What on earth does that mean?' Claire spun around to face her sister who was sitting in the middle of the back seat.

Catherine knew exactly what she meant. She had even begun writing about her experiences in her songs.

Catherine usually wrote about longing, or loss or hope, not actual concrete experiences. This was different and she found that, rather than scaring her away from song writing because of the enormity of what was happening to her, it was making her creative juices flow.

'I mean she's doing it in style, duh! Will you go to the Marc Jacobs store and genuflect in front of it for me please?' Jo begged.

'We're all really proud of you,' Claire said, squeezing Catherine's knee.

'Dad's not,' Catherine said sadly.

Mick had made an excuse not to come to the airport. Said that his stomach was playing up and he needed to stay in bed.

'He's just acting up.'

'When is he going to the hospital? Is someone going with him?' Catherine asked.

'Tomorrow, I think, but he won't say exactly when. He's being a martyr, saying he wants to go on his own.' Claire shrugged in a what-can-you-do way.

'Right.' Catherine hung her head guiltily.

'When he decides he's going to accept our help then we'll help him, won't we, Jo?'

'He's got an appointment tomorrow then?' Jo asked, suddenly serious.

'Yes, at Christie's. He said it yesterday. Was I the only one there?'

'Right . . .' Jo said, not really listening to Claire.

Catherine studied Jo; she looked as if she was hatching a plan.

'What are you thinking?' Catherine asked.

'Nothing.' Jo snapped out of it. 'Not thinking anything.'

'Right, go and don't come back until you're rich and famous.' Claire said as she found a parking space.

The three sisters climbed out of the car. 'And I've set Sky Plus for the weekend . . .' Jo said impishly, 'And I'll call you and tell you if we're on.'

Catherine's stomach performed its now familiar churn. 'Oh God,' she groaned. Saturday saw the first airing of *Star Maker* this year. Now that she was down to the final six, her audition was bound to be aired.

'Next time you come back through those doors, you'll be recognised by everyone. How mad is that?' Jo asked.

Catherine closed her eyes. 'I'm not sure if I'm ready for it.'

'Ha!' Jo laughed. 'Bit late now.'

She was right, it was.

'Anyway, sis, break a leg, Scottish play and all that, as Dad would say, because he's so into the theatre.'

Catherine thought about her dad for a moment. 'Tell him I'll be back soon and that if he needs anything then he can always ring me.'

'Right, yeah, we'll tell him.' Jo said, throwing a look at Claire that suggested this piece of information wouldn't go any further.

'Come here,' Jo gave Catherine a huge warm hug. Claire joined in.

'Good luck, sis.' Jo pulled Catherine's case out of the boot and handed it to her.

'Oh, and if you see Maria in there sweeping the floors then let us know. I've always thought this air hostess thing was all in her head.'

Catherine laughed and waved to her sisters and walked towards the automatic doors with trepidation at what the weeks ahead held for her and her fellow competitors.

Just as the doors were opening two photographers ran up to Catherine and began snapping away. A reporter thrust a Dictaphone into her face. 'You're in the final, Catherine, how does it feel?'

'I don't know what you mean,' Catherine said panicking, craning her neck to see if Jo and Claire might come to her rescue, but they had gone, she was on her own. Catherine made her way to the check-in desk, the reporter and photographers followed, drawing stares from the holiday makers queuing up for their flights. Catherine wondered what to do, it was embarrassing enough being hounded by people firing questions at her and being photographed, but ignoring them while they did so wasn't something she could keep up for long. 'I'm just going to London for the weekend with a friend.'

'Right, pull the other one,' the reporter said harshly.

Just then Kim came round the corner and seeing Catherine trying to fend off the reporter, dived behind a pillar. Catherine wanted her to come over to take some of the pressure off her but she knew she couldn't. If they were seen boarding the plane together and this woman had done her research and had Kim down as someone who was going through to the finals too, she would have her story and Kim and Catherine would be in trouble before they even got to New York. So Catherine braved it out in the queue.

A little boy in front of her turned and said, 'Excuse me, are you famous?'

Catherine laughed and said, 'No, they think I'm someone else.' She just had to get to the front of the queue, get checked in and then she'd be all right, she reassured herself. But something was worrying her, something which totally stood to reason but she hadn't really thought about until now. Once you were famous you were public property and intrusions like this would become, if not commonplace, at least something she couldn't complain about when they did happen. And if one thing was for sure, by accepting her place in the final six of *Star Maker: Transatlantic*, Catherine was now officially signing herself up for fame whether she liked to admit it or not.

Chapter 11

Catherine stared out of the limousine at the New York skyline as they drove towards Manhattan. This famous city, one that was etched in her memory from childhood films through to the terrible events of 9/11 seemed so familiar, and at the same time, so other worldly.

'Wow!' Catherine said, without realising that she had spoken.

'What's wrong with you?' Star asked.

Star had been her usual charming self on the flight over. Having had a few days away from the others Star had cooled down again and decided that being cool and distant was the way to go. Catherine had decided to leave her to it. In her opinion they had been treated like royalty by the cabin staff on the flight over from the UK; Star didn't seem to agree. 'They shove us in business class? What about first class?' she sniffed.

Catherine had never been on a flight that lasted more than three hours. In fact, she'd never been anywhere further than Spain and she'd only been there twice. Now here she was, flying to another continent, business class. Each girl had their own seat that made into a bed, they were served champagne before the plane had even taken off, they were given the option to have a back massage, a foot massage or a facial – Catherine had all three – and the food they were served was definitely the best meal Catherine had ever eaten: smoked salmon roulade followed by a cooked-to-perfection steak with mashed potato and sticky toffee pudding for dessert. Star had turned her nose up at it, saying that she didn't eat plane food. Kim had asked if she ate fancy food, but Star had just ignored the joke and buried her head in her copy of *Vogue*.

As the limo powered across the Manhattan Bridge, Catherine turned to Star. 'Sorry, I just haven't seen skyscrapers before.'

Star sniggered as if Catherine had just admitted that this was the first time she'd clapped eyes on a wheel. 'What? Where have you been?'

Catherine stiffened, 'Manchester, Star. I haven't lived all over the world like you.'

'But surely Manchester has skyscrapers, London does.'

'Canary Wharf might have, but London doesn't, not really,' Kim interjected.

'Who asked you?' Star asked, throwing Kim a withering look.

'Right,' Kim said calmly in her broad Yorkshire accent. 'Let's get one thing straight: you use that mouth of yours again on me and I'll punch your lights out. Got it?'

Star, for the first time since Catherine had met her, was speechless. She gathered herself and, pretending not to be bothered, looked out of the window.

'Star, I said, "Got it?"' Kim wasn't going to let Star get away with her queeny demeanour any longer, it seemed.

'Got it,' Star squeaked.

'Good.' Kim turned to Catherine, 'I've never really seen skyscrapers either. Not all together like that. It's mad isn't it?'

Catherine felt as if she was free to speak now without being ridiculed by the worldly Star. 'Yes, they look so packed together. Why don't they build on the other islands? Why does it all have to be concentrated on this one little bit of land?'

Star cleared her throat as if she was about to say something, but a hard stare from Kim quickly put paid to that.

They drove into New York City and Catherine took in the familiar sites of jammed roads, yellow taxis, newspaper stalls and towering buildings. One moment they would be in an area that looked like somewhere you shouldn't step foot into alone, the next they were driving through parts of the city with glistening shop fronts and picturesque stucco houses with huge steps up to the grand wooden front doors.

'Times Square, ladies,' the driver said through his microphone. He couldn't simply turn around and tell them because there was bullet-proof glass between him and the girls. Probably to stop him turning round and shooting the likes of Star, Catherine thought.

Looking out at the bright neon lights and the hundreds of people crossing the street in different directions, Catherine's head buzzed with everything she had to take in. Adverts screamed from every billboard, people flooded in and out of the touristy shops. Theatres were tucked away along side streets but their hoardings shouted the names of the shows. Once through Times Square the limo driver turned a corner and pulled up at a set of lights.

'What's with the horse?' Kim asked. There was a shire horse pulling a carriage parked in front of them.

She pressed the button to speak to the driver. 'What's with the horse?'

'They're a pain in the ass. That's what's with the horse. For tourists, they ride them round Central Park and then they shit all over the road and I get it stuck in the tyres.' The girls laughed at the driver's turn of phrase and his strong New York accent. The driver then launched into a story which culminated in him telling the girls that he had been engaged to Liza Minnelli but couldn't go through with it because she couldn't cook.

'Here we are,' the cabbie said, looking up at the gothic building facing out onto Central Park.

'Is this the one that was in Ghost Busters?' Kim asked.

'No, no, no . . .' The driver shook his head.

'It's where John Lennon lived, where he was shot . . .' Star said assuredly. 'The Dakota building.'

'No, that's the one up there,' The driver said, pointing up the road.

Catherine stepped from the car. Kim and Star followed her. 'Are we staying here?' Catherine took in the magnificent building.

'You certainly are.' Richard Forster answered. He was standing with his hands in his pockets, beaming at the girls. He had a camera crew in tow.

'I'll introduce you to the guys when we get inside but they'll be trailing you pretty much around the clock now that the competition is on.' Richard gave them a Machiavellian smile.

Catherine looked at the crew. There was no sign of Andy as yet, thank God she thought. After what Jason had told her, Andy was someone she needed to avoid, so she should just stay clear and let him get on and flirt with whoever else came his way.

Jo had been up for two hours and it was only nine o'clock in the morning. She now knew what jet lag must feel like. She didn't want her dad to leave the house when she was asleep, but she didn't want him to suspect that she was going to follow him to make sure that he was OK either.

Mick came into the kitchen wearing a suit. 'Where you off to?' Jo asked, confused.

'The hospital. Make us a brew Joanna, would you, there's a love.'

Jo resisted a sarcastic remark. Mick might be ill, but old habits died hard.

'Why are you wearing a suit?'

'Thought I'd spruce myself up. Them consultants think they're above us all you know, but if you go in wearing a suit and with your head screwed on then they have to talk to you on their level, not as if you're some halfwit who's just walked in off the street.'

Jo felt a pang of pain for her dad. He just wanted a bit of respect and that was totally fair enough, she thought. It didn't matter that he got on her nerves and was totally over the top about things most of the time. On this occasion she thought he was absolutely right. He wanted to be treated with dignity and was doing everything he could to make that happen.

'Why don't I come with you dad?'

'I won't have it, Joanna. I'll let you know how I get on when I get home.'

'But what are you even going in for today?'

He hadn't even told them that, he was being so vague about everything. It was certainly out of character – Mick would usually go to great lengths to describe the most trivial ailment – but maybe this time he just wanted to get on with things and for his daughters to leave him be until he was ready to talk about the cancer.

'A thingy . . .' he pointed at his stomach, 'a scan thingy.'

'Haven't you had a scan already?'

'They do them a lot. Just to check. You know.'

'No, I don't know. Explain it to me.'

'I don't want to explain it, Joanna!' Mick said thumping his fist on the table making Jo jump. 'I just want to get it over with.'

'All right, Dad, jeez, I'm sorry,' Jo said, feeling both foolish for pushing the matter and annoyed at her dad for shouting.

'Well, don't be going on about it.'

'Right. I won't.' Jo said, rising from the table and heading to the door. 'I'll see you later.'

Jo walked out of the house and into the garage and decided that she'd cycle over to Christie's and wait for her dad and then figure out what to do from there.

Jo preferred cycling to public transport. It was loads better than sitting on the top deck of the bus with murderous idiots and sweaty smack heads. She had once even been hit, by a girl on a bus who accused Jo of 'looking at her' even though Jo had been facing forward and the girl had been sitting behind her. The girl had followed Jo off of the 520 from Flixton and said, 'What were you looking at?' When Jo replied, 'The poster saying "Give up your seat for elderly people",' the girl had slapped her across the face. A big Sue Ellen out of *Dallas* slap. Jo loved watching reruns of *Dallas* as well as *Dynasty* on UK Gold. She didn't, however, like being slapped like someone who had crossed JR's wife.

She dragged her mountain bike out of the garage and set off in the direction of Withington. It was a long cycle, about six miles, but she was determined to find out what was going on with her dad, even if he wasn't willing to say.

Jo cycled through Trafford Park, past the futuristic War Museum and the Lowry Gallery at Salford Quays, past Old Trafford Football ground and along to the tram station that would take her around the outskirts of Chorlton. When she had set off she had promised herself that there was no way she would go to Chorlton, no way that she would swing past her mum's to see if she was in. But when she found herself cycling along tree-lined Seymour Grove and faced with a left turn to Withington and the cancer hospital or a right turn to Chorlton and her mum and Jay's house, Jo pulled the bike to the right. I'll only be a couple of minutes, she bargained with herself. Dad isn't at the hospital till eleven.

She cycled through the main row of shops and on towards Beech Road, the gentrified area where Jay had his huge house. She passed the cafés and the art shops – and would have sneered at them had there been anyone there to sneer with – and cycled up towards the house. Just as she was about to turn the corner, bargaining with herself about how long she would stay around to see if there was any sign of her mum, a familiar sight made her throw her bike quickly down a small alleyway. The manoeuvre was so sudden that her bike went in one direction and Jo fell in a heap in the other. Her dad was climbing out of a taxi and walking along the street, as if doing this was the most normal thing in the world.

'I could do without a camera crew jammed up my arse twenty-four seven,' Star complained, throwing her Louis Vuitton luggage on the bed. This was the first time that Catherine had ever clapped eyes on real Louis Vuitton luggage. Maria had a wardrobe full of the stuff, but as it had been sourced from a man called Fat Kev who worked on freight at the airport, Catherine wasn't too confident about its authenticity.

'They're a bit full on,' Catherine agreed.

They had had a quick pep talk on arrival from Richard and then they had been assigned rooms and roommates. Catherine, Kim and Star were to be roommates again, which was no surprise but it still made Catherine's heart sink a little, realising that she would have to wake up every morning to Star until one of them was ejected from the competition.

Catherine walked over to the window and looked out across Central Park. 'Oh my God, this place is amazing.'

The park stretched out in front of her for miles. People were walking their dogs, jogging, sitting on the bench by the John Lennon memorial, watching the world go by. 'I can't believe it's in the middle of the city.'

'A park's a park,' Star said, like she knew everything.

Catherine stopped for a moment and was about to point out that wasn't actually the case, that this was Central

Park, the most famous park in the world, in New flipping York, but she knew that it would fall on deaf ears. 'Yeah, you're right. It's pretty much the same as Dog Poo park.'

Kim, who had just entered the room, laughed.

'Where the hell is Dog Poo park?' Star asked.

'End of our road in Manchester.'

'Why's it called Dog Poo park?' Catherine looked at Star, was she serious? 'Because there's dog poo everywhere?' Star answered her own question, her face contorting as if this was the most fascinating and disgusting thing she had ever heard.

'Got it in one.'

'Jesus, where do you live?'

'Don't you have dog poo in London?'

'We clean it up.' Star said, pulling her clothes out of her bag and smoothing each garment before hanging it in the giant oak wardrobe.

'We could learn a lot from you, Star,' Kim said, throwing her case on the floor and unzipping it.

Star didn't bother to retort. The dressing down she had received on the way from the airport had obviously done the trick.

There was a knock on the door. 'Hi girls, the dentist is here,' Jesse informed them. Jesse had been to see the girls on their arrival to say hello, but there had been no sign of Andy as yet.

Kim, Star and Catherine looked at one another. 'My teeth are perfect,' Star complained.

'What dentist?' Kim asked.

Catherine had completely forgotten to mention the conversation she'd had with Antonia on the last night in

London; she'd been too wrapped up in what was happening with Andy.

'It's in our contract,' Catherine said, feeling like a *Star Maker* drone. 'We have to have our teeth done. Straightened, whitened whatever it takes to make us look good for the camera.'

'Get lost!' Kim couldn't believe it.

'It's true.' It was true, but Catherine knew it didn't make it any less ridiculous.

Catherine, Kim and Star were back in their room, holding their faces, in varying degrees of agony. Catherine had been informed that her teeth were 'in great shape' but that they needed whitening; a process which involved a large metal clamp, some gum shields, a very bright light and searing pain. Catherine hadn't realised her teeth were so sensitive. Kim had had a similar procedure, whereas Star, with her 'perfect teeth' was now sporting a set of the dreaded Da Vinci veneers. She looked like she had a mouthful of white piano keys.

'Nggnngnnna,' Star moaned.

'What did she say?' Kim asked Catherine.

'I think she said "sadistic bastards",' Catherine giggled and then held her own face in pain. There was a knock at the door and Shoneeka, Meagan and Freya walked in, wearing trainers and gym clothing.

'Hi guys. Oh God, what happened here?' Freya asked.

'Ha, you've been toothed. They got us last week.' Shoneeka said, sitting on the bed. 'So you ready for training?'

'What training?' Catherine asked. Antonia had said she wouldn't have to do any just after her dentist work.

'Core training for you guys, I think, and a run for us. Come on, it'll be fun!' Freya said, and clapped her hands in an insanely happy way.

'No it won't, it'll be a pain in the ass, but I'm not going on TV looking fat, so I'm in.' Shoneeka was evidently resigned to her fate.

'We're lucky,' Meagan informed them. 'The over-twenty-fives have been here for five days and two of them have had a face lift and a tummy tuck. Not good.'

'This isn't right, is it?' Catherine blurted out. Everyone turned and looked at her, surprised by her outburst. 'Sorry, but I just didn't think it would be like this. It's a singing competition, not a model competition.'

'It's showbiz, baby,' Shoneeka said, jumping up and down on the spot ready for her run, 'and you'd better get used to it,' she added, as if she'd been doing this for years.

[illegible]

[illegible]

[illegible]

[illegible]

[illegible]

Chapter 12

Jo locked her bike to a lamp post with her three bike locks (she'd lived in Manchester all her life and knew that a bare minimum of three locks were required). Her mind was racing, what the bloody hell was her dad doing here? He wasn't meeting their mum on a regular basis and hadn't bothered to tell them, was he? She wanted to speak to Catherine but she wasn't about to call her in the States to ask her why their father might be bothering their mother. She took her phone out and began to dial Claire's number, but then decided against it. That would mean explaining that she had also taken a detour to Chorlton to have a glimpse at her mother and how the other half lived. She didn't want Claire knowing that there was any chink in her armour where her mother was concerned; she was barely ready to admit that to herself.

Jo crept along the alleyway and looked along the road, peering directly into her mother and Jay's house. She felt like *Dog the Bounty Hunter* and Sue Ellen spying on *JR* all rolled into one. This was quite exciting, she thought and then remembered that she was just following her poor, sad-case dad and was not about to perform a Dog-style 'Intervention'. She stood at the corner of the road wondering where her dad had gone, when a familiar voice made her jump a mile.

'Jo Jo, what brings you Chorlton-bound?'

Jo spun around in shock to be faced by Jay. The one person she could do with never seeing again.

'Hi! I was just er . . .' she grasped for the right words, what was she doing here?

'Looking for Karen?' Jay offered.

'Yeah, sort of,' Jo nodded. 'Just kind of wondering if she hears from Dad ever.'

Thinking that maybe she should tread carefully around this subject, in case they had no idea that her dad was wandering around near their house.

'Your father? He's in the house having a cup of tea. We find it easier to deal with him that way than to call the police.'

Jo felt sick, the last thing she wanted was to hear smug-arse Jay talking patronisingly about her dad, but what did he mean? How often was he here?

'That all got a bit tired, belling the station every time he came around and anyway, who wants to get the pigs involved, eh?' Jay said, punching Jo lightly on the arm.

What? Jo wanted to scream. What on God's green earth was Dad doing? Had he no shame? and then realised almost immediately that she knew the answer to that: of course he didn't.

'Come in, pull up a pew. I'll make you a brew,' Jay laughed his horrible drain-emptying laugh. 'I'm a poet and I didn't know it.'

'You're a dick and you make me sick,' Jo whispered under her breath.

'What?' Jay asked.

'Nothing,' Jo said, following the nob into his evil artistic lair.

* * *

The tableau greeting Jo as she stepped through her mother's door was verging on the bizarre. Her father was sitting at the marble island in the middle of the designer kitchen sipping tea in his Sunday best, while her mother sat cross-legged on a cushion in the window, chanting.

'Karen's meditating,' Jay said.

'My mum, you mean?' Jo asked, shooting a look over to her mother who was pretending to be in a yogic trance.

'We don't really go in for paternal and maternal labels over here. They anchor a person to a role to which they might not necessarily want to be attached,' Jay said, with a sage nod.

'It's all right, Jay. We got it loud and clear that she wasn't arsed being a mother when she pissed off and shacked up with you. Calling her "Mum" or "Karen" isn't actually going to make that much difference,' Jo said, smiling sweetly.

After her initial encounter with Jay outside, Jo had armoured herself for anything that her mother or Jay threw at her. Jo had long since learned that it didn't get her anywhere being nice or appearing needy where her mother was concerned, if anything it sent Karen flying even further in the other direction.

Karen's eyes flew open. 'Joanna. Nice to see you, but a bit of warning next time.'

Mick was watching the exchange like a little boy watching his parents argue.

'I was just wondering what you're playing at,' Jo turned to her father.

'I was just passing . . .' Mick began.

'You were on your way to . . .' Jo looked at her dad, she couldn't say could she? He wouldn't have told Karen, not if he'd sworn his own daughters to secrecy '. . . to the shops the last time I saw you,' Jo said, thinking on her feet.

'Well, I like the butcher's in Chorlton.'

'Since when? You've not been in a shop since they've started using grams and kilograms.'

'Since years gone by,' Mick said, looking sadly at Karen.

Jay was obviously feeling uncomfortable, 'Would you like to see some art, Jo?'

'Not really.'

'Why, afraid it might challenge your expectations?'

'No, I'm afraid it might just be another turd-polishing exercise . . .'

'Right!' Jay said, throwing his hands in the air. 'I've tried, Karen, God knows I've tried. But your kids are the limit.' He flounced out of the room.

'What has he tried? It's not like he's just taken me to Butlin's for two weeks. It's years since I've seen him and now he's having a hissy fit because I think his art is shit?'

Karen grabbed her daughter by the wrist, 'His art is *him. He* is his art. You can't separate the two. Your words, Jo, can be mortally wounding to the spirit. When you grow up, if you ever do, you might realise that.'

'I've had a look, it's rather good,' Mick said, nodding agreeably.

'Who are you, Brian Sewell?' Karen snapped. Mick recoiled and sipped his tea.

'Don't have a pop at him,' Jo shouted.

Karen pushed her daughter through the kitchen door into a large hallway that led through to the lounge. 'Go in there,' she directed Jo. The lounge was newly decorated, it was all white walls and up-lighting, very *Grand*

Designs. 'Are the Arts Council giving you more than usual this year?' Jo asked, looking around the room.

'What is that meant to mean?'

'It means, how did you afford all of these fancy decorations?'

Karen pulled at her chestnut brown ponytail and narrowed her eyes at her daughter. It was more than a little disconcerting for Jo, as her mother looked exactly as Jo would look if she spent the next twenty years living outdoors on an ocean-going liner. Until Karen had taken up yoga – and there was no way of knowing if that was a new thing but Jo had a feeling it was a fad like everything else with her mother – Karen had been overly fond of cigarettes and red wine, which had aged her somewhat. 'What the hell has it got to do with you?' Karen asked.

And there it was; the sentence that Karen always managed to get to when she and Jo saw one another, the one where Jo knew not to go any further because she didn't want to hear what else her mother might have to say. If Jo retaliated now, saying that what it had to do with her was that she was Karen's daughter, Karen could easily counter with something blisteringly hurtful about her not really being her daughter as she hadn't been bothered with her since she was twelve. Jo knew the facts, the last thing she needed was her selfish mother spelling them out.

'Nothing.'

'That's right. nothing.' Karen said, standing up and walking over to the picture window that looked out on a walled garden. 'So, what's new?'

Jo thought for a minute, was her mother serious? Didn't she know about Catherine? 'Catherine's in New York.'

Her mother's eye flickered. 'Oh yes, your father said something about it. Some singing competition isn't it?' Karen said, as if she wasn't bothered. Something told Jo she was more than bothered.

Jo shook her head. 'Are you for real?'

'What?' Karen asked, lighting a cigarette and immediately waving the smoke away as if it had nothing to do with her.

'A singing competition? It's the most watched TV show in the world.'

'Oh, right,' Karen said, non-plussed.

'Karen,' Jo said, it seemed more appropriate than 'Mum', 'this is a really big deal. Why are you pretending not to be bothered?' She thought she smelled a rat. Did her mother know something she wasn't admitting to? Jo quickly dismissed the idea. Her mum wasn't one for hiding opportunities to cash in or be the centre of attention. If she knew something she would tell them; she wouldn't have been able to help herself. It seemed she genuinely wasn't that interested.

'I am bothered and I wish her well. I'll send a message to the spirits for her.'

'You will, will you? And how will you do that?'

'Jay and I are training to be Shamen.' Karen said matter-of-factly.

'Oh, right. Of course,' Jo said, mocking her mother. If Karen caught her tone, she chose to ignore it. 'Anyway, she'll be on the TV very soon. Hundreds of thousands of people enter it and she's down to the last six in her category. So, well done, Catherine.'

'Yes, well done, her.' Karen said without much enthusiasm.

'In fact . . .' Jo didn't know why she let her mother get to her but she couldn't help herself, 'we're all on it. As a family.'

'You mean all of you?' Karen asked, appalled.

'Yes . . .' Jo said, pleased to have her mother's attention. 'We all went down to support her and Dad sort of kicked off on Richard Forster.'

'Oh my God, what on earth did he say?'

'You'll have to watch it to find out.'

'OK,' Karen said with a sigh.

Jo never failed to be surprised by her mother. There were mothers out there who would sever a limb to see their kids do well on a show like *Star Maker*, but not Karen, she couldn't give a monkey's. The only thing that would interest Karen on TV was a show about herself.

Jo decided to change the topic of conversation. 'What's Dad doing here, Mum?'

'He comes here quite a bit. He sort of roams around outside. We used to call the police but now we just let him in, he has a cup of tea and then he goes.'

Jo's heart sank, she wanted to get her dad by the scruff of the neck and to tell him to stop being such a deluded, soft old sod. What was he doing roaming around down here? And it wasn't as if he could even drive himself here, he must always get a taxi the four or so miles to Chorlton in order to stalk his ex-wife.

'Well, maybe he's got something to tell you, maybe it's because there's something really serious wrong with him . . .' Jo said, pushing her mother to see if there was an ounce of compassion in the woman.

'The cancer. He told me, I know all about it. But perhaps it's not true, perhaps it's all in his mind.'

'What?' Her mother was seriously deranged, Jo realised.

'It wouldn't be the first time that he lied to get his way.'

'You're unbelievable . . .' Jo was genuinely shocked that her mother could think such a thing.

'He's spiritually stunted. Do you know, Joanna, that your father didn't tell me he loved me once after the day we got married? He couldn't, he was an emotional husk . . .'

'Right, we're off,' Jo shouted, marching into the kitchen.

Mick was still sipping his tea and staring out of the window. Jo hooked her hand through his arm and pulled him off the stool he was perched on. 'What the blazes?'

'Out now,' Jo demanded.

'But I need to say goodbye to your mother.'

'You don't need to say goodbye to anyone.' Jo pushed Mick through the kitchen door and pulled it behind her. Once out on the street and safely out of earshot, Jo lambasted her dad. 'What the bloody hell were you doing there?'

'I might ask you the same thing.'

'I was passing through Chorlton.'

'Going where?'

'Nowhere. None of your business. A friend's, if you must know.'

'What friend?'

'Never mind me, what about you? Mum says you go there all the time! That they have to invite you in because they got bored of calling the police!'

'So what?'

'So what? You lied, you told me the other day that you hadn't seen Mum in ages.'

'Myself and your mother don't have to report in to you kids every time we do something.'

'Listen to yourself!' Jo pleaded. 'There is no "you and Mum". You and her are no more. Stop making a fool of yourself, Dad. She doesn't want you. She doesn't want any of us; get used to it.'

Mick stood in front of his daughter and if it was possible for a human being to crumble then that is what he did. He slumped to the ground, his hat falling off his head into his lap, tears streaming down his face.

'Oh God, Dad, I'm sorry, I really didn't mean to upset you. Please don't cry,' Jo said, rubbing his back and smiling tightly at two passers-by who crossed the road in order to avoid the display of sadness they were witnessing.

'I'm gone, Joanna. I'm gone.'

Jo didn't know what he meant but she knew that he must feel terrible. He was sick with cancer, his kids were all grown up and the mother of those kids wanted nothing to do with him.

'You're not gone, Dad, you're here and I'm here with you.' She bent down and hugged her dad; he turned and clung to her like a drowning man hanging on to a piece of driftwood. She felt awful. He seemed so sad, so alone. She hasn't realised, she just thought that he was a bluff old sod who weathered anything that was thrown at him.

She needed to move him away from the area so that neither her mother nor Jay saw him like this. She wasn't going to allow that pair to feel any more smugly sorry for Mick than they already did. Jo looked at her bike and realised she was either going to have to flag a taxi or ride tandem with her dad to the hospital. She thought the taxi would be more appropriate under the circumstances and that the bike would have to be collected another time.

'Anywhere here'll do, thank you,' Mick said in the middle of a wide house-lined road that didn't seem to have a hospital anywhere in the vicinity.

'Where's the hospital?' Jo asked, 'We're going to Christie's,' Jo informed the taxi driver. 'Can you take us to the door please?'

'Christie's is about five minutes up this road, love.'

Jo looked at her dad. 'Why do you want to get out here, Dad?' After Mick's collapse in Chorlton, Jo was being as gentle as possible with him.

'I wanted a walk, that's all,' Mick said, 'A bit of air.'

'But I think it's best that we just get to the hospital and if you want some air then you can walk around the grounds.'

'I don't need baby-sitting, Joanna.' Mick seemed to have forgotten his breakdown in the street and was back to his truculent self.

'OK. Fine. Can you pull over, sorry . . .'

Mick paid the driver and Jo climbed out onto the pavement. As the car pulled away Mick straightened himself out and began to walk. Jo followed in silence.

'I don't want you coming in with me.'

'Why not?' Jo wasn't sure herself that she wanted to spend the next few hours in a cancer hospital but if her dad was going in then she didn't think she had a choice.

'Because I don't. You can get a coffee and I'll see you when I'm finished.'

Jo thought about Catherine and the fact that she had

always had to put up with her father's moods and whims. Jo decided to text her sister and ask what New York was like. She wished she was in New York rather than being forced to go for her coffee alone in Withington. In fact, she wished all of this would just go away and that her dad would be all right and he could just go back to his normal grumpy depressed self, rather than someone who was grumpy and depressed and potentially seriously ill.

'Dad, I'd really like to come in with you. Maybe there are some things that the doctors would like to tell someone from your family . . .'

'Like what?' Mick shot his daughter a look.

'Like how to look after you properly. Like what we should do if something happens.'

'If what happens?'

'I don't know, do I? That's why I want to come in with you,' Jo said, exasperated.

Mick shook his head as if all this fussing and caring was getting on his nerves. Jo walked along at his side, waiting for him to say something. Finally he spoke. 'She wasn't bothered, you know, your mother. About the cancer. I thought she would be, I thought if there was one thing that would make her realise, then it was this.'

'You thought that this would make her realise what?'

'That all this,' he threw his arms in the general direction of Chorlton, 'was a fad.'

Was he serious? 'Fads don't last seven years, Dad. What are you on about?' Then something dawned on Jo; she felt an icy chill run the length of her body. Her eyes must have given it away because Mick quickly began to cover his tracks.

'Nothing, she's not worth bothering about, not when I've got you lot being so good and looking out for me and everything.'

Jo's eye's narrowed and she bit her bottom lip as she tried to hold in what she was desperate to say and tried to add some rational thought before leaping to conclusions about her dad. 'Right, OK,' Jo said, stalling for thinking time.

'Anyway, you get yourself in there and have a coffee,' Mick instructed Jo as they passed a ropey-looking coffee shop.

Jo looked at her dad, 'It's all right, I don't fancy a drink really. Anyway,' she swallowed hard on the sick feeling that had come over her in the past few moments, 'I'm going to come with you and see what the doctors have to say. I want to make sure that they're doing all they can.'

'I'm a big boy, I can look after myself.'

'That might be the case, but I still want to come in with you.'

'Well,' Mick said defiantly, 'I don't want you to.'

'Tough, I'm coming in.'

'No, you're not.'

'Yes, I am.'

'You can't just go swanning in there,' Mick said, flustered.

'I'm not swanning, I'm accompanying my father who is a patient.'

'Well, I don't want you there.'

'Why not?' Jo asked angrily.

Mick threw his arms to his side like a petulant child, 'Because . . .' he struggled for the words, 'I don't want to upset you,' he said finally. Jo buckled. She had been thinking some very dark things about her father in the past few minutes, that he was somehow milking this to somehow garner attention with his ex-wife but seeing him standing here now looking alone and frightened Jo realised that she had judged her dad in the same dismissive manner she always judged him.

'All right, Dad, I'm sorry.' Jo wanted to hug her dad again but it didn't feel appropriate somehow. Instead she pointed awkwardly to the coffee shop and said, 'I'll just be in here, yeah? Shout if you need anything.'

'I'll be about an hour. You don't have to wait; I'll get the bus back.'

'It's all right, Dad, I don't mind waiting.' Jo said.

'OK,' Mick said and then turned and trudged away from Jo, looking small and, dressed in his suit and tie, as if he was attending a funeral.

'How did you get on?' Claire asked, stepping to one side to let Jo into the hallway. Claire's house was like something out of *House & Garden*. It wasn't much to look at from the outside – a detached new build with a garage and a small manicured front lawn – but once inside it was all bold prints and warm, inviting lighting. The kitchen looked like the type that a TV company would hire for Nigella to pretend was her own. Claire could probably hire out Jake and Rosie while she was at it, they'd make great middle-class, celebrity-cook kids with names like that.

'Don't ask,' Jo said, flopping onto a kitchen chair and throwing her head into her hands.

'What? What did they say? Tell me!' Claire said, panic-stricken.

Jo looked up, realising she had unnecessarily worried her sister. 'Oh, Dad said that he just has to receive "on-going treatment" as he put it. I'm guessing it's chemotherapy but he's not using that word so neither am I. But he came out of the hospital in better spirits than he went in.'

Jo told Claire about the morning's events. By the time she had finished, Claire was sitting bolt upright in the chair with her mouth open, holding a spatula that she had been using to bake fairy cakes as if she was held in suspended animation.

'So my bike has now taken up temporary residence in Chorlton,' Jo said, finishing her story.

'And she really didn't give a stuff about Catherine?'

'Didn't seem to.' Jo shrugged.

Claire bit her lip. 'She is unbelievable,' she said quietly. 'You know she wasn't always like this, don't you?' Claire said, as if she wanted to wipe all of Jo's troubles away for her.

'You don't have to lie about Mum to make me feel better, you know, I can handle how she is. I just wish I hadn't gone. It's like picking a scab every time I see her.'

'I'm not lying. I'm not saying she was perfect, she wasn't. But when we were younger, when you were a baby, she was just a mum. Like every other mum. She did mum things; laughed with us, shouted at us. Just mum things, you know?' Claire said sadly.

'I can't really remember.'

By the time Jo was a year old Karen had already started

going to her weekly Women's Forum meetings and going on Poll Tax demonstrations. She might have done lots of 'mum things' but Jo's overall memory of her mother as a little girl was of her being angry at someone or something. She was always going on about empowering herself, Jo recalled. As if she had been shackled to the kitchen sink and Mick had hidden all the lighters so she couldn't burn her bra.

'Do you remember being dressed up like ET?' Claire asked.

Jo loved that film and Claire saying this rang some vague bell but she couldn't place the memory.

'Mum put a sheet around you and stuck you in the shopping basket at the front of her bike. It was a full moon and we all rode along on our bikes telling you we were going to find the spaceship that was leaving from the rec.'

Jo laughed at the thought. 'Mum did that?'

'I thought you'd remember . . .'

Jo felt a sad pang for her childhood. 'No. I just remember Mum being difficult and being more bothered about things going on outside the house than in.'

'That was always a bit of a problem with her, wasn't it?' Claire said, getting up and going over to her cake mix. After a few moments of stirring the mixture in silence, Claire asked, without turning around, 'Did she mention the kids?'

'Yes,' Jo lied. 'She asked how they were getting on and I said she should come over and stop pretending that life in Flixton stopped when she left.'

'She's been over a couple of times,' Claire said. Jo felt

that her sister was making excuses for their mother. 'She's OK when she's here, always buys the kids something nice . . .' Claire trailed off. This was something that they all did, Jo acknowledged; be deeply angry at Karen one minute and the next they would make excuses up for her as if giving their own perspective on Karen's behaviour made it somehow more bearable.

'Does she know about Dad's cancer?'

Jo thought about this for a moment and then decided to avoid the truth for now. 'I'm sure he won't want Mum knowing.'

'That's understandable.'

Jo picked at her nail varnish and wondered why she had just felt the need to lie to Claire. But she knew that if she told Claire that her father *had* told Karen and her mother's response had been less than helpful, then she would have to face two ugly truths: that her mum couldn't be called on to have a heart in any situation and her dad was willing to use his illness as a bargaining chip for his ex-wife's affections.

Chapter 13

'I've just stood in horse shit!' Star complained.

It was their third day in New York and the final twenty-four contestants had been on the go from the moment they arrived. Catherine thought there might have been room for a bit of a look around the city, or at least the chance to be un-chaperoned for more than a minute of the day. But their schedule had been relentless. One good thing about that was that Andy had stayed true to his word and kept his distance. She had seen him once or twice but he had always been accompanying Jason or chatting amiably to another contestant – probably trying to worm his way in to their affections, or their pants – and they had simply avoided speaking.

Catherine was now exhausted. She had been singing for at least three hours each day and in between her vocal coaching lessons she had been primped and preened by a team of stylists and run ragged by Antonia and her team of exercise sadists. She now had bright white teeth and having stuck to her allotted thousand calories a day – and fitness regime – her size fourteen jeans were hanging off her. She also had long hair extensions that made her look, freakily enough, a lot like Jo. Catherine would never have thought that in a million years she would ever look like her younger sister. But then again she didn't think anyone would spend in excess of five thousand pounds grooming her and that she would have complemented the effect by starving herself. It was all beginning to worry her a little. She had just wanted to sing, but now she was definitely letting the *Star Maker* effect take hold.

She and the other finalists were now standing in the middle of Central Park, being photographed alongside the famous horse-drawn carriages for the charity single they had recorded that day for Horse Aid, Richard Forster's favourite charity. He had had to explain that the money went to poor countries where horses were the main work animal in cut off villages, not – as Star had thought – on race horses and Shire horses and the like. The song was terrible, Catherine thought. It was the words from the famous speech by Richard III offering his kingdom for a horse set to the theme tune to *Black Beauty*. Even when they were recording it and trying not to laugh at the over-worthy sentiment of it all, grown men who worked in production had tears in their eyes and Catherine knew that this awful record would undoubtedly sell like hot cakes.

Star hobbled out of the shot with her shoe in her hand, shaking her head.

'We're finished anyway,' the photographer told them.

'What now?' Kim asked Will. Their agenda was so regimented, there was bound to be something.

Will looked at the itinerary on his iPhone. 'Back to the homestead and then we'll just be doing some media training with you for tonight, especially you guys.'

Tonight was the first airing of *Star Maker* and for the past few days the production team had been trying to impress on the contestants that they would have to be prepared for the public onslaught of interest.

'Why us?' Catherine asked.

'You're the under-twenty-fives. The overs never win and no one cares about them. They're just here to make it look like we're being inclusive.'

Catherine took this information in. She was beginning to think that her dad had a point, that this was a machine and she was quietly accepting her place in it. 'Then for the next two weeks until the first live final the day will look like this.' Will pushed his iPhone in front of Catherine. It informed them that they would be up every morning at six, in the gym until eight, they would sing for two hours and break for lunch, sing for another two hours and break for dinner, work through their songs in the evening and lights would be out at ten.

'Every day?' Kim asked. 'But can't we have a day off to go sight-seeing?'

'Oh, you are going sight-seeing . . .' Will tapped the screen '. . . on Thursday, with the camera crew.'

'Can't we go on our own?' Catherine asked, feeling not a little bit caged.

'Believe me,' Will said ominously, 'once this hits the screen tonight, you guys won't want to go anywhere on your own.'

'What do you mean?' Catherine asked.

'You'll be mobbed everywhere you go.'

The girls looked at one another. They didn't need to say anything, they were thinking the same thing; they were scared.

Chapter 14

'Oh my God, I am so excited!' Jo said, jumping in front of the telly. 'Catherine is going to be famous and all the losers from her school will see her and wish that they weren't such sad cases.'

It was the first showing of *Star Maker* and Jo was beside herself with anticipation. The auditions were her favourite bit; the live finals were boring. Who cares about people who can sing – unless it was your sister of course – bring on the divvies who couldn't hold a tune, that's what Jo thought.

'Sit down! All I can see is your fat arse,' Maria shouted.

'That is hardly a fat arse, is it?' Claire asked.

'At least my arse is in the right place, someone seems to have slapped yours and put it where your face should be,' Jo said, flicking Maria a V.

'Jesus, tonight, will you all sit down and give this moment the gravitas it deserves,' Mick huffed. 'Sometimes I wonder were you brought up or dragged up.'

'Dragged up,' the sisters said in unison.

Claire topped everyone's wine glass up. She was eager to ply everyone with as much drink as possible, as she had a pass out tonight. Paul was looking after the kids and she was staying over in Catherine's room. Jo also assumed that her sister wanted to be pie-eyed in order to take the edge off her TV debut.

The *Star Maker* music began to play; a rousing, galloping romp of a tune. Then the voice over kicked in, 'It's back, and this time it's bigger than ever . . . *Star Maker* . . .' There was a pause as the music continued, '*Transatlantic.*'

'Woo hoo!' Jo shouted. The others cheered. The camera panned over the crowd queuing to get into one of the audition venues. Then the judges were introduced.

'It's your best mates, Dad, look.'

'Shut it, Joanna. That lot wouldn't know talent if it sat on them.'

Jo looked at her dad, confused. 'What you on about? They put Catherine through.'

'Well, they were rude to us, weren't they? Shower of shites.'

'What's that got to do with the price of fish? Just because someone tells you to sling your hook, doesn't mean they don't know what talent is. You talk some bollocks.'

'Eh!' Mick protested.

'Oh my God, it's Catherine!' Claire screamed.

'First up. It can't be.'

'It was her, it just showed her for a split second.'

'Maybe we are on tonight then,' Maria said, sounding pleased.

'You just want to see what your orange mug looks like on the telly.'

'I just want to see what your ugly mug looks like on the telly.'

Jo ignored her sister.

'Shrek probably,' Maria goaded.

'Yes, I always get told I look like Shrek,' Jo agreed.

They waited and waited. The first part of the show was full of the usual halfwits who couldn't hold a note but still thought that it was a good idea to go on national TV and sing a Céline Dion number. The second part saw a few people who could sing being put through to Boot Camp.

'Weird, our Catherine knows them,' Jo mused.

The third part was a mix of those who could sing and those who couldn't. The thing that made it different from other years was that the English halfwits were intercut with American ones. They really did everything bigger and better over there, Jo thought, impressed; even their halfwits. After the ad break for the final part of the show, Jo began to lose interest, convinced that this wasn't Catherine's night, maybe tomorrow. She was just about to go to the toilet as she'd been holding a wee in for the past two hours, when Maria squealed and Jo saw that Catherine was on the TV walking towards the judges. They then cut to the rest of her family as if they had been waiting outside all along. 'Oh my God!' Jo screamed.

'She's our sister,' Maria was saying to Jason P. Longford.

'Oh my God, I sound like a right common cow,' Maria said, shocked.

'And?' Jo asked.

Claire shushed the pair. 'And what's your name?' Richard Forster was asking.

'It's Catherine Reilly.'

Jo was sitting glued to the TV, her knees tucked under her chin, biting them nervously. She couldn't believe it, up until now she knew that Catherine was part of the *Star Maker* show this year, but it hadn't really sunk in.

Now, sitting here watching her sister on TV, wearing *her* dress, the reality of the situation was finally dawning on Jo.

Jo had no idea why she was so nervous. Her sister was happily tucked away in New York. Then she realised why she was nervous, as the camera returned to her and the rest of the family. Jason P. Longford seemed uncharacteristically speechless and Mick was taking centre stage ranting and demanding to be allowed in the room. The way the scene was edited made them all look as nuts as their father; all shoulder-barging and out-of-my-way northern bravado. They fell through the door and Mick began his tirade against the judges and each sister let out a loud groan.

'What?' Mick asked defiantly. 'We did her a favour. She got through didn't she?'

'I don't really think it's any thanks to you, do you Dad?'

Jo watched through her fingers as Mick shouted at Richard Forster about being a robber baron and about being out of the music business quicker than he could say Gareth Gates. Then they were out and unbeknownst to any of the Reillys they had been filmed complaining, mumbling and arguing all the way to the car. Then the camera cut to Catherine, who sang and was told she wasn't quite what they were looking for.

'Oh God,' Claire said. 'I'm totally mortified.'

'I'll be pestered by passengers for the rest of my life,' Maria said.

The footage cut back inside and they saw the judges deliberating over Catherine and then deciding to bring her back. The camera followed the young guy who was sent to get her from the car and then Catherine was back in front of the judges again, being triumphantly put through. The judges looked like great guys for giving this poor girl a second chance and Catherine looked like someone who needed all the help she could get as a result of being from the family she was from. The very last piece of footage was of Mick poking his head into the audition room and Richard Forster saying, 'You again?' and Mick replying, 'Wrong door. I thought this was the bogs.' Then the credits rolled.

Jo threw herself on the carpet and rolled around, her hands covering her face.

Claire and Maria sat in stony silence on the settee. Only Mick seemed rather pleased with his TV debut. 'I think we came out of that all right, don't you?' he asked.

'No, Dad,' Claire explained. 'We are the best that they saved to last, don't you see?'

'You know, Dad, the big divs that everyone laughs at?' Jo said. 'Well, that's us now. Good eh?'

'Who cares?' Mick said, waving his hand dismissively.

'We do,' the girls chorused.

'You shouldn't! No one will give that a second thought after tonight,' Mick said confidently.

'Really?' Jo asked, pulling out her mobile phone which she'd purposefully put on silent for the duration of her and her family's TV debut. Twenty missed calls and forty texts. 'Shit,' she said, showing her phone display to Claire and Maria. 'That's everyone I know ringing up or texting to take the piss.'

'And so it begins,' Maria said, with grave portent.

It was the first wise thing that Jo could ever remember her sister saying.

It was four in the afternoon in New York and the viewing figures were in for *Star Maker: Transatlantic* in the UK. 'Wow. Fifteen million people. That's our highest ever,' Richard Forster told Andy.

'That's great,' Andy said enthusiastically. Andy was convinced he was turning into someone he wouldn't have cared for before he started working on this show. He was sure that he was agreeable with Richard to the point of sycophancy, but didn't know what other way to be. Everyone seemed to be sycophantic to Richard.

'Let's go give the news to the girls . . . Oh, and by the way can you ask Star to come and see me later when all this is done?' Richard asked. Andy was intrigued to know why, but of course didn't ask.

Andy followed Richard into the room where the contestants were congregated. 'Right everyone,' he said, 'this might seem dramatic but I don't want you to underestimate what I say. Your lives, as of now, have irrevocably changed. The first *Star Maker* episode has aired in the UK and we hit fifteen million viewers. That's one in four people in the UK that watched. And Catherine,' Andy looked at Catherine as her eyes shot open in alarm at being singled out, 'your family were a massive hit. The message boards are alive with your father's antics.'

Andy wanted the ground to open up and swallow him. Any mention of Catherine's father left Andy feeling terrible.

'Oh,' Catherine said, looking worried. She briefly caught

Andy's eye and gave him the blackest look he'd ever received. She still hates me, he thought.

'Tonight, we'll be watching the first US episode from a TV studio over looking Times Square. The spin is different over here, obviously. Throughout the audition episodes we'll concentrate more on the US than the UK but you'll all be featured, obviously.' Catherine looked ashen-faced at the thought.

'I know that you are all lined up to have media training over this, but I just want to let you know that the interest in you if you get through to the finals will be intense. It's also something that is extremely enjoyable if you choose to go along for the ride. The people who fare badly are the ones who start taking the process – and themselves for that matter – far too seriously. You have to learn to develop a thick skin and take the rough with the smooth. OK?' He looked at the contestants. 'Good, because it's fast track this year. There's always a buzz around this show but this year, with the back-to-back auditions and then straight into the live shows we're expecting an unprecedented response.'

Andy looked out at the girls. They would be famous soon, all of them, even Catherine. And then she'd be so busy that she wouldn't have time to talk to him, even if she had the inclination. Andy decided that he would concentrate on his work and if Catherine wanted to speak to him, then she would, but he was becoming increasingly convinced that she would have better things to do.

Chapter 15

Star Maker: *Transatlantic* had been airing for ten consecutive nights. Even though the contestants had been too busy to have much contact with the outside world, it was apparent that they were becoming – if not famous – then recognisable. There was a definite buzz around the show and, in particular, Catherine's family, but because Catherine hadn't been in the UK to witness it happen, she didn't quite believe it. Catherine had been in touch with Jo who had told her that their dad was something of a minor celebrity in Manchester and the fame was going to his head. It had one good effect in that his spirits seemed to have lifted and he didn't feel as ill as he had in previous weeks.

Catherine was missing her family terribly. She knew that each contestant was allotted tickets in the coming weeks for the live finals, but that hers weren't until the fourth week, if she made it that far. She hadn't even mentioned it to her sisters yet, she didn't want to jinx herself.

She and the other finalists had been ushered into a room that looked as though it should be in the Palace of Versailles rather than a New York apartment. There were gilt-edged mirrors and marble tables that must have been worth an absolute fortune. Richard Forster came into the room and explained to the girls that the American host of *Star Maker*, Tom Soronsen, who was to host the live finals, was about to greet them. Catherine noticed that Jason P. Longford was doing a lot of eye-rolling; he evidently felt intimidated by the American host.

Richard said that once this had been filmed they would be taken off by a famous face that they had yet to meet and they would be mentored by them for the day. There was a buzz of excitement – who would it be? Names were bandied around – Britney Spears, Kelly Clarkson, Rihanna. Richard told the contestants to calm down and all would be revealed.

Until now the whole thing, other than the auditions and the nerve-racking nature of them, felt somewhat tame. The tension and the razzmatazz associated with *Star Maker* was all created in the edit for the first stages of the competition, Catherine now realised. But when Tom Soronsen walked into the room and went straight into his role as host, the atmosphere changed. Catherine could see the other girls straighten in their chairs. Maybe it was the American accent that made proceedings seem altogether more showbizzy than they had in the Cotswolds or London or any time in the past two weeks in New York, or maybe it was that Tom Soronsen was charismatic and known the world over, unlike Jason P. Longford, who was charmless and known primarily to the daytime TV watchers of the UK. Whatever it was, the whole thing had suddenly shifted up a gear. It suddenly felt real: they were here to perform and to compete. Catherine looked around – everyone felt it.

Tom walked through the room, shouting each contestant's name in his punchy American way. When he said

Catherine it made her involuntarily take a breath and her back fizz with goose bumps. 'Cut,' the director shouted. 'Got it in one,' he said watching the footage through his viewfinder.

'I'm such a Goddamn pro,' Tom said, his tongue firmly in his cheek.

Richard took the centre of the room. 'Thank you, Tom,' he said, folding his arms and looking at his groups of hopefuls. 'Right you all have mentors for the afternoon. Guys . . .' he looked at the over-twenty-five men, '. . . you've got Elton.'

'Elton John?' one of them asked.

'How many other Eltons do you know?' Richard raised an eyebrow. 'Ladies,' he turned to the over-twenty-fives, 'you have Anastasia.' The girls turned and excitedly whispered to one another.

'Gents . . .' The under-twenty-five men listened carefully, '. . . you have JT.'

'Justin?' one of the guys asked, jumping to his feet.

'The very same,' Richard nodded. 'And girls . . .' he screwed his face up, 'I'm sorry. I haven't got time to sugar the pill here, so here goes: it's Anya.'

A uniform gasp filled the room.

'I know, I know,' Richard said, like a man who'd heard it all before. 'Everyone loves Anya. Everyone thinks Anya's great. Well, she isn't. Frankly she's a mess.'

Anya – unlike Star – never had to give her surname. She was known the world over as just Anya. Thrust into the limelight at seventeen, she was now twenty-seven and despite a train wreck of a life that had seen her lurch from disastrous relationship to disastrous relationship and hit drug-fuelled lows involving male prostitutes and her second child being given up for adoption, people still wanted to think that she was going to come good again. Recently she had lost a lot of weight and looked something like the teen sensation that she had once been.

'I know it's exciting, thinking that she's going to be mentoring you, but trust me, she won't. She's coked up to the eyeballs and we're trying to bring her round. So here's the drill: we'll do some shots of you all meeting her, she'll wear shades. She'll say the bare minimum and you'll go through your songs with one of our vocal coaches. Then she's out of here and off to a clinic in Arizona to dry out in time for her performance on the live show on Saturday. Any questions?' Richard looked at the group. Catherine realised that they were all sitting staring at him, utterly speechless. 'Didn't think so. Enjoy your afternoon.'

Andy was having the most bizarre hour of his life. He had been charged, alongside Jason, to look after Anya. Andy would have assumed that looking after one of the mentors would have been far too lowly a job for Jason but Jason had jumped at the chance to meet his pop idol. Now, Andy could tell that he was wishing he hadn't bothered. Anya hadn't stopped talking for the past hour, hadn't even seemed to have drawn breath, and her only topic of conversation was herself. She was now in the toilet throwing up violently, having ended her hour-long rant by asserting that if her ex-husband – a famous pop star himself – went anywhere near their daughter she would tell the world that he'd had sex with a horse.

'Is she on drugs, do you think?' Andy asked as he and Jason stood outside the toilet door.

'Is she on drugs?' Jason asked disbelievingly. 'She's off her fucking box!'

Andy caught his eye and they laughed together for the first time since they'd met; both realising the preposterousness of the situation they found themselves in.

The door opened and the young star stood before them, her blond hair extensions matted to her head, her eye make-up smeared all over her face, her breath smelling of sick.

Jason took his Ray Bans out of his pocket and handed them to Anya. 'Stick these on darling, you look like Bette Davis in *Whatever Happened to Baby Jane.*'

Andy swallowed a giggle as one of the world's most famous women lurched in between them. Andy took one arm and Jason took the other and they guided Anya into the next room where they thought the under-twenty-five girls would be waiting. When they shuffled into the room the only person in there was Catherine. Catherine looked stunned for a moment and then bit her bottom lip as if she were holding in a laugh. He could understand why, he was propping up a near-paralytic superstar.

'Ladies and gentleman,' Jason said drily, 'I give you Anya.'

'The others are just on their way in,' Catherine said, pointing at the door.

'Right.' Andy felt embarrassed.

Richard Forster walked in with the other contestants following him, breaking the tension. They all stood and stared at the fallen superstar.

'Well, you didn't have to make such an effort, Anya,' Richard said sarcastically to the bedraggled star.

'Fuck you, Richard Forster,' Anya spat.

'Why, thank you.'

'What I needed tonight was a friend but I got you . . .' Anya said, lurching to one side and slumping in a chair.

'Well, that is a shame,' Richard said, clearly trying to mask his impatience.

'You don't even know that's from a film, do you, Richard? Demi Moore says it to Rob Lowe in *St Elmo's Fire*, Richard!' Anya shouted slurrily, no one knew where to look.

Andy shot a look at Catherine. She momentarily looked back at him and half smiled.

'Right,' Richard Forster got to his feet and grabbed the sozzled star. 'That's it. You're out. Jason, get Christina on the next private jet we have, if not Christina then I'll do it myself.'

Anya got to her feet and then threw her arms around Richard. He stood back, disgusted, his hands in the air looking down at her head on his shirt like someone had just thrown a custard pie at his chest. 'Get her out of here.'

'I thought you loved me,' she giggled and then turned suddenly serious. 'You used me. You pick me up when you want me and then you leave me high and dry.'

Andy looked at his feet. Rumours were rife about Richard's liking for young girls but Andy innocently thought that they were just that, rumours. Was this true? Surely not, Cherie would have his bollocks on a plate if she knew that something like that was going on.

'We've had it with the inane witterings, Anya, you're going home.'

'Too long in the business, Richard? Liked me when I was fresh meat though, didn't you?'

Richard didn't hesitate a moment longer, he grabbed Anya by the top of her arm and frogmarched her from the room. Moments later Richard was back. 'Sorry about that, folks,' he smiled confidently, 'let's just say I don't think Anya will be having a number one again, not outside Turkmenistan. So where were we?'

Andy looked at Jason, who was intently listening to Richard, as was everyone else in the room. They all knew they had just witnessed the end of a once great pop career. Richard Forster wasn't a man to be crossed.

Chapter 16

The day of the first live finals had at last arrived. Catherine had spent all day going over and over the song she was to sing, 'The Edge of Seventeen' by Stevie Nicks. Not something she would have chosen, but she did acknowledge that it was a clever choice. It was an old song that had been sampled by Destiny's Child, so sounded modern.

The American vocal coaches were loud, brutally frank and each more terrifying than the last. They had been putting the girls through their paces since Anya had been unceremoniously sacked from her role as mentor. The public didn't know this, of course. To see the footage of her standing by a piano with each under-twenty-five girl, anyone would have thought that she had carefully guided them through every step of their performance.

The past two weeks had been exhausting but great fun and now they were being driven to the TV studios at Chelsea Piers where there would be an audience of over a thousand people and their performances would be broadcast to the nation. Catherine was so nervous she hadn't been able to eat properly – even her meagre one thousand calories a day – for days. Antonia had spotted her yesterday, tapped her collar bones and said, impressed, 'Wow they're really starting to stick out, good work!'

Catherine hoped that her nerves wouldn't get the better of her for the performance itself. But as soon as the day was over, her thoughts turned to her dad and how things were at home. She had tried to call home three times today but each time had got the answerphone. Finally, she decided to call Jo's mobile. It made an odd noise and then connected.

'Catherine, how's it going?' Jo sounded distracted.

'It's great. How's Dad?'

'Dad is totally fine. Nothing to worry about,' Jo said breezily.

'Are you sure?'

'Completely. Fine. So come on, what's the goss?'

'No goss, really,' Catherine said, feeling relieved that all seemed to be OK at home. She kept bargaining with herself about her dad. If she did well in this then she would be able to make sure he had the best care possible. 'This line is bad. You sound like you're miles away.'

'Duh! I am. Right, I'm going to try again,' Jo said, as if she was trying to get through to someone who had great difficulty understanding the most basic instruction. 'How is New York? With Richard Forster and the *Star Maker* programme? It is the biggest programme on the planet – don't tell me you don't have any gossip!'

'Oh, yes. Right.' Her sister really did have a point. 'Well, there was something that happened that was totally bizarre that I forgot to text you about . . .' Catherine explained the Anya episode and Jo squealed excitedly throughout the story.

'I'm ringing *Heat*!'

'You are not!' Catherine said, panicked.

'That was a joke, you dimwit.'

Out of the corner of her eye, Catherine could see Star

walking towards her. The usually immaculately groomed young woman was dishevelled and looked to have been crying. Catherine watched as Star got nearer, but when she saw Catherine she ducked out of view. 'Listen, Jo, I've got to go.'

'I'll be texting you and watching you tonight and we'll all be voting. In fact, all of Manchester will be voting and Dad's new fan club will obviously be behind you, too.'

Catherine didn't want to think of the sort of nutters her father would be attracting now that he had made his TV debut.

'I'll call back later, after the show.' Catherine looked at her watch. The show aired late in the UK, at half-nine and earlier in the US, at four-thirty eastern time.

'Good luck.'

'Thanks.' Catherine hung up and followed Star. She had been acting strangely for the past few days but Catherine hadn't thought too much of it as they had been so busy and Star acted strangely all the time anyway.

'Star?' Catherine said, following her into their room.

'What?' Star asked, opening her wardrobe and rummaging around in it. Catherine could tell that she was only doing this so that she didn't have to look at her.

'Are you OK?'

'I'm fine,' Star said. She didn't sound fine.

Catherine tiptoed towards her, and Star turned around and said, 'Seriously, I'm fine.'

'Why have you been crying then?' Having three sisters made Catherine an expert at not taking no for an answer.

'I haven't,' Star said adamantly and went back to going through her wardrobe.

'Star . . .' Catherine decided that she was going to extend some kindness to Star. She was prickly and brittle but sometimes she seemed like a lost soul to Catherine. 'I know you probably don't want to, but just to let you know, if you need to talk to someone, you can talk to me.'

Star turned around slowly and looked at Catherine. 'Thank you. But really, I'm fine.'

'OK.' Catherine felt that there was more to this than nerves. Star didn't suffer from nerves, she was the most self-confident person Catherine had ever met. 'Well, are you going to be OK for later?'

'I'll be fine, honestly,' Star nodded.

Catherine walked towards the door thinking that she should give Star some time alone.

'Thanks,' Star said timidly, as Catherine opened the door.

'No problem.'

'Bloody hell, that was close.' Jo said, stepping out of the taxi and looking up at the huge hotel they were booked into for the night, off Broadway.

'It smells.' Mick said, disgruntled.

Maria's bare, tanned leg stretched out of the taxi and she gathered herself as if she was about to step onto the red carpet for the awaiting photographers. 'What does?'

'This place. New York, New York, so good they named it shite,' Mick grumbled.

'Does that make any sense to you?' Jo asked Maria, before turning to her father. 'Right, you, a few rules while we're here. Number one: no moaning. Number two: no moaning and number three . . .'

'All right, all right. "No moaning." I get it.'

'Good,' Jo said firmly. She looked around and couldn't believe she was in New York. The fashion capital of the world. She wanted to soak up every minute of being here, not listen to her dad bang on incessantly about his opinion of the place.

Jo, Maria and Mick had flown from the UK that morning, courtesy of *Star Maker*. Mick had been such a hit with the public both in the UK and the US that his performance at the auditions had become one of the most watched videos on YouTube. He was now being stopped in the street and asked to re-enact his infamous robber baron line. Jo hadn't bothered to impart on Catherine how odd their own few weeks had been. Catherine might be off in the States and be on track to becoming a star, but back home Mick was the one who thought he was famous.

The bellboy helped them to their room with their cases and Maria, who had been to New York before and knew that her dad would be utterly flustered with the whole process of tipping, paid him ten dollars, refusing to tell Mick how much she had handed over. Jo knew she was right to do so, they'd only have to listen to a speech about how much someone should be paid for carrying a few cases up the stairs.

'So what happens now?' Mick said, as soon as the bellboy had gone.

'We're being picked up here . . .' Jo looked at her watch, '. . . flipping heck, in ten minutes out front, to go meet whoever we're seeing from *Star Maker*.'

Mick smiled proudly. 'We're going to be proper famous. Good eh?'

'No, we're not. It's not about us, we're just the freak show that was glad of a free flight,' Jo said. Her father was proving even more of a pain in the arse as a minor celeb than he was as her run-of-the-mill dad.

Jo's phone began to ring again, she hoped it wasn't Catherine – she didn't want to have to lie to her again. The number was a Manchester one, it wasn't Claire's – poor Claire had had to stay at home because Paul was working away and children under ten weren't allowed at the live finals. Jo studied the number and then realised who it was. She'd been waiting for a call back from the hospital. 'Sorry, just need to get some reception somewhere.' Jo walked out of the hotel room and shut the door behind her.

Ever since her last meeting with her mother the idea that her father wasn't being entirely truthful about his illness had been niggling Jo. She didn't even want to admit to herself that he might be being dishonest, so she called the hospital and explained to a nurse there that they were having problems getting their father to accept their support, to the point where he wouldn't even tell them what sort of cancer he had. The nurse had said that she would find out what she could and call her back. She had explained that they were bound by patient confidentiality but that she was prepared to see what she could do, as Jo was a relative and had sounded so upset.

'Hello,' Jo said.

'Hi, Jo, it's Louise Roper, I'm a sister at Christie's Hospital.'

'Oh, hi.' Jo said, feeling suddenly nervous.

'I'm just calling back because I've been looking up

information on your father and we haven't a patient registered with us under the name of Michael Reilly.' Jo felt sick. 'I've searched the archives but there isn't anyone that matches your dad's date of birth or address details.'

'But I dropped him off there the other week,' Jo said quietly, her mind racing.

'He might have come to us for treatment but be registered with Wythenshawe or St Mary's Hospital. One of the other nurses here is looking into it for you,' the sister said. 'I would normally suggest that you just ask him, but it's such a delicate subject that I understand if you want some the facts and that your dad might not be the best person to tell you.'

'You're right. Thank you. You will let me know as soon as you find anything out, won't you?'

'Yes, of course. It might be next week though.'

'OK. Thanks for your help.' Jo pocketed the phone and thought for a moment. Should she go out and just confront her dad now and find out what the hell was going on? On the other hand, he had been confused about where he was registered when they'd spoken about it before, so maybe he was registered elsewhere. She didn't want to stir up a hornet's nest if there was a perfectly reasonable explanation. She decided that she would leave it for now and they should just try to enjoy their time in New York. Anyway, she was looking forward to surprising Catherine later and she didn't want a cloud hanging over the family when that happened.

'Come through, come through,' a voice Jo recognised was saying. She looked up to see the producer guy that they had met on Catherine's first day at Boot Camp. She tried to remember his name . . . *Will,* that was it. They were led into a huge boardroom with floor-to-ceiling windows on all sides with views over Fifth Avenue to one side and Central Park to the other. This is the life, Jo thought.

'Hello there.' Will said with a big smile when he saw Jo.

'Look at you, all big and important in New York,' Jo smiled back.

'Yep, I'm so important that I'm here to make some cups of tea for you guys while you talk to Richard.'

'Richard?' Mick's ears pricked up.

'Yes, Richard Forster. He wanted to see you all. He hasn't got long but he just needed a brief meet before tonight's show.'

Mick puffed his chest out like the man of great importance that he'd like everyone to think he was. 'Well, that's only right.'

'What's the meeting about?' Jo asked.

Maria was standing at the window looking down at the street below. 'Look at all the people, like little ants.'

'Earth to Maria,' Jo grabbed her sister and sat her in a chair next to their dad who was perched at the boardroom table.

'Richard will fill you in when he gets here. Tea, coffee, soda?'

'Ha! Soda. You've gone native already,' Jo laughed.

The door opened and Richard Forster walked in. 'So, guys, glad you could make it; you've been making a great impression on the public, Mick . . .' he leaned across and shook Mick's hand.

Mick looked pleased as punch that he was being treated

to a manly handshake. He's such a bag of wind, Jo thought. One sniff of praise from Richard Forster and Mick's protestations were out of the window. If Mick were a dog he would have rolled over to have his belly tickled by now.

'We're just waiting for one other person and then we can begin,' Richard said, looking at his watch. Jo wondered who this person could be. A moment later her question was answered. The door opened and standing there was the last person that Jo expected.

'Hello, everyone,' Karen said with a smile.

Chapter 17

Catherine and the other twenty-three contestants had spent the afternoon rehearsing at the Chelsea Pier studios where tonight's first live final was to take place. Earlier that day she had stood on the stage where she would sing in front of millions of people, wearing a Juicy Couture tracksuit that a stylist had thrown her into, with her hair in rollers. Catherine had struggled through the first part of the song and was nervous that she was going to mess up tonight. She also knew that the full enormity of what she was about to do hadn't dawned on her yet and was hoping she wouldn't go to pieces as she stepped out in front of the studio audience this evening. Each act would perform once and by now everyone had rehearsed except Star.

'Where is she?' Kim asked, after she had finished her rendition of 'Crying'. Kim had complained to Catherine when she was given this song to sing, but she quickly realised that it suited her voice and her practice run this afternoon had been extremely well received.

'I haven't seen her since this morning,' Catherine said, looking around. In the corner of the studio Catherine saw Andy standing talking to one of the technicians. She couldn't believe that they had managed to avoid one another for two weeks. She had seen him around and watched out for the type of behaviour that Jason said he was known for, but she hadn't witnessed any. On the other hand, Jesse – it was widely rumoured – was working his way through the American girls and the crew from both sides of the Atlantic. Catherine had thought that Jesse had his eye on Star, but it seemed he had his eye on everyone. Andy saw Catherine catch his eye and waved. She waved back, feeling a little bit silly in her rollers. He walked over and Catherine felt nervous and embarrassed. Nervous because despite what he had done, she still quite liked him and embarrassed because of the way she had spoken to him in the back of the car in London.

Andy smiled shyly at Catherine, 'So then . . .'

'So then . . .'

'How's everything? We've all been so busy that I've hardly seen you . . .'

'Yes, it's been great. You know, just knackering. . . And I've got new hair and teeth.' Catherine tapped her front teeth with her finger.

'Very nice.'

'Oh and new bones . . .' She pointed at her clavicles.

'I've noticed that, you need to eat some more. Is it nerves?'

'Nerves and Nicole Richie's diet. Antonia thinks I "look amazing!"'

Andy rummaged in his pocket and produced a Hershey Bar. Catherine hadn't seen any chocolate for weeks. Andy passed it to her as if he was smuggling drugs. She looked around and, checking that no one was watching, greedily stuffed it into her mouth. 'That tastes so good,' she said, with her mouth full. 'Thank you.'

'No problem.'

They stood in silence for a moment, Catherine trying

to swallow the chocolate as quickly as possible and Andy looking like he was trying to find the right words to say.

'Can I just say that I'm really, really sorry about everything that happened in London . . .' Andy blurted.

'You don't have to apologise again,' Catherine said, but was secretly glad that he had. That he hadn't just forgotten about upsetting her as soon as it had happened.

Andy bit his top lip as if he was working out whether what he was about to say was social suicide. 'Oh God, listen, I'm going to say something and if you say no, fine, but I'm just going to say it. Let's go out tonight, please, after the show? I can get them to let you go out for a few hours, I know I can. And we can go wherever you want. And I think we'll have a great time because I think you're great . . .' Andy tripped over his words.

Catherine was stunned. He seemed genuine, but maybe this is why he was so successful in his Lothario ways, because he didn't look like the sort that chatted everyone up. And she did have firm evidence that she couldn't trust him one hundred per cent. She didn't know what to do, she knew she was letting her defences down, but she couldn't help it – she liked Andy.

'You think I'm *great?*' Catherine asked, embarrassed.

'Yes, well, I did . . . sorry that came out wrong, I do. And I know you don't think much of me but I just want to have chance to go out with you, before everyone knows who you are and I know I've left it a bit late and everyone will know you once they see the show tonight but . . .' Andy was getting redder and redder '. . . I never say things like this, and I can't believe I am, so will you?' Andy looked exhausted as he came to the end of his sentence.

Catherine didn't know what to think. Andy *appeared* so honest, she didn't know what to believe. Catherine thought for a moment, one thing she was sure of was that if she didn't go she'd never know.

'Yeah, go on then. I will,' she smiled.

'Oh, that's great,' Andy seemed utterly relieved.

'But only because you gave me chocolate.'

Andy looked as though he seriously thought this was the reason and when he realised that Catherine was joking he relaxed and laughed, 'Oh right, yes. You just want me for my confectionery.'

Andy put his hand to his earpiece. 'Listen, I've got to go. Star's acting up and we need to get her out to rehearse. I'll see you later, yeah?'

'Yes,' Catherine said and then plucked up the courage to add, 'I'm looking forward to it.' But Andy had already dashed off.

Jo was sitting with Maria in a food hall somewhere off Fifth Avenue, waiting for their father to return with the McDonald's that he had set off in search of over fifteen minutes ago. They could have gone anywhere Jo thought, had any manner of food, but Mick wanted a Maccy D's. He was such a culture vulture.

'Yes, it's us!' Jo shouted at a teenager who was pointing a mobile phone at them. She couldn't believe that this was happening here as well as back home in Britain.

'Where's your dad? He's nuts!' the spotty oik asked.

'With your mum, probably,' Jo shot back. 'Dickhead,' she said under her breath.

'Where is our "nuts" dad? That is a very good question,'

Maria asked, from behind her Gucci knock-off shades. 'I should have known it would be like this, New York is bedlam at the best of times, never mind when you're famous.'

Jo held her nose and did an impression of a tannoy announcement. 'Is there a deluded orange air hostess in the building? Deluded orange air hostess? Thank you!'

'I'm not an air hostess. I'm a member of cabin crew and I'm not bloody orange. This is Fake Bake, you dimwit.' She pointed at her fake-tanned arms. 'Victoria Beckham uses it.' She threw her hair back dramatically as if to make a point.

'What, your famous mate Victoria Beckham?'

'I'm not stooping to your level,' Maria said.

'You were already there.' Jo smiled sweetly, she loved the smallest of victories where Maria was concerned.

'Look!' Maria said nodding over at the McDonald's counter where a crowd was gathering.

'What? People, Maria, you've seen people before, haven't you?' Jo asked.

'They're not just people, they're people *surrounding* Dad.'

Jo jumped up. Maria was right. 'Oh shit. I bet he's loving that.'

A few moments later the crowd parted and Mick practically skipped towards them. 'Where's the food?' Jo asked looking at her empty-handed father.

'He's got someone following him,' Maria said. Two young Goths were trailing after Mick with *Sesame Street* puppet bags slung on their backs, stripy over the knee socks and huge bovver boots.

'Don't panic, girls, the food's here. These two lovely punk rockers offered to help.'

Jo groaned as the girls giggled at being mislabelled.

'Can we have our picture now please?'

'Certainly can!' Mick enthused. The girls put the tray down and one handed her phone to Jo to do the honours.

Mick put his arms around his fans. 'Say Robber Baron!' he grinned.

Jo turned to Maria. 'Oh God he's making up his own catchphrase!'

'He's like Timmy Mallett,' Maria said, pulling her shades down to fully inspect what was going on, 'he'll be writing a novelty song next.'

The girls thanked Mick and then wandered off, looking at their phones and giggling, while Jo watched her dad doing some odd pointing thing – jabbing two fingers after the girls.

'What's with the fingers, Dad?'

'I saw Bill Murray do it on a chat show in the eighties. Always thought it looked good, but needed a bit of celebrity gravitas to pull it off.'

'You're not famous, Dad.' Jo said pointedly, as a group of young girls approached.

'Excuse me, are you the family from . . .'

Mick's eyes lit up. 'See!' he grimaced at Jo.

'Yes we are. Now hop it,' Maria said.

Jo burst out laughing. Mick tucked into his McDonald's.

'So . . . one big happy family then, that'll be nice.' Jo said, referring to the meeting they'd just had. Richard Forster had suggested to Mick and Karen that they appear together tonight at the live finals and be a 'united front' for Catherine, he thought it would look 'appropriate'. So that was what the free trip was about. He said that they were not informing Catherine of any of this because at the moment they didn't want to put her off her performance.

Then the *Star Maker* team would feed this news to the papers and give them the story that Catherine's family were all there for her. Jo couldn't believe that anyone had convinced her mother to do this; there had to be more to it than a free trip to New York with her estranged family.

Karen, who had said that she needed a few minutes before she joined them for lunch, walked towards them swinging a turquoise Tiffany bag. 'Oh look, she's *so* skint,' Jo said. Karen was always complaining about her lack of funds.

'She looks like Jackie Collins in that suit,' Mick said wistfully.

'She looks like Joan Collins in *The Bitch*,' Jo said under her breath.

'I heard that, Joanna,' Mick gave his daughter a stern look.

Karen sat down in the chair next to Jo and waved the bag in her daughters' faces. 'Tiffany's!' she exclaimed. She pulled out a box and opened it. It was a pair of Elsa Peretti earrings that Jo had coveted for years. 'One for Maria,' she said passing the box to her daughter, 'one for Jo,' she slipped a box to Jo, 'and one for me.'

Jo opened the box. If anyone else had given her these earrings as a present she would have yelped with joy. 'You can't afford these.'

'You could show a bit of gratitude, Joanna,' Karen huffed.

'What about Catherine and Claire?' Jo asked pointedly.

'Why don't I just buy everyone in New York something from Tiffany's while I'm at it?' her mother snapped.

'I only meant your other two daughters,' Jo said coolly, placing the box to one side. 'So what else did Richard Forster say to you?'

Maria and Jo hadn't stayed for all of the meeting. The

production team were keen to talk to Mick and Karen on their own and Jo and Maria decided to leave them to it. It was dull and they didn't want to have to sit around while their mother planned to be fake and Mick's mind went into lala mode and he thought that he and Karen were finally getting back together just because some TV bods wanted them in the same studio.

'They had a few ideas—' Mick said.

'That didn't come to much,' Karen spoke over him quickly. 'So we just had a nice chat and left, didn't we, Mick?'

'Yes, we did,' Mick nodded. He seemed entranced to simply have his name uttered by his ex-wife.

'Right,' Jo said, throwing her half-eaten burger back into its container; she didn't feel particularly hungry. She knew that neither her mum nor dad was telling the truth but she just couldn't be bothered to dig any more. 'Maria, fancy a spot of window shopping?'

'Yep.'

Jo looked at the Tiffany box on the table. She quickly weighed up what to do. Her mother was an arse who thought she could buy affection if she ever had the money or the inclination; on the other hand, the earrings were exceptionally pretty. Jo picked up the box. 'Thanks for the earrings . . . Karen . . .'

'It's mother to you,' Karen said pointedly.

'Tell yourself whatever you need to hear . . . but it's not.' Jo placed the box in front of her mother. 'And as lovely as they are, if I want some I'll buy them myself. Come on, Maria.'

Maria looked at Jo, then pocketed her Tiffany box and followed her sister out of the food hall.

Chapter 18

The twenty-four *Star Maker* finalists – twelve men and woman under twenty-five and twelve men and women over twenty-five – were standing in the wings waiting for Tom Sorenson to announce their name and for their chance to take the stage. The twelve British contestants were to sing tonight, the twelve Americans the following evening and then two people would be voted off. This was to happen each week until there were six left and then it would go to one show a week.

Catherine was wearing a one-shouldered metallic blue top, Seven for All Mankind jeans which the stylist had assured her was like 'having an ass-lift' and some Stella McCartney wedges, which were surprisingly comfortable to walk in. Her hair was pinned to one side at the front and curled down her back and her eye make-up was smoky blacks and greys. She had seen her reflection and barely recognised herself, especially when she smiled and was almost dazzled by her sparkling teeth. Everyone else was equally groomed. Kim had her hair dyed purple, something which she hadn't liked at first but was now quite pleased with and Star had her long flowing curly hair pinned up in a gravity-defying beehive. She was wearing a large sequinned Christopher Kane shift dress and six-inch heeled gladiator sandals; she looked great but she was in a mess.

She had been pulled into rehearsal and she was still evidently upset. She was taken onto the stage by one of the vocal coaches and asked to sing her song. Star had begun to sing 'Silent All These Years' by Tori Amos, the song she had been allotted earlier in the week, but the band seemed to know nothing of it, they had 'That Old Devil Called Love Again'. This puzzled the other contestants. The song was way too deep for a soprano like Star, and the fact that the song had been changed at the last minute and everyone was acting as if Star should know this had seemed very strange to Catherine. There had been none of the self-confidence that Catherine had come to expect from Star today, she was a wreck. She had tried to speak to her to ask her if there was anything she could do but Star had cold-shouldered her again.

The over-twenty-five women had now all been called and the last of the over-twenty-five men were filing out onto the stage to rapturous applause. Catherine looked at Kim and Kim grabbed her hand. 'Good luck,' she whispered.

'Catherine Reilly!' Tom shouted and Catherine walked out onto the stage. The lights were blinding, the applause deafening and the walk to the stalls where they were to sit for the duration of the show seemed a mile. Catherine looked around, there were people holding placards with her face on it. How weird was that? She could hear people screaming her name. Catherine took her seat and looked at the judges; Cherie was dressed like Cruella De Vil, Carrie was looking sweetly pretty next to her, Lionel looked like a mad professor and Richard was sitting back in his chair wearing an open-neck shirt with a black suit and a tan.

He caught Catherine's eye and then looked behind him. She furrowed her brow, was he trying to tell her something? She looked into the crowd and there, sitting behind the judges, was Jo, Maria her dad . . . and her mum. She was so excited to see her family, but what on earth was her mother doing here? Jo waved as if she was trying to shake her arm off. Maria jumped up and shouted, Mick pulled up his jumper to reveal a T-shirt with Catherine's face on it and her mum simply raised her hand and waggled her fingers as if she was the lady of the manor.

Jo was mouthing something, Catherine studied her sister and worked out that she was saying, 'We wanted to surprise you. Sorry about Mum.'

Catherine winked at Jo. She couldn't believe they were here and she certainly couldn't believe Jo had managed to keep quiet about it. Jo had been texting Catherine non-stop all day, pretending to be gearing up to watch the final on the TV.

The rest of the contestants came to the stage and then Richard Forster stood up and welcomed everyone on both sides of the Atlantic to the new series of *Star Maker*. Catherine nearly had to pinch herself, she couldn't believe she was actually onstage. 'I genuinely believe that this has been a great idea of mine this year . . .' he said with a smile, as the crowd jeered his egomania in a pantomime fashion. 'Seriously,' he continued, 'this year, bringing the best of British and the best of US talent together has been a real success. It's upped the ante. Everyone wants to win.'

He made it sound as if it had been constantly competitive behind the scenes, whereas they saw so little of each other when they were rehearsing that it really didn't feel that way. Being here on the stage now she knew that the competition was definitely on. The pressure in the room was immense.

'OK, Cherie, would you like to start?'

'Thank you, Richard,' Cherie said, not looking at her husband.

'They've had a bust up,' Kim whispered. 'Jesse said he heard them arguing earlier.'

Catherine quickly looked at Kim, who nodded knowledgably.

'My first act is . . . Jamie.' Jamie was a thirty-five-year-old father of two from Scotland whose wife had left him. He had a lot of support and a lot of public sympathy. He wasn't, however, a very good singer. He belted out 'You're the Voice' by John Farnham and received rapturous applause. Cherie could barely be heard over the crowd, 'That was amazing, and you are amazing. The public love you and you've got a long career ahead of you.' More cheers went up from the crowd. Catherine looked at Jo who was pretending to stick her fingers down her throat.

'That was truly inspirational,' Carrie said. Jo pretended to gag again, Maria jabbed her in the ribs.

'I think that you have definitely captured the public imagination,' Lionel said, 'but that song choice didn't really do it for me.'

Richard was staring at his panel of judges as if they were all stark-raving mad. 'Are you all tone deaf?' he asked, before turning to the hapless Jamie. 'I'm sorry, Jamie, you're a nice guy but you look like an accountant and you sound like a constipated club singer.'

There were boos and jeers from the crowd. Catherine looked at Jo who was falling about laughing, it made her want to laugh too, but she knew the camera would pan on to her and she would look like the cruellest person ever, so she bit the inside of her cheek until the urge to yelp with pain was greater than the urge to laugh. Jamie shuffled back to his seat deflated. It didn't matter what the other judges said, it was Richard Forster's opinion that mattered. Catherine felt nauseous; she was going to have to face this grilling very soon.

Catherine fell into something of a trance as different singers went up and received lavish praise or cruel criticism, rarely anything in between. When her name was finally announced she looked up as if there had been some mistake. She walked towards the microphone, her legs trembling like a baby deer's, and looked out at the audience. Seeing her dad and Jo and Maria made her proud, but seeing her mum gave her such a confusing mix of pride and disdain that all she wanted to do was prove that she was good enough. Good enough to be here, good enough not to be left behind and ignored. The familiar first bars of the song began to play and Catherine grabbed the microphone and began to follow the well-choreographed routine that she had been over a hundred times this week. But now, instead of feeling like it was something that she had learnt, she felt that it was something that was hers. She moved around the stage, singing and dancing with all of her heart. The song was over before she had time to be nervous and as she stopped and looked out at the cheering crowd and the equally cheering judges, Catherine felt her heart thumping wildly in her chest.

'That was amazing, Catherine,' Richard was saying, though he was finding it difficult to be heard. 'It's a tired phrase, but I'm going to use it anyway, because you really did make that song your own.'

Catherine looked to the other judges, they all heaped praise on her and Catherine looked out at the crowd and her mum was on her feet clapping, along with her dad and her sisters. Gone was Karen's toodle-pip wave, she looked genuinely proud of her daughter. Catherine walked back to her seat unable to believe how well her song had been received.

When it was Kim's turn to sing, she gave a pitch-perfect performance and was praised accordingly. The final act of the evening was Star. Catherine watched her roommate walk nervously to the microphone. Here was the girl that only a few weeks ago Catherine would have put all her money on to win, approaching the microphone as if it was the last thing in the world she wanted to do. What had happened to her? Catherine wondered. Maybe she would come to life as soon as she started singing, just as Catherine had.

The music began to play and Star tried her absolute best to make the song work for her, but it just didn't match her voice. Catherine shifted uncomfortably in her seat. Star was dying in front of millions of people and Richard Forster, who was ultimately responsible for her song choice, was looking at her blankly as if he didn't care what happened to her. She was in his category, he should care, Catherine thought. But he made money whatever happened: it was his show.

Star finished the song. Richard spoke, and for the first

time he was able to be heard over the less-than-enthusiastic response from the audience. 'You've had a tough week, Star, but I think you brought some of it on yourself.' Star looked at the ground and a tear plopped to the floor.

'Brought what on herself?' Cherie demanded angrily. 'You're her mentor, you should have chosen a better song. You changed the song at the last minute. Why Richard?'

'Well, Star, my good lady wife is on your side. That's always good to know.' Richard sat back and folded his arms.

'Cherie's right, Richard, you've let her down with the song choice,' Carrie said, shaking her head.

'Look, she's a soprano, I thought we'd mix it up a little,' Richard shrugged.

'Oh, you mixed it up all right, you changed the song at the last minute. How's that for mixing it up?' Cherie threw back at him.

Something serious must have gone on behind the scenes, that much Catherine knew, but what? Star wasn't saying, Richard certainly wasn't saying. Was he hoping to have Star voted out by giving her a terrible song choice, or looking for the sympathy vote by changing her song at the last minute?

'Would you like to say anything, Star?' Carrie asked.

Star couldn't look at her mentor who was sitting with his arms folded staring at her as if he was daring her to level something at him. 'I just think I let myself down. That's all.'

Kim looked at Catherine, they were both thinking the same thing; what on earth was going on?

* * *

Catherine was having her make-up reapplied by a young make-up artist that she hadn't met before. There were so many people that worked on the show. She had hoped there would be time to see her family, but the contestants had been whisked backstage and told that they couldn't see anyone until the show was over. 'I've been really looking forward to meeting you,' the young woman said, as she swept a blusher brush over Catherine's cheeks.

'Me?' Catherine had asked looking around, half expecting Mariah Carey to be stood behind her.

'Your family were so fun on the TV.'

'Oh, you saw it?' Catherine had said, feeling panic-stricken, but of course everyone had seen her family, it was just that she'd been in the *Star Maker* bubble and hadn't been exposed to the impact her dad's performance had had.

'Everyone saw it. You were great and they were great. My God, you'd have your own show on MTV if you lived in the States,' the woman said, sitting Catherine down and studying her face.

The Reillys? Bloody hell, Catherine thought; like *The Osbornes*, but more dysfunctional.

The make-up artist laughed as she began to apply foundation to Catherine's face with graceful strokes '. . . And then your dad called Richard a robber baron. And I'm there with all my girlfriends and we're like, "What's a robber baron?"'

'I was like "What's a robber baron?" too,' Catherine admitted.

'We just *loved* him!'

Catherine didn't know how to respond. No one ever said they loved her dad. Maybe his larger-than-life characteristics, both good and bad, were perfect for TV. They just weren't very helpful in everyday life. 'He's in the audience. I haven't had chance to talk to them yet.'

'Right, Catherine, you OK?' Richard Forster poked his head around the dressing-room door.

Catherine nodded. 'You've got ten minutes with Jason now. He'll just be asking you about New York and how you feel about getting this far, the usual guff,' Richard said.

A runner scurried in front of Catherine, heading towards Richard with a mobile phone. 'Manny Rowntree.' The girl announced. Manny Rowntree was the best known and most ruthless PR man in show business. Anyone with any dirt to dish, or dirt they didn't want dishing went to him. He was at least as famous as his clients.

Richard took the call and listened to what the PR guru had to say. He looked over at Catherine. He flipped the phone shut, 'Could I have a moment alone with Catherine?'

The make-up artist left and Catherine sat in the chair feeling very worried. Richard walked towards her and leaned against the wall. 'The call I've just taken was from Manny Rowntree. You know your family are here . . .'

'Yes, I can't wait to see them . . .'

'We flew them over.'

'Thank you, I really appreciate it.'

'No need to thank me. They've been a great success and they're very amenable.'

Catherine furrowed her brow; she didn't like the sound of 'amenable'.

'The *News of the World* is running a story tomorrow. It's about your dad's battle with cancer. One of the weekly magazines has picked it up over here as well. It might not be what you want, but it's what they want and I think that you need to think about – as I've said before – how this can benefit you.'

Catherine felt sucker punched. 'No! They can't. How could they know something like that? They can't just print something like that without his permission, that's illegal.'

'They've got his permission. They've got both their permission.'

Catherine felt the words swim past her. 'Both who?'

'Your mum and dad. It was your mother's idea.'

Catherine wanted to be sick. How could this be happening? How could her mother do something like this and how could her father agree to it? And what were they doing even speaking to one another?

'So, I think now would be a good time to think about how you handle it. I know you think that I'm being cynical, but I'm a realist. Your father is ill. He's about to tell the country himself. So what do you want to do?'

'I want to be sick,' Catherine said and ran out of the studio, making it to the sink in the ladies' toilets just in time.

Andy was excited about his date tonight. Or at least he thought he could call it a date. Maybe Catherine thought that they were going out as friends? No, he was being stupid. He had found out somewhere really impressive to take her, courtesy of Richard Forster, and he knew that she would be on a high after her performance and having sailed through to the following week. While Andy was waiting for Jason to finish interviewing the contestant who had been voted out this week, a lady called Jodie from the over-twenty-five category, he saw Catherine come offstage.

'Hi,' he smiled, 'well done.'

'Thank you.' Catherine smiled her twinkly smile. 'Listen, Andy,' she said, suddenly serious, 'I'm really sorry but I won't be able to come out tonight. My family are here and there's something that my mum and dad have done that I really need to talk to them about . . .'

Andy was crushed. He could tell she was making excuses. Tonight had been life-changing for all of the contestants, he could tell just from their faces after they had performed. Why would she want to go out with someone like him now?

'Oh God, don't worry. It was just a drink. We can go for one any time. We don't even have to go for one,' he gabbled, 'we're both busy.'

'Yes, we are.' Did she seem happy? Disappointed? Andy couldn't tell. 'Anyway, I'll just see you tomorrow or whenever,' Catherine said, walking off.

'Yep. Whenever,' Andy said. He watched her walk away, wondering if he'd just been blown out for good. Of course he had, he thought, he was way too heavy-handed earlier when he told Catherine how much he liked her.

'Come on, Andy . . .' Jason came past in a flurry of activity, shaking him from his thoughts. '. . . that's the first nobody interviewed and out of the competition,' he waved his hand in the direction of Catherine as she disappeared into the wings. 'No doubt she'll be next.'

'No she won't. She's too good,' Andy said adamantly.

'Tell yourself whatever you need to hear. No one's bothered about her.' Jason said, waltzing off without waiting for Andy to follow.

Chapter 19

The first live final had come to a close and the obnoxious Star girl that Catherine had told Jo all about had been saved by the public. Jo couldn't understand why, she had looked like an overmedicated mental patient and she had sung like a yodelling goat herder. The first person to be voted off *Star Maker: Transatlantic* was Jody, a thirty-two-year-old woman from Reading. Poor sod, Jo thought, she just didn't have the regional support or the sympathy vote or the outstanding talent that the other British contestants had.

Jo was having a brilliant time. She was sure she already spotted Brittany Murphy and Bruce Willis in the audience and now she was on the look out for someone young, male and famous to get a snog out of, just to make her friends back home pea green with envy. But first she needed to see Catherine. Her sister had been whisked away as soon as her performance ended and as the crowd now dispersed, Jo was wondering when she was going to appear.

'Catherine looked stunning, didn't she?'

Karen was sending a long-winded text, probably to the nob, Jo thought. She wondered what Jay thought of his partner coming all the way to New York with her family, but then decided not to ask because the answer, whatever it happened to be, would rile her.

'She looked like you,' Mick said to Karen.

'Oh, shut up, Dad, you sound like a sap,' Jo hissed.

'I'll say what I like, Joanna. Anyway, I thought she was cracking tonight, our Catherine. Really cracking.'

'That's good to hear,' Jo said, relieved that her dad was pleased for Catherine.

'Catherine!' Jo jumped up and down in her seat, seeing her sister walk onto the stage.

Catherine waved and began to run over, but realising she couldn't run in her shoes, took them off and continued barefoot.

'I can't believe you're here!' Catherine was evidently delighted.

Jo couldn't believe she'd managed to keep it quiet, as soon as they found out they were coming she had wanted to blurt it out.

Catherine hugged Maria and then gave her dad a quick hug and her mum a polite kiss on the cheek. 'So, how did you like tonight?' Catherine asked.

Jo noticed that her sister didn't seem to be able to look her parents in the eye.

'It was ace. And Richard Forster is about sixty and has had loads of surgery, which I would have put money on, but they put loads of make-up on him and he pretends to be in his early fifties in interviews, the saddo.'

'You've seen him before.'

'Not from two feet away . . . So, how are you?'

Catherine took a deep breath and looked at her mum and dad. 'I was all right . . . until someone told me about what you two have done.'

Jo glanced at Maria, she didn't seem to know what was going on either.

Jo was sitting on the flight back to the UK still ignoring her parents. She couldn't believe that they had stooped so low. Karen had refused to talk to her daughters about her reasons for agreeing to participate in the story, but Jo knew already knew what it was: money. She had still yet to see a copy of the offending article; she wasn't sure she even wanted to.

Maria was peering over the top of the seats, looking as if she was trying to work out if she recognised someone. 'Jenny?' she asked quietly. When she didn't get any response from the air stewardess behind them she tried again a little louder. 'Jenny?'

The woman looked up and nearly dropped her coffee. 'Oh my God, Maria. It's you! We were just talking about you.'

She looked at Karen and Mick and then started acting in the same way Maria had acted when she met Richard Forster for the first time, as if they were famous. 'Oh hi! Great to meet you both. Mr Reilly, we're all really sorry about your . . .' she searched for the word, finally settling on, 'trouble.'

'I'm fine,' Mick said with a wave. 'Nothing a good strong whisky wouldn't help with.' Mick laughed.

'Oh, of course, of course.' Jenny forgot about the woman she was serving and poured Mick a large whisky.

'Lovely,' he said. 'Have you any more of them snack things love, I'm half starved.'

'Oh, of course,' Jenny said, firing packet after packet of crispy snacks at Mick. Jo looked at Maria, who was evidently as bemused as she was. 'And Mrs Reilly?'

'It's Ms White,' Karen said. 'I'll have a Bloody Mary, thanks.'

Maria leant forward and put her hand on Jenny's arm. 'Have you read the paper? Is that what all this is about?'

'Yes. We've all read it. I've got it at the middle station, shall I get it?'

Jo swallowed hard, did she want to see it?

'Please,' Maria said nervously. 'We couldn't get it in New York.'

They all sat in silence as Jenny went off to fetch the paper. Jo didn't want to speak. She just wanted to kill both her parents.

Jenny handed the paper to Maria. 'You're so brave,' she said to Mick, a lump in her throat.

Mick nodded without meeting her eye and tried to grab the paper from Maria.

'*Star Maker* Finalist's Brave Dad,' Maria began to read. There was a picture of Mick, sitting in a chair, looking like he had just been instructed to look as miserable as possible, with Karen standing behind him with one hand on his shoulder. 'The tears behind the laughter . . .' Maria continued.

Jo looked at her parents, they were truly unbelievable, 'The tears behind the laughter?' she asked.

'What?' Mick asked.

'And look at this,' Jo pointed at the picture. 'This makes out like she's your rock!' Jo jabbed the paper in the direction of her dad.

Karen leaned forward in her seat. 'Right, listen to me. Now that this is in the paper, the whole bloody country will vote for our Cath and me and your dad have made a bit of money and might I remind you that your father is poorly,' Karen said snottily.

'That's not what you said when I met you in Chorlton, is it, Mum?'

Mick looked out of the window. He didn't want any confrontation, Jo could tell.

'What did she say?' Maria asked.

Jo weighed up whether she should say something or not; she had nothing to lose.

'She said she thought he was faking it.'

Mick stood up, knocking his drink over. 'I'm sitting somewhere else. I can't be doing with you lot,' he said angrily. As he shuffled his way out of his seat, Jo heard a young boy behind them say, 'Dad, that's that man off the telly!'

Jo put her head back and closed her eyes. She didn't want to see or hear anything more about her father and his new role in the public eye.

When Catherine had seen her family sitting together in the audience she had been so excited, imagining that they would spend time together that week and hoping that her mum might give some of her time to her daughters. But as soon as she found out about her parents' new media profile Catherine was happy to discover that they were on the first flight back to the UK the following day. That morning Catherine had checked the internet, something she had been avoiding, but was drawn online by a morbid curiosity. She put *Star Maker* into the search engine and then typed Mick and article after article came up on the screen about her father and his illness, all taken from the interview that her parents had given. How had Mick gone from not wanting to tell anyone to wanting to tell the world? The only answer that Catherine could come up with was, her mother. One good thing had come out of it though – it let Catherine see that her father was able to surround himself with people to look after him and he really didn't need her help.

Catherine decided she needed a walk. Kim had gone for a run and Star was still in bed, so she slid out of the room and walked over to Central Park and sat on the bench by the John Lennon memorial. It was a beautiful warm summer day, the first time Catherine had had some unscheduled time alone in New York.

'You were great!' a girl said to Catherine as she skated by.

It took Catherine a moment to realise she was talking to her. 'Thank you.'

'Give your dad my best,' the girl shouted over her shoulder, 'he's a brave guy.'

God, was it really breaking news here already? Did people really care about her father's illness? And were they really bothered? Catherine couldn't be sure, one thing she did know was that it felt very odd that all of this was happening to her.

Catherine threw her head back and breathed in deeply. It was great to have a day off. Because the Americans were performing later today, the UK finalists had a rare break. There were no runs to be undertaken or scales to be practised. They just had to be styled and made up for this afternoon and then when the show was over they could even go out into New York they had been informed, as long as they went to one of the designated, *Star Maker*-approved bars or clubs.

'Hi.' Catherine looked up. Andy was standing in front of her eating an ice cream. 'How are you?'

'I'm good,' she said. She didn't know how to be with Andy, one minute he seemed to be into her, the next he didn't. Last night he had seemed almost relieved that she couldn't go out with him. Then she had seen him chatting to some of the American contestants and one of them hugging him, and he hadn't seemed too keen to shake her off.

'Is it OK if I sit down?' Andy asked. Catherine shuffled up to make room for him.

'It's hard to believe we're here, isn't it?' Andy said, looking at the Imagine memorial; a large round stone engraving on the ground in front of them.

'I know. I've read about this place because my dad used to like the Beatles when we were younger.' Mick had liked lots of things when Catherine was younger: music, football, enjoying himself. But over the past decade he had seemed to have forgotten about his interests and concentrated on everything that blighted him.

'Why would you shoot someone because you liked them?' Andy said, referring to John Lennon's killer.

'Because you wanted to be famous,' Catherine said and then looked at Andy, who looked slightly worried by her comment. 'Oh God, don't think that I think like that about fame. I think the person that shot John Lennon was sick and thought that he could be revered through shooting someone famous. Actually, I think fame is a load of cobblers.'

Andy laughed. 'That's good to hear, but I think you might be on the wrong show, then.'

'I know. I'm the original lady who protests too much. Don't want to be famous? Then don't go on *Star Maker*. I know. Got it in one.'

They fell into comfortable silence for a few minutes, watching the people entering and leaving the park as they passed by.

'How's your dad?' Andy asked tentatively.

Catherine sighed. 'On the one hand he's all right. This, the show, all seems to have given him some focus. On the other hand I want to strangle him because he and my mum, who I really don't want to talk about, have sold their half-made-up sob story to the *News of the World*. So his secret is well and truly out because he not only wants to tell everyone he knows that he has cancer, but the entire country too.'

'Why would he do that?'

'God knows. Money? Attention? I really have no idea.'

Andy turned to face Catherine. 'Right, tonight. Please can we go out together? I think you need cheering up and is it OK if I don't take no for an answer?'

Catherine laughed at Andy's politeness. 'Yes, it's OK.'

'Good. Then that's settled. Straight after the show we're heading into town.'

The taxi sped through Central Park and pulled along the Upper East Side turning at the corner of Central Park and delivering Catherine and Andy into the hustle and bustle of Columbus Circle. Where they were staying, on the Upper West Side, New York seemed airy and green, and Columbus

Circle was a taste of New York madness, the sort she was used to seeing portrayed on the TV, the New York she had expected to see when her plane touched down.

As Catherine jumped out of the taxi arguing about paying and eventually insisting that Andy take a ten-dollar bill from her, Catherine looked out over the park and stopped in her tracks. The sky was blood-red as the sun set, and the hustle and bustle made Catherine feel as if she was at the centre of the universe.

'Look at that,' Catherine said to Andy.

'Apparently it's a lot more impressive from up there,' Andy said, throwing his head back and pointing to the top of the towering hotel they were about to enter. 'I've booked us a window table,' Andy said eagerly.

Now was not the best time to tell Andy that she was scared of heights, Catherine realised. They walked into the marble atrium and both gazed around. 'We look like a right pair of hicks,' Catherine said through her teeth like a ventriloquist.

'Speak for yourself, I think I bring an air of sweaty sophistication to the place,' Andy said. It was so warm that he had to pull his shirt away from his skin in order to circulate the air. Catherine could feel her heart begin to pound. She knew she was scared of heights, but it wasn't something that posed much of a problem living in Manchester where until recently – when the Hilton tower opened – the highest building could have been scaled with a step ladder.

They stepped into the lift and it began to climb at speed. Catherine had never felt anything like it. In the UK lifts didn't travel very fast, but here, where they had to contend with nearly one hundred floors, they needed to be fast and efficient. Catherine wanted to be sick. People who were scared of heights shouldn't be sealed in a metal tube and shot into the sky at ninety miles an hour, especially not on a first date when they were meant to be acting all cool, calm and collected.

The door opened and the poshest bar Catherine had ever seen in her life – and that included in films and magazines – was laid out before her. 'After you,' Andy said.

'No, after you,' Catherine squeaked.

'Are you OK?'

'Yes,' Catherine said. She wasn't. Her mouth had dried up and she felt as if the ground beneath her had been replaced by marshmallow. Andy stepped out and held the door for Catherine. She realised that she was walking as if there were giant cracks in the floor to be avoided.

'Andy Short,' Andy told the maître d', who looked at him as if he belonged somewhere less salubrious than the bar of the Mandarin Oriental.

'It's a window seat, sir,' he said, glancing at Catherine.

A window seat? Catherine thought; she was going to flip out at this rate. She grabbed the bar and walked around it, like a baby cruising along the furniture. Andy walked towards the window and Catherine followed, what she really should have said to Andy was that as she was scared of heights so this wasn't a very good idea, but she didn't want to look like she was ungrateful to him for bringing her to this swanky palace, so she persevered. As she approached the floor-to-ceiling window she tried to concentrate on the New York skyline, the amazing view over the park and the setting sun. But she couldn't stay focused. All that Catherine could think about was looking down. She knew it would be a bad idea, but she just couldn't help it. So she looked. The ground rushed up to meet her and Catherine fainted for only the second time in her life, both times in front of Andy. The last thing she remembered hearing before she hit the ground was the waiter saying, 'Aren't you one of the contestants on *Star Maker*?'

Catherine came to a few minutes later. When she looked around there was a crowd staring at her. 'What's going on?' she asked.

As she spoke, the crowd cheered.

'We thought you were out for the count!' The maître d' said, with over-the-top bonhomie.

'She looks so cute in real life,' Catherine heard someone else say. 'Like a little doll,' she heard another voice agree.'

'I do hope her father is OK, he's been so brave, I was reading about him on the internet.'

Catherine struggled to sit upright. She grabbed Andy's hand. He was kneeling at her side and she whispered in his ear, 'Please . . . get me out of here.'

'She's not very well, let's just get you back,' he said to Catherine, pulling her to her feet.

'Let me help . . .' A burly man stepped forward to help, 'I loved you last night, you rocked,' he told Catherine. Other people in the ever-increasing crowd agreed. Catherine could hear even more murmuring about her father and then she was in the lift.

'Thank you. We'll be fine from here. I just want to get her back, it's been a very busy week . . .' Andy said as the doors shut. Catherine looked at herself in the lift mirror. She was pasty white, even through her fake tan.

'What the hell just happened?' Catherine asked in amazement.

'I think you're famous.' Andy said, looking at her reflection in the mirror; they both burst into fits of laughter.

'Well, where are we going to go then, so that I don't get hounded by my adoring public?' Catherine said, pretending to be a prima donna.

Andy thought for a moment. 'I've got just the place.'

The Cobbler's Thumb was an Irish pub down a back alley, about five minutes walk from Columbus Circle, but once through the door it looked like it was a million cultural miles away from New York. Andy held the door open for Catherine and she stepped through, thinking that this was possibly the first time in her life a man had held a door open for her. When she was with her dad he always marched through first and left the door to swing violently back at her; Catherine had actually become quite good at catching it before she got smacked in the face.

Once through the door Catherine and Andy were greeted by a cacophony of fiddly-de-dee music the like of which Catherine was sure hadn't been heard in an actual Irish pub in the last thirty years. Andy looked at Catherine and raised an eyebrow.

'Come on,' she said, pulling him inside.

'Howaya?' the American barman asked in a fake Irish accent.

'Good,' Catherine answered.

'And yer man?'

Catherine looked at Andy. 'How's yer man?' she asked cheekily mimicking the barman.

'Fine.' Andy nodded, 'Grand, even.'

The barman didn't realise he was having his leg pulled.

'What's your poison?' The barman's accent was slipping, he was oscillating between Irish, American and pirate.

'He's going to say "O be sure", in a minute,' Catherine whispered to Andy.

'I'll have a pint of . . .' Andy looked at the bar.

'Guinness?' the barman offered.

'No, just lager, thanks.'

'And what can I get for the colleen?'

'Same please,' Catherine said, smiling. *Colleen?* Where was this guy from?

'We don't serve pints to ladies.'

Catherine laughed out loud. 'Really?'

'Sorry, missus, we try to keep some standards.'

Catherine looked around. The place was a dump, with bikes nailed to the walls, rows of dusty copies of *Ulysses* perched on bookshelves and a copy of the Proclamation of the Free Irish State peeling off the back of the bar.

'Of course,' Catherine nodded. 'I'll have a lager in a lady's glass, please.'

She and Andy stood in giggly silence until the barman had served them and then they retired to a booth. 'What's he on?' Andy asked.

'Oh God, he reminds me of when Dad used to drag us down to Chorlton Irish club when we were kids. My dad's parents over from Ireland, and every now and then he'd get all misty-eyed for a country he'd never lived in and we'd have to go and listen to some terrible band play "The Fields of Athenry".' Catherine laughed remembering.

'Isn't it funny how people like to pretend to be Irish?'

Andy mused. 'No other country in the world has that effect on people, does it? '

Catherine laughed. 'My sister Jo pretends to be South African sometimes.'

'Really? Why?'

It's hard to explain why Jo does a lot of things, Catherine thought. 'She just likes the accent, I think.'

Andy nodded as if this made perfect sense to him. 'It is a good shouting accent. "Release the hounds!"' he said, in a perfect South African accent.

Catherine laughed. 'That's even better than Jo's!' she said, impressed.

'Thanks, I have hidden talents,' Andy said with mock seriousness. 'So then. You're scared of heights . . . What else should I know about you before I can't speak to you any more because everyone else is trying to get a piece of you?'

Catherine thought for a moment, what else was there to know about her? 'Not a lot.'

'Tell me about your dad.' Catherine looked at Andy and could tell by his face that he thought he had made a mistake. 'That's if you want to . . .'

'He's poorly, that's all there is to it. I'd rather not talk about him, if that's OK.'

'Course, yeah. No problem. Bad idea,' Andy said quickly. 'OK, tell me about singing. What made you enter?'

Catherine began to explain and then realised that it was her dad's announcement that he had cancer that had forced her to enter the competition. She immediately felt guilty. What sort of daughter would do that? She began to tell Andy what had happened and found herself half an hour later, still sitting, sipping her drink from her lady's glass and explaining everything to Andy about her family and her role within it.

'You shouldn't feel guilty!' Andy said, 'There's nothing to feel guilty for.'

'Well, I do.'

'Is it Catholic guilt?'

'What?'

'Well, your dad's parents were Irish, just wondering if you were Catholic.'

'Sort of. We went to Catholic school and used to go to church but I only go there to sing now. Anyway it's not Catholic guilt, it's guilt guilt.'

'I think you're really hard on yourself,' Andy said gently and touched her hand. It was then that she realised she was crying. Catherine wiped her eyes.

'Sorry, you must think I'm a wreck, fainting, crying. Nice first date.'

'It's a great first date,' he smiled. 'I'm really enjoying myself.'

'This isn't very New York though, is it?' Catherine said after a while.

Andy looked around. 'No it isn't,' he said touching the bike wheel behind them.

'I've hardly seen anything of New York since we've been here, I mean I know we're here, but I could be anywhere.'

'Shall we go somewhere else?' Andy asked.

'Where?'

'Come with me.' Andy said, standing up and taking Catherine's hand.

* * *

'Where are we going?' Catherine squealed. Andy had walked her from the taxi with his hands over her eyes. Catherine could tell they were near water, there was a freshness to the air that she hadn't felt since she'd arrived in New York.

'I just wanted to show you a bit of New York but I'm rubbish at doing this blindfold thing. They always do this in the films and it looks easier,' Andy said, taking his hands away.

Catherine gasped. The Statue of Liberty was lit up on the other side of the Hudson River. The lights from the city glinted on the water.

'Wow!' Catherine sat down on one of the benches that line the Battery Park Esplanade. Andy sat next to her.

'I was trying to think where to take you, you know, a pub or club, somewhere that New York was famous for, but I thought you might get recognised again so I just thought here would be a nice idea.'

Catherine looked at Andy. What a really thoughtful thing to do, she thought.

She was just about to thank him when he turned to her. 'I think that we're both quite shy really, aren't we? I mean, I know that you get up and sing in front of people but you're like me – shy – when it comes to things like this.'

'Things like what?' Catherine looked into Andy's eyes.

'This,' he said, leaning forward and kissing her.

Catherine moved in towards him as he put his arms around her. And they sat, alone in the half-light and kissed and it was the most perfect moment that Catherine could ever remember.

Chapter 20

It had been five days since Jo and her family had returned from New York and in that time Mick had managed to become the man of the moment. Claire said it reminded her of when Eddie 'the Eagle' Edwards shot to fame. Jo didn't remember this Eddie guy but apparently he had been a hopeless ski jumper who – with true Dunkirk spirit – had represented Britain at the winter Olympics years ago and come, predictably, last. The country loved a loser and the bigger the loser the better. Well, Mick was a loser and the country had already loved him for having the David-taking-on-Goliath balls to challenge Richard Forster; now that they knew had cancer he was fast approaching national treasure status.

Mick was in the dining room. He'd been mooching around in his dressing-gown all morning. 'I don't think I need representation, thank you,' Mick said to the person on the other end of the phone. 'Good day to you.' He replaced the receiver and whistled chirpily as he entered the kitchen.

'Who was that?' Jo was sitting at the kitchen table, cutting open the sleeves of a Fair Isle cardigan that she intended to turn upside down, sew together and make into a skirt.

'Max Clifford again. I told him last time, thank you for those buns you sent and words of kindness but I'll be looking after my own public appearances.'

Max Clifford's firm had sent a basket of muffins to the house. Mick hadn't been able to work out why someone would send 'buns' and had even got Jo to go online and find out how much 'a tin of buns from London costs'. When Jo located the firm that had delivered them and told her dad the hefty price tag, Mick nearly fell over. He was evidently pleased that someone would go to the trouble of trying to court his business and to do it with buns seemed to be going the extra mile.

The portable TV was on in the corner of the room. Something on it caught Jo's attention. It was Carol McGiffin talking on *Loose Women*, 'No . . . I'm sorry but I just can't imagine under what circumstances it would be a good idea to sell your story to a newspaper about having cancer. I just can't . . .'

'But he didn't, did he?' Jackie Brambles interjected. 'He just went along to support his daughter and all this has come out.'

'Well, if he was just supporting his daughter then he should have just stayed at home and voted for her,' Carol McGiffin was adamant. There were boos from the audience.

Jackie Brambles turned to the camera, 'We are of course talking about Mick Reilly, whose hilarious appearance in support of his daughter on *Star Maker*, we have recently found out is tinged with sadness, as he has cancer . . .'

'That bloody McGuffen woman, I don't know who she thinks she is with her toy boy and her "I married Chris Evans" she does my bloody head in . . .' Mick huffed. The fact they were talking about him seemed perfectly normal to him though, oddly, Jo realised.

'Well, I have to say . . .' Jane McDonald began.

'Oh, not her, "I'd rather have a cup of tea than sex", we've heard it all before. Get back on your boat,' Mick complained to the TV.

'I like him, he's got balls and a good fighting spirit. Good on you, Mick, if you're watching, I'm rooting for you!' Jane McDonald gave a thumbs up on the screen.

'I've always liked her,' Mick said, backtracking.

'I can't believe they're talking about you on *Loose Women*,' Jo said, genuinely amazed. Even though her father had featured in a number of papers and magazines this week and the phone had barely stopped ringing with offers of personal appearance opportunities, Jo still couldn't come to terms with it. Things like this didn't happen to people like them.

'Heard anything from Mum?' Jo asked. She was half expecting her mother to be the next guest on the show.

'No,' Mick said, avoiding his daughter's eye.

'Told you.'

When they had arrived at Manchester Airport, Jo had turned to her dad as her mother had pulled her bag down from the overhead compartment and said, 'We won't see her for dust.'

Karen had jumped in a taxi and promised to call and only Jo, it seemed to her, had known not to hold her breath. Maria and Claire had both asked Jo if Karen had been in contact and Maria had even told Jo that she thought that they had all had a lovely time together. It had made Jo sad to hear this – she wished it was true but she knew it wasn't. Karen just looked after number one.

Jo's phone began to ring.

'Tell them I'm out,' Mick said. 'I'm off for a bath.'

'It's my phone, why is someone going to ring you on my phone?'

'Because,' Mick pointed at the TV, 'I'm all over the shop.'

Jo gave her father a withering look. 'That's the most accurate thing you've said in a while.'

Mick tutted and walked out of the room, the cord from his dressing-gown trailing on the floor. There was a suspicious-looking substance on the tip of it. Jo curled her lip in horror and then – seeing the tub on top of the work surface – realised it was Nutella. Her father really was a slob.

She answered the phone. 'Hello.'

'Hi, is that Joanna Reilly?'

'Speaking.'

'It's Nurse Roper from Christie's.'

Jo's stomach lurched.

'Is it your dad that's been in all the papers this week?'

'The very same.'

'Right . . . In that case, I think you might want to come down to the hospital because I really don't want to do this over the phone.'

Jo's heart fell into her boots. 'OK, tell me where to be and when.'

'Here we are standing on top of the Empire State Building with some of the finalists of *Star Maker*!' The presenter shouted excitedly. Star, Catherine and Kim and three of the over-twenty-five men were standing on the observation deck being buffeted by the wind. Catherine was finding it difficult to match the interviewer's enthusiasm after her last vertiginous experience at the top of a New York building. She had been mentally preparing herself for the experience all morning and was now performing breathing exercises while having an argument with herself that went along the lines of *What's the worst that can happen? I could climb over the projective barrier and throw myself off lemming-style, that's the worst that could happen.* This was about the thirtieth interview the *Star Maker* contestants had done this week and Catherine had been requested for each one. Not only did it mean that she was finding it difficult to concentrate on her rehearsals for this week's live show, but it also meant that resentments were beginning to surface towards Catherine. She had tried addressing it with Will and Richard but they had told her that she needed to stop complaining and get on with it. Her stock was high at the moment, thanks to the interest in her dad and her performance on the previous show.

'So, Catherine,' the interviewer thrust her microphone in Catherine's face, 'You're the hot favourite at the moment, how does that feel?'

Catherine shifted awkwardly. 'I wouldn't say that. It's very early days and there are lots of strong singers in the competition, like Kim and Star,' Catherine said amiably. Star gave her a dirty look and Kim smiled at Catherine but Catherine could sense that all the attention she was getting was irritating her.

'Well, we here at Rock Music Radio would!' the woman turned to the camera, beaming. 'And one thing I'm sure that all of the great British and American public out there is wondering . . . how's your father?'

'He's fine, thank you for asking,' Catherine said uncomfortably.

Mick was sitting in the back garden scouring the day's papers. 'Look at that picture. Do I look like that?' Mick put the paper to the side of his head and pulled a face. Jo didn't answer, she was trying to choose her words carefully, because she was so angry she wasn't sure she would be able to get the words out.

'Dad, I don't know how to say this, so I'm just going to come right out and say it.' Jo gathered herself. 'Have you got cancer?'

The colour drained from her father's face. 'What sort of bloody question is that?'

'A straight one.' Jo held her dad's gaze. 'Well?'

'Why would you ask something like that?' Mick shifted in his seat.

'Because you don't seem to be receiving any treatment, you won't talk about it and you aren't registered as having had treatment anywhere in Manchester. So I'll try again: have you got cancer?'

'Who told you that I'm not registered?'

'A nurse.'

'There's such a thing as patient confidentiality, you know.'

Jo pressed on. 'Have you got cancer?'

'I can't believe you would even think to ask me such a thing,' Mick said, unable to maintain eye contact with his daughter.

'Answer the question, Dad: have you got cancer?'

Mick curled his lip at Jo and shook his head as if bitterly disappointed with her. 'I thought I had.'

'What do you mean, "thought"?'

'I just mean that I "thought" I had. I could feel something inside me.'

'But you haven't got it, have you?'

'The doctor says I haven't, but they can be wrong, them doctors.'

Jo slumped onto the garden bench next to her father and looked out over the small lawn where they used to play as children. 'Do you know what it's been like for us thinking that you have cancer? And all this crap in the papers and all this crap with Mum . . .' Jo paused, thinking about her mother's role in this. 'She knew, she told me she thought you were lying.'

'She didn't!' Mick sounded panic-stricken. 'She didn't, she thinks I'm sick, she doesn't think I'm a liar.'

Was that it? Was that what all of this boiled down to? That he didn't want Karen to think badly of him? Never mind the hurt he had caused his daughters, never mind the fact that he'd profited from this and dragged his sorry story through the papers.

Jo turned to face her dad. 'Is that why you did it? To get Mum's attention?' she asked quietly, desperately wanting the answer to be no.

'She never took me seriously. Not like that idiot she's shacked up with. Him and his oh-so-important art. I had something oh-so important wrong with me, or so I thought. I could feel it inside me, couldn't I? So I told her. Thought she might see sense . . .' Jo put her head in her hands. '. . . but she didn't, all she wanted was him.

Even when she came with us last week it was all about the money so that she could get Jay some spuds for his potato prints or whatever he's doing next . . .'

Mick's attempt at humour didn't work. Jo just stared at him. 'Have you any idea what you've done?'

'Oh, leave me alone, Joanna,' he said belligerently.

'Leave you alone? I will, but they won't.' She pointed at the tabloids. 'When this gets out, because it will, Dad, these things always do, then all these people who've been wishing you well and rooting for you are going to feel like fools and they'll turn like that.' She clicked her fingers. 'And you're going to wish you'd never opened your mouth,' Jo got to her feet and walked away from her dad.

'I thought I had it.'

'Well, Dad, to use one of your tired old phrases, "You know what thought did, don't you?"'

'Well, that was just great,' Star snapped at Catherine as they made their way through the crowd that had gathered at the entrance to the Empire State Building to see the *Star Maker* finalists. It seemed that every day they became of more interest to the public. Catherine tried to walk through the crowd but people were shouting her name and shoving bits of paper towards her, hoping for an autograph. Just the idea that someone would want her signature seemed bizarre to Catherine. She was hardly Kate Winslet. Catherine turned round to see what Star was referring to but she was busy having her picture taken with some of the fans.

'In the car,' one of the *Star Maker* security guards said, giving Catherine a shove. She landed in the back of the limo and looked out to see just how many people had been waiting for them to put in an appearance.

'There's hundreds of them,' Catherine said breathlessly.

'Because Richard makes sure that people are tipped off as to where we'll be,' Star said, climbing in next to Catherine. Kim followed.

'Really?' Catherine asked.

That couldn't be right could it? He spent so much time pretending that he was protecting the contestants from the press that it seemed ridiculous to her that he would be tipping them off.

'Of course, really,' Kim said. 'He runs every aspect of the show, you must know that by now. From the song choices to what we wear to who interviews us. Come on, Catherine, he brought your mum and dad over and got them to sell their stories to the papers.'

'That was different.' Catherine didn't even believe her own words. Why was it different, that was exactly what had happened.

'And it's done you no harm,' Star said bitchily.

Catherine's nostrils flared angrily and she sat forward in her seat, glaring at Star.

'How dare you! My dad is sick, I'm not trading on it. I wish it wasn't happening. As for Richard having anything to do with it, I didn't ask him to do it and I certainly didn't ask my parents to get involved.'

'Well, they did, and now everyone loves you,' Star said, holding up her mobile phone with a copy of that day's *Daily Mirror*. There was a picture of Catherine as a child with the caption, BORN TO BE A STAR. That picture had been in the loft for years. The only way the papers could have printed it was if one of her family had taken it to them. Catherine's mind raced, she was becoming suspicious of everyone – she hated being like this. She had just wanted to sing, now she realised just how naive she had been. How had she ended up as the centre of a media storm? She was sure it would blow over very quickly when some real news came along and people would soon forget about her but while she was at the centre of all this attention, she hated it.

Catherine sighed. She didn't have anything to come back with so instead looked out of the window at the Manhattan streets and wished that none of this were happening to her. She just wanted her life back and her dad to be well. None of this – money, fame, celebrity – could make that happen.

Catherine's phone began to ring, she reached into her bag and pulled it out – Jo. 'Hi, Jo, have you any idea how that picture of me got out of the loft and into the *Daily Mirror*?'

'Yes, Dad sent it to them, sorry.' Catherine's heart sank. She couldn't believe he'd do such a thing. 'I forgot he'd even done that until I saw the paper today. Some journo rang up and asked for childhood pictures of you and Dad just handed them over . . . Listen, Catherine, that's not why I'm ringing.'

'Can you put Dad on please . . .?'

'No, Catherine, I can't.'

Catherine was so angry with her father, what did he think he was playing at? It was almost like he was enjoying all of this. 'Jo, please.'

'Catherine, I need to tell you something. Are you on your own?'

Catherine looked at Kim and Star, 'No, I'll call you back in fifteen minutes.'

Catherine ran into the apartment building, telling Kim and Star that she would see them later. She didn't know where was the best place to call Jo from, so she ran down the stairs into the basement where the utility rooms were. She waited for one of the washing machines to finish its spin cycle and punched Jo's number into the phone, wondering what on earth could be wrong.

Jo picked up straight away. 'Hi.'

'What's wrong?'

'This is going to be really hard to take, Catherine, but it's the truth, just try not to freak.'

Catherine felt all of her muscles clench. 'What? Just tell me!' she demanded.

'Dad hasn't got cancer.'

'What?' Catherine slumped against a tumble dryer.

'He hasn't got cancer, Catherine. He's not listed anywhere in the Manchester area. He has never received treatment. He's lying.'

'But there must be some explanation for it.'

'There isn't. The only thing I can work out is that he was trying to get Mum's sympathy.'

'By saying he had cancer?' Catherine put her hand to her face, she couldn't believe this. Her father had had her running around after him for months, she had been worried sick and all for what? For nothing. 'I'm coming home, I want to see him and I want him to look me in the eye and tell me why he did it.'

'No!' Catherine could hear the concern in her sister's

voice, 'You are *not* blowing this because of Dad, I won't let you. You can sort it out when you come back.'

Catherine thought about it, 'But that won't work, Jo, will it? It will end up coming out, everyone will hate Dad and feel sorry for me, or maybe even hate me and think that it was all a set up. Besides, I can't wait for however long it takes for me to be kicked off the competition before I confront Dad.'

Jo was quiet for a moment, 'OK then,' she said finally, 'I'll bring him to you.'

'How?'

'With the money that he got for his story, that's how. Now go and do some practising.'

'OK,' Catherine said, hanging up, grateful to Jo but feeling utterly let down by her father.

Jo climbed out of the taxi and walked along Beech Road. She turned along the alleyway where she had left her bike weeks ago. Only the handle bars were missing. *Result,* she thought. She wasn't sure how she would get it home in that state, but that wasn't her most pressing concern; she needed to speak to her mum. Jo walked purposefully to the door and knocked. She didn't feel sheepish, or apologetic or, at the opposite end of the spectrum, bolshie as she had in the past, she just felt she had a right to say her piece. Jo waited. A few moments later the door was opened by Karen. She stood back to let Jo into the house. Neither one said hello.

'Coffee?' Karen asked.

'No, thanks, I'm not stopping.'

'Well, that's good because I've got a lot on . . .'

Jo would usually make some barbed remark about how busy her mum must be sitting around all day watching daytime TV and doing yoga but she didn't; she wasn't angry with Karen anymore, what she felt was more complicated than that. 'OK, I'll keep it brief.'

'I was right about your dad, wasn't I? He hasn't got cancer, he's having himself on.'

Jo knew that entering into a discussion with her mother about anything she cared about was like pouring oil on a fire. 'I'm not here to discuss that. You and Dad have been in the papers saying he has, so you'll be the one that has to deal with it.'

'That's very caring of you, Joanna,' Karen arched an eyebrow at her daughter.

Jo desperately tried to stick to her train of thought, not to get emotional with her mum, as hard as it was. 'I'm not getting into that with you, I've just come to say that I think we're done, Mum.'

'What do you mean, you "think we're done"?'

'We've all spent the last eight years wishing you back. And for what? I don't need a mum, not one like you anyway. You come to New York with us and the only thing you're there for is to make a fast buck out of Catherine . . .'

'That's not true,' Karen cut across Jo. 'I was there to support Catherine and when the opportunity to make some money came up I thought why not? As did your dad, might I add.'

'And we all know that if you said "jump off a cliff" he would. But you, you know exactly what you're doing. You never once told Catherine you were proud of her. I watched you. You just smiled at her, like she was in another room and you were looking at her through glass or something and then that was it, you were bored, like you always get bored. Well, it's OK, that's all I wanted to say. We've all got each other, as much as you're bothered about that. And that suits us fine. So from now on, we'll leave you alone.'

Jo walked to the door. She could feel her hand shaking so she jammed it in her jeans pocket.

'What if I want to see you, what about that?'

'But you won't, will you, Mum?' She turned around and looked at her mother, trying to keep the hurt from showing in her eyes. Karen shrugged and looked away, her eyes watery. 'There's my answer.'

Jo walked out and pulled the door gently behind her. She had gone to Karen's promising herself that she wasn't going to bang and crash and argue and she hadn't. She should be pleased with herself, but she just felt numb. There was no happy outcome where her mother was concerned; there was just heartache and long gaping periods of wondering in between. Hopefully now, Jo thought, that would at least be something they wouldn't have to experience and they could all get on with their lives in relative peace.

Chapter 21

Andy had had the best week of his life. He and Catherine had been getting on brilliantly, he was working in New York on the biggest show in town and he had managed to go out in the sun everyday without burning to a crisp. Things couldn't get any better he thought. Will had asked that he join him, Jason, Cherie and Richard for a meeting at two so he was planning on having some lunch from the deli near the park first. He was standing in the corridor waiting for the lift for what seemed like an age. When the doors finally opened, Star almost fell through them; it was obvious she had been crying.

'Star, are you OK?' Andy asked, trying to grab her as she barged past him.

'Please leave me alone,' she said, trying to wrestle her arm from Andy's grasp. The fact that Star said 'please' made Andy think that maybe he should pursue this; Star never said please. He followed her into her apartment and through into her bedroom. 'What are you doing?' Star demanded. 'I asked you to leave me alone.'

'But you're upset, I just wanted to see that you're OK.'

'Well, I'm not, all right? I'm not.' The fight went out of Star's voice, she hung her head and began to cry, her shoulders heaving. Andy didn't know what to do. There were no girls around to call, no female runners on hand. He walked towards her and then backed away; he hated to see anyone this upset, but he also knew that there was a fair chance he would get his head bitten off if he got too close to Star. He tiptoed over as if he was walking through a minefield. Star stood on the spot, her shoulders pulled into her head, as if trying to make herself smaller.

'What's happened?' Andy placed his hand on Star's back. She didn't answer, she just kept crying.

'Come on, Star, you can tell me.'

She looked out from under her hair, her pretty face blotchy and red from crying. 'If I tell you, you cannot tell a soul, you have to swear to me.'

Andy nodded, nervous about what he was about to hear. 'I promise, I won't tell anyone.'

Catherine had been sitting in the park for over an hour trying to calm down. She had tried to contact Andy but his phone had been switched off so she presumed he was in a production meeting. She and Andy had been getting on brilliantly since the other night. He was kind and sweet and charming and she fancied him rotten. Catherine never thought that she'd feel like that about someone. She knew she sounded like an old spinster, but she'd thought that if she ever did get a boyfriend it would be because they were friends and then came to some agreement about making it more than that. She didn't know how people got to the stage where they were besotted by one another. But now she knew. She thought about Andy all the time and couldn't even be bothered to act cool and pretend that she didn't; it was written all over her face. She had even told Kim and Star about him and had to stop herself from inserting his name into every conversation. 'What's that you're eating? Cornflakes, oh Andy eats cornflakes too!' She wished that he was here now with her, so that she could talk this through with him.

Catherine had wanted to ring her dad and shout at him, to tell him that she had wasted too much of her life looking after him and he had lied to her. But they didn't have conversations like that in their house. They just buried things and pretended they hadn't happened. Only Jo got everything out in the open. If Catherine hadn't entered *Star Maker* and it had come out at home, just between her family, that Mick had been lying about having cancer, then they would have all tried to sweep it under the carpet. Mick would pretend that he genuinely thought he had cancer but that it had gone and everyone else would dance around the story, and after a while even Jo would fall into line. Well, it wasn't going to happen that way this time; once the news got out that Mick had been lying, Catherine knew that he was going to be fed to the tabloid lions.

Marching through the grand old apartment building where they were staying, Catherine's anger began to bubble over. Thoughts of making sure her dad took his tablets every morning – what tablets were they – Smarties? A vision of her and her father on the moors flying kites – what a dupe, she thought. She needed to speak to someone about this. She pulled her phone out and dialled Andy's number again; this time it rang but there was no answer. Catherine headed for her bedroom, she was going to get a shower and try to get herself into the right frame of mind for that afternoon's rehearsals.

* * *

Andy pulled Star into his arms, she was a shuddering mess. He had never seen anyone this upset. 'Why haven't you said anything before?' he asked.

'What could I say? "Richard Forster has been making me sleep with him so I don't get a bad song choice"?' Star asked, her hair stuck to her face.

She had just told Andy that since they had arrived in New York, Richard had been making a play for her. He had asked her to come to his room and she had gone. At first she was flattered by the attention but then Cherie had seen her coming out of Richard's apartment – the couple insisted on separate living quarters – and had followed Star, demanding to know what was going on and telling her that if she went within a foot of her husband she would make sure she never worked again. Richard, on the other hand, made it quite clear that *unless* she came within a foot of him – slept with him, in fact – he would make sure she never worked again. At first Star hadn't believed him and just tried to avoid Richard. But at the first live show, when he had changed her song on the day of the performance, Star realised he meant what he said. But she also knew that Cherie meant what she said. Since then, Star had been a bag of nerves. She had been called to Richard's living quarters three times and had slept with him twice.

Star could barely get her words out, she was so upset. Andy put his hand to her face and clumsily pushed her hair back. Star put her arms around him and fell against his chest. He felt terribly sorry for her. How could someone force someone else to sleep with them? Where was the pleasure in that? Andy felt nothing but disdain for Richard

Forster; he might be one of the richest men in the world but he was nothing, in Andy's opinion, if this was how he operated.

'Thank you, Andy,' Star said, still clinging to him.

Andy rubbed Star's back. 'No problem,' he said.

The bedroom door opened and Andy turned round. Catherine was standing there with her mouth open, unable to believe what she was seeing.

Catherine ran through the long oak-clad corridor and down the stairs. 'Catherine, come back!' Andy shouted down the stairwell.

She kept running. She knew it was too good to be true. He was probably trying it on with everyone, and she'd told Star all about him the other day, saying how much she liked him; what a fool. She took the stairs two at a time.

'Catherine!' Andy shouted.

She could hear him catching up with her. She turned and ran along the bottom corridor leading out of the door. Andy was hot on her heels. Catherine kept running. She got to the doorway where outside a crowd of photographers and reporters had gathered. She ran out into them, fully expecting them to be waiting for someone else. She felt the crowd close in on her, pointing Dictaphones and shouting questions over one another.

'Catherine, how does it feel to have been lied to by your own father?'

'Have you spoken to your father, Catherine?'

'Catherine, did you know that your father didn't have cancer? A few people are speculating that you hatched the plan to do well in the competition.'

Catherine reeled around, trying to take in the enormity of what was happening. Everyone knew. She felt a hand around her arm and she was dragged backwards through the crowd, back into the apartment building. 'Thank you. That will be all,' Andy said, slamming the door shut.

'What was all that about?' Andy asked.

'I might ask you the same thing,' Catherine snapped.

'What does that mean?' Andy looked utterly confused.

'Jason told me what you were like, he said you were off with a different girl every night, and like a div I didn't listen to him.'

'Off with a different girl every night? Star was upset, I was comforting her.'

'Nice try, Andy. You sound like an MP who's been caught with his pants down.'

'I was. Go ask her.'

'I'm not going to ask Star anything.'

'She's had a terrible time. Richard Forster—' Andy stopped short.

'Richard Forster what?'

'Nothing. It's not my place to say. Look, you've just got to believe me. I really like you, honestly. And what the bloody hell was Jason on about a different girl every night? I'm not like that! I couldn't be like that if I tried . . .'

Catherine looked at Andy, his eyes were pleading with her to believe him. 'That stuff down at the park with my hands over your eyes, I was so nervous, I thought you were going to tell me to get stuffed, but I just wanted to do something nice because I think you're amazing and I was scared that you'd get famous and wouldn't want to talk to someone like me anymore.'

'I'm not like that,' Catherine said, half flattered, half offended.

'Well, I'm not like how you've just described me either. We're both just normal, aren't we? Caught up in this mental world where you get mobbed by paparazzi and people will do anything for fame.'

'I wouldn't. I'm sick of all this. All I ever wanted to do was sing.' Catherine felt sick to the stomach that her family were now being dragged through the press and people seemed to want to know everything about her. 'And look at me, I'm not eating, I'm worried sick about what's about to come out in the British papers. It's awful.'

'What do you mean?'

Catherine told Andy about her dad.

'Oh God, I'm so sorry.'

'I should be thrilled, shouldn't I? He hasn't got cancer, he's fine. But he's lied to all of us. And all because he wanted to get my mum's attention.' Catherine shook her head. 'The silly old idiot.'

They walked back to the room. When Catherine opened the door, Star – who was sitting on her bed – pulled her knees up to her chin like a frightened child. 'Star?' Andy asked, 'Could you reassure Catherine that nothing was going on between us?'

'Andy!' Catherine said, embarrassed.

'With him!' Star said rudely and then, realising that this sounded harsh, recovered with, 'Sorry, he's just been really lovely. I was upset and he talked to me.'

'Upset about what?' Catherine asked.

Star looked at Andy, the look said, *should I say?* Andy shrugged.

'It's OK, I'd rather not talk about it,' Star said, climbing under the covers.

Andy looked at his watch, 'I'm really sorry, I have to go to this meeting, I'll see you in a bit?' he asked Catherine. She followed him to the door. He kissed her and she felt a jolt of excitement run through her. 'We'll talk more later, OK?'

'Yes,' Catherine said. She really needed to talk to someone. As Andy left, Catherine wished that her family were all tucked up somewhere safely and not about to enter the full glare of a wronged media.

'Andy, glad you could make it,' Richard said. He was sitting at the head of the boardroom table at the *Star Maker* offices on Fifth Avenue, wearing an open neck rugby shirt.

'Right, just a few things to run through for this weekend . . .' Richard went through his list of who should stay and who should go and how he was to engineer the departure.

'Star?' Cherie asked pointedly. 'You were very keen to get rid of her last week, but the dear old public kept her in. This week I notice . . .' Cherie looked at her notes, '. . . that she is singing "Nessun Dorma". The public don't know as yet that she can sing opera so when they hear that she's guaranteed to go through. What's changed?'

Richard glared at his wife. 'Nothing's changed, I just think she should stay in.'

'Really?' Cherie said, as if to say, pull the other one.

'I think you're absolutely right, Richard. He really is a good judge of what the public wants, isn't he?' Jason P.

Longford said, in the biggest display of arse kissing that Andy had ever witnessed.

Andy stood angrily in silence. He should say something shouldn't he? He knew what Richard was like. And as for Jason, he was beyond contempt, too. Telling Catherine he was playing the field. Why would he do that? The only conclusion that Andy could come to was because he was miserable himself and couldn't bear to see anyone else happy.

'Moving on,' Richard scanned the room. 'I heard Catherine speaking to her sister on the phone this morning and it turns out daddy dearest hasn't got cancer after all.' There was a quiet gasp from the room.

'You heard?' Andy asked.

'Yes, I heard. There are cameras in the basement, Jesus, where have you been?'

Of course, Andy thought, Richard the ultimate control freak liked to keep tabs on everyone, even at this late stage in the competition.

'So, I've been onto the press and the coverage is going off the chart apparently.'

'You told the papers?' Andy said.

'Of course I told the papers,' Richard said, as if he was dealing with an imbecile. Andy wanted to tell Richard to shove his job, that he couldn't work like this, but he was no use to Catherine if he was in the dole queue. He was better weighing up his options, he thought. So he settled back and listened to Richard's plans for making and breaking people this week and wondered what he would do about all of this, if indeed he would do anything.

* * *

Star finally confided in Catherine. Catherine had told Star about her dad and the fact that there was a gaggle of paparazzi baying for her blood. Star had listened and taken it all in and then sat bolt upright in bed and said, 'I might as well tell you, your boyfriend will only tell you anyway.' And informed Catherine of what Richard Forster had made her do. Catherine felt sick.

'And he's given me "Nessun Dorma" this week because that will keep me in, apparently.'

'But why didn't you just say no?' Catherine said and then felt terrible as soon as the words were out.

'Because I'd be back in Hackney living in my mum's shit flat. That's why.'

Catherine stared at her, 'Hackney? But I thought your mum lived in Fulham?'

'She doesn't.'

'And all the stuff about living all over the world?'

'Look, Catherine, not everyone's got a family like yours.'

Ain't that the truth? Catherine thought.

'You're all really tight and your dad might be a total nightmare but he does things for the right reasons.' Catherine had never thought about it like that, but there was some truth in what Star was saying. 'My mum doesn't give a flying shit what I do. About the only thing that she says to me is, "Mandy, get me ten B and H from the shops."'

'Mandy?'

'Yep. Mandy.'

'I'm surprised that hasn't come out in the papers.'

'Me too, no doubt I'm next and the fact that I've said my parents are dead, well, that'll go down a treat won't it?'

'Your mum didn't mind that you said she was dead?'

'No, it was her idea, that was the truth.'

Catherine walked over to Star's bed and sat down next to her. 'It'd mean the world to you to win this competition, wouldn't it?'

Star nodded. 'But I can't go on like this. I'd rather leave than let that disgusting old ming-head near me again.'

Catherine hoped that there was a way to sort this out without Star having to leave.

Chapter 22

It was the day of the live show and Catherine was preparing to sing that evening. It had been difficult. The past few days had been fraught with people trying to get to Catherine to ask her opinion on what her father had done. Catherine had managed to keep a dignified silence. Her anger had been quickly transferred from her father to Richard Forster when Andy had told her that it was Richard who had gone to the press. She needed to bide her time if she was to have any comeback against Richard, it wasn't something she could take him into a quiet room and talk to him about – she knew he would have her thrown off the show. Her song this evening was 'Angels' by Robbie Williams. She didn't like the song and was dreading singing it.

Catherine came off the stage fiddling with her microphone pack, Andy walked over to her. 'Are you all set for tonight?'

'Yep.'

'You sure?' he studied her face.

'Never been surer. Are you?'

'I think I've got it covered.' He leaned forward and kissed her.

Catherine was very nervous about tonight but she knew she had to go through with it. She looked down at her phone, there was a text from Jo. 'We're here – with the most hated man on the planet.'

Mick had had a terrible time since the news broke that he had been lying. Jo said he'd even made the national news in the 'And Finally . . .' section where they usually talk about pandas that have learned to rollerskate. Mick was being held up as an example of everything that was wrong with society today. Her poor dad had fallen on his sword and told the media back home that Catherine had known nothing of this. That she genuinely thought he had cancer. He had also added that so did he, but nobody bothered to report that.

'Oh my God, that was the worst journey ever!' Jo said marching towards Catherine, wearing a *Star Maker* security badge. Now that they were very much part of the *Star Maker* story they had been collected in a car from the airport. Catherine looked behind Jo to see Maria, Claire and her father looking incredibly sheepish. She ran forward to hug her sisters in turn, leaving her father for a moment. There was no sign of her mother.

'It's nice to be back in the Big Apple, courtesy of Dad's blood money,' Jo smiled.

Catherine looked at her dad, who was trying to shrink away with mortification. 'So, Dad . . .'

Mick shuffled towards his daughter. 'Can we have a few minutes?' he asked the others. Catherine took her dad into the seats and sat next to him.

'I'm so sorry, Catherine,' he said, unable to meet her eye. 'I got carried away.'

'Carried away?'

'I know it sounds terrible, but that's what happened,' he looked at his hands, ashamed. 'And then, once I'd said it I felt like I couldn't go back. And as daft as it sounds now I thought that maybe your mum might come back if there was something real to come back for.'

Catherine took a deep breath, she was getting increasingly angry. 'There was always something to come back for, Dad, she just didn't want it.'

Mick hung his head. 'You're right, love, you're right.'

Catherine wanted to be kind to her dad, she always gave him the benefit of the doubt but she was boiling with rage towards him, for what he'd done, for his stupidity, for his selfishness. 'I might be right, but I'm still sitting here feeling sorry for you, aren't I? Being expected to weather whatever you throw at me because you're allowed to do what you want, Dad, and sod the consequences.'

Mick looked stunned. 'What does that mean?'

'It means you treat the house like a dumping ground, conning yourself that you're going to make loads of money on eBay. You pretend that one day you might go back to work but we all know you have no intention of it. You treat me like your wife when I'm your daughter and I shouldn't even still be living at home – I should be having a life . . .' Catherine had never felt so angry, but she was trying her best to keep her voice down, 'And then when I do actually achieve something that means that I do something that I want to do, you sabotage it for me and not with just any old thing, no, you've got to tell the world about your pretend cancer. Well, well done, Dad, because if you wanted to mess things up for me you've done a pretty good job of it. I can't step out of the door without getting a camera in my face and being accused of engineering the whole thing.'

'But I've told them you didn't know anything.'

'That doesn't stop them asking!'

Mick put his head in his hands. Catherine had promised herself that she wouldn't get angry with her father that she would try to be calm with him, but she couldn't help herself.

'I am so sorry, Catherine,' he looked at her, his sad eyes heavy with tears. He looked genuinely crushed. 'I never meant to cause you any upset.'

'But you have,' she said quietly.

They both sat in painful silence for a few moments. Then Mick tentatively put his arm around Catherine. 'I'm sorry, love. You mean the world to me. And I'm so grateful for everything you've done for me, honestly I am. And I don't blame you if you never believe a word that comes out of my gob again but I promise I'll never lie to you – to any of you – again.'

Catherine felt tears sting her eyes – her dad *never* apologised; she tipped her head back to prevent herself from crying.

She turned to her dad, her anger disappearing, and felt so sorry for him that she hugged him. 'Has it been hard?' she asked finally. 'Are you being pestered by the press?'

'Pestered? They were hiding in the wheelie bin yesterday!' Mick sighed. 'But as they say, today's news is tomorrow's fish paper.'

'I think it's chip paper.'

'Right-o, well, whatever; that's me: chip paper. Hopefully.'

Catherine knew that as long as she was in the competition then her family would be under the intrusive spotlight of the press. And there was no one she could blame but herself. 'I think you're right, Dad, it'll all blow over.'

'Thanks, love.' Mick said, touching his daughter's hand. The intimacy of the gesture shocked her.

'What for?'

'For everything, love. For everything.'

'We're live from New York and you're watching *Star Maker*!' Tom Soronsen said to the camera; the crowd went wild. Catherine peeped out from a gap in the wings to see her family all cheering, even her dad. Claire was waving a banner with Catherine's head on it and hitting people in the face with it in her excitement.

Andy came up behind Catherine and wound his arm around her waist. 'Good luck.'

'Thank you.'

'Are you sure about this?'

'Yes, are you?'

'Absolutely.'

Catherine's name was called and there was a huge cheer from the crowd. She walked onto the stage and waved. Kim followed her as they took their seats. Kim leaned towards Catherine. 'Is everything OK?'

'Yes, fine.' She said, she hadn't told Kim of her plans as she didn't want to put any unnecessary pressure on her.

Once all of the finalists had taken their seats Tom turned to Richard. 'So, it's been a busy week?'

'It certainly has. I think it's fair to say that there's been as much interest in what goes on off screen as the show itself.' He spun around and looked at the Reillys. 'But you know, we have to ride these things out.'

Catherine was fuming, he had been the one who had informed the press and now he was acting as if he was just running some humble singing competition.

'So what have you got for us tonight?'

'First up is Star and I think you'll see a distinct improvement,' Richard grinned. He looked up at the screen where each contestant would talk about themselves and their week for twenty seconds before they performed. Instead of Star waxing lyrical, the video that began to play was of Richard sitting in his room and Star entering. Catherine looked at Richard's face, which had drained of colour, Cherie put both hands on the desk and looked at her husband. Then as quickly as the image was flashed up it was replaced with the original footage as she, Andy and Star had agreed. Catherine felt giddy with excitement. Richard Forster looked as if he was about to explode. Kim was elbowing Catherine in the ribs, evidently wondering what was going on.

Andy and Catherine had decided to play Richard at his own game. They had activated the camera in his room and when Star had gone to see him as instructed they had taped it. She had feigned illness and not slept with him but the full tape was damning enough to ruin Richard Forster's reputation for good and he knew it. They had decided to only play a taster of it, so that he knew that someone somewhere had it.

Everyone praised Star for her performance and Richard was more full of praise than he had ever been, making light of the technical problems that he blamed for the video confusion. Star returned to her seat and smiled at Catherine.

As each contestant got up to perform Catherine studied Richard, he was nervous because the show was live and he knew that at any time the video might be played in full. Catherine knew that there would be a lot of behind the scenes activity now with people running around trying to work out who had planted the footage at the beginning of Star's tape.

Kim pulled off another stunning performance and the atmosphere in the studio as it got closer to Catherine's time to perform was electric.

'Catherine Reilly!' Tom announced, Catherine walked over to her spot on the stage.

'Well, Catherine, the last few days have been something haven't they?' Catherine smiled weakly. Tom looked down the camera. 'And do you know now that to be found to be lying about something is now known as "Doing a Mick"?'

The audience cheered, Catherine looked at her dad, who had sunk so low in his seat she could only see the top of his head.

'Anyway guys, here's Catherine . . .'

The VT rolled and Catherine looked at herself talking about how her time in *Star Maker* was shaping up. It was like watching another person, she was so shiny, it wasn't her. She wasn't willing to give up everything for her fifteen minutes of fame. She'd had a great time and experienced things and been to places she never thought she would but the past few days had soured everything for Catherine.

Catherine hoped that Andy had managed to perform the music swap as they had planned. It began to play. Great, it isn't 'Angels', she thought. It was the music to one of Catherine's own songs that she had had recorded herself. Richard Forster's face dropped. *What the bloody hell is this?* Catherine saw him mouth to the other judges.

'This is a song called "All I Ever Wanted",' Catherine said quickly and then began to sing. She had never in her life put such an effort into a performance. She soared to the high notes and gently let her voice fall away to the lower notes, there was so much passion and emotion in the lyrics but only now, standing here on this stage, was she able to do it justice. It was an emotional song and one that she could sing with true conviction. She looked over at her family. She could see in her sisters' eyes that they knew what this song was really about – Catherine had barely even admitted it to herself – their mother. To anyone else it would have sounded like a broken-hearted love song, but it wasn't; it was about their loss as a family.

Catherine could see Jo wiping away tears. Mick hung his head. Claire put her hand to her neck as if smoothing away the lump in her throat and Maria was simply sitting with tears streaming down her face. Catherine had never felt so close to her family. And she didn't miss her mum as she sang. She was sad for everything that had happened, but she didn't miss her.

The song ended and Catherine looked out at the crowd, people were on their feet cheering. Jo was jumping around hugging Claire and Maria. Mick was on his feet clapping his hands over his head.

Richard Forster looked around scowling. 'Well . . .' he said sharply, 'everyone seemed to enjoy that, Catherine, whatever the hell it was.'

There were boos from the audience.

'Listen, we spend all week practising "Angels" and you sing this, whatever it was meant to be.'

'It was beautiful, don't listen to him,' Cherie said.

'Thank you,' Catherine smiled appreciatively.

'There are rules, Cherie, and you don't just change your song choice at the last minute,' Richard snapped at his wife.

'You did last week with Star,' Catherine said bravely.

'What I do and what you do are two very different things,' Richard said, crossing his arms. 'Where did you get that song from?'

'I wrote it myself,' Catherine said, trying to keep her nerves at bay. There were gasps and cheers of appreciation from the audience.

'Well, you know that that is against the rules.'

Catherine put the microphone in its stand, 'Yes I do and I know that I'll have to leave the show now, but I just wanted the chance to sing my own song and I wanted the chance to say as well that my dad isn't a bad person, he didn't mean to lie.' She knew he had but she didn't have the air space to explain the ins and outs of her dad's reasons. 'Things have just been blown out of proportion and I think that if I stay in the competition it will only get worse.'

'You can't just leave!' Richard Forster said, getting to his feet.

'I can.'

'You're under contract!' he barked.

'And I've just broken it by singing my own song,' Catherine said. She couldn't believe how forthright she was being, but she felt she had nothing to lose. The audience were watching amazed, their heads going backward and forward as if it were a tennis match.

'You don't call the shots around here, young lady.'

Catherine looked over at Star, who nodded. 'Richard, everyone likes you being Mr. Nasty, shall we show them how nasty you can be?' Catherine asked sweetly, looking back at the screen. Richard glowered at Catherine, he now knew that somehow she was behind the video of him with Star and he couldn't risk that coming out.

'I don't know what you mean, Catherine, I've been a pussy cat.'

There were murmurs from the audience. Everyone wanted to know what Catherine meant. He nodded at Tom who stepped in and took Catherine by the hand.

'Anyway, I think you'll all agree, that Catherine has been a great contestant and we wish her well. Let's hear it for Catherine!'

The crowd cheered wildly and Catherine headed offstage. She was escorted straight off the premises by security. She hadn't thought that she'd be allowed to hang around, but her feet barely touched the floor.

Once unceremoniously dumped outside, Catherine looked around; there was no crowd, no paparazzi, no one had made it to the stage door in time to ask her anything. Across the road was a Mustang, the driver beeped the horn. It was Andy.

'Thought you might need a lift now you're a nobody . . .'

Catherine scurried across the road and jumped in the car. Andy kissed her.

'How are you feeling?' he asked.

'Exhilarated, crap, nervous, excited . . . lots of things. You?'

'Jobless, but hey, there's always another role as a gofer, especially with the reference that Richard Forster will have to give me . . .' he said, holding up a DVD case marked 'Star'. 'I think that Star will probably do all right in this competition, don't you?' Andy asked with a sly smile.

Catherine grinned back, 'I hope so.' She leaned forward and kissed Andy again, this time a longer, lingering kiss. 'So where to now?'

'I've taken the liberty of booking us into a little place I know, an Irish bar . . . where no one in the world will recognise you because they're all stuck in the 1950s.'

'The Cobbler's Thumb?'

'The very same. They've got rooms about the bar, classy eh?'

'Can't wait,' Catherine giggled.

'I've booked us under Mr and Mrs Smith,' Andy grinned. 'Because you can't be too careful when you're famous.'

'When you're a has-been, you mean?'

'I don't think I've heard the last of you,' Andy said, his eyes twinkling.

'No?'

'No, I think you're going to be around for a very long time.'

Catherine leaned in and kissed Andy again. A few moments later he pulled the car away from the studios and headed towards The Cobbler's Thumb, gladly leaving the rest of the world to the glitz and glamour of *Star Maker*.

Chapter 23

Six Months Later

Jo walked into the lounge with a bucket full of burnt popcorn. She was useless at making the stuff but it didn't stop her trying.

'Joanna, have you burnt the arse out of the pan again?' Mick complained. 'How many times do I have to tell you?'

'Dad, knock it on the head.' Jo said, offering the bowl around the room. Funnily enough, Claire, Paul, Rosie, Jake and Maria all refused. 'I've not missed anything have I? She's not been on yet has she?'

'It's ten in the morning, why do you need popcorn?'

'Because we're watching Catherine on telly, duh! It's like being at the cinema, it's an occasion.' Sometimes she despaired of her family.

'No, she's not been on yet. Anyway, she's been on loads of stuff, you don't make popcorn every time.' Catherine had appeared on everything from *This Morning* to *Friday Night with Jonathan Ross* since she exited the *Star Maker* competition.

'Yes, but this is special, we get to watch slimy chops have to kiss her bum. It's going to be class.'

Star and Kim had got down to the final two and Star – Jo had thought rather predictably – had won. But they knew that Richard Forster wasn't going to let someone with so much ammunition against him lose. Since the final Kim had secured a record deal with a big label and Kim and Catherine were still firm friends. The biggest surprise for Jo was that Star and Catherine had remained in contact and that Star hadn't binned her sister the moment she was pronounced the winner. She was actually all right, for a mental stuck-up southerner who was willing to pretend her parents were dead to get on in a show, Jo thought.

As for Catherine, her song, 'All I Ever Wanted' had been released on the internet and had become one of the fastest selling downloads of all time. It was still in the charts – spending longer there than Star's song, which had recently slipped out. Everyone who interviewed Catherine asked her who the song was about, and a few had questioned whether it was actually about her mother. Recently, the story of how Karen had left Catherine and her sisters to live with Jay, enjoying a lavish lifestyle courtesy of the Arts Council, had made it into the national press. This, coupled with the fact that she had made money from her initial story with Mick and had now been turned on her by the very paper that bought the story, meant that Karen was having a hard time walking down the street without someone offering an opinion as to what a disgrace she was. Jo was pleased to see that Catherine had kept her mum at arm's length since returning from New York and not taken her up on any of her invitations to get together. Jo was sure that they were just so that Karen could write a new version of events in her head to make herself feel better about how she had behaved and had nothing to do with wanting to build bridges with the members of her family.

Catherine was now working on her album. She was

without doubt the success story of this year's *Star Maker*. Not that you'd know it to see her, Jo thought, half proud, half despairing. She had even tried to go back to work in the call centre at first. Jo had told her she was like those embarrassing people who win the lottery and then are back working shifting pallets round a factory the next day, saying, 'It won't change me . . .' Catherine was now in talks with an influential American indie label about making her album with them, after turning down a number of the bigger labels.

Catherine and Andy were now very much an item. Jo had never seen her sister be like this about a member of the opposite sex. She could see why she was mad about him though, he was kind and considerate and funny in a geeky kind of way and he thought the world of Catherine. Andy had moved to Manchester after returning from his stint on *Star Maker*. As he was freelance he had had to come down to earth with a bang. One week he was ushering Bette Midler from her helicopter the next he was in Urmston job centre. He hadn't had to wait too long for work, though. He was now working as a runner on a show at Granada Studios called *So You Think You Can Base Jump?* and it was his job to take C-list celebrities to the top of famous buildings and watch them parachute off. He was still hoping to get work experience as a cameraman but Jo couldn't understand why. If she could spend her days watching the likes of Dane Bowers take their lives in their own hands she'd love it.

Andy and Catherine had decided that they would see where Catherine's work took her in deciding where to move next but whatever happened, she knew they'd be together. They were just one of those couples – finishing each other's sentences, having hysterics over something that happened to them when no one else knew what they were talking about. It would have been sickening if Jo hadn't been so pleased for her sister.

Catherine had moved back home when she returned from New York and was still living there officially, but she had barely spend at night at the Reilly residence. She was either off being interviewed in both the States and London or she was with Andy.

Mick had found himself in the (for him) unfortunate situation of not being able to moan. He was so ashamed of his behaviour and having been outed as someone who would pretend to have cancer, that it seemed to Jo that her father might never whinge again. Old habits died hard of course and she would see him now and again thinking about complaining about something, but a look from one of his daughters was just enough to set him back on the path of non-grumbliness.

This morning Catherine was about to be interviewed by her nemesis, Jason P. Longford, on his new – and surprisingly popular – morning chat show and Jo knew Catherine was really looking forward to it. It was as if she'd come full circle and Jo was looking forward to watching Catherine make Jason squirm.

'Here she is!' Jo squealed. Catherine walked onto the stage and waved at the studio audience, they all cheered.

'Well, Catherine, you're looking well,' Jason said with a big beaming disingenuous grin.

'Thank you,' Catherine smiled back. Jo cheered, her sister was enjoying herself.

'So one thing I'm sure everyone must be asking you is, how is your dad?'

'He's absolutely fine,' Catherine said weathering the question well. 'He hasn't made an illness up for a few months now.'

Jo held her breath but the audience laughed.

'I'm a laughing stock,' Mick grumbled.

'You certainly are,' Claire nodded.

The furore surrounding their father had died down surprisingly quickly. People took Catherine at her word that her father hadn't intended to lie, and the rumours surrounding Richard and Star after the half-shown video meant that Mick was old news. Jo couldn't help thinking that he was slightly disappointed.

Jo herself had benefited from Catherine's *Star Maker* experience; she was still in touch with Will who she'd got off with in a drunken haze after Catherine's last appearance on *Star Maker*. He was trying to persuade her to be a contestant on his next project called *Catwalks and Catfights*. It was going to be like *America's Next Top Model* but a million times better, he told Jo. She had told him she'd believe that when she saw it. She was still toying with the idea. She could wear her own designs and prance around being obnoxious and getting shouted at by the likes of Janice Dickenson. She hadn't told any of her family other than Catherine though; she knew that the idea would be pooh-poohed immediately.

'And you now have a hit record that has outsold the winner's song on downloads alone.' Jason beamed at Catherine; Jo knew it was sticking in his throat being nice to her sister.

'Yes, I can't believe it's happened really,' Catherine said shyly.

'Aw, she's gone soft,' Jo complained. She had hoped Catherine would make him squirm because he'd been so rude to her during the competition.

'So, have you got any advice for anyone out there wanting to apply for next year's competition?' Jason asked, placing his hand on her arm like they were life-long friends.

'I'd say go for it, don't listen when anyone tries to put you off. Even if they're really rude and insistent.'

Jason looked at her wide-eyed; he couldn't believe she was going to drop him in it.

'Oh my God, look at his face, he knows Catherine's going to tell everyone what a horror he was.'

Catherine looked at Jason and held his gaze. 'But on the whole, people are really supportive and you've just got to believe in yourself.'

'She didn't pull him up! Aw that's rubbish,' Jo complained.

'No, it's not. She was dead right,' Mick said proudly. 'She didn't pull him up because she didn't need to. She doesn't go in like a bull in a china shop, she picks her battles.'

Jo thought about it for a moment. Her father was right. Catherine didn't need to have a go at Jason P. Longford live on air, it was enough that she had succeeded. She had always picked her battles, Jo realised, like with their mother, she didn't go looking for a fight with her because she knew she wouldn't get anywhere. She just got on with life and helped bring Jo up and looked after her father and then took her opportunity, this one big opportunity when it arose. Jo felt a lump rise in her throat; her sister really was a star.

'Living well is the best form of revenge,' Mick said wisely, tucking into a half-eaten pork pie that had been sitting on the chair-arm for the past hour.

Jo raised her bowl of popcorn in the air. 'To Catherine, who in 2009 put the Reillys on the map . . .'

'. . . And then took us back off it again!' Mick added and everyone cheered again before settling down to watch Catherine perform her very own hit song.

Ebury Press Fiction Footnotes

Turn the page for an exclusive interview with Anne-Marie O'Connor . . .

What was the inspiration for Star Struck?

That poor girl who came onto the *X-Factor* show in a dress her dad had made her which made her look like one of those lacy doll toilet roll covers from the '80s. She looked less like a pop star than anyone the British public has ever clapped eyes on and then proceeded to sing an entire song in one off-key note. The producers had obviously decided she was TV gold but it was her family that were the most shocking thing about the whole episode – they genuinely believed she was good and piled in to tell Simon et al exactly what they thought of their put downs. It made me begin thinking about people who have their fifteen minutes of fame and then have to go back to their lives and deal with being that person who was laughed at by the entire country. Then my editor Gillian suggested that it would be far more interesting to have the mad family but give the auditionee some talent and watch them proceed in the talent competition. So that's what I did.

Have you ever felt tempted to enter a talent show? If so, what was your talent?

I've never entered a talent competition as such but I used to sing solo as a child in the church choir and would have to sing in front of visiting dignitaries and at weddings and the like.

I did however once, when I was living in Dublin, audition for a group in Ireland called The Irish Sopranos. Contrary to what my surname may suggest I have a big Bradford accent and sound more like a Dingle than a Corr and I think the clue to what they were after was definitely in the title of the band! I got in there and as soon as I opened my mouth I could see them thinking 'Noooooooo!' After I'd sung I rather pathetically asked, 'I'm sorry, did you need me to be Irish?' I can only assume this would be like auditioning for the Lippizzaner Stallions and saying, 'I'm sorry, did you need me to be a horse?'

Dream Casting time: who would play Catherine in the movie of Star Struck? Any other thoughts on the rest of the cast?
Catherine would be played by a young Shirley Henderson, Jo would be played by some undiscovered sarcastic talent who is currently living on an estate somewhere thinking that her family don't understand her and Mick would be played by John Thompson.

X-Factor or Britain's Got Talent?
It depends. *X Factor* is slicker but doesn't have room for unicycling dogs. So I think it would have to be *Britain's Got Talent.*

Which book are you reading at the moment?
At the risk of sounding worthy I'm reading *An Evil Cradling* by Brian Keenan about his time in captivity in Beirut. It's been staring at me from my bookcase for about eight years and I've finally made myself read it and brilliant it is too.

Who are your favourite authors?
Roald Dahl – brilliant as a kid to discover him after years of thinking everyone other than me and my friends were missing out because we didn't a) go to private school b) hang around in a group of five or seven, or c) have a magical tree at the bottom of the garden inhabited by a man adorned with pots and pans and another with the moon for a head. Enid Blyton has a lot to answer for. For comedy I love Marian Keyes and Alexi Sayle's

short stories. Recent novelists I've enjoyed have been Lionel Shriver, Jonathan Franzen and I've re-read some Graham Greene which I didn't really get when I was younger but loved this time round - my Catholic guilt must be getting more acute.

Which classic have you always meant to read and never got round to it?
The entire Dicken's collection probably. When my dad retired he started reading the classics and has totally put me to shame. I do think though that it is easy to feel a bit thick if you haven't read every book ever written before 1935. So I've had to come to an uneasy truce with myself and admit that life's too short to read *Jude the Obscure*.

What are your top five books of all time?
It's hard to choose five and there's always the risk of just putting classics so that everyone thinks you're really well read and la-di-da. So here are five books which have been really important to me over the years for different reasons.

1. *The Twits* by Roald Dahl.
2. *The Secret Diary of Adrian Mole aged Thirteen and Three Quarters* by Sue Townsend.
3. *1984* by George Orwell.
4. *Rachel's Holiday* by Marian Keyes.
5. *Small Island* by Andrea Levy.

Do you have a favourite time of day to write? A favourite place?
It would be nice to slope around waiting for the muse to descend but I'm dictated to by my son, so when he's asleep or in nursery. And I love writing in Manchester Central Library and at the National Media museum in Bradford. The café there is brilliant.

Which fictional character would you most like to have met?
I know he's loosely based on reality, but Macbeth. I'd say, 'You know that missus of yours, I wouldn't listen to her, she's not all there.'

Who, in your opinion, is the greatest writer of all time?
It's so hard to say because different generations have different writers that are important for that time. I also think that writers in all their forms should be recognized for their power with words and that there is sometimes a worthiness unjustly attached to novel writing. Political speech writers, film writers, journalists as well as novelists – anyone who can move people and make a positive difference to someone's life is a great writer – I suppose that's a long winded way of saying I don't think there is one 'greatest writer'.

Other than writing, what other jobs have you undertaken or considered?
I've had every job going. I've going to sound like a Victorian orphan but I had my first job aged twelve – a paper round. I enlisted the help of my brother who was seven at the time. As I only paid him 50p a week for his services he rightly mutinied one evening and left me to it in the pouring rain.

My first Saturday job was in Bradford meat market aged fourteen surrounded by men who had worked too closely with raw meat for too long. Everything was an innuendo. I hated that job. I got £1.50 an hour, had bits of meat stuck under my finger nails by the end of the day and had to wear a tabard like a dinner lady. After a year of this I managed to wangle a job at a shop called Guy Watson's (anyone of a certain age from Bradford will remember this institution). It was a gift shop/joke shop/borderline soft porn shop. I worked there for four years and loved it. I used to volunteer to stock-take and see how many chocolate willies I could eat before I was told to go on my break. I then worked in numerous factories around Bradford during the summer holidays from university. The shampoo factory where you weren't allowed to pack medicated shampoo for more than half an hour because it made your nose bleed. The card factory where one of the women had 'bitter' and 'lager' tattooed above her nipples. When I enquired why she simply said, 'For my husband.' The catalogue factory where two lads were sacked for trying to sneak out with fifteen football tops on each.

After all this, when I graduated I was dying to work in an office and have a 'normal' job but I soon realized that all jobs have their quirks. I worked as a secretary in a school in Moss Side which was a brilliant job and a great place to work but then I worked out I could earn at least six grand more by calling myself a PA so that's what I did until I started writing about seven years ago. I worked in Manchester and then in Dublin as a PA. When I returned to Manchester to try my hand at writing I supported myself by being a waitress -this was my favorite job of all. Everything happened in that restaurant and it was brilliant for pinching characters. From the sleazy businessman I overheard saying to his secretary while evidently trying to get into her pants, 'I'm a human being first and a businessman second' (GAG!), to the old lady who lived in a home down the road but used to pretend she'd just jetted in from Monaco whenever she came in. This was one job which might not have paid much but stood me in good stead for becoming a writer.

Which book has made you laugh? Which book has made you cry?
Marian Keyes always makes me laugh. She is hilarious. There was something she wrote about the Irish compulsion to sing at the drop of a hat that made me sick laughing. The last book that made me cry was *Sophie's Choice.*

Which book would you never have on your bookshelf?
I'd happily take some of my husband's books to the tip. There are a lot of drug lords and psychopathic nut jobs that write books and they make their way into our house. Anything that starts 'From the mean streets of Liverpool to the crack dens of Calcutta to the showers of St Quentin, this is the story of one man's journey from poverty to international crack baron . . .' for me can go and live in the bin. I think that men like these books for the same reason they like *Police, Camera, Action*. Whatever that reason may be . . .

Is there a particular book or author that inspired you to be a writer?
Not really a book or author. My friend Danny Brocklehurst is a TV/film writer and we used to share a house years ago. He used to get up and eat his cornflakes in front of *Trisha* and start work at ten while I would leave the house at eight and cycle into the city centre and get rained on nearly every day. I quickly began to think, maybe there's something in this writing lark . . .

What is your favourite word?
Div. I'm not even sure it's a real word but it covers a multitude of sins.